For G

BEAUTYWOOD
BOOKS

TOBY JUGG TOURS

THE BEST IN THE SOUTH WEST

Travel to Europe by luxury minibus

- Visit the war graves of Northern France
- See fairy-tale buildings and fascinating architecture
- Wander through the historic cities of Belgium
- Marvel at the stunning scenery
- Experience a day of farm life and share a hearty Belgian feast
- Sail on the canals of Amsterdam
- Sample Belgian chocolate, French cuisine and the gastronomic delights of Amsterdam

- Enjoy the robust beers and refreshing lagers of Northern Europe
- Stay overnight in comfortable hotels
- Ten nights. Twelve places available. Contact Tommy Judd for details

1

'Can I have some butter on this toast, Keith?'

Lil picked up a slice of toast and bit into it. The butter melted over the perfectly crusty edges.

'It's already dripping with butter, Lil.'

Keith, the owner of Keith's Kaff across the road from Clover Hill Retirement Home, winked in Lil's direction and raised his voice cheerily, making sure that everyone else in the café – a young mum with a toddler, two men in work-clothes eating sausages – could hear every word.

'It's bone dry,' Lil waved her arms theatrically. 'This toast could be classified as a murder weapon, it's so hard.'

Keith wiped a table with strong arms, inked with tattoos. He was around forty, certainly no more than half Lil's age. He called back, 'I'm watching your figure for you, darling.'

'No one's watched my figure in years,' Lil retorted.

It was part of Lil's routine to cross the road every day, have breakfast in the cosy café set back from the main road and pretend to give Keith a hard time. He would flirt with her in return. It was what they always did. She'd tell him that there wasn't enough butter on the toast and he'd retaliate with a laconic remark about watching her figure or old people being better off without the high cholesterol, and she would reply with the same comment every time.

'I'm nearly in my grave already, Keith, so I may as well go with a smile on my face and my toast dripping with butter. Didn't you know, that's the meaning of life: butter?'

And today, as ever, Keith, his hair slicked back, murmured, 'You know you love me, Lil.'

To which she replied, 'Always and forever, sweetie,' before he wandered back into the kitchen whistling.

'What about some peanut butter, darling?' Lil called after him. Then, in mock-desperation, she yelled, 'Marmalade?'

Lil chewed toast and pulled her book from her huge, round, cat-faced handbag. She'd wander back to Clover Hill and see what Maggie, her neighbour, was doing. There wasn't much happening today in the recreation room: no yoga for seniors, and the hair-dresser didn't come until Monday. Today was Friday.

The cartoon picture on the front cover of the novel showed a cheerful woman in a low-cut blouse, a tight-fitting riding jacket, muscular thighs in jodhpurs and a whip in her hand. She was riding on the back of a dark-haired man who was crouched on all fours, a shocked expression in her eyes. The woman's blonde mane flew wildly from beneath her riding hat and, in the hand that didn't hold the whip, she was using the man's tie as reins. Her smile was one of wild abandon. The man was wearing little else other than his tie and a small pair of briefs: Lil noted that his caricature-body was well-toned. The title of the book was *Fifty Shades of Hay*. Lil was halfway through the book and was really enjoying the plot: Annette, the gorgeous, lascivious heroine, certainly knew how to frolic in the hay with all sorts of different people. Lil liked books with a lot of nooky in them; it fascinated her to read about women's raunchy exploits. They seemed to be in charge of their own love lives nowadays. She shook her head; sadly, there hadn't been much passion in her own life. And things had changed so much since 1953.

She pulled out the old photo that she had always kept in a frame but, since Cassie had it laminated, she'd used it as a book-mark so that she could keep it with her. The black and white image beneath the laminate was cracked, despite her efforts to care for it over the years. It was the only photo she had of Frankie. They were relaxing together on a rug on the grass, probably sharing a picnic – she couldn't remember. He had his arm wrapped around her, pulling her closer to him, smiling. It was as if he thought she belonged to him. He was handsome and carefree, with dark, curly hair and a happy appearance. He was in his soldier's uniform – of course he would have been: he had been in the US Army, stationed in the UK back in the fifties, after the war. And Lil was sitting upright next to him, her dark hair pinned up at the sides, serious, shy, not sure if she was allowed to smile although she'd felt deliri-ously happy. She had truly loved him, even though they'd only shared a few months together.

Lil closed her eyes and thought about the man in the photo-graph, her Frankie. He'd been four years older than her; he was twenty then. He'd be eighty-six now. Lil wondered if he was still alive. She turned the photo over. The paper on the back was yellowed, and faded writing in a cursive style proclaimed the snap was Lily and Frank, 1953. Lil returned it to the novel, marking the page where Annette and Rory, the gigolo jockey, were currently adjusting each other's riding tackle in the paddock.

'I wonder if I should have worked at a riding school. Or lived on a farm.' Lil brushed crumbs from her lips. 'I'd have liked the country life, all those animals.'

But it was too late to change her lifestyle now: she was at Clover

Hill and that was fine. She liked the other residents; each day she met Maggie from next door for a cuppa in Keith's Kaff so that they could complain about Maggie's dreadful husband, Brian; she had her independence. Usually, she couldn't be bothered to use the little hotplate in the tiny kitchenette and Keith across the road cooked good, reasonably priced food, as long as you could supplement it with lashings of ketchup.

Besides, Cassie, Lil's beloved Cassie, more like a sister than a daughter, lived only a mile away at the bottom of Clover hill. Having Cassie living so close was a blessing and Lil always looked forward to Cassie's visits and the updates about what she'd been doing; Cassie was a performance poet now and Lil was really proud of everything she'd achieved in her life. Lil had so many photos of her: one of her at sixteen, smiling as she won the literature prize at school; graduation, at Bristol; another in her thirties, surrounded by the children she had taught English in Africa and China; another, on Stage Two at the Edinburgh Festival years ago. And now Cassie was a frequent visitor, often bringing Lil's favourite sweets, the green chocolate triangles.

But, despite all that activity, Lil found she was often a little bored. Routine was fine for some people but Lil craved distraction, something to amuse her, and at such times Lil always had Jenny Price, Duty Manager at Clover Hill, whose office she would visit in secret. It was Lil's favourite pastime, finding new opportunities to do random acts of kindness for Jenny, who always seemed unhappy. Lil glanced at the clock. It was past ten thirty. She wondered if Jenny would be out of her office and if she'd forgotten to lock the door again.

Lil crossed the road at a steady pace and pushed open the gate that led to Clover Hill Retirement Home. She had a comfortable flat on the second floor, consisting of a modern lounge-diner, a prettily decorated bathroom, a bedroom and a kitchenette in the sheltered housing block overlooking the beach and the railway line in Salter-ley. It was more luxurious than the place she'd had as a young mum, with a shared kitchen, a tin bath, and an outside toilet, so Lil considered she'd done quite well for herself.

As she wandered through the gardens, beyond the house to the sea below, Lil remembered the harder times. In 1953, she had been sixteen; she had only known the handsome, dark-eyed American soldier for three months. Sex wasn't something she had fully under-stood: it had only happened once, a frenzied fumble in the car park of a pub in Heyford. Frankie had been sent back to the States two weeks later; he hadn't known she was expecting the baby. Lil sighed. If that was love, it had all occurred far too quickly and then it had been shoved to one side, never to occur again. She had decided that love broke your heart and when children came along, they occupied your every moment and became all the love you needed. There was no time for much else.

Her parents had been furious with her, quickly embarrassed by the tightness of her skirt, the expanding waistline, and the neigh-bours' whispered judgements. Lil's mother had narrowed her eyes and told Lil that she'd made her bed, so she could darn well lie on it now. Her words had pointedly suggesting that Lil had already been lying on a bed with someone she shouldn't and now she was in the trouble she deserved; she'd brought shame on the family in the process and should be made to suffer all over again. Lil was too young and too naïve to plead that she wasn't quite sure how it had all happened, but she was very, very sorry.

Lil's father had allowed her to stay in the house, to bring the baby up under his roof until she could find a place of her own. Lil's mum had informed her bitterly that she was now soiled goods and no man would look at her again, not with a child in her arms. So Lil had believed her, forgotten about love and concentrated on little Cassandra Rosemary Ryan. She had chosen the first name weeks before the birth when she came across it in a book: it was the name of a Greek goddess. Her daughter would be a blessing.

She hardly remembered the actual birth, except that she'd been terrified. For the first few days, she had gazed in disbelief at the soft bundle in her arms; from that moment onwards, she'd had little time to think of anything but Cassie, each day a treadmill, lurching from feeding, washing baby clothes, then later helping with homework, making ends meet with small cleaning jobs, dancing each night to Buddy Holly and later The Beatles in the little room with her beloved growing daughter. It was only after Cassie had left home that Lil had worked full time, managing to scrape together every penny she could, determined to start her own business. She had bought a B&B much further south, in Salterley, Devon, by the sea, and that was where she had stayed until she'd moved to Clover Hill. Romance had been the last thing on her mind: she hadn't wanted her heart broken again.

Lil pressed the eight-digit code on the keypad and the door opened. She stepped inside and was immediately too warm: the heating was on, despite the summer sunshine. The small office was on the ground floor, opposite the entrance, but Lil knew she'd be quickly aware of Jenny approaching: the click of the door, the echoing footfall, the scent of floral perfume that made her nose twitch. Lil would have time to make her escape. Her fingers were already on the door handle – one turn, one push and she was inside: Jenny had forgotten to lock it, as usual. She left the door ajar to make sure that she'd hear Jenny's clattering heels a mile off.

She sat in the swivel chair and twizzled round one way, then the other, and then whizzed at speed. She glanced at the desk. It was untidy again, although Lil had sneaked in three days ago and tidied it for her. Jenny had left her diary open on today's date, Friday 26th July, 2019. Lil noticed the debris on the desk: a chocolate wrapper, an unwashed coffee cup and an almost-empty carton, which had probably been last night's takeaway food. By the smell of the smears of sauce, Jenny had ordered chow mein. Lil began to tidy the surface, arranging things in order, pushing rubbish into the already-overflowing basket, wiping the coffee stains from the desk with a tissue from the pretty box Lil had secretly planted several weeks ago. She sniffed: the honeysuckle air freshener she had left back in June was still working, but Lil made a mental note to replace it soon.

Lil glanced around for something else to do to brighten Jenny's life at Clover Hill. It was hard work and a huge responsibility, being Duty Manager, caring for so many residents, and Jenny always seemed to carry the world on her shoulders. Lil had never heard her laugh, but she imagined her smiling, however briefly, when she discovered the little things Lil did to make her life sunnier. She gazed around at the Cliff Richard 2019 calendar on the wall, a collection of photos of the singer in his younger years. Cliff was Mr July at the moment, in Bermuda shorts, smiling boyishly with pearly teeth. Lil had left the calendar hanging in Jenny's office back in January: she knew Jenny was a huge fan of Sir Cliff. She glanced at the empty tin of mixed biscuits she'd left for her at Easter. Lil had recycled it as a container for pens and pencils in May.

Lil plucked another tissue from the box and started to polish Jenny's telephone. It was dirty, with greasy fingerprints on the glossy black plastic. Lil rubbed hard and then an idea came to her. She could ring up and order a pizza for the duty manager's supper. Jenny would still be in her office this evening and Lil imagined she'd enjoy a nice Hawaiian pizza. She pictured Jenny's face brightening with delight when it arrived, the delivery girl telling her that it had been ordered on her behalf. Jenny still had no idea that it was Lil who sneaked around doing all the secret random acts of kindness.

Then Lil heard the echo of footsteps.

She sidled out of the office and rushed towards the stairs. She'd go and share her morning news with Maggie. She'd rescue her from Brian, who'd be sitting in the chair smoking and watching seventies TV. *Charlie's Angels*, most likely. Then they'd share a cup of tea, a laugh. She always cheered Maggie up.

Lil disappeared up the steps and around the corner just as Jenny, in a black jacket and sensible skirt, paused at her gaping office door and frowned: the door was ajar.

2

Cassie Ryan walked into The Jolly Weaver a smile on her face, looking forward to the evening. In one hand she carried her banjo case, the other was tucked through the elbow of Ioannes Anastasiou, always called Jamie, her housemate. The pub was full, as it always was on 'Friday night is Open Mic Night'. Cassie deposited her banjo at the usual table, helped Jamie to a seat and, as he stretched out his legs, she moved to the bar where a middle-aged man and a woman were busy pulling pints. Duncan, the barman, his hair darker than ever despite his fifty-something years, came straight over. 'Beer and a port and lemon, Cass?' Cassie nodded. 'I'll bring it over straight away.'

Cassie returned to the table. She thought Jamie seemed a little tired tonight but, dressed in a jacket, bright shirt and best jeans, he looked smart and handsome, and he was always so keen to support her. He never missed one of her performances.

Jamie murmured, 'The usual crowd is here.'

Cassie gazed around. The members of The Weaver's five-a-side football team were in the corner, the four youngsters making lots of noise. At a larger table were several members of the Salterley tennis club. Cassie recognised a few of them. A dapper man in a shiny-buttoned blazer and silk cravat noticed her and waved a hand in recognition. Cassie waved back.

'Who's that? I've seen him before somewhere,' Jamie asked.

'Ken something...' Cassie murmured. 'He gives lectures in the library. I went to hear him talk about some historical king ages ago. He's our age, sixties, possibly late fifties, who knows?'

He smiled. 'Is there anyone in this pub who doesn't love you?'

She patted his shoulder. 'Everyone knows me through Open Mic.' Her eyes shone. 'Can I help it if I'm the star?' She indicated the stage area. 'Our drinks will be here in a moment. Let's enjoy the performance.'

Alice Springs was on the little stage at the moment, wearing a khaki shirt, knee-length shorts and a hat with corks hanging around the brim. She was singing 'Tie Me Kangaroo Down Sport', marching on the spot, smiling and shrieking into the microphone in an accent that had never been heard anywhere near Canberra. Alice's real name was Janice Cuthbertson and, other than an uncle who had emigrated to Melbourne in the sixties, she had no link with Australia whatsoever. As she finished her performance, the locals offered an energetic cheer; such was the way with the drinkers in The Jolly Weaver. They were a good-hearted crowd and, on a Friday night at half past nine, their whistles wetted, they were usually fairly easy to please.

Duncan, the barman, helped Alice Springs down from the makeshift stage and grabbed the microphone, flashing a smile. 'Thanks, Alice,' he muttered, riotous applause drowning his next words. He began again, murmuring into the mic. 'So, as you all know, my wife, Kerry...'

A wolf whistle pierced the air; it had, no doubt, come from one of the young lads, Pat, Jake or DJ, who were sitting at the back with the other two members of The Weaver's five-a-side football team.

Duncan's face shone as he adjusted his tie. 'Well, you know I like to keep my Kerry in her place behind the bar pulling pints...'

There was an uproarious cheer from every corner; one lone voice, that of the five-a-side team's lean and hungry striker, Emily Weston, her blonde ponytail swishing with every movement as she thumped the table, could be heard yelling, 'You're still living in the nineteen seventies, Dunc.'

'But Kerry wants to sing a song and, as you all know, what Kerry wants, Kerry gets, so normal service will be interrupted for the next ten minutes,' Duncan protested.

Kerry, his wife, was next to him, a willowy redhead in a short dress, tugging the microphone from his hands and waving him back to the bar. Despite the tumultuous applause, Jamie managed to whisper audibly in Cassie's ear, 'She's going to sing "Funny Face" again.'

Kerry fiddled with her hair and purred. 'This song is special: it's for my wonderful husband, Duncan...'

Cassie moved her lips closer to Jamie's cheek. '"Funny Face" it is...'

Jamie gave an expression of excruciating pain as the karaoke backing track whined through speakers, the persistent screech of a violin and a slide guitar, and then Kerry began crooning in a cracked voice, waving her hands and gawping mournfully at her spouse, as if the lyrics of 'Funny Face' personified their love. She was more than slightly off-key. Duncan leaned on his arm at the bar, staring back, besotted. Jamie reached for his glass, draining the last of the port and lemon as if it were lifesaving medicine. Cassie squeezed his knee encouragingly and he, in turn, rolled his eyes. Kerry threw her arms in the air for the big finale, missing the last high note completely, her voice more piercing than ever, and the audience offered ecstatic applause as she bowed in appreciation.

Then she was back behind the bar and there was a flurry of

punters buying pints and bags of crisps. Cassie turned to Jamie. 'Are you all right?'

He winced. 'The left leg's playing me up a bit tonight but it's nothing a refill won't cure.'

Cassie raised her glass and tilted it towards the bar and Duncan was by her side. 'Are you ready to go on, Cass? You're my final act of the evening.'

She nodded. 'Another port and lemon for Jamie, please.'

'I'll sort it. And there will be a pint of Otter waiting for you here when you've entertained the troops.'

Cassie took her place on stage, carrying the banjo, aware that everyone was watching her. She was resplendent in the spotlight tonight, wearing tight black velvet trousers and a red patchwork velvet jacket, her snow-white cloud of hair tied with a purple bow. Tumultuous clapping echoed around the bar, some people banging the table with their fists. Cassie whispered in a voice soft as silk, 'All right, you lot, calm down. I'm here now.' Her eyes shone with mischief.

Someone at the back started thumping the table and chanting her name: Cassie Ryan. No doubt it was Pat Stott, a tall young man in his early twenties with a bright thatch of red hair and china blue eyes that stared as if he were perpetually amazed. Pat was always laughing, his external ebullience hiding his naturally shy personality. He had a big voice and a big heart: everyone in The Jolly Weaver knew he was too good-natured to be a really effective goalkeeper, but he was the best the five-a-side team could find.

'So, here's a song about old people's daytime TV,' Cassie crooned, picking up the banjo that stood by the side of the stage.

Someone shouted, 'You're not a day over forty, Cass...'

'I'm sixty-five years old,' she retorted.

Pat was wolf-whistling again.

Cassie's voice was syrup through the loudspeakers. 'So, is there anyone here who watches much daytime TV?'

Tommy Judd shouted that it was all repeats, but in less demure language, then Cassie offered a mischievous lopsided grin. 'Well, here's my take on daytime TV and, in particular, the type of adverts we have to put up with in between all those repeats...'

With a conspiratorial wink, she began to sing, her voice tuneful, playfully changing from loud to soft, and the room was silent.

> *This daytime TV will be the death of me*
> *I watch Pointless, The Chase, with a smile on my face*
> *All the soaps on repeat while I put up my feet*
> *But the advertisement break is more than I can take.*
> *It's all...*

She winked at the audience, took a melodramatic breath and launched into a frantic chorus.

> *It's all dentures, dementias,*
> *Silver surf adventures*
> *Watering cans, funeral plans*
> *Stannah Lifts, pointless free gifts*
> *Receding hairs, reclining chairs,*
> *Reading glasses, old-age bus passes,*
> *Inflation, cremation, with too much elation*
> *Hot meals, just order 'em – and more Carol Vorderman:*
> *We won't get some peace without Equity release*
> *Now life's at a junction – erectile dysfunction!*
> *Book a final resting place and go back to The Chase*
> *These ads are depressing – with my head they are*
>   *messing*
> *Old folks are a burden – it's on the ads, I just heard 'em*

Daytime TV makes my blood boil – all I have left is to...

Cassie paused, winked at Jamie, and sang,

...shuffle off my mortal coil.

The room erupted in whoops and cheers. She rode the wave of noise, then continued with a crescendo.

All this talk of cremation, it turns me to violence.
So, I'll turn off the telly. Ah, that's better...

She made a mischievous face and whispered,

Silence.

Cassie stopped playing abruptly, then she rolled her eyes in mock surprise. She acknowledged the hoots of laughter then gave a little bow. The walls of the bar echoed the applause.

Cassie leaned forward, the bright velvet jacket opening to reveal a multicoloured shirt underneath, as she murmured, 'As you all know, I don't intend to grow old gracefully – just disgracefully.' She shrugged theatrically. 'But that's just a little song I wrote recently to start off proceedings.' She placed her banjo on the stage floor carefully. When she faced the audience again, she was serious.

'Now for a poem I wrote during my years working as a teacher in Africa. This one is a sad story inspired by one of my students, and it's called "Death Waits at the Door".'

Everyone in The Jolly Weaver sat motionless, drinks in hand, as Cassie explained that the poem was dedicated to Adama, a boy she'd taught English to in Senegal years ago, a gifted scholar who'd died prematurely of a disease that could have been cured had simple medical care been available. Her voice was hushed but every word was clear. In the corner of the pub, Duncan's father, Albert Hopkins, sat hunched over a single-malt Scotch, wearing a heavy overcoat, a tear in his eye. Then Tommy Judd, one of the five-a-siders, a particularly hefty and dirty defender, was shushed when he tried to ask if anyone wanted a refill. Cassie's voice was soft in the microphone but clear as ice in the silence.

> *Death is outside; you can hear his breath in the grasses:*
> > *hush*
> *You know him, and he knows where you are*
> *His fingers are twigs and his hair is seaweed blowing*
> *Listen. He stands within silence.*
> *He is the space between then and now*
> *He is close by; he raises his arms for you*
> *The earth is not yours but you are his*
> *He makes spaces for those before you, all patience*
> *Dark places are his and his mouth is full of soil*
> *His kiss fills your waiting soul soon – now –*
> *With solid certainty.*

Cassie bowed her head slightly and everyone applauded, Ken from the tennis club in the blazer and cravat rising from his seat. Jamie had heard most of her poems before; he had been there when many of them had been written and rewritten, but he felt the familiar surge of warmth. Cassie was special; he lived in her house; she reminded him to take his medication every day and she let him have the room with the best sea view. He watched her as he sipped his drink, his eyes soft with admiration. Cassie was the most sweet-natured, generous and talented person he knew; she was honest, outspoken, a free spirit who had no idea how much he cared for her, how much his feelings had grown over the two years he'd lived in her house, and, he reminded himself, one day he'd find the right moment to tell her exactly how he felt. Jamie sighed and watched Cassie as she wandered back to the table, beaming, and he met her gaze, holding out a hand. 'Wonderful, as ever, Cassie.'

Duncan placed two freshly filled glasses on the table as Cassie sat down. He pressed her shoulder. 'Thanks, Cassie – I don't know how you do it. You make them laugh and then you make them cry. The Weaver wouldn't be the same without you.'

'My pleasure.' Cassie brought the glass to her lips and slurped. 'I'm writing a new song about pollution for next week.'

'Great.' Duncan was pleased. 'Crisps?'

Cassie nodded. 'Salt and vinegar – two packets, please.'

'Oh, maybe I shouldn't...' Jamie put a hand to his stomach, beneath his jacket.

'So, fish and chips on the way home is out of the question?' Cassie pouted mischievously.

Jamie sighed. 'Do you know, five years ago I could probably have walked up the hill from here to our house in fifteen minutes? Now, even with this stick, it takes me a full twenty – more if we stop for chips.'

'It's good exercise, a bit of gentle walking,' Cassie said encouragingly. She sipped her beer and glanced at Jamie. He was handsome, his dark hair now grey, his face tanned. He had lost a little weight, she thought, despite the delicious meals he cooked, mainly Greek dishes he'd learned from his parents who had both been born in Cephalonia. She was fond of him: he was good company, tirelessly supportive of her work, a kind and lovely man, and she couldn't imagine life without him. He was hunched over his drink, finishing the last mouthful. Cassie touched his arm. 'We should be getting off home, Jamie.'

Someone was on the stage, gabbling enthusiastically into the microphone. Cassie glanced up at Tommy Judd, dressed in too-tight jeans and a too-tight T-shirt. Tommy, the organiser of the five-a-side team, had convinced himself, despite his forty-two years, that he was still as young and fit as he had been twenty years ago. His team-mates disagreed; he drank too much beer, he was overweight, but what he lacked in speed he made up with over-exuberant tackles and the ability to frighten opposing strikers with his ferocious expressions. Cassie turned her attention back to Jamie. 'Are you feeling all right?'

Jamie nodded. 'I'm a bit tired, Cass. I'll sleep in tomorrow. What are you planning to do? Visit Lil?'

'Oh, yes. I never miss a Saturday.' Cassie rolled her eyes. 'I can get the update on her random acts of kindness. Last time I was there I had to listen to Jenny Price telling me that someone regularly sneaks into her office, tidies it when she's not there, and leaves her little gifts. Poor Jenny's scratching her head, but I know it's Lil. Bless her heart, I love her to pieces.'

'She's certainly very sprightly for a woman in her eighties. I mean, I'm not sixty-five yet and I can't gad about like she does.'

'Lil's eighty-two, but she doesn't have MS, Jamie. You do brilliantly.'

'Do you never feel you need a break?'

'What from?

'From us – from caring for me, caring for your mum. It must be exhausting.'

Cassie lifted her arms wide, a gesture that seemed to throw any anxiety to the wind. 'What else would I do but spend time around those I love?' She glanced around for her handbag, a patchwork velvet satchel with a long strap. 'We should be going.'

A chirpy voice came from near her elbow. 'Nice performance, Cass.'

A slightly deeper voice agreed. 'I liked the sad one about the little boy who died.'

Cassie gazed up into two pairs of eyes and two young members of the five-a-side team, their hands on each other's shoulders, grinned back.

'Jake, DJ, how are you both?'

'Great,' they chorused together.

Cassie smiled. The two men were in their early twenties and notoriously inseparable: Jake Mathers was shorter in stature with long, intensely black hair falling over his eyes and Donovan Niati, always called DJ, was taller, a tangle of dreadlocks on top of his head, shorn at the sides. Jake was dressed completely in black, his smiling face making him look like a happy vampire. DJ, in contrast, was tall and lean in designer jeans, a gold chain around his neck, the shining map-shaped pendant in the form of the island of Jamaica symbolising his father's place of birth. Jake had his arm around DJ's neck in a stranglehold and they were both tussling.

'I enjoyed the song about old people,' Jake told her, loosening his grip on DJ.

'She's performed all over the country, haven't you, Cass – Glastonbury?' DJ was impressed. 'My days, wasn't it the Edinburgh Festival last year?'

Jamie nodded proudly. 'She's done Edinburgh several times. She headlined once in the poets' tent at Reading. She's even been on TV – I know – I was there doing the sound.'

Jake beamed, pushing a hand through his fringe. 'So, what about Tommy's minibus trip? Are you going?'

Cassie frowned. 'Tommy's minibus trip?'

'He's organising a holiday abroad.' Jake rubbed the pallid skin on his forehead with his fist. 'He was just telling everybody over the mic – he's running a bus trip for the pub.'

'Kerry won't be very pleased,' DJ observed. 'Dunc's going, so she'll be on her own in the bar. The five-a-side team are well up for it all, clubs, pubs, we're getting a game against the Belgians too, according to Tommy.' He offered an optimistic smile. 'You should come, Cass, Jamie. It'll be a blast.'

'There are loads of places left...' Jake added.

'I'm surprised it's not overbooked.' Jamie sighed. 'I'd have loved to go on one of Duncan's beer fests a few years ago. My days of waking up in a hotel room in Rotterdam with someone's cheesy feet up my nose are sadly a thing of the past.'

Jake rummaged in the pocket of his black jacket and tugged out a roll of leaflets. 'Well, have one of these anyway. We promised Tommy we'd hand them out. Take care, you guys.'

Cassie watched them walk away, their arms around each other's shoulders. She glanced at the piece of paper with a photocopy of a map of Europe, advertising Toby Jugg Travels. It was typical of Tommy Judd – a joke about his name pertaining to drinking beer, another one of his crazy schemes. It occurred fleetingly to Cassie that the jaunt would probably end with the entire busload of The Jolly Weaver being locked up for several days in a Belgian jail with poor Kerry having to raise the bail.

She turned to Jamie. 'Shall we go home?'

He reached for his walking stick. 'Ready as I'll ever be.'

They ambled towards the door, in step. Many of the customers were saying last goodbyes; others had already drifted home. Kerry was still washing glasses and Duncan was clearing tables, waving to friends, calling out cheery good wishes. Tommy was handing a leaflet to an uninterested woman with a neat haircut, a loose floral scarf and a blue sweatshirt with the logo of Salterley tennis club.

In the corner, Albert was huddled in his huge overcoat. He appeared to be asleep, then he opened an eye, gazed around, rubbed his chin, sipped the last mouthful of single malt and waved a hand to his son for a refill.

3

Lil and her neighbour, Maggie Lewis, were sitting at a small table in Keith's Kaff drinking milky coffee. Lil was wearing a long cardigan over her T-shirt and jeans; she knew Keith had switched the heating off for the summer. Maggie wore a loose, sleeveless dress and was complaining about the heat and how hardly any of last year's summer clothes currently fitted her. Lil patted her hand sympathetically and suggested that she looked great but, if she had put on a pound or two, Keith's cooking might be to blame: he made his cakes very sweet and the biscuits were always sprinkled with sugar.

Maggie shook her head sadly. 'No, I comfort eat, Lil. Anything sweet relieves the boredom. It's Brian. He drives me mad.'

'I thought he never spoke to you.'

'He doesn't. He sits in the chair all day in the flat, watching the little television, all the old programmes from the seventies and the eighties. It's blaring out all day long and he's ogling *Charlie's Angels* and chain smoking.' She sighed. 'It's no company for me. I'm all alone and bored.'

'You have me, and yoga with Geraldine once a week – and that nice young man from the art college to teach us how to do macramé,' Lil protested.

'It's not enough though, Lil – I still have to go back to Brian afterwards, the stench of smoke and his dull poop-poop laugh from the armchair every five minutes. It's like living with Thomas the Tank Engine.'

'Why ever did you marry him?' Lil asked.

'We loved each other, a long time ago – he was gorgeous. We used to dance together. The first time we met we smooched to Elvis Presley, "Love me Tender". I was whirled off my feet.' Maggie patted her hair, cut in a tidy style, and fingered a small pearl earring. 'Then we married and I had Darren six months later. Then Ross and Paul came along, only eighteen months apart, then Gemma, who wasn't planned, and Brian was working all hours for British Telecom – but we all got on so well together. Family life was wonderful – I loved being a mum. But when the kids left one by one and Brian retired, we came to live in Clover Hill...we just settled into silence and a daily routine and...' Her voice trailed off, her face sad.

Lil thought she ought to finish the sentence. 'You've grown apart?'

'It's got worse over the last two years. He just watches TV now and I do all the running about.' Maggie sipped cold coffee. 'I try to make the best of what I've got, although I never have anyone to talk to. But you're next door, thank goodness, and you cheer me up. And my kids come to visit with the grandchildren, so I have that to look forward to.'

'Thank goodness for our kids, Maggie.' Lil nodded. 'I'm so glad I have my Cassie. She'll meet us here soon.' She stared at the half-drunk coffee and pushed the mug away. 'Do you know, she invited me to live with her before I moved here? We've always been good company for each other, but she needs her own life, so I chose to come to this place instead. I'm glad I did too.'

'How long have you lived here now?'

'Oh, years. I ran the B&B for ages: Cassie came home from her travels, after teaching abroad, and we ran it together for a while. She made a name for herself on the circuit with her performance poems, going all around the country, and she'd bought her little place down the road, so I moved here. I've always been independent. I fancied the idea of sheltered accommodation where I could do my own thing. I like it, especially having nice neighbours like you.'

'And what about the man Cassie lives with? They aren't married, are they?'

Lil shook her head. 'No, you won't get our Cassie settling down. She wasn't brought up that way. She's had plenty of offers, mind, but she's a free spirit, like me. Men let you down sometimes. I think most men find Cassie a bit too headstrong – she does her own thing. Jamie, the chap who lives with her, is just a friend. He's really nice.'

Maggie gazed at the clock on the wall. 'Well, I suppose I'd better get back to Brian, to the silence and the stench.'

'Why? Stay here and have another cuppa.' Lil was baffled. 'He won't have noticed that you're not there.'

'He never does,' Maggie mused. 'It's just habit, I suppose. It's nice to spend time with you, though. You make me smile. Time away from Brian makes me realise that I'm still alive.'

'Cassie and I will call round for you later and we'll walk down to the sea. I love watching the waves roll in.'

'Me too – the fresh air and the view are lovely.' Maggie eased herself upright. 'I'll look forward to that. I'd better bring a coat. The wind's chilly today. I'll see you later, Lil.'

Lil watched her friend walk through the café and stop at the door, calling a cheery greeting to someone who was approaching. As Maggie left, a snow-haired woman in a black velvet cape and jeans with huge holes in the knees rushed in holding a bunch of flowers and a box of chocolates. Lil leaped to her feet, ignoring the twinge in her hip. 'Cassie.'

'Great to see you, Lil.' Cassie hugged her mother, feeling the small woman's arms wrap around her: Lil felt as fragile as a sparrow.

'A latte for my Cassie, please, Keith,' Lil called.

'Coming up, gorgeous,' Keith yelled back from the kitchen.

Lil was beaming. 'Sit down, Cass, tell me all about it. How's the outside world doing? Do you know, I meant to come to The Jolly Weaver last night to see you perform but I was a bit tired. I should have got a taxi or asked Jenny Price if her Tim would give me a lift.'

Cassie put her lips close to her mother's ear. 'Talking about Jenny Price, she stopped me on the way here. She was very surprised...'

'Oh?' Lil showed her daughter the innocent expression of an angel.

Cassie knew the look so well. 'Her office was spotless.'

'How strange.'

'The poor woman was mystified by how it had suddenly become so tidy.'

'Really?' Lil placed a hand over her mouth, batting her eyelids. 'She had a takeaway pizza delivered to her office last night too, and she'll have no idea where it came from...'

Cassie hugged her. 'You are just so lovely, Lil.'

'I feel like the elusive Scarlet Pimpernel, you know: they seek her here, they seek her there... It relieves the monotony too.' Lil sighed and put a hand to her hair, the same soft snow-white hair as her daughter's but thinner.

Cassie shook her head. 'What about a hobby?'

'I do yoga with Geraldine and macramé once a week with a handsome art student.'

'That's not much – you need a proper hobby.'

'I've got hobbies – I come to the Kaff to tease Keith, and help Jenny with random acts of kindness. That keeps me mentally agile. I keep an eye on Maggie next door and help her recover from the intense boredom of living with her Brian, bless her.'

'You could learn a language or take up drawing.'

'Life drawing might be all right.' Lil leaned back in her seat. She thought of the cartoon man with the horse-riding woman on his back in the novel she was reading. 'I'd happily sketch a lithe young man with muscular thighs. A proper model, a big naked man, that would be good.'

Cassie gazed in disbelief. 'Shall I buy you some art materials today, then?'

Lil patted her hand. 'Talking of which, Cass – have you got a piece of scrap paper and a pen?'

Cassie rummaged in her bag and handed her an A5 sheet, with one blank side, and a biro. 'Here. Are you going to do a sketch now? Shall I pose?'

'No, I have to make a list. There are just a few things I need you to get for me.' Lil turned the paper over, pen poised thoughtfully. 'Some of that face cream for the over forties and some more sweets, the chocolate triangles. Oh, and some hand cream, the jasmine one. There was something else I wanted...'

'We can finish it later,' Cassie suggested. 'How about a walk back to Clover Hill, through the garden, down to the path and we can look at the sea?'

'That would be smashing.' Lil eased herself up. 'I'll have to get a warm coat if we're going outside. We'll call for Maggie. And you can tell me about the poems you've been writing. Did you write that new song about pollution?' She moved forwards precariously, making sure her hip joint took no strain. 'Come to think of it, we could do with a bit of global warming. There's a bitter wind outside. It comes off the sea and cuts through right to your bones...'

Cassie caught her eye, the mischievous twinkle, and nodded. She was reminded at these times how much she loved her mother, how resilient she was, how wilful. That was how Lil had kept going all her life, basic bloody-mindedness – it was how she'd dealt with adversity and challenge, how she had pulled through. Cassie took her arm, feeling the thin body against hers, the fragile bones. The surge of love and respect she was feeling became momentary anxiety. Lil was eighty-two; Cassie would not have her mother forever. She hugged her tighter, sensing Lil lean against her gratefully, and they moved together in step towards the door.

'It's not going well, Jamie.' Cassie chewed the end of her pen and adjusted the huge red reading glasses perched on her nose. 'It's too didactic. You can't make pollution funny and you can't preach to people as if they know nothing about the subject when so many people do. Maybe the tune is wrong – I think it has a comedy feel to it with the fast banjo and that's not right.'

'Sing me what you've got so far. This is almost done.' Jamie stirred the sauce for the moussaka he was making, easing his body round to gaze at Cassie, who was sprawled in her chair, her arms across the table. She moved herself to an upright position, picked up her banjo, gave a small cough and launched in, her voice strong and passionate as her fingers tickled a jolly tune.

> *It's sadly fantastic*
> *That we need to get drastic*
> *We have so much plastic swamping our seas...*

Cassie stopped, her face pinched in an expression of frustration, and shook her head. 'It's trite. One for the bin, I think.'

'It might work, Cassie – maybe slow it down a bit, make it mellow,' Jamie suggested, piling salad in a serving dish. 'It's a bit pessimistic, but that's the effect you're striving for.'

Cassie watched him lift the salad bowl with both hands and she sighed. 'I think I need to come back to it. I've started a poem about dreams. It has potential. I might return to that one. I'm just – feeling a bit stale at the moment.'

Jamie walked over to stand behind her chair, placing his hands on her shoulders, pressing down gently. He closed his eyes, breathing in the sweetness of her scent. 'You work hard. Maybe you need a break. Go for walks, take time out. You know, spend some energy caring for yourself?'

'I haven't had a holiday in years, not a proper one.' Cassie closed her eyes and inhaled. 'The moussaka smells delicious.'

'It's ready for the oven. And meanwhile, I'll open a bottle of red. Then you can tell me all about Lil and the mischief she's been up to.'

* * *

Lil adjusted her reading glasses, sipped her tea and stared at the list she was writing. She couldn't remember what the other item was that she needed Cassie to buy for her: hand cream, face cream, chocolate triangles. What was the other thing? She scratched her head for a moment, thinking – that was it, shampoo, some of that stuff that made white hair glossy. She wrote in her careful handwriting: *shampoo*. She touched the piece of paper she was writing the list on, the one Cassie had pulled from her handbag, and turned it over. Something was printed on the other side.

She stared at it. It was a poster of some sort, advertising Toby

Jugg Tours, and there was a colourful map. Lil brought her the leaflet closer, tracing the coastlines with her finger: France, Belgium, the Netherlands. She read the small print: the holiday would visit three countries, there would be beautiful scenery, chocolate to sample, beer, you could even visit a farm, and there would be a minibus to take you from one place to the other.

Lil rubbed her chin thoughtfully. A holiday would be nice. Mobility wouldn't be an issue in a bus: she could take plenty of cushions. Cassie could do with a break too. Lil thought she had looked a bit tired; her eyes had been circled with dark smudges.

She listened to the television blaring from Maggie's flat next door. Brian was watching *The Sweeney* again and Maggie was probably watching Brian. Then, suddenly, Lil was clapping her hands together. An idea was forming. She had no mobile and using the phone in the flat was much less exciting. Lil glanced at the clock and wondered if Jenny Price would be in her office. If not, the door might be unlocked and she could just slip in. It would only take a few minutes and she'd leave her a chocolate triangle, just to say thanks. She grabbed the leaflet from the table and whirled towards the door, noticing that her hip had temporarily stopped aching. That was a good sign: she was revitalized – she had a plan.

4

Cassie strode into The Jolly Weaver, immediately noticing the group of people crowded around two tables pushed together in the corner. Tommy stuck a pen behind his ear and yelled, 'Over here, Cass.'

She sailed past the bar and Duncan called over to her. 'I'll bring you a pint and join you in a moment. Kerry can hold the fort.' His wife muttered something and he gave a short grunt, as if he had been told off. Cassie sat down at the table, moved a beer mat towards her and gazed from face to face.

Tommy pulled the pen from behind his ear and put a tick next to Cassie's name on his notepad. Cassie noticed the other people around the table: next to Tommy, Emily Weston, the five-a-side striker, waved her fingers in greeting, her ponytail swishing. The other members of the team smiled: tall, lean DJ Niati, Jake Mathers dressed in vampire black, then Pat Stott, grinning shyly.

She also recognised Sue Wheeler, who ran the Salterley tennis club. Sue was short and slim, her hair cut stylishly straight at her jawline. She had an intelligent expression, tight slacks below a cashmere jumper and a loose turquoise scarf. The man next to her was Ken Harrington, tall, slim, light-haired, probably in his late fifties, a similar age to Sue. He was wearing a smart blazer with brass buttons, a green silk cravat knotted at his throat. He lifted a hand and waved. Cassie recalled his talk in the library a year ago, about Richard the Third. It had been quite lengthy.

In the seat next to him was a broad-shouldered, muscular woman with auburn hair in a sweeping style. She introduced herself.

'Denise Grierson. I'm new to the area.' She glanced at the man and woman next to her. 'And new to the tennis club. I've recently moved into Larkside Avenue, just down the road from Sue.'

She offered a little wave of her hands as she spoke, clearly self-assured. Cassie noticed that Denise pronounced Sue as *Syoo* and she noted the imperceptible nod of approval from Ken Harrington and how Sue's nose turned up at the end, as if she could smell something unpleasant. Duncan sat next to Cassie and put two pints of beer on the table, one for himself and one for her. He rubbed a hand across his hair, which had recently been cut shorter, a helmet of thick fur. 'Right, Tommy. We're all here. I think we can start now.'

Tommy studied a sheet of paper and began to examine each name.

'Cassie's here, tick... Duncan, co-organiser... tick. Then there's me, Tommy... tick. Others from my five-a-side team... Emily... DJ... Jake... Pat, tick... Tennis club members, Sue, Ken... Denise, the new lady, all here. Not present – Lil Ryan plus one. That makes... one missing, oh, Albert... he's here, good.' He glanced at Albert, who reached for his pint of beer, oblivious, supped a mouthful and closed his eyes. 'Right, everyone...'

Cassie lifted her pint. 'Before we begin, Tommy, thanks for your text inviting me here. But I'm not sure why. Something about a holiday?' She was aware of the others' eyes on her. Emily Weston, slender, fresh-faced, who could be no older than twenty-two, winked at her. Jake whispered something to DJ and sipped his half-pint of lager.

Tommy stretched his arms and cleared his throat. 'Okay. We're here today because we've all signed up for the Toby Jugg tour of northern Europe – Toby Jugg, that's me – it sounds like Tommy Judd and it's a tubby beer mug. 'Nuff said, ha, ha. Well, France and Belgium and – what's the other place? Ah, Amsterdam – the place famous for canals and bicycles and... other things.'

Jake and DJ met each other's eyes and laughed. Pat sat up too quickly and almost spilled his lager.

Tommy continued, using his sheet of paper as a prompt. 'So, there are thirteen of us going, which leaves plenty of space at the back for luggage and – beer – or any souvenirs we might bring home. Dunc's co-organising, the five-a-side football team including me – I'm the driver, of course, being fully-qualified.'

Jake and DJ nudged each other, then DJ mimed a driver careering round corners. Pat laughed too loudly.

'Then we have the tennis club – well, three members of the tennis club – welcome, Sue, Denise and Ken. Oh, and Albert, will be joining us.' He pointed to the older man wearing a large overcoat who had been dozing next to a glass of beer. He opened sparkling blue eyes, smiled in acknowledgement and lifted a finger in greeting.

'That's ten,' Ken observed.

'And Cassie and your two guests.'

'Ah...' Cassie took a breath. 'That's the part I'm not clear about. While I'm delighted you phoned and asked me to be here, I have no idea where any of this comes from. I haven't signed up to go on a holiday.'

'Your mother rang me up – she said to text and ask you to attend this meeting on her behalf.' Tommy wiped a hand across his sweaty forehead. The temperature in the bar had become warm.

'My mother?' Cassie leaned forward. 'I see...'

Tommy nodded. 'She sounded like the Queen on the phone. She booked three places.'

'Three? Me, Jamie and my mother?'

'No, you, Ms Ryan and a Mrs Maggie Lewis.'

'Maggie?' Cassie covered a smile. 'I'm going on a coach trip to the Netherlands with Lil and Maggie? Well, I'm – speechless.'

'She's already paid the deposit.' Tommy wriggled uncomfortably in his seat, wondering if Cassie might withdraw from the trip and leave him in the lurch having to fill another seat. He'd found it hard enough to convince Sue and Denise from the tennis club to go and they'd only agreed because Ken Harrington, who seemed an authority on all things cultural and had once been a town councillor, had said he would take a place simply to see the architectural delights of Bruges and Amsterdam.

'Okay.' Cassie sipped from her pint glass. 'It seems we're going on holiday together, me, my mother and Maggie.'

'And the five-a-side team,' Pat added. He was an earnest young man with the sweet, round, red face of a cherub. 'It will be great. We're going to get a game against the Belgians. Dunc's organised it.'

'Well, Kerry has,' Duncan admitted. 'I've had to promise her a fortnight in the Costa del Sol to make up for me being away for nearly two weeks. Of course, her sisters will come down and help her run this place. She always has a good time when Katy and Michelle are here.'

Sue Wheeler crossed neat legs. Her voice was strong, booming. 'You say there will be cultural opportunities, Tommy – art galleries and fine wine. Have those been booked in advance or do we need to organise them ourselves before we go, my dear?'

'I can book galleries online for us all.' Ken Harrington spoke in a deep, well-modulated voice. 'And I can help to choose some quality restaurants for those of us who appreciate fine dining. Don't

worry, Sue,' Ken continued slowly and deliberately, in an authoritative manner. 'There are several good hotels along the way. I've
advised Tommy about the best accommodation and food; we
should be in for some excellent *cordon bleu* meals. I've been to
France a lot and, I have to say, I'm your man when it comes to
knowing my *poulet roti* from my *boeuf bourguignon.*'

Duncan spoke up again. 'I want to sample as much beer as
possible.' He winked at Tommy. 'It's purely business though. I want
to find some fresh suppliers, improve my stock, keep up my link
with the European brewers.' He noticed the wide smile on Tommy's
face, which had quickly replicated itself on those of the youngsters,
Pat, Jake and DJ, so he added quickly, 'My dad's coming, of course –
he needs a break too and I can't leave him with Kerry. She has
enough on her plate running this place. Obviously, Dad's not
particularly sociable, as you all know – he prefers his own company.
He's eighty-one now, but I'm hoping the fresh air will be good for
him.'

Albert appeared to be asleep, then he opened one eye and
closed it again. He huddled inside his large overcoat and began to
snore lightly.

'My mother and her friend are a similar age – well, I think
Maggie's almost eighty.' Cassie folded her hands together. 'As long
as we can keep them comfortable in the minibus, lots of loo stops
and rest time...'

'Oh, my minibus is top notch,' Tommy spluttered. 'And I'll put
extra cushions in for the golden oldies...' He stopped himself,
offering an apologetic shrug.

'Well, I'm not sure we should be taking pensioners.' Denise
Grierson huffed dismissively. 'I'm only in my fifties and I wouldn't
want to be responsible for someone with health or mobility issues.
Perhaps there should be an age limit, say, sixty years old, just for

safety.' She gazed hopefully at Ken, then at Sue. 'It makes sense. What do you think, *Syoo?*'

Sue crossed her legs the other way. 'As long as everyone is in reasonable health and has holiday insurance, Denise, I don't think it matters.'

'It matters that we don't exclude people for no good reason, though.' Cassie sat up straight. She took a breath, making herself speak calmly despite the rising frustration. Injustice always made her cross and she knew she had a tendency to speak her mind without hesitation. 'My mum is very fit for her age. But if you believe that Lil and Maggie and I – because I'm sixty-five – will be a liability, just say so now and we won't come.' Cassie glanced at Tommy. 'You're organising it, Tommy. What do you say? I'm happy to take my mum and her pensioner friend to a nice comfortable hotel in Paris for a long weekend where there will be plenty of culture and *cordon bleu* cooking and excellent places to visit. I can get them luxury hotels and health insurance and no one else will run the risk of them expiring suddenly in the back seat of the minibus during the journey.' Cassie paused; she had already said too much.

Silence fell over the table for a few moments. Denise gazed at her expensively sandalled feet. Sue coughed; Emily pressed a hand over her mouth to cover a grin, DJ ruffled his locks and Ken fingered his cravat. Then Tommy slid his pen back behind his ear. 'I think your mum and Dunc's dad and the other lady will be fine, Cass...'

Denise spoke up again. 'And can I be assured that the best accommodation is booked, with comfortable rooms and good breakfast and single en suites for those who are by themselves? I mean – I don't want to find myself sharing with someone I don't know...' Her eyes moved suspiciously to Cassie and away again.

'Well, we'll sort out rooms each time we visit a hotel. My wife,

Angie, booked all the accommodation online, and she's a secretary at the school,' Tommy protested. 'Some of them are small hotels and won't always have single rooms.'

'We'll be fine.' Ken's voice was reassuring. 'Besides, if we get into difficulty, my French is a little rusty but I used to be quite fluent...'

Cassie pressed her lips together. 'When do we go, Tommy?'

'Two weeks' time, the 9th of August.'

'Going clubbing in Amsterdam will be brilliant,' Jake enthused. 'Lots of girls to impress.'

'It'll be a great laugh,' DJ agreed.

'And we'll drink lots of interesting beer and play football,' Pat said hopefully.

'I'm looking forward to scoring a few goals against the Belgians,' Emily announced. 'And I've always wanted to go to Amsterdam.'

'I can hardly wait,' Cassie said. In truth, she was trying to imagine what sort of venture this holiday would be, with the young five-a-side team, the middle-aged tennis club members, Duncan, his dad, her mother, Maggie and herself. She couldn't imagine. But, Cassie thought, ever the optimist, there would be interesting scenery, sightseeing, good food and the chance for Lil to enjoy herself. More to the point, she might even find some time for herself and the inspiration to write a few good poems.

'It's no good, Lil. I'm not going.'

'Of course, you are – we'll have a whale of a time, you and me.' Lil stared at Maggie, who was open-mouthed as they sat opposite each other in the café. Keith, his hair slicked back, tall and morose in his chef's uniform and a little white cap, placed a plate of toast and two cups of tea on the table in between them. Lil turned to him. 'Where's the butter?'

'On the toast,' Keith quipped, the empty tray in his tattooed hand.

'That tiny smudge?' Lil was flabbergasted.

'You know you love me, Lil.'

'Always, darling. But can't I have a bit more butter? Please, Keith? I've always had a taste for those bad-for-you things that have loads of cholesterol in them...' Lil watched him slope away and winked. 'Don't say you're not coming, Maggie.'

'I can't come.' She stuck out her bottom lip. 'I can't leave Brian.'

'What do you mean, you can't leave Brian? You can. You simply pack a case and we go.'

'But he needs me.'

'What for? To give you secondary smoke? To make your hair and clothes smell of cigarettes? So you can turn up the remote for him while he's busy leering at *Charlie's Angels*? You need a break, time for yourself, a good pampering.'

'You might be right.' Maggie shook her head. 'But I've never been to Northern Europe.'

'Well, now's your chance.'

'What about Brian?' Maggie sighed. 'What about his other needs?'

Lil's eyes widened. 'Do you mean bedroom action?'

'I mean company – he needs another person in the house.'

'Maggie, just for once, think of yourself. Put yourself first. If you do that, Brian might do it too.'

'I'm not used to being selfish.'

'Then get used to it – think of all the fun we can have: the food, the drink, the sights, a boat trip on the canal.'

Maggie sulked. 'He won't let me go if I ask. I bet he'll say no.'

'You don't need to ask him.' Lil hooted so loud that Keith came out from the kitchen. Lil blew him a kiss and lowered her voice.

'Don't worry about Brian. Don't even tell him. Just go. He probably won't even notice.'

Maggie's lower lip was trembling. 'But...'

'But nothing. He takes advantage of your kind nature. He can get his food here in the café. You deserve a break.'

'Do you think I could go, really?' Maggie was weakening.

'Of course. The deposit's paid. We can ask Jenny if her husband Tim will take us into town to buy some new clothes. Or we'll go shopping online. Either way, we can afford it. I have enough in my bank account for a few years yet – as long as I don't live to be a hundred and four...' Lil winked. 'Besides, I want a holiday and you need one and my Cassie deserves one, so that's it, decided. We'll have a great time, you and me. Europe here we come.'

Maggie nodded, still anxious. 'Brian won't be happy.'

'Good. He needs a wake-up call. He'll miss you like mad and recognise you for the lovely woman you are.' Lil moved closer to her friend. 'This is the plan. We'll sneak out without telling him. We'll pack the night before; you can leave your case in my flat and you can just tell him you're going to the toilet, then we'll get on the minibus and go. No "goodbye, Brian", no "I'll miss you, my darling". Just close the door, forget him for a few days and we'll have the time of our lives. What do you say?'

'We won't even tell him we're going?'

'Precisely.'

'We'll just go? Say nothing at all?'

'Exactly.'

'But what happens when he notices I'm not there?' Maggie gasped.

'Maggie.' Lil took a deep breath. 'I've lived without a man in my life for longer than I can remember. I've got nothing against them. They are lovely beings, men, but sometimes they get it wrong and they let you down. Brian needs to be reminded what a sexy, wonderful, fun wife he has. And he will – once you're not there. So – what do you say?'

Maggie thought for a moment and then a grin started to spread across her face. She leaned over and squeezed her friend in a too-tight hug. 'I say – let's do it, Lil. I think it's the best idea you've ever had. I can spoil myself, put myself first for once. A minibus holiday in Europe? Bring it on...'

5

Cassie watched as Jamie poured wine. The soft red liquid splashed into the bottom of the glasses, making an almost imperceptible glugging sound. She gazed around at the honey-yellow lighting of the taverna, the illuminated serving bar at the far end of the room, the framed posters on the wall of Zeus and Athena, and back to the spanakopita on her plate. She lifted a fork. 'Well, this is nice, Jamie – what a treat. Thank you.'

'I love coming here. It's a friendly place and I can practise my Greek with the waiter. And it reminds me of my parents and the times they took me to see my *yia-yia* when I was a child, my grandmother. She spoiled me rotten every time we went to Cephalonia.'

Cassie chewed thoughtfully. 'All that Greek food must have been delicious. It was a great idea to have dinner here.'

'My pleasure.' Jamie beamed. 'It's a special occasion.'

'Because I am going away tomorrow?'

'Oh, no – I just want you to enjoy yourself as much as you can...' Jamie gazed at Cassie, taking in the halo of snow-white hair, the red bow she had tied around it, the long triangular earrings, the emerald silk dress. He thought she was lovely.

'Are you sure you don't want to come with us?' Cassie met his eyes. 'It won't be the same without you. I could ask Tommy to squeeze one more seat in – that's just a bit less space for luggage and beer...'

He shook his head. 'No, you go and have fun with your mother. Have some bonding time, the two of you. Do some writing...'

'Will you be all right by yourself?'

'I'll be perfectly fine – you know I will.' Jamie smiled broadly, hiding the thought that the house would be quiet without her.

Cassie patted his hand. 'So – this meal tonight? Is it a bon voyage, Cassie, have a lovely time or a sort of Last Supper because I'm going away with Lil and it could be an absolute nightmare? Do you feel sorry for me?'

'Not at all.' Jamie lifted his fork, meeting her gaze. 'This is a special occasion. It's two years today.'

Cassie frowned. 'Two years since what?'

'Since you took me in as your house guest.'

'What else could I do? You had nowhere to go.' Cassie shrugged. 'When you rang me and said Anna wanted you to leave, I had to offer. I mean, I have a three-bedroomed house and there was only me in it.'

Jamie smiled. 'You've been great though, Cass. I don't pay rent. I don't help much around the house...'

'I don't need rent. You're a great cook. I eat the best food Greece has to offer. And you listen to my poems and songs and tell me the truth about them. Nobody else would put up with me.'

'I love living with you...' Jamie exhaled slowly. 'I've had some difficult times in my life, Cass. My marriage turned out to be a car crash and I have MS.' Jamie thought about reaching out, touching Cassie's hand, then he changed his mind. 'I just hope you didn't take me in because you felt sorry for me.'

'You are wonderful, Jamie. You don't need anyone's sympathy.

I'm always so impressed with how you manage everything. I've never done particularly well on the relationship front either. Men find me too single-minded and outspoken.'

'Oh, I think you're perfect as you are.' Jamie changed the subject quickly, stretching out his hands. 'My fingers tingle a bit today.' He reached for his wine. 'Thank goodness Mariposa said it's okay to have a drink every now and then. A man has to indulge once in a while.'

'I love the way you call your doctor Mariposa.'

'I can't call her Dr Gonzales; we're far too intimate for that now. She knows everything about me.'

'So, you bought me dinner to celebrate the anniversary of the end of your marriage?'

'No, I'm celebrating living here with you now.' Jamie's eyes shone.

'I remember when we first met, I had a performance on TV in the afternoon and you did the sound check. After rehearsals, you bought me lunch in Shepherd's Bush. We got tipsy on ouzo and staggered back to the studio...' Cassie smiled.

'Then you performed so powerfully, as if not a drop had touched your lips. You were inspired.'

Cassie nodded. 'No, I was well rehearsed. And I had no pre-performance nerves at all after the ouzo.'

Jamie was on a roll. 'And remember, we met up again at Edinburgh and that rapper was trying to chat you up.'

Cassie remembered, smiling. 'Jazzy Ed with the earrings and the kaftan and the crimson hair. I went out with him for two weeks. He complained that I was more interested in my poems than in him.' She laughed. 'He was right.'

'And we met up again in Brighton, and Manchester – remember Liverpool in 2016?'

'Sheffield – I loved the gigs I did there.'

Jamie sighed. 'And then in 2017, it all blew up. Anna wanted me to go.'

'I remember you ringing me.'

'I was in a panic. I had nowhere to live.'

Cassie smiled reassuringly. 'I never thought you were in a panic – you seemed so calm, so sure of what you were doing. And we'd always got on well.'

'These two years have been lovely, the best. You're quite special...' Jamie wondered what to say next and how to say it. He thought of spilling his feelings, a rush of too-long-hidden emotion, but as he took a breath his courage failed. He raised his glass instead. 'To you, Cassie, to your generosity, your kindness, your loveliness...'

Cassie took in his shining eyes, his handsome face; he was smart in his elegant suit. 'To me and you, Jamie – the odd couple. We rub along all right together, don't we?'

'Cheers. *Yamas,* as my dad used to say.' Jamie chinked his glass against hers and offered a rueful smile. 'To rubbing along.'

Cassie agreed. 'Absolutely. That's better than most housemates do.'

'Housemates.' Jamie repeated the word softly. He wondered if now was the best time to tell her how he felt, but his mind couldn't formulate the right words. He sighed again. It would keep. He murmured, 'Oh, I hope we're a bit more than just housemates, Cassie.'

* * *

Maggie's luggage was packed, standing upright like a sentry behind the front door to Lil's flat, next to Lil's bulging pink suitcase, stuffed with clothes and a couple of novels she hoped to find time to read, her treasured black and white photo flattened between the pages. It was almost nine o' clock in the morning; the minibus would arrive at nine exactly. Lil was ready: she had her jacket on, a warm pullover, stretchy trousers that would be easy to travel in and some comfortable ankle boots she'd recently bought online. She was waiting for Maggie, who had promised to be there at a quarter to. She was ten minutes late.

Lil swung her handbag onto her shoulder, the round one designed like a cat with green felt whiskers, and decided she should take action. Leaving her door open, she went into the corridor and noticed Maggie's door was ajar. A bitter stench came from inside and the haze of hanging cigarette smoke caught in her throat. There were other smells, heavy sweat from clothes, grease from fried eggs. Lil peered through the crack in the doorway into the lounge, staring straight towards the television, blaring loudly. An armchair faced the TV, its back to her, and Lil could see the top of Brian's head, a wispy grey tuft poking over the back. Smoke curled from his head as if he were a sleeping dragon. She crept through the lounge, her feet soft on the patterned carpet, moving towards the kitchenette. She could glimpse Maggie inside, washing dishes. She was wearing slippers. Lil slithered behind the kitchen door, pushing it closed but being careful not to let it snap shut.

She stared into Maggie's surprised eyes and mouthed, 'Come on. We'll be late.'

Maggie mouthed back exaggeratedly, shaking her head. 'I'm not coming.'

Lil put her hands on her hips and frowned, whispering, 'Why not?'

Maggie's eyes bulged. She pointed to the living room, her expression frantic. 'I can't do it – I can't leave Brian.'

Lil grasped Maggie's hand in one lightning move. 'Be brave. We've agreed we'd go. You need a holiday. Come on – one step at a time.'

Maggie gesticulated towards the living room wildly as Lil tugged her arm. Maggie tottered forwards, bumping into the stacked plates in a rack on the draining board. One slipped into the sink followed by another and splintered, making a sudden crashing noise as a plate broke in half. Both women stood still, frozen, holding their breath, waiting for Brian to respond. There was no sound except for the continuous rattle of the television.

Maggie shrugged elaborately, her eyes panicking. 'What do I do now?'

'Follow me.' Lil waved her hand towards the door. 'We're going.'

'He needs me.'

'What for?'

'I'm his wife. I have to stay with him. I'm all he's got.'

'You're all you've got.' Lil grabbed Maggie by the shoulder and marched her through the kitchen, into the lounge and out of the door. Brian stayed where he was, smoke coiling, the back of his head stiff against the chair. She continued to propel Maggie until they were inside her flat, standing by the two upright cases. Lil forced her friend to look into her eyes.

'Right, well done. You've made it. Now we're going on holiday.'

Maggie collapsed against the wall. 'Oh, dear – I almost chickened out.'

'Are you all right?'

'I think so...'

Lil took a breath. 'How do you feel?'

'Thank goodness you came for me, Lil. I scribbled a note for him but then I froze – I just couldn't do it by myself.'

'What happened?'

Maggie exhaled slowly. 'My feet wouldn't carry me out of the flat. It's as if he has some sort of magical power, keeping me there...'

'You need this holiday so badly. And it will do both you and

Brian a favour,' Lil said firmly. 'Come on, Maggie – the minibus will be waiting.'

'You're right. I am in a rut. And as you said, Brian won't notice I've gone for hours.' Maggie pointed at her feet and groaned. 'Oh, no. I've still got my slippers on.'

'Have you got shoes packed in your case?'

'Yes – some trainers and a smart pair.'

'Then you'll do as you are. The slippers will be comfortable to travel in. We can always buy shoes in Europe – they have supermarkets and shops.'

Maggie protested again. 'I haven't got a coat, Lil.'

'I'll have something you'll look fabulous in.'

'Your coat won't fit me.'

'Of course, it will.' Lil beamed, reaching across to a hanger behind the door, and offered Maggie a choice of two. 'Which is it to be? The faux leopard or the anorak?'

'I don't know,' Maggie wailed. It was impossible to make a decision. Lil's mind worked quickly – the leopard faux fur was a generous style that swamped her own small frame. She thrust it into her friend's arms. 'Right, you'll be warm and gorgeous at the same time. It might be August but that wind is cutting. Now let's go.'

Maggie struggled into the coat. She ran her fingers over the soft faux fur and smiled weakly. 'Do I look like a film star?'

'You look glorious. Now come on.'

Maggie wavered, her mouth open. 'I haven't done anything by myself in years...'

Lil grabbed a case and shoved it into Maggie's hand, picking up the other and propelling her forwards. 'Okay. I've got the luggage, I've got you. We're as ready as we'll ever be. Let's hit the road. Europe here we come.'

Maggie allowed herself to be pushed forwards in the furry coat, the case dangling from her hand. She groaned, one tortured word. 'Brian...?'

'He'll still be here when we're back. This is the beginning of the new independent Maggie,' Lil offered and slammed the door behind her. The hallway smelled of lingering cigarette smoke, sweat and fried eggs. Lil marched Maggie past the door of her flat and a triumphant smile broke out on both their faces. They were on their way.

Lil shuffled up the steps and onto the minibus, sitting behind Cassie, who was in the front seat next to Tommy, who was driving, his belly against the steering wheel. Lil tugged Maggie next to her, wrapping an arm through hers, both for comfort and to stop her changing her mind and running back to Brian. Lil glanced over her shoulder and waved to the other passengers: a debonair man in his fifties in a smart blazer and cravat seated next to a frantic man, who was ticking names on a list; two middle-aged women were sitting together but leaning away from each other, holding up magazines; three lads and a young blonde woman were sitting at the back. The youngsters called 'Hello,' and the young man with longish inky hair that Lil thought made him look like someone from a Dracula movie shouted, 'Hi, Lil. Hi, Maggie.' She was impressed that he knew their names.

Opposite her sat an elderly man with sparkling blue eyes, huddled inside a huge overcoat. Lil pulled out a packet of chocolate triangles from her handbag and held the bag across Maggie's lap towards the older man by way of introduction. Maggie took one. Lil leaned further forward, making Maggie gasp inside the faux leopard coat.

'I'm Lil. Have a chocolate triangle. They are nice, quite chewy and I find they don't stick to your teeth.'

The man gazed at her a moment but said nothing. Lil wondered if he didn't understand English, but she liked his face, his twinkling eyes. She rattled the bag at him for emphasis and he mouthed a word half-formed, then he reached out a hand and took a sweet, gazing at it for a few moments before unwrapping the green foil and staring at the chocolate that was melting between his fingers.

'Go on,' Lil murmured. 'Knock yourself out.'

She watched as he pushed the chocolate triangle into his mouth. He leaned back in his seat, chewed slowly and closed his eyes. Maggie took another sweet before Lil hurriedly replaced the packet in the bottom of her handbag.

Fifteen minutes passed as suitcases were stowed in the space at the rear. There was loud, excited chatter. DJ and Jake were teasing Pat in the back seat, Emily was texting and Ken was telling everyone around him who would listen about Pont-l'Evêque, a particularly delicious if smelly Norman cheese. Then everyone was comfortably settled and gazing expectantly at Tommy, who called from the front of the minibus. 'Right, are we all here?'

'I hope so,' Duncan answered on behalf of everyone else. 'I've just counted heads.'

'Okay,' Tommy said matter-of-factly. He twisted round, meeting rows of expectant eyes. 'I'm Tommy Judd, the organiser of this tour.' He puffed out his chest. 'So, let's just go round and do introductions, shall we?' He raised his eyebrows. 'Since we're going to be getting to know each other very well.'

'I'll begin, shall I?' Ken touched his silk cravat with light fingers. 'Ken Harrington. I'm a historian and an author with an interest in architecture and foreign travel. I intend to practise my rusty French and eat gourmet food.'

'Sue Wheeler.' Sue shifted her neat figure and boomed, 'Salterley tennis club. I'm the social secretary.'

'Thanks, *Syoo*.' Denise took a breath. 'I'm Denise Grierson. New to the tennis club and the area. I want to...' she gazed around '... expand my social circle.'

Pat chimed from the back of the minibus. 'I'm Pat Stott, the goalkeeper.'

'He wants to expand his social circle too.' DJ laughed. 'He hasn't had a girlfriend in ages.' There was silence as Pat's cheeks glowed. 'I'm DJ Niati,' DJ added. 'And I can't wait for all the laughs we're going to have in Amsterdam.'

'Me too,' Jake agreed. 'I'm Jake and I'm looking forward to the clubs and the night life and the football.' He elbowed DJ and they both nodded in agreement. 'And meeting all the Dutch girls...'

'Emily Weston.' Emily smiled confidently. 'I'm going for the football game. And because Pat and DJ and Jake are three of the nicest guys in the world, despite being completely immature.' She winked as DJ hugged her.

'Duncan Hopkins, the barman,' Duncan muttered. 'You all know me. I'm only here for the beer, as they say.' He pointed to the older man in the overcoat, who was staring through the window. 'That's my dad, Albert. He doesn't say much but he'll be happy if you buy him a pint.'

Cassie spoke up smoothly. 'Cassie Ryan. And I'm looking forward to getting to know you all even better.'

'Likewise,' Ken murmured, picking an imaginary speck of dust from his pristine blazer.

There was a silence, then Lil gazed around the bus. 'Ah. Hello. I'm Lil,' she said. 'Lil Ryan. I need a holiday. I haven't been anywhere for a long time.' She gazed at Maggie. 'And this is my friend Maggie Lewis. She needs a break from her Brian.'

'I do,' Maggie agreed.' And I'm having one...'

'Right. Introductions over. And we're off,' Tommy yelled excitedly. He started the engine and raised his voice to an even louder pitch. 'Happy holidays, everybody.'

A rousing cheer came from the back of the bus as Tommy reversed eagerly out of the car park. There was a bump, a light crunch and another whoop from the back seat.

'My days, you've hit something,' DJ shouted as he twisted round.

'It's a blue car,' Jake added.

'A blue Volkswagen Up!' Emily explained. 'We've dented the front bumper, I think.'

'Oh no – that's Jenny Price's car.' Lil was alarmed. Her immediate instinct was to go and find Jenny and hug her.

'Her pride and joy.' Maggie's eyes were wide with fear, as if she was imagining Jenny's reaction. 'There will be hell to pay. Oh dear – things haven't started well.'

'Leave it with me,' Cassie murmured, sliding out of the front passenger seat. 'I'll pop in and explain. We can sort out everything else once we're back.'

'Shall I come with you?' Lil asked, concerned. 'Poor Jenny.'

'No, stay where you are. I'll sort it out, Lil.'

'You haven't been drinking, have you, Tommy?' Duncan asked.

'No...' Tommy's ears reddened.

Pat's face creased with laughter. 'We haven't even got out of the car park yet and Tommy's in trouble.'

'You have passed a proper minibus test, I hope?' Ken asked.

'Of course.' Tommy was purple with embarrassment.

'We won't fall behind schedule will we?' Denise frowned.

Sue waved a hand as if dismissing an annoying fly. 'I have to say, it wasn't exactly the start to my holiday that I was hoping for.'

'Sorry, everyone,' Tommy spluttered. 'I wasn't expecting a car to be parked there.'

'It is a car park, my dear,' Sue reminded him, with an expression of dissatisfaction.

'Do we have a second driver, someone who has taken the appropriate test – just in case?' Ken asked.

'That would be me,' Duncan offered. He didn't intend to drive the minibus; he'd be too busy sampling the local beers, purely professionally of course. He said nothing more.

Tommy shook his head. 'I've driven this thing loads of times – I did that trip last year to Alton Towers, remember, with the football team?'

DJ shouted from the back seat. 'The one where Jake puked all the way home?'

Emily elbowed him. 'I don't remember you clearing it up, DJ. You left the bus claiming you felt queasy and I had to sort it all out.'

'I'd been eating a burger – I think the beef must have been off,' DJ protested.

'Can we please not mention being sick?' Denise huffed. 'We haven't left the car park yet. And what's that awful smell?'

Everyone turned to stare at Pat, who had produced a beef pasty from his bag and had started to tuck in. He stared at the accusing faces. 'I was hungry. All that talk about burgers...'

'We really ought to be on our way to Portsmouth,' Ken suggested, glancing at an expensive timepiece on his wrist.

'I agree, Ken,' Sue boomed.

'We'll make good time, don't you worry.' Tommy waved a hand. 'I know the way, all the shortcuts. This little minibus can belt along when I get her up to speed...'

'Oh, we don't want to be speeding.' Denise frowned.

Lil elbowed Maggie and whispered softly. 'This is great, isn't it? Better than watching Brian watch TV. Much more entertaining.'

Maggie nodded, holding out her hand. 'And the chocolates are nice.'

Cassie was back in the minibus. 'Right, I've spoken to Jenny and we've agreed she'll take the car to a garage where her brother-in-law works and he'll fix it. I don't think there's much damage done and we'll sort out any payment when we're back.' She breathed out. 'So – let's go.'

Tommy started the engine again, edging forward and then reversing while Jake shouted instructions from the back seat. 'Left hand down, now stop. Stop! No, no, go left now. Back a bit, no, a bit more – stop, stop, Tommy, stop!'

DJ burst out laughing. 'Right, you're there now, Tommy – the road is that wide grey tarmacked thing just in front of you now. My days, do you think you'll be all right driving by yourself?'

A dismissive snort came from the driver's seat and Cassie's calm voice could be heard whispering something about how Tommy should programme the satnav. Lil patted Maggie's arm.

'We're off, Maggie. Portsmouth here we come. I can't wait. We'll have such fun.'

Lil noticed the concern in Maggie's eyes and reached into her cat handbag for the packet of chocolate triangles. As she looked up, she noticed Albert in the seat opposite turn to her and hold out his flat bony hand with a hopeful expression. He offered her a charming smile and she smiled back.

It was early evening, after five, the minibus was safely stowed in the car deck, and the ferry was in motion. Duncan and Tommy had led everyone into the bar and the five-a-side team, Lil, Maggie and Duncan's father, Albert, were sitting around a large table full of drinks and crisp packets, chattering. Further down, perched at a high table on stools, Cassie, Sue and Denise were sharing their hopes for the holiday while waiting for Ken, who was at the bar, having offered to buy them all a drink.

'The thing is—' Sue was applying fresh lipstick '—I have been working far too hard. I manage a group of florists and, my dear, you wouldn't *imagine* the work it takes to keep them all up and running. I only hope they won't mess up my ordering system while I'm away.'

'It's the same for me, *Syoo*,' Denise pointed out. 'I am solely responsible for paying so many people's wages on time. I make sure everything is done properly. It's a matter of professional pride.'

Cassie was sympathetic. 'I think you both deserve a break from work. It sounds exhausting.'

Sue nodded. 'You're a professional poet, aren't you, Cassie? I've seen you perform in The Jolly Weaver so often. Last Christmas, the entire tennis club – all twenty of us – came to the Boxing Day open mic session. Do you remember – we all got up to sing the "Twelve Days of Christmas"?'

'I remember it well.' Cassie's eyes shone. 'I think every number after six was the maids a-milking.'

Sue boomed loudly. 'We'd been on the sherry just a little.' She glanced at Denise. 'That was all before you arrived in Salterley, Denise.'

'I do enjoy singing though, *Syoo*. It's been said many a time that I have a good voice.'

Sue sniffed. 'Cassie sings well. I've heard you. And you play the banjo, don't you, my dear?'

Cassie nodded. 'Light relief from the poems. Lil gave me the banjo when I was a little one and I picked it up straight away. As some famous Irish musician once said, any *ould shite* can play a banjo...' She glanced up as Ken arrived carrying a tray of glasses. He put them down in front of the three women.

'Here – two G and Ts, a grapefruit juice for me and your pint of bitter, Cassie.'

She reached for her glass and took a deep drink. 'Thanks, Ken – that's very nice of you.'

He sat down and adjusted his cravat. 'It's my pleasure.' He beamed at the women. 'The wine on these ferries is bog-standard. I can't drink it. Grapefruit juice is so refreshing.'

Sue cleared her throat. 'You're married, aren't you, Cassie? I've seen you in The Weaver with a man, the one with the walking stick. He's your husband, isn't he, my dear?'

'Housemate,' Cassie muttered between sips. 'He's called Jamie.'

Denise breathed out in a huff. 'Oh, I'm divorced now, thank goodness. You're the same as me, aren't you, *Syoo*?'

'I left my husband two years ago, Denise. And I have to say, my life has improved tremendously. He was a scumbag.'

Denise opened her eyes wide, as if a little shocked by Sue's strong words. 'I left Bob last year and moved here. He was a scumbag too.' She gazed hopefully at Ken. 'Are you divorced, Ken?'

'I'm afraid so.' He shrugged sadly. 'My ex-wife, Caroline, and I didn't really share the same concept of partnership. She was very quiet, domestic: she stayed home baking while I needed more stimulation from external things – museums, travel, and meeting interesting people.' He raised an eyebrow in Cassie's direction. 'It's good to be in the company of someone with an artistic bent.'

Cassie swallowed more beer.

'I wanted to talk to you all,' Sue began, 'because I think we four share a common interest. While I'm delighted the others are going to enjoy a fabulous ten days drinking and playing football, I'm here because I want to immerse myself in the culture and I think you are all of a similar mindset, my dears.'

'Absolutely, *Syoo*,' Denise enthused. 'Certainly, I know that we members of the tennis club share the same passions.' She glanced at Cassie, who met her eyes and smiled.

'I've been reading about Belgium a lot, the cities we'll visit, the architecture, the history.' Ken raised his eyebrows. 'I'm very keen on history. I do lots of lectures at the local library in between writing my books. When Duncan the barman rang me personally and told me about this trip, I said I'd be delighted to come along and share my knowledge.'

Sue sat upright. 'Oh, you're an author?'

'Yes, I am.' Ken nodded, sipping his grapefruit juice. 'I do quite nicely – it keeps the wolf from the door.'

'That sounds idyllic.' Denise sighed. 'Writing and travelling all the time. It certainly beats sitting in a smelly office behind a computer.'

'So, as I was saying, my dear.' Sue waved an authoritative finger. 'I imagine we four will spend a lot of time together; we have all that in common, love of museums, art, architecture, fine food and wine. So, I thought we'd make a little pact, sort of set up a friendship group, and keep an eye out for each other.'

'I do like a good robust wine,' Denise agreed. 'Don't you, Ken?'

'I have spent a long time studying wine,' Ken admitted, brushing imaginary dust from his blazer. 'I have a good palate, I'm told.'

Cassie waved her pint. 'I'll drink most things.' She noticed Denise's sharp glance of surprise. 'But I don't think we should write the others off as philistines just yet.'

'Oh, no, not at all,' Ken agreed.

'I didn't mean...' Sue began. Denise was shaking her head in horror.

'For instance—' Cassie waved a hand, always ready with an opinion '—young Emily's an engineer who designs submarines. Jake is a plumber and he's also a part-time artist; he sketches incredible likenesses. And DJ...' She leaned forward to make her point. 'He has a degree in animation. Pat works with his father in the family business, carpentry, but he also makes and paints little models of soldiers. He has a keen eye for detail. And...' Cassie glanced at each face '...my mother is not without her talents, I can assure you.'

'Indeed – I was chatting to your mother briefly down on the car deck,' Ken chipped in. 'A most interesting woman. I'm looking forward to getting to know her better. It might provide a fascinating insight into past times, you know, primary research for a book.'

Cassie raised an eyebrow. 'Oh, Lil's interesting all right.'

A whoop went up from the table where Pat was balancing an empty beer glass on his forehead and Lil was on her feet, waving her arms and trying to distract him, to make him lose concentration, while Maggie applauded. The plastic glass fell on Pat's lap and everyone cheered again.

Sue leaned forward, preening. 'Well, I wanted to share this with you, my dears. The tennis club has a social fund and, as social secretary, I've been allocated a small contribution to buy everyone a meal when we're in France. You know, a way of bonding and sharing food, breaking bread together on behalf of the tennis club.'

'What a wonderful idea, *Syoo*.'

'Of course, I'll make up any shortfall myself,' Sue added in a loud voice.

'I'd like to contribute too.' Ken scratched his ear. 'I don't do enough within the tennis club nowadays, as I'm so busy writing. But I can help you to select the perfect place for us all to dine, somewhere the cuisine is top rate. It would be a tremendous experience, sitting together, sharing the best that France can offer us on a plate.'

'And as I'm also hoping to be a long-term club member, I'd like to chip in too – a gesture of warmth, friendship and bonding.'

Denise glanced at Ken, checking his expression for approval. 'The three of us could be hosts.'

'It might be just the way to start the holiday, my dears?' Sue suggested, folding her arms neatly.

'Or even a good way to end it, *Syoo*?' Denise added enthusiastically.

Cassie watched her mother place the empty plastic beer glass on her forehead and attempt to balance it there while Pat was gurning into her face to break her concentration. She met Sue's eyes.

'That's a really lovely idea. I'm sure we could all bond together over some nouvelle cuisine.' She watched the glass tumble from Lil's head and onto the table with a crack. 'I think this holiday is going to be an interesting journey for us all.'

7

Three hours later, the minibus, packed with weary travellers, descended the ferry ramp into the sunset and headed for the centre of Cherbourg via the bridge. They arrived at their hotel, L'Etable, where they were welcomed by a tall man with huge forearms, wearing an apron, who introduced himself as François. He showed them to their rooms, after which the five-a-side-team, Duncan and Albert went to the bar for a beer and a burger, despite the protestations of the three members of Salterley tennis club, who wanted them all to accompany them to a great little restaurant two streets away. Lil complained that she was tired and her hip was killing her, so François kindly offered to bring sandwiches to the room she was sharing with Maggie and Cassie. They sprawled on single beds, their cases unpacked, ate cheese and onion rolls and shared a bottle of red wine. Suddenly, Lil's hip was much improved.

'You should've gone with the tennis club, Cass, or at least had a burger with the others in the bar.' She winked at Maggie. 'We aren't going to allow ourselves to be a burden to you this week. You enjoy yourself. I intend to, even if it does mean I have to get an early night every so often. All that travelling was quite tiring today.'

'It was balancing the beer glasses on your head that wore you out, Lil,' Maggie mumbled, half a cheese roll in her mouth. 'It made me laugh though. I feel a bit guilty that we're not all eating out together on the first night of our holiday.'

'It'll be a busy day tomorrow, so it's a good idea to rest tonight.' Cassie slid from her bed to the floor and stretched out her legs, then reached for the wine bottle. 'Tommy said we're visiting the beaches of World War Two. Then we're travelling north and staying in a lovely little hotel in Amiens. We'll all eat together there tomorrow, when we're all rested. There's plenty of time to get to know everyone well.'

Lil closed her eyes for a moment. 'Ah, it feels so nice to be away from home.' She sighed. 'Don't get me wrong – I love my little flat and the Kaff and Keith's toast and sneaking in the office to do random acts of kindness for Jenny Price, but it's just so nice to remind myself that there's a world beyond the front doorstep of Clover Hill.'

'And it's nice to be away from Brian.' Maggie folded her arms determinedly. 'The air is cleaner. It's not just the cigarettes and the fried stuff – it's the way the smell of him occupies every corner. His clothes and the stench of his body fill every space. I'm just a lodger who does the cleaning and the laundry and makes tea in the kitchenette. I'm fed up and unappreciated.'

Cassie agreed. 'I have a feeling this break is going to do us all good, Maggie. I'm glad Lil persuaded you to come.' She took a sandwich from the plate on the bed in front of her mother. 'I think we all needed a holiday.'

'They are such nice kids, too,' Lil observed. 'I was enjoying the game with Pat in the bar. He says it's even better after a few pints and chasers, but I only had the one drink. They've all got a good sense of humour, those youngsters. I noticed you were entertaining the tennis club on the ferry, Cassie.'

'Do you think they might be a bit snooty?' Maggie asked. 'I haven't really spoken to any of them yet.'

'Aloof?' Lil suggested by way of interpretation. 'I'm not sure the women like each other much, or anyone else for that matter, and that man, Ken, is definitely too keen on himself.'

'Oh, they're fine, once you get to know them. I think it will be a nice mix of people. We'll all get to know each other better over the next ten days,' Cassie decided. 'The tennis club members have offered to buy everyone dinner on the last night of the holiday. I think it'll be a lovely celebration.'

There was a knock on the door. Maggie stiffened; the fear in her eyes made Cassie wonder if she thought it might be Brian, who had somehow followed her and was here to take her home. Cassie answered softly, 'Just coming,' and opened the door to see fresh-faced Emily, wearing a jacket, jeans and a T-shirt, smiling broadly.

'Hi, Cassie. DJ, Jake, Pat and I are just going into the town for a stroll. We thought we might pop into a supermarket if there is anywhere open and pick up a few snacks for the journey tomorrow: crisps, cans of cola. Was there anything you wanted?'

'That's kind,' Cassie said.

'Chocolate triangles,' Lil yelled from the bed.

Maggie swallowed a mouthful of wine. 'I'd like a bar of chocolate – or some crisps. Or both, if you don't mind.'

Emily pushed back a wisp of hair. 'Anything for you, Cassie?'

'No, thanks.' Cassie smiled. 'But it was kind of you to ask. I think Lil and Maggie plan on getting an early night. I'm going to find a quiet space and ring home. I'll see you tomorrow. Sleep well, Emily.'

* * *

Half an hour later, Cassie was on the landing, holding the phone to her ear. 'So, how's it going?'

Jamie's voice came back to her as clearly as if he were standing at her shoulder. 'I'm fine, Cass. How was the journey?'

'After the initial collision with Jenny Price's car, it was fine.'

'What happened?'

'Ah, no real damage was done. Tommy's not a bad driver. We had lots of stops on the way for Lil and Maggie to go to the toilet and buy sweets and move about a bit.' She smiled. 'It's like taking kids on holiday.' Cassie was thoughtful for a moment. 'Not that I've had any children to take on holiday myself.'

'What about all those children you taught when you worked abroad?'

'The kids in Senegal and Guangzhou didn't really have trips out with me and, anyway, they were much more polite and self-disciplined than Lil could ever be.'

Jamie's voice was warm with affection. 'I want you to make sure that you have a great time. Relax, enjoy yourself, write a few poems, drink some wine.'

Cassie made a soft sound through her lips. 'You make it sound idyllic. There are twelve other people on the bus, all with their own idea of what a good time looks like.' She sighed. 'Maybe we should have just had a holiday, the two of us.'

'One day, perhaps.' He was quiet at the other end for a moment, then he spoke softly. 'I made dolmades tonight. What did you have for dinner? Oysters? Escargots?'

Cassie shook her head. 'A cheese sandwich and a bottle of cheap red with Lil and Maggie.'

He tutted. 'Seriously, I want you to have a fab time. I want you to come back refreshed and revitalised.'

'I will.' She wanted to be sure, so she asked again. 'Are you going to be all right?'

'I'm the one who is eating good food – you're the one with the butties and plonk,' Jamie replied. 'But, please, don't worry about me. What are you doing tomorrow?'

'Cemeteries and the beaches where the Americans landed in World War Two.'

'That sounds really quite grim,' Jamie murmured. 'Is that your sort of thing?'

'Yes, I don't see why not. It's fascinating. I might write a poem or two about it. It'll be inspirational, I'm sure.'

'Well, just make sure you have a good laugh too – it shouldn't be all doom and gloom. Are all the other people on the trip nice?'

'Lovely,' Cassie purred. 'But not as lovely as you.'

'You can be such a flirt,' Jamie chided gently.

Cassie thought he sounded flattered. 'Well, I'll call you tomorrow, Jamie – and tell you all about it.'

'I'll do my best to keep body and soul together until then.' She heard him laugh softly.

'I'll bring you a tacky souvenir home,' she retorted.

'Make it a nice bottle, and we'll share it.' There was warmth in his tone. 'Seriously, though, have some fun.'

She heard the phone click at the other end. Cassie put her mobile phone in her pocket and turned back to the room. She hoped that her mother and Maggie were already tucked up in bed but, as she creaked the door open, she could hear Lil regaling her friend with the story about the time when she ran the B&B and she had to throw one of the guests out, a Mr Ernest Postlethwaite from Pontefract. Cassie pushed open the door to see Lil and Maggie huddled on one bed, drinking red wine from the toothbrush glasses, chattering like schoolgirls.

'What did he do wrong, your Mr Postlethwaite?' Maggie asked, eyes wide.

'What, other than complain about the over-fried bacon and steal my cutlery?'

'He did that, Lil? That's terrible.'

'Oh, yes, but worse was yet to come...' Lil licked her lips, enjoying her own performance. 'One night when I was asleep, he pushed through the door marked Private, came into my room, and got into bed with me.'

'Oh, no! What did you do?' Maggie was alarmed.

'Well, he was hardly Omar Sharif or I'd have let him stay.' Lil slurped wine. 'I was in my shortie nightie. He had hairy ears. So, I asked him what he thought he was doing and he said he'd been sleepwalking and he'd taken a wrong turn and he couldn't help it as the poor lighting on my landing made him very disorientated. So I told him he could just sleepwalk back to his own room or he'd be sleeping for a very long time.'

'You didn't.' Maggie gasped.

'Oh, she did.' Cassie pursed her lips. 'Lil was no pushover. Never has been.'

'You never married though, Lil?'

'No, I had a lucky escape,' Lil joked, then she sighed. 'I kept myself busy instead. Even when Cassie left I – I don't know, maybe I didn't find the right man, maybe I was too independent.'

'Too independent, yes, and stubborn, like me, too set in your ways.' Cassie smiled.

'Do you think men prefer a woman to be a pushover, like me?' Maggie asked sadly.

'Never.' Lil shook her head. 'Love's a lottery though – sometimes the right one gets away. I decided I'd avoid getting my fingers burned a second time.'

'Or maybe we just haven't met anyone who is equal to the job?' Cassie laughed, defiant.

'Cassie, love.' Lil patted the bed next to her. 'Come and sit here, pour yourself another glass and tell us the one about when you were performing your poems in London and you met that politician and he made an improper suggestion...'

'He wasn't a politician, Lil, he was a banker.' Cassie moved over to where Lil was holding out the bottle.

'I love these stories.' Maggie rubbed her hands enthusiastically. 'I've really missed out on all this stuff, you know, romance and fun and frolics. Sometimes, I think my life has been a bit boring.'

Lil smacked her lips together. 'Well, Cassie certainly hasn't missed out. My girl has travelled the world and she's done so many interesting things. She tells a good story too, our Cass – she knows how to keep the best bits back until the end, don't you, love?'

Cassie watched Lil fill up her glass to the top before emptying the last of the wine into the other two glasses. Lil fished out a second bottle from next to the bed and grinned wickedly. Cassie noticed the soft gleam in her mother's eye; it was going to be a long night.

* * *

The next morning, in the huge breakfast room, a quiet couple in their early twenties were holding hands across the table, and a smart woman in a suit was talking in fast French on her phone as she sipped black coffee, her legs crossed neatly. François, still wearing the apron and his shirt sleeves rolled showing huge fore-arms of Popeye's proportions, was carrying a loaded tray to a table covered with a white cloth, where Pat, DJ, Tommy, Emily and Jake were eating rolls and drinking coffee. At the table next to them, Sue, Ken, Denise and Duncan were spreading jam on bread and slurping tea while Albert stared around, still in his huge overcoat. Cassie breezed in, offering a cheery good morning to everyone. She was followed by Lil and Maggie, both wearing huge sunglasses, walking precariously and sitting down without scraping their chairs. Ken leaned across.

'Good morning, ladies. I can recommend the soft rolls.'

Lil pulled a sour face. 'I can't eat anything. Just black coffee for me, and lots of it.' Her voice became a croak. 'Never again...'

Maggie adjusted the sunglasses and groaned. 'We were up until two, telling stories and drinking wine.' She forced a smile 'I feel like a film star, boozing until the early hours and laughing. It beats watching *Charlie's Angels* and *The Sweeney* with a cup of cocoa and going to bed at nine.'

DJ was impressed. 'Massive respect, Lil, Maggie,' he called out. 'We should have come over to your room and brought a few cans, made a session of it. We just played cards until midnight. Pat lost every time.'

Tommy reached for a bread roll. 'You have to have the knack with cards, like I do. I'm your man when it comes to the winning hand.'

Lil piped up from behind her shades. 'I doubt it, Tommy. I think you and I should have a few games of poker. But I have to warn you – I don't lose, ever.'

'A challenge.' Tommy beamed.' I'm up for that, Lil.'

'A fool and his money...' Cassie muttered beneath her breath.

Ken gave a small cough, his eyes sweeping over everyone. 'We're visiting Omaha Beach today. I've been reading about it. And the cemetery isn't far away from the beach. It should be edifying.'

'And the weather is perfect, too, my dear – bright and sunny,' Sue added, crossing her legs.

'Oh, I think it will be quite chilly on the beach, *Syoo*.' Denise shivered. 'I'm taking a warm coat.'

Duncan nodded. 'It's the beach where all those poor soldiers battled. I imagine it will be quite eerie there.'

Lil glanced across to Albert, whose soft eyes closed imperceptibly for a moment as he reached for his teacup.

'I'm looking forward to it.' Ken waved a hand. 'My next historical novel is about a young man called Private Pattison who is in action in World War Two, an American hero. He's in love with a beautiful nurse who dies in his arms.'

'Very Hemingway,' Cassie agreed, not noticing Ken's horrified expression.

'It will be an original – I'm going to set it on Omaha Beach and I'll research it today,' he insisted. 'He will be injured, Pattison, and the beautiful nurse will tend to his every need in the military hospital.'

'Every need? Do they have a bit of how's your father in the hospital bed behind the curtain?' Lil chimed from behind the sunglasses. She was beginning to perk up.

'Oh, good grief, no.' Ken was aghast. 'It's not that sort of book.'

Lil disagreed. 'Either Pattison is too wounded to woo the nurse or he's not a believable soldier.' She muttered to herself. 'He should have some love on the night rounds with Nursey. Then two months later, Pattison goes back to Oklahoma and Nursey finds herself all alone with a baby on the way... that would be a good story.'

Maggie nodded. 'Oh yes – there's no stopping these men once they get that gleam in their eyes.'

Denise agreed. 'My experience exactly. And then, several years later, they change. All they want to do is dig the garden and read the newspaper.'

'Or watch TV,' Maggie added.

DJ and Jake exchanged glances, their eyebrows raised. Emily chimed in. 'Perhaps you just haven't met the right man yet, ladies. I promise you, there are a few good guys out there who defy the stereotype.'

'I'm sure you're right, Emily,' Cassie agreed.

'So, ah, everybody...' Tommy held out his cup as François filled it with coffee. 'We have quite a full schedule today.' He cleared his throat over the chatter but no one was listening. The couple at the far table got up, holding hands, and walked to the exit. The smart woman followed them, still speaking rapidly on her phone. Tommy gazed at the twelve remaining people still eating breakfast and chattering excitedly and tried again. 'So, everyone, today we will visit the beach, the cemeteries beyond and if we get time we'll go to Bayeux before we drive to Amiens.'

'Oh, yes – we must see the Bayeux tapestry.' Denise purred. 'I do like cultural visits, as you know.'

'It's always worth a visit to Bayeux, ladies – I've been several times,' Ken agreed.

Tommy presented his most official expression. 'We are staying over at Amiens tonight. We are booked into a hotel with a funny name – I can't remember – called La Mort Pirate or something like that.'

'I don't care where we stay, Tommy. One hotel is as good as another as far as I'm concerned – I can sleep anywhere.' Pat's mouth was full of bread. 'But we'd better not bother with the card games later, DJ. I was cleared out of euros last night.'

'I've booked a big table for us all in the restaurant for dinner at eight,' Tommy explained. 'We will get slap-up nosh after the grave-yards and the beer is good there. It'll be brilliant. It's a nice hotel, very comfortable, it gets good reviews.'

'La Mort?' Pat gaped at Emily. 'What does that mean? Isn't it French for love?'

'That's l'amour,' Emily replied.

'So, what does it mean?' Lil asked.

Cassie waved a hand, as if it was unimportant. 'It means death. Tommy thinks we're staying at a hotel called The Pirate's Death, apparently. Or The Dead Pirate. Not sure which would be worse.'

'My days,' DJ murmured.

'Do you think the place is haunted?' Maggie's eyes bulged.

Lil snorted. 'I'm not superstitious. As long as the Grim Reaper has got a few bottles of wine in his cellar and the food's good, it's all fine with me.' She stood up and adjusted her sunglasses. 'Right, that's breakfast done. Come on, Tommy – get the minibus out. Maggie and I are ready to hit the beach.'

8

The breeze buffeted Cassie as she stood on Omaha Beach. She was staring up at the huge memorial anchored in the sand, a series of tall angular shapes formed like wings or sails, the steel glinting in the sunlight. She sighed and muttered the title, 'Les braves,' beneath her breath. Emily came to stand beside her, followed by DJ and Jake, their hands in their pockets. They were still for a while, thinking, then Jake said, 'It's so sad.'

DJ read the sculptor's words aloud. '"I created this sculpture to honour the courage of these men. Sons, husbands and fathers, who endangered and often sacrificed their lives in the hope of freeing the French people."' He shook his head sadly. 'Poor lads.'

Cassie turned up the collar of her jacket against the breeze. Emily pulled a phone from her pocket and took some snaps, standing close to the sculptor's words and photographing them several times.

'Incredible, when you think about it,' she said softly. 'All those women left behind waiting, and they had no idea what happened to their men, not really. I expect they all had a telegram and were told the soldiers had been killed in action but what else would they know about how it happened? Nothing, not ever.'

Cassie moved closer to Emily and placed a hand on her shoulder. 'How's Alex doing?'

'He's out in the Middle East.' She pushed wind-blown tendrils from her eyes. 'He's fine. We talk on the phone when we can.'

DJ breathed in. 'It must be tough having a marine as a boyfriend, Em.'

Emily nodded. 'It has its moments. But I'm glad I'm here with you guys – it takes my mind off worrying.' She gazed around at the beach. 'Well, not here exactly – this place gives me the creeps.'

'I saw the beginning of *Saving Private Ryan*. I was terrified just sitting in the cinema.' Jake's voice was a whisper, the pummelling wind drowning his words.

DJ agreed. 'The first half an hour was almost unwatchable.'

Emily's voice was low. 'It brings it home, doesn't it, just what an incredible sacrifice those young soldiers made?'

'I'm sure Alex will be all right.' Cassie wrapped an arm around Emily.

Emily nodded. 'He enjoys the life.' She forced a brave smile. 'We miss each other though. But we both know what we've signed up for, being together. He'll be home soon.'

'You're both incredible young people,' Cassie murmured. Her head was buzzing with words, images; she gazed at the stretch of sand, so still, so quiet, the tiny grains whipped up by the wind, whisked and dropped, just like soldiers' lives, separate stranded souls. A poem was forming in her mind, a rhythm, moving phrases and sounds making her thoughts race, words jumbling, colliding and then finding a place and a pattern. Cassie moved away by herself and stared into the distance. Maggie was strolling alongside Sue and Denise, the three of them not far from the monument, looking out to sea. Tommy, Duncan and Pat were down by the waves in a line, wearing black jackets and jeans, standing like three crows, gazing ahead. Albert sat on the sea wall, huddled in his overcoat, looking around.

Cassie thought about Omaha Beach, how empty and quiet it was, and tried to imagine the chaos of boats arriving, soldiers rushing and ducking down for their lives, bullets spraying, shattering, skimming the sea. She closed her eyes and thought of the different sounds, the yelling of commands, voices screaming in pain, ricocheting bullets; she visualised the clash of colours, blood red against blue water and dirty yellow sand, heaped bodies in uniform, the dull steel of helmets, the duller grey of each face against the sky, the cavernous gape of each mouth yelling in silence as the battle raged louder over their cries. It would have been noisy, like hell, like Hades. Cassie wanted to write it all down.

Then her eyes caught the movement of a speck in the distance, two specks, walking slowly together. Her mother was arm in arm with Ken, taking steady paces against the background of a line of waves and the vast open expanse of blue sky. Cassie watched them edge forward, their heads down, Ken in a navy overcoat and a smudge of blue cravat, Lil wearing a red hat and a brown jacket, huddled against him for warmth. Cassie smiled momentarily; it occurred to her that Lil needed this holiday, to step into the bigger, busier world outside Clover Hill, to meet new people. The familiar thought came to her: that her mother had missed so many opportunities in life; she'd become a mother in her teens, forced to throw her energies into bringing up her small daughter alone, in cramped accommodation on a meagre amount of money.

But Cassie hadn't been allowed to miss out as a child. She'd never known her father but she hadn't particularly needed one. Her mother had been everything to her. They'd played together, danced, cooked, painted walls and pictures, told and written and acted out stories; they'd been to plays, they'd shopped together, they'd laughed and cried at the same films in the cinema, eating from the same bag of popcorn. Lil had encouraged her daughter all the way, from the grammar school to university in Bristol, through the regular, animated letters Cassie had received during the tremendous times she'd been teaching abroad. She and Lil had always been close; as Lil had always said, they were more like sisters and Cassie didn't mind that at all.

Her mother had thrown all her energy into the B&B after Cassie had left home and Lil had built a thriving business, probably at the expense of any romantic attachments. Lil always had plenty of friends, but Cassie believed that her father had hurt her so badly that she wouldn't risk love again.

Lil's fierce independence had rubbed off on Cassie. Of course, she'd had boyfriends, lovers; Cassie had even lived with a significant other twice: Mo in Dakar, Jon in Guangzhou. But she hadn't stayed with either of them for long; she had a track record of being headstrong, unwilling to commit to one person, to take the final step that allowed you to trust someone. Cassie wondered if it was due to her father or, at least, due to the absence of him.

Lil had told her from a young age that her daddy had 'gone away to America' or 'gone back home'. As a child, Cassie had imagined an elusive stranger, a lean silhouette of a man in a long overcoat and a hat that shaded most of his face, who had slipped into the distance and dissolved forever. Cassie knew his name: he was Frankie Chapman, a man with dark curly hair, clean-shaven, a strong jawline, wearing a uniform. She had seen him in the photo, his arm around her mother; it had been her idea to laminate it so that Lil could use it as a bookmark. She knew Lil stared at it all the time. Cassie shook her memories away and moved back to DJ and Jake, who were chattering and offering chewing gum. She took a piece.

* * *

Lil was still leaning against Ken, taking small steps in time with his deliberately slow paces and feeling the sea breeze press against her cheeks. Ken's arm was very comforting; it allowed her to move steadily as he held her upright, offering warmth and support. She nodded her head as he spoke softly in her ear.

'It was in June 1944, Lil. Right here, exactly where we're walking now. It's hard to believe, isn't it, that such a peaceful place as this was a scene for one of the bloodiest battles imaginable?'

Lil nodded. 'I would have been about seven years old. I remember sitting in the kitchen by the radio with my mother and father and my brother, Edward, who was two years older than me, listening to the broadcasts. Sometimes, Mr Churchill used to tell us what was going on; sometimes it was just the man's voice reading the news. We were living in rural Oxfordshire. It was difficult to imagine a war going on while we were there. They had it harder in the towns and cities. For me, it was more about the things you couldn't get, rationing of the things you could, and there was always a sense that the enemy was going to march into the village carrying guns and your life would change forever. I remember being scared a lot of the time. My mother kept chickens so that we could have a few eggs. I never had a banana though. Later, the Americans were living nearby – they stayed on after the war – and there was always some chocolate or bourbon. Everyone liked it when Americans came to stay.'

Lil was thinking about Frankie. He had come to stay and they had fallen in love. If he had known about the baby, her life would have been different. She was sure they'd have married; he'd have taken her back to America, they'd have been very happy. Lil breathed out slowly, her heart heavy.

She gazed up at Ken. 'During the war I was still just a kid. I didn't start work until I was fourteen. I was training to be a hair-dresser. Of course, I had Cassie as a teenager, so I had to grow up quickly, and the pregnancy put paid to any idea of hairdressing. I was a child, really, until Cassie popped out. It's funny, when you think about it. Growing up happened in one big rush of childbirth.'

Ken nodded thoughtfully. 'The war must have been hard for children.'

'It was harder for all those young men who were away fighting.'

'There were 2,400 American deaths here at Omaha.' Ken cleared his throat. 'The Germans lost 1,200 men. One particular division, it was the 352nd I think, lost 20 per cent of its soldiers. They had few reserves, the Germans.'

'It's so sad.' Lil put the knuckle of a finger to the corner of her eye. 'It didn't matter which side you were on, did it? Those boys just didn't go home. How awful must it have been.'

'The book I'm thinking of writing will probably end with the battle here on Omaha. Private Pattison's nurse will have been killed and he will be in a boat, the battle raging all around him, and he'll have no fear any more; he'll be like a machine, because his love is dead, so his heart is hard.'

'I think he'd have some fear,' Lil murmured. 'Oh, yes, dead love or not, he'd be very afraid.'

Ken nodded. 'His nurse is going to be called Celia. Celia Maxwell. What do you think of that for a name? Does it fit the time period, do you think? She'll be a redhead.'

'Poor Celia. Redhead and dead,' Lil sighed.

'And I have to decide whether our Private Pattison makes it through the battle on this beach. I was thinking he'd survive – but then again he might be injured, or even die.'

'He might,' Lil agreed.

'So, what would you advise, to make the novel more powerful for the readers? How would you end it, Lil?'

She spoke without thinking. 'He won't make it, Private Pattison. No, he won't go home to his family again.'

'Yes, I agree. The most poignant ending of all, Private Daniel Pattison lying on the beach, water washing over his body, darkening his uniform, his blood seeping into the sand and turning the waves red. What do you think? And as Daniel Pattison utters his last breath, Celia's name is on his lips?'

'That would be a very likely ending, Ken. But one thing, perhaps, that could make it better...'

Ken lifted his eyebrows. 'Yes? What would you change, Lil?'

'Don't call him Daniel. Daniel is too serious a name, too manly. You want something that shows the young man as they were: bashful, inexperienced, a bit awkward, good-natured, warm-hearted, always kind.'

Ken nodded. 'You're right. Yes. Not Daniel – Pattison's not a Daniel.' He gazed across the beach, searching for the others. 'What about Tommy? Or Pat? Albert, even.'

'No. He has to be Frankie,' Lil said, her mouth set determinedly. 'That suits him best. Call the young man Frankie.'

* * *

A light rain had started to drizzle as they arrived at the Hotel Pirate Jacques just before six o'clock. They had eaten lunch, visited the cemetery, taken a tour round Amiens three times because Tommy was lost and Maggie was desperate to go to the toilet. The minibus pulled into the hotel car park.

'Here we are, Tommy – this is your Hotel Death,' Pat announced.

'I think we've had enough death for one day, what do you think, Denise?' Sue asked in a loud voice.

Denise agreed. 'All those soldiers lined up in all those rows in the cemetery – some weren't even eighteen.'

'I'm looking forward to a shower.' Jake shuddered. 'I got cold at that graveyard.'

'It isn't really called Hotel Death, this place?' Maggie asked anxiously. 'I've been worrying about it all day, what with all those crosses and Stars of David and the different names and religions in the cemetery, all of them mixed up together.'

'No, it's called the Hotel Pirate Jacques. There's nothing to worry about in this hotel. It's named after some pirate called Jacques,' Emily explained. 'Tommy must have read the itinerary and made a mistake.'

DJ and Jake were quiet now; both of them had large notepads on their knees and were sketching. Emily peeked over their shoulders. 'What are you drawing?'

'Characters to animate later for work.' DJ was engrossed. 'Aliens.'

'I'm sketching a soldier,' Jake murmured. 'An old one and how he would have looked when he was young.'

Pat took a breath. 'That's so realistic, Jake – it's exactly like Albert.'

Maggie hunched her shoulders. 'Will the hotel be creepy?'

Cassie patted Maggie's hand. 'You'll love it, Maggie. Tommy's chosen well – it was spectacular in the photos online. Apparently, there's a story about some pirate who lived hundreds of years ago and he was doing a dirty deal in the hotel bar. His enemies came in and caught him, a fight broke out and he was killed on the spot. Literally – there is a bronze slab that marks out the exact place. Poor old Jacques.'

'Is the place haunted?' Pat asked, eyebrows raised.

'It'll be haunted by the English tourists tonight,' Lil piped up.

'I'm looking forward to dinner at eight and putting on my glad rags and having a darn good time, what do you say, Maggie?'

Maggie shuddered. 'It was cold on the beach. I'm glad I had your furry coat.'

'I'm ready for a shower and then dinner.' Tommy raised his voice, turning round from the driver's seat to glance at his passengers. 'Right, we're here. We go in, we say hello to the owner, who is called Mireille, and then we'll sort out the rooms, who's pairing up with who tonight. After that—' a smile broke across his face '— we'll all meet up in the bar at half seven and I'll buy everyone a drink.'

A rousing cheer came from the minibus, and an immediate shuffling from seats and clattering of cases. From halfway down, Maggie's small voice squeaked, 'Can I get off first, please? It's been a long day and I just have to pay a visit...'

Lil was on her feet. 'Come on, Maggie – you and I will go in, talk to Mireille and tell her we're all here. DJ and Jake can bring our bags in with theirs – is that all right, lads? Albert, you'd better come with us too. Let's go in, find the loo, shall we? Then maybe we can have a swift drink in the bar to warm us all up before we go and get glammed up for dinner.'

9

They had been allocated rooms on the second and third floor. Mireille had told Cassie as she led the group to the narrow stairs that the third floor was haunted by Jacques the Pirate. Although most of the others didn't speak French, eyebrows were raised when the serious-eyed owner said, *'C'est hanté par le fantôme pirate.'* Pat's eyes had widened in real terror.

By seven o'clock, the English tourists from The Jolly Weaver had showered, changed their clothes and taken over the bar. Mireille had invited them to choose their food from the menu before they took their seats in the restaurant at eight. Lil watched as DJ, Jake and Pat took turns to stand on the brass spot that proclaimed, *'Le pirate Jacques a été tué ici, 1745',* pretending to wave a cutlass and fight off the enemy, and then Pat offered to buy a round of drinks. Cassie accompanied him to the bar to help him with the French language. Lil watched as he was approached by a young woman who met his eyes with a gaze of pure boredom and murmured, *'Oui?'*

Pat became tongue tied, waved his hands, said, 'Pint,' several times, becoming louder and more embarrassed.

Cassie whispered, 'Just say beer.'

Pat held up five fingers and said, 'Beer – *s'il vous plâit*,' and the barmaid nodded and moved to the pump. Pat's face glowed with pride.

Cassie was speaking to Mireille while Tommy was staring at his list, trying to work out who had ordered which meal from the menu they had been given, stuttering to Cassie in English. Lil felt a familiar glow of pride as she observed Cassie organising the food in fluent French while Tommy floundered at her side, staring at his list of names and frowning at the menu.

Lil watched Cassie, who was dressed in a colourful patchwork velvet jacket, a long skirt to her ankles and a black top. A black scarf adorned her cloud of white hair. Chunky beads rattled in her ears and bracelets jangled on her wrists as she chatted to Mireille as if it was the easiest thing in the world. Lil was aware of herself, small and unobtrusive in a black dress and jacket, sipping a glass of orange juice. She and Cassie were two of a kind, peas in a pod. Lil was smaller now, less flamboyant, but Cassie hadn't inherited much from Frankie. Lil wondered if Cassie ever thought about her father. Lil doubted it; Cassie had no need for a father. She assumed he was in the past for Cassie, where he had only existed as a name. Lil sighed. She still thought about Frankie every day. She wondered if he was alive, if one day he'd knock at the door and his dancing eyes would meet hers as he breezed in. 'Hi, Lily – it's me. I told you I'd be back.'

Lil was pulled from her thoughts by a gentle hand on her arm. Ken pointed to the orange juice. 'Can I get you another?'

'Ah, no, I'm fine, Ken.' Lil glanced at his glass; he was drinking red wine. 'I'm just watching Cassie order the food.'

'I was doing exactly the same.' Ken held a mouthful of wine as if sampling it, then swallowed quietly. 'She's very impressive, your daughter. Where did she learn to speak French so well?'

'Senegal, mostly – she taught there for ten years.' Lil's eyes moved to Pat and his friends; they were encouraging him to talk to the young barmaid. Jake was persuading Pat to practise saying, *'Voulez vous couchez avec moi?'* which he insisted meant, 'You have lovely eyes,' and Emily was chiding the boys, putting a protective arm around Pat. DJ was still talking about the ghost of the pirate and how he hoped it would haunt their room: he and Pat and Jake were together on the third floor, next door to Duncan.

Lil noticed Pat's expression, nervous and flustered, although whether it was due to the ghost or the barmaid, she wasn't sure. Her gaze moved to Sue and Denise, who were in the corner talking to Maggie, who was fascinated by their conversation about the clothes they'd wear for the tennis club's autumn ball, which would be in October. Duncan was sitting with his father, asking him loudly if he wanted another pint of beer before they ate; Albert was staring ahead, seemingly deep in thought.

Lil met Ken's eyes. 'What have you ordered for tonight? I've asked for the beefsteak and chips.'

'I have ordered the *tripes à la mode de Caen*, a local speciality, which is cooked in Calvados.'

Lil wrinkled her nose. 'What's that?'

'Tripe in brandy.'

Cassie had finished at the bar and she and Tommy joined Lil and Ken.

'Ugh, tripe.' Tommy was disgusted. 'That's innards, isn't it?'

'An acquired taste,' Ken admitted. 'What are you having, Cassie?'

'A simple quiche with salad.'

'I have to have chips every day.' Tommy rubbed his stomach. 'My metabolism is so fast I have to eat lots of carbohydrates and high-fat foods to keep my strength up.'

'Me too.' Lil winked at Cassie, her eyes straying to Tommy's belly where the shirt stretched.

He held up his glass and added, 'And beer, to keep me hydrated.' Lil couldn't help laughing.

Mireille called something across to Cassie, who raised her voice and called out, 'Our table's ready and food is about to be served. We can go through to the restaurant.'

Ken offered Cassie an arm. 'May I accompany you to dinner?'

Cassie shrugged and took his arm, glancing over her shoulder to check where Lil was. She had been accosted by DJ and Jake, one on each side, both chattering to her at the same time.

Then she returned her gaze to Ken; she hadn't heard what he was saying. He raised an eyebrow, his tone debonair. 'I was hoping you could tell me all about your time in Senegal over dinner. Perhaps afterwards we can share a Calvados or two. It's such a warming liqueur.'

'It is,' Cassie agreed. 'Calvados is an acquired taste and a bit strong for some people but, a couple of years ago, I was at a poetry festival and several of us finished a whole bottle after a performance. I have quite a liking for it now.'

Two hours and a small glass of Calvados later, Cassie was in her room lying on the bed, attempting to write a poem. She had enjoyed her meal and Ken had been very attentive, urging her to talk about her travels in Africa and China, occasionally regaling her with his latest idea for a novel about a man who was a missionary, who fell in love with a beautiful nurse in Africa who died of malaria. Cassie had hoped she hadn't offended Ken by being too outspoken: she'd remarked that Hemingway had written a similar story and that it was a little outdated for the white middle-class hero to be saving the subordinate female characters. Ken had leaned closer and told her quietly that he valued her opinion as a 'fellow artiste'.

Cassie had phoned Jamie as soon as she'd reached her room. Lil was still in the bar, talking with the youngsters. In fact, Cassie assumed everyone else was in the bar. Pat hadn't stopped talking about the barmaid throughout the meal and Jake and DJ hadn't stopped teasing him. Apparently, the young woman was called Marie-Ange. Emily had been trying to find out if she might be interested in having a drink with Pat, and DJ and Jake had turned it into an excuse to bait him mercilessly.

Back in Salterley, Jamie had seemed well and cheerful; he had listened to Cassie chatter about her experiences on the beach and how she wanted to write a poem in the character of a young soldier on Omaha Beach, but she was anxious that her work was becoming quite melancholy. Jamie had suggested hopefully that perhaps she was missing him and Cassie had agreed. Jamie had been a bit quiet then; he'd mentioned that he'd picked up his acoustic guitar again, more to exercise his fingers rather than through any desire to play. Cassie had wondered if she'd made him feel a little lonely. She had said a warm goodbye and promised she'd ring him again tomorrow.

She went back to the poem, reading the first lines aloud, as a performance.

> *I thought of you, love,*
> *As the guns rattled*
> *As the boat tipped and the cold waves lapped my feet.*
> *I saw your face for a moment, the trace of a smile...*

She pressed her lips together. 'Do I want to kill him off this early in the poem? Maybe he should be addressing someone in particular, not his lover – perhaps his father? Maybe his lover is too sentimental an idea.' She sighed. 'What do I know about fathers? Okay – what about – *I thought of you, Mother...?*'

There was a soft rap at the door. Cassie looked up. There it was again, a single, gentle knock. Cassie eased herself up from the bed and moved across the room. When she tugged the door open, Ken was standing outside in a fresh shirt and cravat with a hopeful expression, holding up a bottle and two glasses.

'May I come in?'

Cassie blinked. 'Ken?'

He showed her the bottle again. It was dark green with a wired cork. 'Champagne.' He moved his head a little by way of explanation. 'It's a nice one. I thought we might...'

'Ah.' Cassie shook her head. 'That's really thoughtful, Ken, but I'm working. I'm halfway through a poem...'

Ken waved the bottle yet again. 'Perhaps this will help to get the creative juices flowing.'

'Thanks, Ken, but not now.' She pushed the door a little so that she could see less of his face and he could see less of hers. 'I'm going to finish my work and have an early night. Thanks all the same.'

Cassie could see Ken's eyebrow rise and the side of his mouth turn up in a hopeful smile through the slice of open doorway. 'Another time, perhaps?'

'Perhaps,' Cassie said softly and closed the door. It shut with a crisp click.

She put a hand to her hair and frowned. Why had she said perhaps when what she'd meant to say was no, not at all? Ken was a pleasant man but she wasn't keen to be alone with him in her room. She was momentarily cross with herself for not being clear that no would always mean no as far as late-night drinks and Ken were concerned. Then she felt a moment's regret; perhaps he was just being friendly. Perhaps he was just lonely, reaching out to someone who was by herself and she had misjudged his intentions. That wasn't fair.

Cassie went back to the poem about the soldier but it wasn't really working. She screwed the paper into a tight ball and tossed it into the waste bin. She thought for a moment and gave one single cynical laugh. Ken wasn't her type at all. But, after all these years, despite knowing what sort of man *wasn't* her type, she'd never really decided what her type *was*. It was about compatibility, Cassie decided, and she'd never met anyone who'd been just right, no one who'd truly understood her outspokenness, her creative energy, and valued her for the person she was. Cassie shrugged. She'd have an early night. She wouldn't give Ken's appearance at the door another thought.

Lil's feet trod softly as she walked down the corridor along the second floor and glanced at the rickety stairs leading up to the third, in shadow. It was ten o'clock. She wanted to visit Cassie, to check that she was all right in the room by herself, find out if she'd written her poem.

She gazed again at the dark staircase stretching upstairs. The air had suddenly become cool and it felt much spookier to be alone in the darkness, a single glowing light illuminating the wall along the corridor. Lil's feet creaked on the wooden floor as she moved softly towards Cassie's room, the boards making an eerie elongated moan. The shutters rattled at the far window, and the temperature had dropped. Lil shivered inside her dressing gown. Her fingers were stiffening in the cold. Then she stood still, listening hard. She thought she'd heard a sound, a soft moan, coming from the floor above. She took a step forward again. A muffled bang, a soft slapping sound came from upstairs, then a dull rattle. Lil wondered if it was the clink of chains, a cutlass, perhaps.

Then suddenly, a whisper on the wind became a low evil croak, a voice that moaned, 'Patrick Stott – I'm coming for yoooooooooou.'

Lil glanced up to the third floor as a door banged open and slammed shut; then she saw a shock of shining red hair as a muscular young man in boxer shorts and very little else rushed out of a room and charged towards the stairs. It was Pat, and he was running away from something that had frightened him.

'Pat?' she called. 'Have you seen the pirate?'

As he thudded down the stairs, he noticed her standing in the corridor below; Pat shrieked once, then he stopped still on a wooden step, frozen with fear. He jerked his body upwards, staring down at Lil with round eyes, then he murmured, 'Oh, Lil. I thought you were a ghost in that dressing gown.'

'No, it's just me.' Lil watched him shivering halfway up the stairs, taking in his muscular frame and the well-fitting boxers. Pat almost smiled, then he became aware of his lack of clothing, and placed his hands strategically. He hesitated as if he didn't know what to say. 'I – I was just getting in the shower,' he explained. 'The lads played a joke on me...'

Then suddenly there was a loud roar as the third-floor door was flung open again, two white-clad figures leaping out from the shadows, moaning and rushing down the stairs, their heads and bodies covered with sheets, yelling, 'Arrr, Pat lad!' DJ and Jake, pretending to be ghosts, grabbed Pat around the neck and all three started to shout and tussle. Lil wondered if they would tumble downstairs, men, sheets, boxers and all. It was just like a comedy show on TV.

Then Pat was running back upstairs, grumbling that they should leave him alone, and Jake was shrieking with amusement and impersonating a pirate again. Pat's voice was high with shock and irritation, then suddenly there was another voice, gruffer and deeper, from another room, telling the boys to shut up and go back to bed because his poor Dad was trying to get some sleep. Jake was apologising, 'Sorry Dunc – we were having a joke – we didn't mean to wake Albert,' and DJ's laughter rang out again.

Lil smiled, watching from her vantage point on the second floor. She'd pop to see Cassie quickly, ask about the poems, then she'd go back to her room. Maggie would have the kettle on and they'd share a chat and a complimentary sachet of hot chocolate before turning in for the night. Maggie seemed more cheerful now she was on holiday, and Lil wanted to keep her that way by discussing exciting plans for the next day. She'd check Pat was all right the next morning, buy him a burger for lunch. In fact, she vowed she'd make a special effort to keep an eye on Pat throughout the rest of the holiday, treat him like a grandson. Jake and DJ would go too far left unchecked and she'd noticed Pat's sensitive side. She would keep him safe.

Lil glanced into the gloom. Suddenly she stopped still. There was a movement, a length of shadow outside one of the rooms down the corridor, definitely a man, leaning forward with something in his hand. She narrowed her eyes and stared into the darkness lit by a single misty yellow lamp. She was sure that the shape was standing outside Cassie's door. Lil caught her breath. Cassie was alone: she had a single room. The man was outside, waiting: the pirate.

She stared harder and breathed out slowly, rubbing her eyes to make sure. The man was knocking again in a very quiet, conspiratorial way. He had a bottle in his hand, not a sword, and he held two glasses. It wasn't Jacques the Pirate; it was Ken Harrington.

Lil watched for a moment as Ken waited and she saw the door open. Cassie's voice came from her room, kindly and soft. Lil sighed and decided that what Cassie got up to was none of her business; she should go back to her own room. She walked down the dark corridor, back to Maggie, back to a cup of hot chocolate. When she gazed back over her shoulder to check, Ken was still there, whispering and waving a bottle.

10

Lil made sure she sat next to Pat at breakfast time the following morning, offering him half of her eggs and toast, telling him how handsome he was, how girls found red-haired men attractive. She was delighted that Maggie, on the other side of her, was chatting enthusiastically to Sue about what a lovely time she was having in France and how fresh the air was in Normandy. Lil felt a warm glow of pleasure that she had dragged her friend away for a break. She imagined Brian calling out from his armchair for Maggie to fry him some eggs in the kitchenette and she pictured his surprise when Maggie didn't reply. Lil glanced around the table, listening to the different sounds of laughter echoing in her ears: Duncan and Tommy's hearty guffaw, DJ and Jake's good-natured back-and-forth banter, Sue's loud hoot and Ken's pleasant chuckle.

Ken was currently telling Albert about the place they would visit today, asking him if he knew anything about the World War One cemetery and if he had some second-hand stories about the Great War from his parents. Lil noticed Albert's hand on his cup as he brought it to his lips and set it down, his grip shaking and his blue eyes watery; he seemed troubled. His lips didn't move but he leaned closely and nodded as Ken explained that the cemetery they'd visit was one of the most famous and would provide a useful resource for his research: he'd offer the library a talk and slide show when he was back in Salterley.

Lil swept her eyes across the table to Cassie, who was deep in discussion with Emily about French history and, in particular, the battles against the English. Lil listened carefully to the audible shreds of DJ and Jake's conversation and guessed they were talking about Marie-Ange, the barmaid whom Pat had wanted to impress; it appeared that Emily had spoken to the young woman on Pat's behalf and discovered that she was engaged already. Jake and DJ agreed that it was best not to tell him; Pat would be a great catch for someone but not Marie-Ange.

Lil narrowed her eyes, swerving her gaze back to Ken, and noticed that he was peering at Cassie every few moments as he spoke to Albert, who had hardly touched his breakfast. Ken was talking loudly about his knowledge of the wars, constantly checking to see if Cassie had heard and was impressed; the answer on both counts was negative.

Lil nodded to herself; she liked Ken, but he was unlikely to pass the son-in-law test. She'd never had a son-in-law, but she believed no man would be good enough for her daughter. She wondered, her forehead furrowed with anxiety, if Ken had spent the night with Cassie, if there was a romance blossoming. Perhaps it was already past the early courting stage and they were already lovers. She was determined to find out.

Lil tried to concentrate; Pat was saying something to her about his love of models. Lil assumed he was talking about the barmaid and raised her eyebrows in a question. Pat tried again.

'I hand-paint them myself. I make them from moulds and use special paint. I have hundreds of them.' He shrugged thoughtfully. 'Not enough for the Battle of the Somme, sadly.'

'Oh, model soldiers. That's fascinating – it must be very difficult, painting all those little eyes and mouths and the hair...' Lil reached over and poured Pat some more coffee, then slid her hand across to DJ's plate, swiping a whole piece of buttered toast while he was chatting with Jake, placing it surreptitiously in front of Pat. 'Here – he won't miss a bit of toast. Get it down you – there's plenty of butter on this slice.'

'Thanks, Lil.

Lil sighed. 'Those boys tease you too much, Pat – last night, I thought they'd scared you half to death.'

Pat's face was pink. 'Ah, don't worry. That's normal behaviour for those two. I'm used to it.' He winked.

An hour later, Lil took her seat on the bus next to Maggie. Cassie was placing cushions around them, popping a rug over Lil's knee. Lil patted her hand and Cassie met her eyes.

'Are you comfortable?'

'Oh, yes, I'm just perfect here. Of course, I had a great night's sleep after all that sea air.' Lil narrowed her eyes craftily. 'Did you sleep well, Cass?'

'Like a baby.'

Lil recalled the image of Ken by Cassie's door holding a bottle of champagne and two glasses. She pressed her lips together; a man didn't take champagne to a woman's room at night unless he was planning to stay until the morning. Lil offered her best attempt at a nervous smile.

'I'm not sure I could have slept in a room by myself, not in that haunted hotel.'

Cassie shrugged. 'It didn't bother me.' She tucked the blanket around Lil's legs. 'Anyway, I don't mind if I have a single room or not. We'll change each day according to what sort of accommodation the hotel has. Single, double, triple, I don't mind. Who knows who I'll be sleeping with tonight?'

She headed away towards her own seat further back. She heard Ken's rounded tones pipe up. 'Cassie. How are the poems going? Why don't you sit here with me and we can talk about literature?'

Cassie frowned. 'I promised Emily I'd help her to translate an article about Omaha Beach she's found in a magazine. We'll catch up for that chat later.'

'I'll look forward to it,' Ken replied smoothly. Lil shook her head.

'Do you have any more of those chocolate triangles?' Maggie squeezed her hand. 'I'm getting quite a taste for them.'

Lil nodded, pulled from her thoughts, and rummaged in her bag. 'How are you feeling, Maggie?'

Maggie pushed sunglasses down on her nose and struck a pose. 'I'm determined to rock the film-star look. I'm on holiday and free and happy. What do you think? Am I a dead ringer for Audrey Hepburn?'

'More Liz Taylor, definitely,' Lil said brightly.

Maggie pouted. 'She became plump as she got older too.'

'We'd better limit these chocolates to five a day, then. Just to keep our movie-star figures intact.'

Lil pulled out two green-foil-wrapped chocolates and offered one to Maggie. As she glanced at the seat beyond her, across the aisle, Albert was smiling and holding out a hand. Lil dropped a chocolate into his palm and winked. Albert winked back. Tommy had started to speak to the group, his head twisted round from the driver's seat.

'Right, everyone – we're off on the eastern road to the cemeteries at Thiepval. We'll spend most of the morning there, then we'll have early lunch in a restaurant where they do a particularly good Norman cider. After some refreshment, we're going to drive across the French border and into Belgium, to our next hotel in

Bruges. I'm hoping we'll get a bit of sightseeing done there before our evening meal. Any questions?'

'Are we going to grab a burger for lunch, Tommy? I'm already starving.' Pat's voice came from the back.

Duncan rubbed his head and piped up. 'The area is particularly famous for cider. There will be all sorts of dishes with cider in, like pork, and there are puddings full of Calvados, the apple brandy.'

'I intend to take a bottle of Calvados home. It's very pleasant,' Ken added.

'I'm hoping to taste some cider and take some back with us,' Duncan agreed. Lil thought his expression was a little guilty; she wondered how much he was planning to sample.

'A nice lunch will be particularly welcome after an hour at the cemetery. Although it's a sunny day, there's definitely a chill in the air. What do you think, *Syoo*?'

'I have a warm coat, Denise. I don't intend to catch a cold, my dear. And some solid shoes – there will be some walking to be done.'

Lil heard Denise sniff. 'I'm sure these heels will be fine. The ground isn't damp.'

Maggie's eyebrows shot up, two high arches in her forehead. 'Oh, not too much walking, I hope? I might just stay in the minibus and rest if there is.'

'Don't worry.' Cassie's voice came from behind them, soothing and soft. 'I'll walk with you and Lil– we only need to go as far as the memorial. You will be able to see everything from there and it's not too far.'

'That's good,' Maggie purred, glancing in Lil's direction hopefully. 'I don't suppose there are any more of those green sweets? I think I can risk one more.'

* * *

The cemetery at Thiepval was accessed through a huge archway containing a book of memories, which visitors were asked to sign. Cassie paused to read some of the comments. Lil shivered and hooked an arm through Maggie's, snuggling up to the borrowed faux-fur coat.

Maggie sighed. 'I don't really understand the attraction of these graveyards. They depress me.' She and Lil watched the group ahead of them. Tommy, Duncan and Albert were walking slowly towards the mound of grass in front; DJ, Emily, Jake and Pat had reached the clump of trees to the right and Sue, Ken and Denise were reading a sign in French just beyond the entrance. Denise was lifting a foot and inspecting her shoe unhappily.

'It's about remembering the awful sacrifice of young lives, Maggie.' Lil sniffed, wiping her nose. 'My uncle was in the First World War. He was shot; he didn't die at the time, but the bullet stayed in his body and it killed him eventually.'

'One of Brian's relatives was killed in Passchendaele.' Maggie nodded, then her face fell as she remembered. 'I wonder how Brian is.'

'You haven't phoned him?'

'No. He can contact me. I'm being strong, just like you said.'

'Well done.' Lil chewed her lip. 'What if he's gone to the police and reported you missing?'

'He won't.' Maggie seemed sad. 'I left a note by the side of the bed to say I'd gone on holiday for a few days and, if he doesn't find it, Jenny Price knows where I am. But I don't suppose Brian will bother to text.'

'That's awful,' Cassie spluttered.

'I know, shocking.' Maggie put her hands on her hips.

'No, he'll be missing you something rotten, Maggie.' Lil shook her head. 'That's the whole point. He loves you but he needs to remember that he does...'

'No, *this* is awful – someone has written something in this book – some Colonel Firth has written "Tally-Ho, chaps!" as a comment. Belittling such a huge sacrifice of young lives, likening the war to a stupid chase…'

Lil lowered her voice. 'She's very opinionated, my Cassie – and very compassionate. I brought her up that way.'

'She is.' Maggie nodded. 'I hope you're right, Lil. I hope Brian is missing me…'

'Of course he is.' Lil threaded an arm through the crook of her friend's elbow. 'He knows he has a gem in you. He just needs reminding.'

Cassie linked an arm through Lil's spare one and the three of them moved forward. Emily, DJ, Jake and Pat were already disappearing into the woodlands.

'Do you think Emily is the girlfriend of one of those nice boys?' Maggie mused. 'She's so pretty – she could have her choice of them.'

'I like them all,' Lil agreed. 'Pat's my favourite though – I have a soft spot for him. He's so good-natured.'

'Emily's boyfriend is a marine. He's on active duty at the moment,' Cassie explained. 'It's nice she's here with her friends. She keeps the boys in line. They all get on well because they play football together.'

Lil seized her opportunity. 'What about Ken? And Sue and Denise? They are all single.'

'A *ménage à trois*?' Cassie raised her eyebrows. 'Imagine that…'

Lil studied her expression for a sign of jealousy and found none, so she said, 'Do you think he's that sort, Ken?'

'He's lonely, I think.' Cassie shrugged. 'But then, most people are lonely at some time in their lives.'

They walked on in silence. Lil wondered if Maggie was thinking about Brian and if Cassie was thinking about Ken. She was aware of the strange silence that had settled on the cemetery. There were many visitors already, several who had walked up to the tall white monument, and yet the vast open area had an eerie stillness, as if the entire cemetery had taken a breath and was holding it, waiting to exhale again.

They stopped suddenly at a grave for no particular reason, and Lil read the name on the headstone. 'William Stanley Barlow, twenty years.' She shook her head. 'That's so young.'

'One here, too. Wilfred Lynch. Seventeen.' Maggie hooked an arm through Lil's. They edged forward.

'Ooh, look,' Maggie whispered. 'There are three names here – three young boys, eighteen and seventeen – Richard Smollett, Thomas Kingsley and John Warren. How come all three are buried together? They aren't brothers.'

'Perhaps they were friends and died together?' Lil glanced at Cassie for an answer.

Cassie sighed softly. 'Perhaps no one could tell which one was which.'

Lil met her daughter's calm eyes and caught her breath. 'War is such a terrible thing. Your father...' She turned away, suddenly cold inside her coat. Lil felt Cassie drape an arm around her.

'He was a soldier, Frankie Chapman. I know. But you two met after the war had finished – in the nineteen fifties. There were still some soldiers around, where you lived...' Cassie pulled her mother closer, a tiny frame beneath her grasp.

Maggie muttered, 'I had an aunt who had an American boyfriend during the war. He was so generous – he used to give her stockings and chocolate.'

Lil nodded. 'Frankie was like that – generous.'

Cassie waved an arm. 'The monument is over there. Do you want to have a look at it?'

'Will it all be in French?' Maggie asked.

Cassie gave an imperceptible shake of her head. 'No. We can walk over there easily, if you like.'

'The others are already there.' Maggie squinted into the distance. 'All right.'

Lil pointed to a row of graves a few yards away. She was intrigued; there were no headstones, just wooden crosses. 'What are those graves, Cassie?'

'*Inconnus*. Unknown soldiers – ones they couldn't identify, I suppose...'

'I'm going to walk down there,' Lil muttered. 'I won't be long.'

'Okay,' Cassie agreed. 'Maggie and I will catch you up.'

Lil hugged her coat close to her and tugged her handbag over her shoulder. She put her head down against the wind and pushed forward, gazing to the right, towards the clump of woodland. The treetops were bent over, pushed by the strength of the gusts, but there was no noise. Lil imagined the sounds of battle in the woods; exploding bombs in craters, dirt flying up in a black spray; the yells of soldiers, the crack of gunfire. The noise seemed to boom inside her head as she forced her way towards the row upon row of simple wooden crosses. She stood still, gazing at the graves as far as her eye could see, lines upon lines of them, reaching far back into the distance. On each one, the word *inconnu* was engraved into the wood. Lil sighed, wondering; each of these young men would have had his own story.

Slowly, she eased herself down into a crouch and stared at one humble cross, noticing the one behind it and the next one, rank upon rank. She whispered softly, 'I wonder what happened to you, young man. And all your friends. I hope you can rest in peace now.'

A single tear was cold against her cheek. Lil wiped it away with a stiff finger. She heard a footfall behind her and knew that Cassie and Maggie had caught up with her.

'I'll just be a minute, love,' Lil said in a soft voice.

A hand rested on her shoulder, a brief comfort, and she was glad that Cassie understood her need to take a moment. Lil closed her eyes, offered up a silent prayer for the young men, and she felt Cassie's hand lift away. She rested her lids a moment, then opened her eyes and stared up into a vast blue sky, flecked with clouds.

'Right, I'm ready. Shall we go back to the bus now, Cassie?'

Lil eased herself upright on tired legs and turned round with a smile of recognition already on her face. The wind blew her hair and she shivered. There was no one there. She stared towards the monument and saw Cassie and Maggie in the distance making their way towards her.

11

The food had arrived at the table of the Basse Cour, a little restaurant ten miles north of Thiepval, and everyone was tucking heartily into the main course apart from Albert, who was very quiet, and Lil, who was deep in thought. All the other holidaymakers were chattering excitedly.

'I've ruined a perfectly good pair of shoes. The heels are caked in mud.' Denise glanced at the young waiter who had just placed a *pichet* of cider on the table in front of her. 'Could I have wine, please? I'm not fond of cider.' She tried again. '*Vin, s'il vous plait.* Red, please, waiter – only one glass – I'm hopeless if I drink too much at lunchtime.'

'Oh, me too,' Sue agreed loudly. 'It just makes me want to sleep. But I'm going to try the cider. It's what all the locals drink, my dear. And besides, Cassie has a pint of it and if she thinks it's good, then so do I.'

'I agree,' Ken murmured.

'It's just me drinking wine, then,' Denise grumbled. 'I can't believe that place was so muddy. Those shoes cost me a lot of money. I hope the grime will come off and I can find a good cobbler to mend the heel.' Denise gazed around for sympathy but no one seemed to notice her anxiety.

'You could buy a pair of clogs in Amsterdam, Denise.' Pat became dreamy. 'I fancy a pair myself. Perhaps a beautiful Dutch girl with yellow plaits and one of those white hats with the turned-up corners might fit me up with a pair.'

Albert supped noisily from of a huge glass of cider. Duncan was thoughtful, speaking to himself. 'This cider is incredible. I wonder how well it will travel in the minivan. I'm going to order a few bottles to take back.'

Tommy shook his head. 'You won't get a lot of it in the minibus. They could send some barrels over later.'

'It's best in bottles, Tom.' Duncan finished his pint. 'It's a shame you aren't able to sample it. It's good stuff.' He was tucking into the main course.

'I'll buy some to take with me for later to quaff in my room before I go to sleep.' Tommy sipped his orange juice. 'Just looking at you lot is making me feel thirsty.'

Albert wiped moist lips, made a soft noise of pleasure and smiled.

DJ patted his arm. 'Do you like the cider, Albert? It's tasty stuff, isn't it?'

Albert nodded. Maggie raised her voice. 'I might have one of those. Is it good?'

Albert moved his head slightly without taking his mouth away from the glass and murmured, 'Mmm.'

Lil turned to Cassie, who was sitting next to her. 'I can't stop thinking about what happened at the cemetery, Cassie. I haven't told anyone else. They'll think I've gone mad. But I was sure that was you and Maggie standing behind me, your hand on my shoulder.' She shuddered with the memory. 'Am I losing the plot?'

'No, not at all.' Cassie draped an arm around her mother's

shoulders. 'It's a common experience in these places. Lots of people report, you know, the sense of another person, a presence. I might even write it into a poem.'

'Oh, I don't know what to think.' Lil still felt cold inside her warm clothes. 'What if it's a prediction? You know, there I am in the graveyard and the Grim Reaper is waiting for me. Maybe it was a warning.'

'No, don't think that.' Cassie hugged Lil again. 'Those places are very atmospheric. I know just how you felt myself. There's nothing to worry about – you just got caught up in the emotion of it all. Ghosts don't exist, Lil...'

But Lil wasn't sure Cassie understood at all. Lil put her hands to her head, her thoughts bulging inside her mind, and closed her eyes. She was eighty-two years old. She was in good health apart from a few aches and pains in her joints and occasional palpitations, but she couldn't last forever. She had pushed thoughts of impending death away so far but the spectre always returned, sometimes at night when she lay awake and alone in her room, sometimes when one of the Clover Hill residents passed away, sometimes when she looked at old photos and realised that she had been alive for a long time. She sighed.

When she opened her eyes, Lil noticed Albert across the table, his eyes fixed on her. She wondered if he wanted another wrapped chocolate. His lips moved slowly and then he pushed his drink across the table, a glass of cider, half empty. She noticed his expression, warm and worn and full of geniality, as he held out the glass and put it down within her reach. He nodded to her and she picked it up and took a sip. It was tangy, a little fizzy on her tongue, and then she tasted the sweetness of apples. She stared into Albert's eyes. He closed his lids for a moment and then met her gaze, his eyes soft, the colour of the sky. She knew he'd understood that she needed a friend. She sipped again and smiled.

'This is lovely, Albert. I'm going to order one.'

The waiter was at her shoulder. Maggie piped up, 'Oh, yes, and one for me too, please.'

Several other voices joined in the request for more cider: DJ, Jake, Emily, Pat, then Ken, Sue and Duncan.

Denise shrugged unhappily. 'I may as well have one, then.'

Tommy gazed at Cassie and made a sad-dog expression. 'If you're ordering for everyone, Cass, can I have another orange juice?'

Cassie winked at him and spoke to the waiter, who nodded happily and rushed off to fetch more drinks.

* * *

An hour later, after a hearty meal and several bottles of cider, everyone trooped to the minibus, Tommy leading the way, disgust on his too-sober face and Duncan bringing up the rear, calling out loudly in English to two French waiters who were struggling with thirty-six bottles of cider in three cardboard boxes. Everyone watched as the bottles were placed carefully in the back of the minibus behind the luggage, a soft-cloth suitcase placed on top to stabilise them. Duncan slipped several euros into the top pockets of the waiters with an enthusiastic smile. '*Merci*, my boys.'

Tommy had already started the engine and Cassie, who had only consumed half a pint of cider and was one of the more clear-headed passengers, clambered up beside him to help him with directions. They were off to Belgium and Tommy had claimed woefully that all the signs seemed the same.

Two rows back, Maggie leaned her head on Lil's shoulder and promptly fell asleep. Lil took out her romance novel, smoothing the photograph between the pages, and began to read. Across the aisle, Albert was resting, his eyes closed. Sue had sprawled in the seat between a calm Ken and a disgruntled Denise, hooting loudly about wonderful Bruges and how she was so looking forward to sightseeing later that afternoon. DJ, Jake and Pat were laughing and rolling around in the back seat, tipsy from the cider. Jake was teasing Pat about the two puddings he had eaten, plates full of apples stewed in Calvados with piles of whipped cream, and Pat was carrying a bottle of spirits under his arm, promising to share the apple brandy later that evening if the other lads behaved themselves.

Denise made several loud comments about how morbid the cemetery had been and how she'd like to visit some nice ancient ruins in Bruges and go on a proper sightseeing cruise. Emily was busy texting on her phone and sending photos of the local scenery. As Denise slid off her damaged shoes, DJ thumped Pat's arm, asked everyone loudly if they could smell rancid cheese, shouting out random words for types of French cheese at the top of his voice and making exaggerated gestures. After DJ and Jake had yelled 'Camembert' for the third time, 'Brie' twice, and mooed five 'Groooyeres', Denise put her soiled and broken shoes back on her bare feet. She muttered the words, 'Not very mature,' which made the boys laugh even louder, and stared, red-faced, through the window.

Emily leaned forward. 'I'm sorry about my friends, Denise. They can be a bit high-spirited, especially after Normandy cider.'

Jake apologised hurriedly. 'Oh, I'm so sorry, Denise. I thought it was Pat's feet. They always ming in those trainers. Pay no attention to me and DJ.'

'We both drank too much.' DJ shook his little locks emphatically, suddenly sober. 'We didn't mean to be offensive. We're really sorry if that came across as rude.'

Denise nodded, turning away, and the boys settled down quietly with their sketch pads, having mouthed 'Sorry' to Emily. Lil glanced over her shoulder, pushing Maggie gently to one side, and noticed Ken was craning his neck. He was watching Cassie, who was oblivious as she was helping Tommy negotiate a busy road by pointing out the sign for Bruges. Lil frowned. Ken's expression was, she thought, one of extreme lust. She was sure of it; she had just read about the a very similar one in her book.

An hour passed. Lil gazed around the bus. Ken had begun a monologue to anyone who might be listening about the importance of primary research when giving a talk on the two world wars and the interim years. Sue's eyes were closed and Denise had flopped onto Ken's shoulder. DJ was asleep now, his sketchbook in his arms, his head on Jake's black-clad knee. Jake was snoring. Pat was slumped across Emily's chest as she thumbed through photos on her phone. Albert hadn't moved, mouth still open. Duncan was also on his phone but his eyelids were drooping.

Maggie had resumed her former position, asleep against Lil's body, smiling happily, making little snorting noises through her nostrils. Lil was pressed against the window and gazed out at the scenery whizzing past. They were close to Belgium; the border wasn't far away. She gazed at the farmlands, flat stretches of fields in various patchwork shades of green, scrubby sparsely wooded hedges, vast tree trunks with dull grey barks and leafy branches stretching like long fingers towards the clouds. Lil wriggled against Maggie until her arms were free, then she opened the book at the saved page and gaped at a photo of herself, serious-faced, staring at the camera while a cheerful soldier wrapped an affectionate arm around her shoulders.

She tried to remember who had taken the photo. Was he called Sonny or Sammy or something else, Frankie's friend? She couldn't remember. She and Joyce, another trainee hairdresser, had double-dated with Frankie and his soldier friend at first. She remembered the warm feeling of being the one Frankie had picked; he was better looking, the kinder one; he had the nicest smile.

Lil read her book for a while, rereading the scene in which the heroine and a man she hardly knew made passionate love in a barley field. Lil marvelled at the words that were used, cheeky phrases she'd never known at seventeen, expressions her mother would have been appalled by, actions that would have had her labelled a hussy and worse in the 1950s.

She was thoughtful for a moment. Although she'd missed out on all this new liberation, and the opportunity to behave as you wished, she'd raised Cassie to be a strong woman who knew her own mind and behaved just as she liked. Cassie was perfect: she was confident, independent, kind; she was fair and positive and cheerful, and it was all down to Lil. She could be proud of that, at least.

Then Lil imagined herself and Frankie in the field of daisies, amongst the cornflowers and cowslips, the heady sweet smell of grass making her sigh. She and Frankie had cared about each other, but the meeting of their bodies had been all about innocence and blunder. She'd hardly known what was happening, then it had all been over and Frankie had promised he'd love her forever. But of course, he hadn't loved her for much longer; before the month was up, he'd been called back home. The war had long been over but Frankie had still been in the US army, so he'd had to obey orders. Lil had been suddenly alone, fighting her own new terrifying battle. But Cassie was her treasure, her best gift from Frankie; she'd never regret that.

Her eyes were closing. The only thing she could hear was the thrum of the wheels on the road, a regular, rhythmic whirr. Cassie's low voice, offering Tommy directions, came from the seat in front, warm and reassuring, and Lil felt herself drift off.

It was warm in the minibus, like being cocooned in a womb, the wheels throbbing like the pumping of blood in veins. Lil opened her eyes. Tommy had just shouted to everyone. He had seen a sign; it was ten kilometres to Bruges. Cassie was murmuring that the roads were becoming busier and Tommy decided that a detour down a quiet road might be the best way forward. He declared how nice it was to drive through Europe, suggesting that the area they were in was very safe for tourists. He began telling a story and Lil strained her ears to listen. The book was on her knee and Maggie was almost lying on top of it, squashing the pages. Lil eased her friend away and leaned forward to listen to Tommy.

'I went to Cairo with Angie last year to celebrate an anniversary – our twentieth, it was. We had a great time but, do you know, I never felt safe there.'

Lil knew Cassie had shrugged although she couldn't see much of her behind the headrest. Cassie said, 'I've been to Cairo. It's quite safe. There are security police everywhere and they do a great job. I always felt comfortable...'

'But haggling doesn't suit me – I like to have just one price – and Angie said...'

'Oh, haggling's great fun,' Cassie protested. She glanced at the steering wheel shaking in his grasp. 'This road is quite bumpy, Tommy. Maybe we should slow down a bit. This area is rural and there are potholes...'

'We're all right, Cassie.' The minibus bounced along a rough patch of tarmac. Lil felt her teeth snap together. Tommy raised his voice over the whirr of the engine as he accelerated. 'Angie was always looking over her shoulder in Cairo. She knew someone who was going to Sharm El-Sheikh a few years ago and their holiday was cancelled – it was in the news, do you remember?'

'I think I remember something...' Cassie murmured. 'It was around 2015, some passengers on a jet...'

'Angie never felt safe, wherever we went. You know, Cass, we were on a bus to the pyramids in Cairo and she was convinced that something would happen. All the way there, she kept on saying to me, "Tommy, what if something bad happened, what would we do?"'

'You should holiday in Brighton,' Cass offered. 'Or Bruges. Perhaps Angie would feel more comfortable.'

'I suppose – but anywhere you go nowadays, all sorts of things can happen – air crashes, murders, bombs, explosions.'

'I don't think you should worry too much,' Cassie suggested. 'I think most places are fairly safe – you have to be very unlucky to—'

She was interrupted by a loud bang from behind that seemed to come from the back seat. The sound of the blast ricocheted through the minibus and there were several shouts and a loud scream. Another bang was followed by two more in quick succession. Tommy swerved the van to the side of the road, pulling into a muddy stretch, an open gate that led into a field.

There was another pop, then someone's voice, Pat's, yelling, 'I've been hit! I'm covered in blood. Can anyone do first aid? Emily? My shirt is soaked – I'm injured. I might be dying.'

Everyone turned around to see Pat on the back seat slumped forward, shocked, clutching his chest, his shirt dark with a wet stain.

Maggie whirled round. 'Lil, Pat's been shot.'

Ken shouted, 'Can someone fetch the first-aid box? We have an injury here, people.'

Sue yelled, 'I'm a first aider. I'm coming. Stay where you are, my dear. Take deep breaths and try to be calm.'

Denise was on her feet. 'I'm trained in first response. Hang on – I'm just behind you, *Syoo*.'

Then Emily's clear voice came from the back seat. 'Don't worry,

Pat – you'll live. There's nothing wrong with you. You're definitely not bleeding – unless, of course, your veins are full of Normandy cider.'

12

Duncan was dumbfounded and disappointed: the corks, despite being firmly wired, had blown clean off and blasted through the cardboard-box containers, frothing all over the soft-topped suitcase that had been placed on top for stability, and all over Pat in the seat just in front. Pat drank the remainder of one of the bottles there and then, Duncan proclaiming that the smell of cider was as good as any perfume – it would drive women crazy with desire. Denise was very unhappy; it was her soft-cloth suitcase that had been directly in the line of fire and the material had been soaked in a gush of airborne liquid. Tommy picked up the case and said, 'Oh, no – whose case is this? I think the cider has soaked through.'

Denise snatched her suitcase from Tommy, worried that he was about to open it, emphatically declaring, 'The whole minibus stinks like a brewery – and I don't need you rifling through my underwear.'

Duncan gave Denise his best apologetic smile and promised to buy her a brand-new suitcase in Bruges, and to get everyone a drink later to make up for the smell. Denise sighed sadly and leaned back in her seat.

'Are you okay, Denise?' Cassie called out. 'Is there much damage done?'

Denise pushed her soft case to her feet, her shoulders hunched. 'Everything's soaked.'

'We'll help you sort it out at the hotel,' Cassie promised, and Lil held out her bag of chocolate triangles.

'Have one of these,' she called. 'Chocolate always cheers me up.'

Denise gazed through the window. 'No, thank you.'

It was three o'clock when the minibus crept like a scolded child into Bruges, the interior of the vehicle reeking of cider. Tommy turned into one of the backstreets just off Market Square, where Cassie told him the hotel could be found. Since entering the town, the passengers had been staring through the mud-spattered windows, their noses pressed against glass, marvelling at the beautiful buildings, Ken telling everyone that they simply had to explore the town before dinner to embrace the mediaeval architecture. Sue suggested too loudly that anything would be better than breathing in the overpowering stench of Duncan's booze, the smell of which still clung to the air like an invisible mist. Five of his bottles had detonated, jiggled in the back of the minibus on the bumpy road and warmed by the afternoon sun to the point of explosion.

Tommy parked the minibus behind the hotel and, keen to ingratiate himself with his passengers, turned around in the driver's seat to make an announcement.

'Right, we're here. The Hotel Oud Huis.' He stared around him, scrutinising each expression, hoping for confirmation that he had done well. He was rewarded with a smile and a thumbs-up from Maggie. 'So – we can leave our things in our rooms and then we're at leisure until dinner at half seven. Right, everyone – we can hit Bruges.'

Denise muttered something about needing four hours in a

launderette to wash all the clothes in her luggage. Duncan coughed abruptly. Tommy continued.

'We have dinner booked in a restaurant at seven-thirty and then, at nine-thirty, we're off to The Trappiste, an underground thirteenth-century cellar that serves great beer. And tomorrow we have the morning free to do as we wish before we leave for the farm visit.'

Ken raised his voice. 'I'm going to the Basilica of the Holy Blood. It's a beautiful place, apparently unmissable. The building dates from the twelfth century. It has a fascinating history I'd be glad to share, if anyone would like to accompany me.' He glanced hopefully at Cassie, but she was gazing out at the frontage of the hotel, oblivious.

'Well, with the rest of the time left this afternoon, my guidebook suggests you can either go to The Old Chocolate House, if you feel you need a rest – they do hot chocolate and lots of different cakes.' Tommy glanced at Lil and Maggie. 'Or there's the Belfry tower with its 366 steps.' He rolled his eyes as if he was exhausted just thinking about the idea of climbing to the top. 'Or they do very nice chips – they call them *frites* here – and there's some Belgian chocolates to be sampled before dinner – after all, we are on holiday so we can forget the waistline.' He grinned at Pat. 'Some of us are going to the brewery tour – that's pre-booked at the Halve Maan brewery for four o'clock; I've reserved six places for those of us who like that sort of thing. Other people might want to explore the old buildings – architecture and stuff.' He smiled at Ken and then at Sue. 'I'm going to the brewery – it will be really interesting.'

'Too right,' Duncan agreed, moving from his seat with such sudden energy that Albert woke up with a start, opening his eyes wide and closing his mouth.

'But we can talk about all this when we get inside the hotel. I'll allocate rooms when I've spoken to the owner, and we'll go from there. We'd better get a wriggle on.' Tommy was hopeful. 'Everyone feeling all right?'

'Great, thanks,' Lil replied. She caught Cassie's eye and winked. 'I don't mind what I do until dinner but I'm definitely not climbing to the top of 366 steps.'

* * *

Thirteen people stood outside the brick-fronted shop with the pretty awning and a sign that advertised the best chocolate ever. Tommy shoved his hands deeply in his pockets and sighed.

'Right, only six of us can go to the brewery. I rang them to double-check numbers.'

'Well, I have to go, obviously. I'm the barman.' Duncan shuffled his feet. 'We ought to get a move on – it's almost four o'clock.'

'I don't mind – I'm happy to offer my place to someone else,' Cassie said.

Ken offered his most charming smile. 'I'm going to the Basilica. Who'd like to come along with me?'

'I will. It will be splendid, my dear,' Sue hooted.

'Me too.' Denise was a little chirpier now Duncan had given her more than enough money for a new case and her clothes, newly rinsed, were drying in the Oud Huis laundry room, courtesy of the kind hotel owner, Rosselin, who had offered to sort it all out while Denise went out with her friends.

'I'll come with you too,' Emily offered. 'I'm not a great beer drinker – I'd rather look at architecture than the inside of a brewery, to be honest.'

'I'm up for the beer tour.' DJ beamed.

Lil breathed in the delicious aroma of cinnamon and chocolate. 'I'm staying here for the hot chocolate. Maggie and Albert will stay too.'

Tommy counted on his fingers. 'Four plus three is seven; take that away from thirteen leaves six. Perfect. We have six places pre-booked for the tour. You're coming with us, Cassie.'

'Great.' She beamed, not noticing Ken's disappointment.

'Right, we'd better get going then, my group,' Ken announced, suddenly in teacher-mode, and turned to walk away, followed by Sue, who began chatting to Emily, and Denise, who scuttled behind them.

Duncan was on his way. Tommy, Pat, DJ and Jake were already following Duncan. Cassie hugged her mother. 'We'll be back in a couple of hours. Are you happy to stay here?'

'Of course – there's chocolate,' Maggie spluttered.

'We might have a wander into Market Square, but we'll be back here for half six at the latest,' Lil promised. 'We'll only be a few minutes away. We won't stray far, Cassie. You needn't worry about us.' She guffawed, a new idea in her mind. 'Unless we get an offer from some Belgian Romeos.'

Albert looked a little stunned by Lil's remark, so she pushed an arm through the crook of his and murmured, 'We'll all stick together and take care of each other, Albie. Come on – I'm up for a hot chocolate. What are you having, Maggie?'

'Chocolate, of course.' She beamed.

Cassie turned to follow the others, waving to Lil, who raised an arm and watched them disappear around a corner. Then she faced Maggie and Albert, a mischievous gleam in her eyes. 'Right. We've got rid of the kids. Come on, you two – it's fun time!'

'Why? What are we going to do, Lil?' Maggie's mouth was open.

Lil pointed at the menu in the window. 'I'm going to start with a Grand Marnier hot chocolate and see what happens. We could have a Snickers topped with whipped cream and then go into Market Square for some chips. After that, Bruges is our oyster – and we can paint it red.'

'How will we do that?' Maggie's brow puckered – she was confused by Lil's mixed metaphor – but Albert nodded, shuffling forwards towards the door of the café, towards the bright light that glowed inside, a shining gold mine, the sweet aroma of chocolate. Lil nudged Maggie, and they followed him in.

* * *

Cassie sipped lager from her glass and glanced at DJ, suave in designer jeans, Jake wearing black and Pat sporting a new 'I heart Halve Maan' T-shirt. They had almost finished their complimentary beers. 'So where have Duncan and Tommy gone?'

'Trying to buy the local brew.' DJ shrugged. 'Tommy said we should have taken the longer tour – they only do one a day but you get to do a full tasting. Duncan and Tommy are talking to one of the managers about sampling a few different beers so that Duncan can take some home. I'm not sure he can buy beer in bulk here, but the manager is going to put him in touch with a supplier who can send it back. Duncan's suddenly become very keen on Belgian beer.'

'The tour was good, though – the way they roast the hops and the lovely smell and the big steel vats.' Jake glanced around at the airy room, the wooden display unit, pristine shelves and gleaming bottles of beer with attractive colourful labels.

Pat's face was red. 'All those steps down to the vault, though – I needed this beer by the time I'd climbed back up.' He finished the last of his lager, a frothy trail running down the inside of the glass. 'I think I'll have another one. Cassie, how do I ask for beer in Belgian?'

Cassie winked. 'Use the same word, *bier* – or you can say *pintje*.'

Pat sauntered off towards the bar, pleased with himself.

Cassie turned to DJ and Jake. 'It must be tough for Emily, with Alex away.'

Jake noticed Cassie's concern. 'He's been in the Middle East for a couple of months. She's enjoying her holiday here with us but I think sometimes she's very worried about him. She keeps it fairly quiet though – she doesn't say much to anyone.'

'I would be worried too, if I were in her shoes, especially when the phone calls don't get through.' DJ scratched his head and sighed.

Cassie murmured, 'Emily's such a warm person, so loyal to you boys.'

'She's probably my best friend,' Jake said, then he turned to DJ and hugged him. 'Apart from you.'

DJ smiled. 'Em's great. My days, when we were rude to Denise, she was straight in there, apologising for us. We'd had a little bit to drink. And we didn't mean anything by it – I really thought the stinky feet were Pat's.'

'Poor Denise – I'm not sure how much she's enjoying the trip.' Cassie sighed.

'We'll make an effort to cheer her up,' DJ promised, brown eyes earnest. 'I'll buy her a pint tonight.'

Pat arrived with a tray, beaming, carrying four glasses of beer.

'I said *"bier"* then *"pintje"* and held up four fingers,' he said excitedly, his cheeks pink. Cassie glanced over their shoulders and saw Duncan and Tommy approaching, deep in conversation, clearly pleased with themselves.

Duncan put both hands on his hips. 'Kerry will go mad. I'm spending far too much on beer. But we'll have some fantastic varieties of Belgian ales in the pub for a few months.'

'That's what we came for, Dunc,' Tommy agreed, then, aware that Cassie was smiling, he assumed an innocent expression. 'And a holiday, of course.'

'I'm looking forward to staying at the farm tomorrow,' DJ said excitedly. 'We might even get a five-a-side game with some of the locals.'

'It will be great,' Pat agreed. 'Is that it now? Is the tour over?'

'I thought *Halve Maan* meant half a man,' Jake murmured. 'But then I saw the logo. It's half-moon...' He tugged Pat's new T-shirt playfully.

'We'd better be going.' Cassie raised her eyebrows. 'It's probably time.'

'Yes,' Tommy rubbed his belly, thinking of the beer he might drink if he could stay. 'We promised to meet Ken's group in the square and the others in the café.'

Cassie met Duncan's eyes. 'I wonder how your father's coping with Lil and Maggie for company.'

'Oh, they'll be just fine,' Duncan protested. 'The three of them are probably sipping hot chocolate and talking about – knitting or something.'

'You don't know Lil.' Cassie shook her head. 'We'll be lucky if they are still where we left them. I wouldn't be surprised if they got into trouble.' She smiled brightly. 'Let's just hope they haven't broken the law or upset anyone – I wouldn't put anything past my mother.'

13

'Belgian chips are just the best.' Lil took a chip from the wrapper that Maggie was holding out and blew on it. She glanced around. Market Square was busy; people were rushing past, some with their heads down against the breeze, others chattering on phones. A couple were strolling, eyes locked, holding hands. A woman pushed a pram, her eyes glazed as if she was dreaming. Lil nibbled the chip, enjoying the sensation of it burning her lips, and stared at the sculpted statues mounted on stone, the pretty colourful buildings with their high pointed fronts, the shops with green awnings, the grey flagstones and the little tables where people were sitting, hunched over huge glasses of beer. She gazed back at her companions. Maggie was smiling, grease on her lips, and Albert was chewing rhythmically, a chip in each hand, holding them up out from his body as if he were about to play tiny drums.

Lil sighed. 'The others will be ages yet. What shall we do?'

Maggie wasn't listening. 'These chips are even better than Keith's. And we've had hot chocolate. I won't want any dinner tonight. I'm having so much fun, Lil – I'm glad you forced me to come on holiday.'

Albert took another chip; he was still chewing steadily in his round-and-round motion, his eyes expressionless. Lil nodded slowly; an idea had come to her. 'Right. If we don't do it now, we won't ever do it.'

Maggie was still lost in her thoughts. 'I wonder how my Brian is getting on. It's a shame he's missing out on all this fun.' She sighed softly, contentment shining in her eyes. 'I love it here in Bruges.' She pushed two more chips into her mouth. 'I might not want to go home.'

'Have you heard from him, Maggie?' Lil asked. 'He'd be so jealous if he knew you were here.'

Maggie wrinkled her nose. 'I've sent him a few texts – three, in total – I thought I'd better. But he's not good at texting. Do you think I should ring him?'

'No. Maybe send him a postcard saying, "Wish you were here". You've told him where we are and that you're safe.' Lil winked at Albert. 'We're having a good time by ourselves, aren't we?'

'We are.' Maggie polished off the last of the chips and beamed.

Albert edged closer to Lil, bending his head in her direction, cocking an ear. Lil raised her voice. 'Come on – the tennis club will be here soon – and the beer drinkers. I'm not letting them think we've been stuck here in the middle of the square waiting with nothing better to do. We have plenty of time – the clock on the belfry tower says it's twenty to five. I know what we'll do. We'll show them that we're not past it yet.'

'Past what?' Maggie was licking her fingers. 'Where are we going?'

Albert moved closer to her elbow and Lil turned and stalked away, the others following her step for step.

Her voice trailed back in the breeze. She put on an authoritative voice, deliberately mimicking Ken's teacher mode. 'We're going to explore the fabulous thirteenth-century architecture of Bruges.'

Maggie and Albert could hear her laughing softly. 'We'll have a few good tales to tell the others when they catch up with us. They aren't the only ones who can have some fun.'

* * *

An hour later, Cassie rushed out of the café and called to the group assembled outside. 'They aren't in there. The waiter was very helpful – he remembered them. He said they left ages ago.'

Sue was anxious. 'It's gone half past five. They said they'd meet us either here or in the square.'

DJ and Jake had just arrived at full-pelt. 'We've just been all round Market Square, twice.' DJ was breathing deeply. 'We couldn't find them.'

Jake nodded. 'They were nowhere to be seen.'

Duncan stared at Cassie and rubbed a hand through his hair. 'Do you think they're all right? Perhaps they have got lost. It's not like my dad to wander off.'

'They could be anywhere.' Cassie sighed.

'Can you ring your mum, Cassie?' Emily was hopeful.

Cassie shook her head. 'She doesn't have a mobile. She never uses one.' He grew serious. 'They can't be far away.'

'We should split up and search for them, 'Ken suggested. 'We'll all return back here in fifteen minutes and check in.'

Tommy's voice was strained with the burden of responsibility. 'Good idea, Ken. It won't look good if I've lost three old...'

'We'll go in pairs,' Ken interrupted him swiftly for the sake of propriety. 'Come on, Cassie – you and I will head towards the belfry.'

'We'll check the area with the chip shop over there,' Jake suggested to DJ and Pat nodded eagerly in agreement.

'I'd better come with you,' Emily added, her blue eyes round with anxiety.

'We'll go towards that building with all the flags, shall we, *Syoo*?' Denise shivered as a gust of wind blew her hair across her face.

'The town hall,' Sue corrected her in a loud voice.

'Right, Tommy, you and I'll check inside all the bars, shall we?' Duncan was already on his way. 'Just in case Dad has stopped off for a beer...'

Ken gave a little cough and offered his arm to Cassie. 'Shall we go?' She slipped her hand through the crook of his elbow and they strolled forward, their movements in step like any other couple. Ken called over his shoulder to Denise and Sue. 'We'll meet back here in half an hour, shall we? Preferably with Lil, Maggie and Albert intact?'

* * *

'Lil, I can't climb any more steps.' Maggie was blowing air through her mouth at a fast rate, the sound of her breath echoing inside the tower. 'I'm too full of hot chocolate and chips. They are wedged in my stomach like a bowling ball and I can't move.' She sighed and folded her arms, tucking her hands underneath her armpits. 'How many have we done now?'

'Two hundred and seven – that's seven more than when you last asked me.' Lil puffed, determined. 'That leaves 159 steps. Come on.'

'I need to stop,' Maggie wheezed, plonking herself down on a step. 'I'm all finished.'

Lil sat down next to her. 'Let's take a rest for a moment. You'll be all right, Maggie – just give yourself a moment. They should have installed a lift in here for seniors.' She took a few deep breaths. 'Are you all right, Albie?' He nodded and Lil reached for his arm. 'We should keep going. They'll be locking up soon.'

Maggie wailed, 'If they've not locked up already. We'll be stuck in this cold tower by ourselves all night.'

'The view from the top is magnificent. That's what the man on the desk said,' Lil recalled

'Breath-taking – he said it was breath-taking. But that's because you – you…' Maggie panted. 'It takes all your breath to get up here. I've got none left. I'm puffed out.'

Lil moved back against the stone wall as a man and a woman possibly in their sixties pushed past, muttering, 'Excuse us,' in perfect English. Lil glanced at the man's smooth head, a few little hairs stuck up on top, and thought he looked exactly like the cartoon of Homer Simpson. She almost called him back to ask if he'd left Marge at home. She watched the couple move slowly down the steps into the darkness below, the thought uppermost in her mind that she'd honestly rather be travelling down than upwards. But she was determined she'd get to the top.

'They close this place at six. We should get a move on.'

'I can't,' Maggie breathed. 'I'm done in. You two go.'

Lil wrapped her arms around her friend. 'Okay – we won't be long, Maggie. You stay here on the step and rest while Albert and I drag ourselves to the top. I'm determined to see Market Square from the belfry tower.' Lil grabbed Albert's arm. 'I'll get there if it kills me. It's not too far now – come on, Albie.'

'It might kill you. A hundred steps is miles away.' Maggie's face crumpled.

Lil's voice was soothing. 'We'll be back before you know it. You'll be safe here. Just take a moment to get your breath back.' Lil tugged Albert's arm. As they crept up the steps together, she was conscious that her hip ached with every pace. Lil counted the remaining steps in her head as she muttered, 'It's cost me twenty-four euros to get us in here and I'm damned if I won't get my money's worth. Come on, Albie – keep up.'

Fifteen minutes later and after several pauses, Lil and Albert gazed down on the expanse of Bruges, spread out below them, from the viewing point. Lil caught her breath.

'This is nice, isn't it?' Lil was conscious that he was smiling, standing close to her, his shoulder touching hers through their coats. 'You can see across the town – buildings and shops, churches and the river. And down there in the square, all the people like little tiny insects scuttling round doing their own business, going goodness knows where.' She leaned against Albert; her hip was twinging, but it felt good to have another warm body to rest against. Albert placed a hand on her arm as they peered through the window. Lil's thighs were throbbing with the effort and the muscles in her calves ached. She thought that she'd be stiff as a wooden board tomorrow, but it had been worth it for the view.

'You wait until I tell Ken how lovely it is up here, looking down on this fairy-tale place, feeling just like one of the gods gazing on the earth below and thinking, aren't they silly, all those small people, rushing around too fast, going nowhere and I'm up here resting and thinking and watching the world go by?'

She met Albert's eyes and he winked at her. She winked back, then turned to survey the square below and the buildings beyond. Lil breathed in the beauty of the view and murmured, 'I wish we had longer in Bruges, Albie. We have it all here, don't we? Chips and chocolate and this beautiful view. I could stay here for a week and still have things I'd want to see.'

He nodded, moving his mouth slowly, showing small teeth behind parted lips, and then he uttered one word, a whisper. 'Lovely.'

Lil watched him for a moment, the joyous expression on his face as he gazed down at the view. He was lovely too, and good company; she had the feeling he knew exactly how she felt, looking down on the world from a high place. She met his sky-blue gaze

and felt the urge to hug him. Instead, she said, 'We'd better go back
down all those steps and find Maggie, bless her. Then I suppose we
ought to catch up with everyone else. There's dinner tonight
followed by drinks in some special beer place.' She offered him an
arm. 'So – shall we go?'

They trudged slowly, making their way to the top step. Lil
turned around, just to gaze at the view one more time before she
left it behind her. It was a beautiful fairy-tale land below and she
felt like an eagle, hovering above. She wondered sadly if she'd ever
see Bruges again.

Cassie and Ken walked briskly towards the tower. Cassie was
thinking about Lil, hoping that she hadn't fallen over or had an
accident or wandered into an area in the outskirts of Bruges, dragging Maggie and Albert with her and losing her bearings. She
wouldn't put anything past her mother; Lil was excessively enthusiastic and demonstrated very little in the way of caution. Cassie was
suddenly conscious that Ken had been talking to her for some time,
his voice a soft hum in the background.

'It's called the Belfort tower. Bruges used to be an important
centre of the Flemish cloth industry. The tower caught fire in 1280.
They added the belfry in the late 1400s. There was a spire on it with
Saint—'

Cassie smiled. 'You know so much about Belgium.'

'I read lots of books.' Ken beamed, pleased with himself. 'Do
you read a lot?'

'All sorts: novels, biographies, non-fiction. I pass them on to Lil
afterwards, but she won't read anything except those bonking books
she loves so much.'

Ken froze, his eyes wide, with shock or interest Cassie couldn't tell. '*What* sort of books?'

Cassie spluttered a laugh. 'I call them bonking books. Modern comedy-romances with lots of sex in them. Lil loves to read that stuff.' She was suddenly thoughtful. 'I think she's missed out on a lot of life in some ways. But she's amazing – her energy is overwhelming.'

'I can see where you get your *joie de vivre* from.' Ken stopped and gazed at her in admiration. Cassie pushed a hand through the white hair where it had come loose from the colourful headband as the wind lifted it across her face. Ken gave a small cough. 'Have dinner with me tonight, Cassie. Just you and me, away from all the others. I could...' Cassie sensed that he was thinking of a way to persuade her. 'I could tell you all about the new book idea I've just had, set in Belgium. It's about an intrepid young journalist who has a little white dog and solves mysteries in the company of a retired naval officer and a retired maths professor...'

Cassie couldn't help laughing. 'Oh, just like *The Adventures of Tintin*?'

'Ah...' Ken tried again. 'Well, I could tell you all about the beautiful buildings of Bruges... I've been reading up...'

Cassie took a breath, thinking that an evening of Ken's monologue about architecture might not be her first choice of entertainment. She imagined she'd be smiling and nodding a lot of the time. She made her voice gentle. 'I think we should probably all spend this evening together as a group, Ken, in the restaurant Tommy's booked. After all—' she offered him a smile as consolation '—we've all been doing our own thing for most of the afternoon and Tommy's very keen we all go to The Trappiste and sample the beers.'

Ken nodded sadly. They were approaching the tower; the clock at the top showed that the time was ten to six. Suddenly Cassie yelped with excitement and called out, 'There she is. Look.'

She pointed a finger and then wriggled free of Ken's arm, rushing towards an older woman with a cloud of white hair who had just appeared through the entrance to the tower, a wide grin on her face. Lil was followed into the square by Albert, who was smiling and shuffling his feet. Finally, a third figure in a faux-fur coat hobbled forwards with a slow, painful sway.

Lil called out: 'Cassie – I thought you'd got lost. We've just had a great time. Albie and I climbed to the top of the tower and looked down. The view was magnificent, all the little people and all the little buildings – you'd have loved it, Ken. But we might need to help Maggie walk back to the hotel, bless her – I think she's pulled a muscle in her bum coming down those last three steps...'

14

'This is just the best place yet. The first round is on me, folks.'
Duncan's eyes shone and twelve other pairs watched him as he
fumbled in his jeans pocket for his wallet. 'I've spent too much on
beer today and Kerry will kill me anyway, so I'm sure a few more
euros to treat my friends to some special craft ales won't matter
much in the grand scheme of things...'

They were sitting around tall barrel tables inside The Trappiste,
a hops-scented bar with high vaulted arches accessed by walking
down stone steps into a cool medieval cellar. Huge chandeliers
hung from the domed ceilings, shedding soft, yellow light. Maggie
had not accompanied them: she had complained of aches and
pains throughout dinner and decided to stay in the hotel to rest her
feet, her legs, her hips and her back, all of which she said were
giving her excruciating agony. Lil had to agree that she was
exhausted too. She'd promised that she'd only have one drink, then
she'd return to the room she and Maggie were sharing and bring
her a beer back. She'd have a long soak in the en suite bath and
sleep like a log.

Lil had finished the *Fifty Shades of Hay* novel and just started

Frolics in the House. She had moved the old photo of Frankie with his arm around her to the pages of the first chapter. She was currently reading about the capers of Jill, a young, innocent politics intern from Colorado, and Garfield, her hard-boiled forty-year-old employer, who was also Minister for Foreign Affairs. She glanced across at Denise, who was listening to Ken, her mouth turned down, and decided to lend her the book when she'd finished: it might cheer her up.

Ken was holding forth about his visit to the basilica, enthusiastically explaining that he had been impressed by the relic of the Holy Blood of Christ, allegedly collected by Joseph of Arimathea. Sue agreed: the building had a most powerful atmosphere; she had felt a definite sacred presence, a sense of being in a sanctified building. Denise mumbled about feeling nothing but cold because the place was so draughty. Sue turned her sweetest smile on Ken and boomed that she'd had a wonderful time. Tommy perked up at the word draught, his eyes searching for Duncan, who was on his way back from the bar with a tray brimming with frothing glasses of beer. Behind him, a shining sign over the bar composed of little yellow lights spelled out the word *bier*.

Cassie arrived, just behind Duncan, carrying another loaded tray. As if by magic, DJ, Jake and Pat appeared from nowhere and grabbed a glass each, sitting down at the huge barrel tables. Albert, sitting next to Denise, swathed in his old overcoat as always, reached out a gnarled hand, picked up a pint of Kerst Pater and brought it to his mouth, froth settling on his top lip like a pale moustache.

Sue and Denise had chosen a lager called Malheur; Cassie had jokingly warned them against it, suggesting that no drink would be called 'unhappiness' without good reason. Denise had taken two gulps and retorted that it was delicious, and she intended to have several more Malheurs before retiring to the room she would share with Sue, which was, unfortunately, directly above the street and she would probably be kept awake for half of the night by drunken brawling youths. Sue countered that she hoped she wouldn't be kept awake by someone's incessant snoring. DJ and Jake were joking together, drinking Delirium; Ken and Lil sipped glasses of La Trappe Blond and everyone else was sampling the Cosmic Tripel. A few tables away, a young man with long hair had started to play a banjo and several people in the bar were singing along.

Sue leaned towards Ken, and purred, 'I'll give you a taste of my Malheur if you'll give me some of your Trappe Blond, my dear.' Ken's eyebrows shot upwards as he passed his glass to Sue, who winked at him and swallowed a large gulp of his beer.

Denise sat upright and flicked her hair. 'I'd like to taste some of yours too, Ken. After you, *Syoo*.' She spoke too loudly, knitting her eyebrows and glancing at Cassie.

Cassie held out her glass. 'You're welcome to try some of my Cosmic Tripel, Denise.'

'No, thanks.' Denise frowned.

'I'll sample some of yours, if you like.' Ken gazed at Cassie hopefully.

Across the table, Albert had finished his pint and Tommy was on his way to the bar for another round, waving to Cassie in the hope that she'd come and help him. She stood up, placing a kiss on the top of Lil's head as she brushed past.

Lil was busy chatting to DJ and Jake. 'So, what do you all do for a living?'

DJ scratched the stubble beneath his tiny locks. 'I'm doing some work on an advert for a kids' breakfast cereal, animating aliens from a far-off planet.' He wrapped an arm around Jake and laughed. 'He's my model.'

Jake shrugged. 'I'm just a plumber. Emily designs submarines, which must be way more fun than cleaning out U-bends for a living.'

'Jake's a great artist, though,' Emily enthused. 'He did a wonderful portrait for my mum of our dog, Goldie.'

Lil frowned. 'Your boyfriend is a marine, isn't he, Emily?'

'Yes, he's away at the moment.' Emily was suddenly serious.

DJ patted her arm. 'I'm glad we came on holiday together. We'll have some fun, Em. Better than moping at home.'

'Emily never mopes,' Pat butted in. 'She's really strong.'

'Thanks, Pat.' Emily gave him an affectionate hug.

'Pat stays at home after work, Lil. He just makes model soldiers.' Jake laughed. 'So, we need to find him a nice girlfriend. Everyone agreed?'

Lil was delighted. 'What sort of girl are you looking for?'

Pat glanced up as Tommy placed a tray of beers on the table and shrugged. 'I'm not sure what my type would be.'

'Someone who'll put up with him,' DJ spluttered.

'Someone who likes men with red hair,' Jake joked.

'She just has to be female.' Tommy had overheard, joining in the banter as Pat's cheeks glowed red.

'Don't be mean,' Emily interrupted them all and put an arm round Pat, whose shoulders dipped awkwardly. 'Pat's lovely – he'd be a good catch for any girl.'

Pat sighed. 'I'd just want someone who loves me for who I am. She wouldn't need to be glamorous or rich, just kind and good-natured. She'd be the sort who'd be a good mum one day, and she'd want to share everything equally, decisions, housework, bills...'

He glanced around the table. Everyone was listening to him. Even Albert, who was holding his fresh glass of ale, was nodding sagely.

Lil gazed around. 'Where's Cassie?'

Heads turned in unison to where Cassie was talking to the long-haired young man, who was smiling and nodding. He passed his banjo to her then stood up and announced through a microphone to everyone in the bar. 'This is Cassie from England. She's going to sing a song she wrote for us all in this bar, just two minutes ago.'

Cassie surveyed her audience, a huddle of drinkers who had turned their eyes on her with interest. She held the banjo close to her body and strummed a few notes, then she beamed and announced, '*Goeden avond*, hello, I'm Cassie Ryan.'

A hearty applause echoed around her. Duncan and Tommy led the cheers, their fists thumping the table. Emily shouted out, 'Go, Cass.'

Cassie turned to the long-haired young man, who was sitting nearby. 'Thank you, Maxim, for lending me this lovely banjo. So, a while ago, I was standing at the bar with Duncan waiting to be served with these fantastic Belgian ales...' Another whoop came from around the bar. 'And as I was listening to Max singing and playing, I just came up with this little ditty.' Her fingers drifted to the strings, plucking various notes, a lively opening tune. Then she began to sing a folksy song, her voice strong, her eyes rolling with mischief.

> *I know a man from The Jolly Weaver,*
> *He loves his wife – he'd never deceive her*
> *But now we're here I'm sure he'd leave her*
> *For the fabulous beer in Bruges.*

There was laughter from the English drinkers and a shout of protest from Duncan. Cassie continued to sing, her fingers expertly picking the strings.

> *So here we all are, enjoying a tipple,*
> *A Trappe Blonde and a Cosmic Tripel*

After several more our livers will pickle
With the fabulous beer in Bruges.

Tommy's wild belly-laughter could be heard from across the room. Ken was clapping furiously, and Duncan was shouting something loudly. Cassie launched into a third verse.

We've had a great day, the town is delightful
The buildings and history, completely insightful
But we can't drink more or we'd all be quite full
Of the fabulous beer in Bruges.

By the final line, everyone in the bar had raised their glasses and was singing along, then there was an eruption of cheers, applause and hooting. Cassie gave a little bow before handing the banjo back to the young man, who kissed her hand and smiled so widely his cheeks creased.

Cassie came back to sit at the little barrel tables, all eyes on her, everyone clapping. Ken puffed out his chest proudly. 'Well done, Cassie.'

Pat was open-mouthed. 'Did you just make that up there and then?'

'Pretty much,' Cassie admitted, sitting down and reaching for her ale. 'It wasn't that difficult.'

'It's our theme song.' Tommy's face shone. 'Weaver's booze cruise in Bruges. Try saying that ten times after you've had a few drinks.'

DJ and Jake immediately tried to repeat the words, becoming tongue-tied after several goes. Denise wrinkled her nose. 'This is hardly a booze cruise, Cassie. I think it's a mistake to imply that it is. While we're enjoying the cultural richness of each place we visit, our interest in the alcohol is purely intellectual.' She held up her beer, then took a deep draught. Her glass was almost empty.

Cassie's eyes shone. 'I saw the banjo and I just had to play it. I asked Max if I could borrow it. He was very sweet to let me.'

'She has a banjo at home,' Lil muttered. 'I gave it to her. Her father left it behind at my house when he moved away.' She shrugged. 'He didn't leave anything else.'

Ken arranged his cravat at his throat. 'That was a lovely little ode though. But tomorrow, we have free time in the morning before we move on and I'm going to climb the Belfort tower. Who'd like to accompany me?' He gazed around the table, his eyes falling on Cassie. She was chatting to Emily.

'Too many steps for me, Ken,' Duncan admitted, offering a glowing smile. 'I'll probably be sleeping this lot off.' He waved his glass mischievously.

'I'll come, my dear,' Sue boomed.

'Count me in,' Denise added.

'I can recommend it.' Lil had perked up; she winked across at Albert conspiratorially. 'Albert and I had a great view from the top, didn't we, Albie?'

Albert moved his mouth softly, his lips forming the word, 'Lovely,' before bringing his beer glass to his mouth.

* * *

The next morning, Lil was seated between Albert and Maggie on a bench on the banks of a canal. Ken had taken a small group to the tower, Cassie insisting that she'd have to climb to the top of the belfry now her mother had done so. DJ, Pat, Emily and Jake had gone shopping for souvenirs. Duncan hadn't made it to breakfast. Tommy had told everyone to meet back at the hotel by twelve and then he'd disappeared into Market Square to buy some 'local produce' to take home with him. Lil jokingly suggested he didn't buy anything that had wired-on corks and was likely to detonate in the minibus.

Lil was listening to Maggie complain about how much her legs ached. Albert nodded; he had been shuffling his feet even more slowly this morning. Lil was aware her hip hurt, but she thought the walk to the canal would help with their mobility. As they sat in the sunshine and watched the swans glide past, leaving ruffled water behind them, she was glad to sit quietly and appreciate the beauty of the Minnewater with green trees and tall churches reflected symmetrically in the mirror-clear surface.

'I gave in and texted Brian.' Maggie groaned. 'He hasn't answered any of my messages.' She turned a distraught face to Lil. 'I've texted him four times now and – nothing.'

'He will.'

'What would you do, if you were me?' Maggie was distraught. 'Living with a husband who doesn't care – who doesn't even know I've gone on holiday?'

'He does care, Maggie. He just needs to open his eyes and realise that he has a lovely wife, and learn to pay attention to her again. He's probably thinking that right now.'

'Are you sure?' Maggie was sad. 'He hasn't noticed me properly in ages.'

'Forget him for now and concentrate on enjoying yourself. It's Maggie time.'

Albert nodded. Maggie was thoughtful. 'Maggie time, yes. Do you know, I've never put myself first, not in all my married life.'

'Well, start now.' Lil shrugged. 'I know you love Brian and I'm sure he worships you, once he stops to think about it. But when you get back, the rules will have to change. Less of *Charlie's Angels* and more of Brian's Maggie.'

'Maggie time. You're right, Lil,' Maggie agreed. 'And look at this lovely place, this beautiful river. It's made me feel much calmer, being here on holiday. I'm having a good time and I'm valuing myself; for the first time in ages, I know I'm worth more than being stuck in the background. I'm not going to be Brian's servant any more. I'm starting to see things from a different viewpoint.'

'Go, Maggie. I'm so pleased.' Lil linked an arm through Maggie's and then through Albert's. 'And talking about a different viewpoint...' she gave them a hopeful smile '...let's cross the bridge, shall we, and see how it looks from the other side? I'm sure we three can help each other to drag our aching old bones a bit further and then I'll buy us all a nice cup of coffee.'

15

Everyone had taken their places on the minibus. Cassie was strapping Lil in safely, arranging cushions, checking that she was comfortable. There was laughter in her eyes as she said, 'Did you really go across the bridge together? All three of you, arm in arm?'

'What's so funny about that?' Lil grunted.

'The idea of you and Maggie and Albert crossing the Minnewater bridge together is hilarious.'

'Why? We're not in our coffins yet. We can still walk...' Lil was offended.

'No, it's not that. It's just that... Minnewater's known as the Lake of Love.' Cassie wiped her eyes.

Maggie stared open-mouthed and repeated, 'Lake of Love?'

Ken's voice piped up from two seats behind. 'The legend tells that Minna was a beautiful young girl in love with Stromberg, a warrior of a neighbouring tribe, but she was promised to someone else, so she ran away and died of exhaustion in her lover's arms.'

'Oh, no!' Maggie exclaimed. 'That's a terrible way to go, dying of exhaustion. I almost died of it myself, climbing the steps of that belfry tower.'

'They say that if you walk over the lake bridge with someone, as you three did this morning,' Cassie explained, 'you will experience eternal love.' She hugged her mother. 'So, there you are, Lil – you, Maggie and Albert, together forever, thanks to the myth of Minnewater.'

Cassie placed an affectionate hand on Lil's arm and kissed the top of her head. Lil snorted softly, muttering under her breath. She watched as Cassie moved to the front of the bus, strapping herself in the passenger seat next to Tommy. Lil wasn't listening when Tommy announced that it would be a short drive of an hour and a half to a farm just south of Antwerp, a few miles from a place called Boom. He explained that they'd be hosted by a local family and they'd really get the flavour of true Belgian hospitality. Lil was deep in thought as the minibus engine began to rumble and the wheels thrummed on the road as they weaved through the traffic.

Lil watched as the beautiful buildings of Bruges were replaced by tall trees and long stretches of fields. She stared out of the window. They were in the heart of the countryside. She listened to fragments of conversation coming from the front. Tommy was telling Cassie that he'd enjoyed the beers he drank last night but was glad that he at least knew when to stop, unlike Duncan, who clearly didn't: the owner of The Jolly Weaver had been incoherent by the time they'd reached the hotel. Lil turned her head to survey the other passengers; most were chattering excitedly or reading, but Duncan was asleep with his head on Albert's shoulder, his mouth open.

In the front seat, Cassie was chatting with Tommy. Lil overheard her talking about Jamie; apparently, Cassie had phoned him last night and he'd wanted to know all about her performance in The Trappiste, and what she'd thought of the beer. Lil wondered why her daughter rang Jamie every night. It was clear that they liked each other. Lil wondered how close they were, and whether she was being selfish, dragging Cassie away on holiday when she might have had more fun with someone her own age. Lil heard the affectionate tone of Cassie's voice; she was fond of Jamie. Lil often wondered what would happen to her daughter after she passed, whether old age would leave Cassie by herself, lonely. But loyal Jamie kept her company; he would care for her.

Lil gazed at Maggie, who was engrossed in her book, a smile on her face. Lil hoped she and Brian would manage to repair their tired marriage, that Brian would make a huge fuss of her when she returned home. Lil was anxious about Cassie being lonely; she was troubled that Maggie might feel alone in her marriage, but suddenly Lil realised that she'd forgotten about herself. Cassie would go home to Jamie and Maggie to Brian. Lil was the one who was alone in the world, and for a moment the idea of loneliness troubled her enormously. Lil was enjoying being on holiday, surrounded by people, having fun; time was flying by. It was so much nicer chatting to other people than being by herself at Clover Hill, watching the clock tick alone in her room. Lil blinked in surprise – perhaps she too needed someone in her life. Or, she told herself, perhaps she was being silly: she had left it far too late.

Lil decided she was worrying too much. She needed something to sweeten her mood. She rummaged in her cat handbag and took out three chocolate triangles wrapped in green paper. She handed one to Maggie, who was laughing intermittently, engrossed in the book she'd just borrowed, *Fifty Shades of Hay*. Maggie opened the chocolate sweet and popped it in her mouth, grunting her thanks. Then Lil turned towards Albert, who was sitting upright across the aisle, Duncan's head slumped against his shoulder. He met her gaze, smiling, and held out a large hand, palm up.

* * *

The minibus jiggled along, making Lil's teeth snap together as Tommy drove down a bumpy track past a rustic sign with the words *Groene Velden* branded into the wood. The farmhouse nestled between trees in the distance, surrounded by acres of fields, some a lush green, some full of golden barley and others a furrowed muddy brown.

Denise groaned. 'This is the part of the trip I'm least looking forward to. I'm not sure what we'll learn of any cultural value here.'

'I disagree, my dear.' Sue's voice was abrupt. 'Spending time with a local family will be fascinating.'

'Tommy said we'd get a game of five-a-side with the farmers,' Pat chimed hopefully.

'There might be home-made scrumpy.' Duncan had woken up, rubbing his eyes.

Ken cleared his throat. 'It's a working farm so we'll get a taste of authentic rural life.'

Denise sighed. 'Oh dear, Ken. I'm imagining mud and cow pats and cold rooms and basic food.' She thought about her words for a moment and tried again. 'It's just that a bit of luxury might have been nice. And none of us speak Flemish or Dutch or whatever it is the locals speak.'

'Cassie has a bit of the language,' Emily protested. 'And most people here speak English very well. We're the ones who should be able to speak their language – after all, we're visiting their country.'

'I suppose so,' Denise conceded, gazing through the grimy window at the vast expanse of grey skies. 'I hope it doesn't rain.'

'The house is really nice.' Jake was pointing to a huge white building. The grass to either side was neatly cut.

DJ agreed. 'I was expecting a run-down farmhouse with a little windmill.'

Jake tugged his friend's shirt playfully. 'And barns, and chickens running about everywhere, and pigs too...'

DJ wrapped an arm around Pat. 'Let's hope there are no sheep here.'

Pat's brow furrowed. 'Why? What's wrong with sheep?'

'Vicious, apparently, the Belgian ones. My days, they hunt in packs here.'

'They don't, do they, DJ?' Pat turned an anxious gaze towards Jake.

Emily winked at Pat. 'No, they don't. We're going to have a lovely time, you wait and see.'

'Look,' Ken called out as Tommy brought the minibus to a halt. 'There's the farmer's wife.'

Everyone gazed at a tall woman in a dark sweatshirt and jeans standing in the doorway, her curly dark hair blowing around her head. She had a strong, honest face, and looked to be in her fifties. Her arms were folded, and she was frowning.

Cassie turned from the front passenger seat and announced, 'She's called Marieke Goossens, according to the information Tommy has. Apparently, there's no Mr Goossens – she runs this place by herself.'

DJ poked Pat with his finger. 'You're luck's in, mate.'

Pat squirmed in his seat, then delved in his pocket and brought out chewing gum, cramming it into his mouth between blushing cheeks. Tommy called to his passengers from the front.

'Right, we're here. Everybody out.'

Cassie climbed down from the front passenger seat, held out a hand to the woman and smiled. '*Goede middag, mevrouw.* I'm Cassie. It's good to meet you.'

The woman shook Cassie's hand firmly. 'Hello. My name is Marieke.' She moved her gaze to each of the people dragging cases from the back of the minibus. 'You are all welcome. My sons and my daughter are at work on the farm at the moment but they will be back later to greet you. I'll show you to your rooms first. There's a room for two, one for three, and two rooms for four persons to share. All rooms have a shower or a bathroom. I have prepared some food for you. Dinner is at eight tonight. You are all hungry after your journey, I think.'

Twenty minutes later, Lil and Maggie arrived in the vast kitchen, having claimed the double room and placed their cases on the beds. A huge iron cooking range stood in the corner, blasting out dry heat; Marieke was standing at the table, her sleeves rolled, sifting flour for pastry. She turned matter-of-factly, wiped her hands on a nearby tea towel and beckoned. 'The food is in the dining room. You can serve yourself. Come this way.'

The dining room was dark. Wooden paintings hung on a pale wall, with an open fire at one end, heavy velvet drapes at the window and a long, dark, wooden table. There were twenty chairs around the table – it reminded Lil of something a king and queen and their guests might feast at – and the surface was covered with a damask cloth; plates and dishes of various sizes were filled with food. Lil gazed at two paintings of horses, both white, with fierce eyes and flared nostrils. She turned to Marieke. 'These are lovely.'

Pat and Emily were at her elbow. Pat caught his breath. 'Magnificent, those horses – like something you'd read about in the Bible – you know, the Apocalypse.'

Marieke's mouth curved in a slight smile. 'My daughter, Thilde, paints them. She loves animals. In the hallway you will see others she has painted – cows, sheep, a pig.'

Lil was wondering whether to offer to buy one for her flat when Maggie muttered, 'Where's the television?'

Marieke shook her head. 'We do not use it much. My father-in-law watches it during evenings; he is seventy-eight and at night he likes to relax. He is out driving the tractor at the moment. You can go into the lounge room this afternoon if you want to watch it.'

Lil studied Maggie's perplexed expression and assumed she was thinking of Brian at home, so she guided Maggie towards the table and handed her a plate. 'It's time to try delicious home-cooked farmhouse food.'

Maggie lifted her plate. 'What are those round meaty things?'

Marieke waved a hand. 'Here we have *frites* and mayonnaise, cold meats, bread, salad, meatballs and some beer. Eat as much as you can. You are welcome. You can have water if you prefer it to beer.'

'Oh, I'll have beer, please, Marieke.' Duncan's voice came from behind Lil's shoulder. He had arrived with Albert, Ken and Tommy, all gazing at the food hopefully. DJ's loud laughter could be heard on the staircase before he, Jake and Pat rushed in and made straight for the food. They tucked into chips stacked high on plates and smothered with creamy mayonnaise as Denise and Sue, their make-up freshly applied, arrived with Cassie and Emily. Marieke smiled and politely told them to *'Eet smakelijk'* and then disappeared to the kitchen.

Cassie was helping herself to salad. 'Marieke says enjoy your meal.'

'These chips are great dipped in mayo.' Tommy was munching. Between mouthfuls he said, 'So – we're all at leisure until this evening. I've arranged a game with the Goossens boys at five-thirty and we'll eat with the family at eight. Marieke says we can go where we like on the farm; we can watch the cows being milked, collect eggs, help her with cooking, take a stroll or just have a nap. She said she's happy to show anyone round the farm if they want to go.'

'Do they have home-made cider here?'

'No, Dunc – but I know Mr Goossens, Marieke's father, brews his own beer. They grow a lot of barley here so perhaps it's like barley wine, strong stuff? We'll meet him later and perhaps he'll show us.'

Maggie yawned. 'I might go for an afternoon nap.'

'I think I will too,' Duncan murmured.

Tommy stretched out his arms and yawned. 'Me too – I'm shattered after all the driving.'

'I might take a stroll,' Denise suggested.

'Great idea,' Cassie agreed; noticing Denise's surprise, she decided to expand her invitation. 'Since we're sharing a room, Sue and Em, why don't we four all go together?'

'I'd be happy to tag along too,' Ken offered.

'I'm going to practise for tonight's game, have a kick-about somewhere.' DJ's brow wrinkled with sudden urgency. 'I hope we brought a football?'

'It's in the back of the minibus.' Emily gave a rueful smile. 'I'd better go and practise my penalties with the boys. Are you coming to watch us play later against Belgium?'

'We'll all be there,' Cassie replied.

DJ, Jake and Pat rushed towards the door. Emily followed them and Cassie's group of four trooped out, closing the door behind them.

Lil shrugged and glanced at Albert. 'That leaves you and me, Albie.' She beamed at him. 'I vote we go and see Marieke, have another beer or a nice cup of tea, and then ask her to take us on a tour of the farm.'

Albert took a step towards her, but she could see he was tired. Lil thought he might fall asleep where he stood. She moved over to him and put her arms around him, squeezing his shoulders affectionately. 'You go and have a rest. We'll watch the kids play football together later, shall we? You'll be refreshed by then. Go on, you pop upstairs and lie down, sleep your lunch off.'

Albert nodded several times in agreement before moving slowly away. Lil took a deep breath. Here she was by herself again, but that had never put her off before. She'd been that way for the last good-ness knew how many years, but Lil told herself she didn't care – she'd make her own way, have her own adventures, as she'd always done. She thought for a moment, then a smile spread across her face. 'I'll take a tour of the farm. That can't do any harm, can it?'

16

Lil had found a pair of old wellingtons by the front door, which she assumed were Marieke's. They were clean and green and looked as though they'd fit, so she pulled them on, tucking her jeans in, and set off over a ploughed field towards a clump of trees and a farm building, an open barn, which she hoped was a milking shed full of soft-faced cows with long eyelashes. Ten minutes later, she reached the barn; her legs ached. Tall trees edged a field in the distance; one had no leaves at all, it was bent over, a gnarled grey skeleton with long bare branches stretching towards the sky. There were no cows, pigs or sheep to be seen, just a steel-framed building with a domed roof and sickly-sweet-smelling hay. Lil wandered inside.

There was a tractor in the corner, bright green with yellow wheels and a little cab for the driver to sit in. Lil suddenly felt tired. She looked around: she could rest in the hay in the corner; it would be soft and she could snooze for a few hours. Then she stared up at the tractor. There was a seat in there, illuminated by sunshine. She clambered up the three steel steps into the cab and onto the hard seat. She sighed, wriggled until she felt more comfortable, cocooned in the firm embrace of the leather backrest, and closed her eyes. The scent of the sweet hay filled her nostrils. The inside of the tractor was warm; sunlight streamed into the barn and little particles of dust twizzled in the beam of honey-coloured light. Somewhere, a crow cawed and another one answered with a single melancholy croak.

Lil dozed for a while, her limbs relaxed, her body slumped in the tractor seat, her breathing regular. When she opened her eyes, her heart leaped: a face was inches away, staring at her. Lil gasped; the man was wearing a trilby hat; his eyes were the intense blue of cornfields; his expression was one of scrutiny, as if he'd never seen a lady asleep in a tractor before. Lil gave a little scream and sat up, glaring at the man whom she supposed to be the same age as she was, fit and lithe, wearing an old duffle coat.

She frowned. 'I thought I'd died and gone to hell and you were old Nick, come to take me away. You gave me the shock of my life, sneaking up like that.'

The man spoke slowly in hesitant English. 'I thought I had found a sleeping princess and I must wake her with a kiss.'

'Don't be silly,' Lil retorted. 'You terrified me, staring at me like that.'

The man raised thick eyebrows. 'You forget something – it is my tractor you sleep in.'

'Ah.' Lil was for once lost for words.

'I also think you are staying in my house.'

'Oh, you must be Marieke's father.'

He shook his head. 'Marieke is the wife of my son, Dirk, who died.'

'Oh,' Lil repeated and then said, 'I'm sorry.' She took in his expression, one that was difficult to read; he was simply staring at her, and she added, 'I'm sorry I fell asleep in your tractor too.'

The man shrugged. 'It is no problem. I wasn't using it.' He held his hand out. 'I am Herman Goossens.'

'Lilian Ryan,' Lil replied, feeling the warmth of his hand, the hard skin against her soft palm.

'Well, Lilian – may I drive you home in my tractor?'

'My friends call me Lil – that is, if you want to be a friend.'

'Why not?' His eyes twinkled. 'So – if you can move over, I can take us back to the house in time for the football game.'

Lil wriggled across, conscious of the tall man who had sidled in beside her and the fact that there was little space for them both. Herman started the engine, a rattling ticking sound. Lil raised her voice over the clatter. 'Are you going to watch the football game with us?'

She hoped she hadn't sounded too interested. Herman was grinning; Lil liked the lopsided twist of his mouth.

'I wouldn't miss Belgium versus England.' He winked. 'Besides, I am one of the players.'

Lil was amazed. 'Aren't you a bit old to play football?'

'Seventy-eight years old and fit all my life working on my farm.' He raised his eyebrows. 'Besides, I am the goalkeeper. I won't need to do anything against your team except stand in the goal and watch. We go now to pick up my granddaughter. She is our super striker.'

Lil wondered how they would fit another person into the cab; she and Herman were already squashed together, too closely for comfort. Lil patted her hair and took a furtive peek at Herman. The tractor bumped across the uneven ground towards a clump of outbuildings where an open-fronted building was crowded with black and white cows. A young woman was waiting close by, wearing jeans and a sweatshirt, her hair a mass of dark curls. Herman slowed the tractor and she swung herself up on the steps, clutching onto the side of the cab. Herman said something to his granddaughter in his own language and Lil couldn't help her thoughts: his voice was a low, sexy drawl. The girl held out her hand to Lil, despite the fact that the tractor was moving again and she was hanging on the side. She smiled shyly.

'Hello. I'm Thilde.'

'Lil,' said Lil, with her most friendly grin. 'I've seen your paintings of horses. They are wonderful.'

'Thank you,' Thilde replied, her cheeks turning pink.

Lil studied her face, wondering for a moment, and then an idea came to her. 'You're playing football this evening, Thilde – and you're the striker.'

'Yes,' she replied, concerned.

'Thilde doesn't care if the English players are big and tough,' Herman observed. 'My granddaughter can find the back of the net.'

Lil nodded. 'And do you have a boyfriend, Thilde?'

Thilde's cheeks became an even deeper pink. 'Oh, no. I work on the farm – I don't often have time to go into Boom to see friends...'

'That's good.' Lil rubbed her palms together excitedly. 'I mean – that's going to be a good game to watch.' She glanced at Herman, wondering if he would wear a tightly clinging football shirt and revealing shorts. The tractor had arrived at the farmhouse, the engine idling with a slow rattle. She met Herman's smile. 'Yes, I'm looking forward to this game a great deal.'

* * *

Cassie gazed out of the first-floor bedroom window, her phone in her hand, listening to Jamie's low voice, enjoying the familiarity of his tone, his words a whisper in her ear. He sounded cheerful, but Cassie knew he was missing her. She glanced down at the football game below. The English players were wearing white tops and shorts, now streaked with mud, and the Belgians sported a red strip. Both teams were rushing around furiously, trying to pass the ball to their female strikers; Emily was fast and tenacious, Thilde strong, focused and determined. DJ and Jake were athletic in their pristine strip, serious and frowning as they attempted to tackle Thilde, who simply dribbled the ball between them as they collided roughly and fell over face first into mud.

Cassie's eyes strayed to Lil, who was standing behind one of the goals, flanked by Maggie and Albert, wearing huge scarves, watching an older man in a purple tracksuit leap up and down to keep warm. Cassie assumed that the Belgian goalkeeper was Marieke's father-in-law. Three tall young men in the red strip, all with curly dark hair, passed the ball to each other, rushing athletically around on the grass. The youngest was around seventeen and the oldest and tallest perhaps twenty-four: Marieke's sons, Teun, Maarten and Damiaan. Tommy was running around waving his arms in a too-tight football shirt and shorts. She watched his clumsy attempt to tackle Thilde, but Tommy was left staring in wonder as she nimbly stepped past him and hammered the ball into the net over Pat's head. Pat fell over in the pretence of trying to make a save, picked the ball up and grinned. He rushed over to Thilde and held out a grimy hand, congratulating her on the goal. They both laughed shyly, their cheeks pink. Emily was on the attack again, leaving Teun on his backside in the dirt as he lurched towards her, too slow. Cassie moved away from the window to concentrate on the phone call.

'So, what are you cooking tonight?'

'Keftedes followed by honey-soaked doughnuts. I've invited Cathy and Mark. They send their love, by the way.'

'I'm glad they're coming over.' Cassie imagined Jamie in the kitchen, cooking for their friends, mixing ingredients and tasting them tentatively. Cassie recalled him cooking dinner for the four of them a couple of weeks ago; they had eaten the same dish of delicious meatballs then. She took a breath. 'Jamie, are you sure you're all right?'

'Of course.' His voice was bright, excessively cheerful. 'Why shouldn't I be?'

'Oh.' Cassie wasn't sure how she could explain the feeling that was scratching at her skin: something wasn't quite how it should be. 'Have you seen the doctor this week?'

'Oh, yes, I saw Mariposa this morning. She's changed my meds. But there's nothing to worry about.'

'Are you sure?' Cassie frowned.

'I'm fine,' he protested, his voice loud in her ear. 'She's pleased with me... and I walked to the surgery and back, by myself.'

Cassie nodded. 'That's good.' She closed her eyes. 'So why do I have the distinct feeling there's something worrying you?'

'Nothing's wrong. I can't wait to hear all about the delicious Belgian feast you're having this evening.'

Cassie protested. 'I wish you were here to share it with me.'

She could hear him thinking for a moment, then he replied. 'It's strange being by myself. The house is so quiet...'

Cassie sighed. 'I'm sure it must be. I miss you too. But Lil's having a fabulous time meeting new people and I'm enjoying visiting all the great locations. Everyone here is really nice and, besides, I'll be home in eight days.'

'Eight?' Jamie's voice wobbled slightly. 'Oh, of course it is. Time will fly.'

'That's no time at all.' Cassie moved back to the window. Thilde had taken up position, her brows knitted, for a penalty kick. Duncan was refereeing, waving his arms and shouting frantically – he had just blown his whistle, a sharp blast that Cassie could hear through the thin glass as Thilde surged forward and kicked the ball.

'I'll ring you tomorrow. I don't want to miss the rest of the game. I promised I'd be there.'

'I'm looking forward to hearing all about it.'

Cassie murmured, 'I'll ring tomorrow evening. Enjoy your meal

– give my love to Cathy and Mark and try not to drink too much wine.'

'I will.'

'Great. Well, take care.'

Jamie's voice was warm with emotion. 'Love you, Cassie.' There was a click. She gazed through the window, still anxious about Jamie. She thought he'd sounded lonely. He was clearly missing her more than she'd anticipated. To be honest, Cassie thought, she'd have enjoyed bringing him with her on this holiday; they'd have had fun sharing experiences together. She was missing him too.

Cassie noticed Lil clapping and cheering: the purple-clad keeper had fallen over as the ball sailed from Emily's foot over his head and into the net. He stood up smiling, his face clumped with dirt. Cassie scanned the scene: DJ had just hugged Jake and Pat, and Sue was embracing Ken, full of excitement. Marieke and Lil were yelling encouragement. Maggie was blowing her nose and waving her handkerchief. Albert simply stared ahead smiling, his chin tucked under a scarf. Duncan was trotting up and down the muddy makeshift pitch, shouting some sort of instructions but no one was paying any attention to him. He was gesticulating wildly and blowing his whistle, desperate to control the game. At the other end of the pitch, Tommy had started to strike muscle-man poses, leaping energetically, throwing himself into the air without a ball then checking to see if anyone was watching just as Thilde sailed past him and thumped the ball over his head, cracking the goalpost. Cassie heard the door click behind her, tugging her from her thoughts. Denise shambled in and threw herself on the bed. Cassie offered her warmest smile. 'Aren't you watching the game?'

'Clearly not.' Denise was stretched on her back, her eyes closed. Cassie thought for a moment. Denise had been quiet during their walk this afternoon; it had been mostly Ken and Sue dominating the conversation, exchanging their views on art and literature and

Ken talking about a new idea for a novel, based on an eccentric male Belgian detective. Ken had seemed unhappy when Cassie had mentioned that it had probably been done before. She moved over to the edge of Denise's bed and sat down. 'Is everything okay?'

Denise said nothing for a moment, then she opened her eyes and pushed herself bolt upright. 'To be honest with you, Cassie, I'm beginning to regret coming on this trip.'

'But why?' Cassie shook her white hair, making the colourful scarf move and the bow on the top flop forwards. She put a hand to her head to straighten it. 'Aren't you enjoying all the fun?'

'No, I'm not.' Denise glared at her. 'Not at all.'

'I'm sorry to hear that,' Cassie said, genuinely concerned. 'How can I help?'

'This sort of holiday's just not for me.' Denise paused. 'I don't seem to fit in. I've nothing in common with the others. I thought coming on this trip would cheer me up – I had a dreadful time a year ago with Bob, my husband, who I found out had been cheating on me for years. The divorce was truly appalling and I left the area I lived in because everyone in the neighbourhood knew what had happened to me. My job is dull, my life is dull and now I'm on holiday and – it's all dull.'

Cassie reached out and laid a hand on Denise's, her voice soft. 'We'll have a great time, Denise – you'll see. We can sit together at dinner—'

Denise pulled her hand away. 'I don't need anyone to feel sorry for me. You, with your clever songs and poems; you're so intelligent, speaking all the languages and helping everybody and Ken thinking you are something special and Sue saying how nice it will be to share a room with you.' Denise paused for breath, her cheeks burning. 'Perfect Cassie. No, thank you. I'm all right by myself.'

Cassie blinked as if she had been stung. 'I'm sorry you feel that way.'

Denise flopped back on the bed and rolled over, away from Cassie, her face to the wall. Cassie watched her as her shoulders shook. She was sobbing silently. Cassie rested a gentle hand on her back.

'I'm going downstairs now but I'll call back up in half an hour or so. We can have dinner with all the others...'

Denise didn't move. Cassie sidled away quietly towards the door, turning back to gaze at the auburn-haired woman curled in the foetal position, her body tense, angry and yet somehow vulnerable. Cassie stepped outside silently, holding her breath; the last thing she heard before the door snapped shut was Denise's voice, her tone desperate and miserable, shouting, 'Please just go away.'

17

Lil was feeling glamorous: she had chosen a long, pale blue dress for dinner and had borrowed a pair of Cassie's colourful dangling earrings. She was like the Queen or, more accurately, like a movie star surrounded by acolytes ready to light her cigarette. Not that she'd ever been a smoker but, with Albert on one side, who had already topped up her wine glass twice, and Herman on the other, passing dishes of food and ladling too much on her plate, she was in great demand. Albert kept smiling and patting her hand and Herman was engaging her in bubbling conversation about how wonderful and healthy life was on a Belgian farm. Lil smiled at both of them and waved her hand regally, in the hope that they'd both persist. It made a pleasant change, after years of being alone; she liked the attention.

She glanced around the table. Everyone had scrubbed up clean after the football game and was in high spirits, chatting and sharing food. Ken was wearing a red silk cravat; Sue had put on a fitted dress and Jake's all-black garb had been brightened with a dark red football scarf. The football players were cheerful although England had lost by one final goal: Pat had been more attentive to the pretty Belgian striker who had launched the ball past him into the back of the net. Marieke's sons, Teun, Maarten and the youngest, Damiaan, were chatting happily to DJ, Tommy, Jake and Duncan, their conversation punctuated by loud guffaws. Ken was sitting between Sue and Denise, but appeared to be giving most of his attention to Sue, whose high, tinkling laugh had become even louder and who seemed to be finding his every comment excessively amusing. Denise, on his other side, was staring blankly across the table although Cassie, next to her, was dividing her time equally between her and Emily. Denise had little to say but Emily was keen to relive a goal she had scored, having tackled the muscular Teun to the ground, sending the ball flying past Herman's ear. Lil thought Denise seemed sad and she decided she'd make a point of talking to her later to cheer her up a bit.

Lil noticed that Pat, his hair freshly washed and glossy, appeared to be eating very little; he was gazing at Thilde, who was gazing back with the same doe-eyed expression. Next to them, Marieke was in full swing, the perfect host, talking to everyone and passing around more food, beer and wine. Lil felt pressure on her hand and turned to Albert, who was patting her fingers. She smiled at him and he held a dish of chips under her chin. Herman patted her arm on his side, offering a dish of mussels. Lil helped herself to both and turned her attention to Marieke, who was addressing everyone around the table.

'Have you all seen *Oud Woot* by the outbuilding across the field?'

'Who is he?' Lil asked.

'It is the name we give to the tree at the end of the ploughed field, the one with no leaves,' Herman explained softly.

'Oh, yes.' Emily nodded. 'It's very sparse, its branches all bare and sticking up into the air, like it's been struck by lightning.'

'Is it a cursed tree?' Ken wondered. 'I could put it in my new novel about a detective – an intelligent Belgian man with a moustache who picks up clues and is very logical...'

'It sounds excellent, Ken,' Sue cooed. Denise curled her lip.

Cassie murmured, 'A bit like Agatha Christie's Poirot...'

'We used to play up by that tree when we were children.' Teun smiled at the memory. 'Grandma Theodora would tell us not to go there because of the terrible story of *Oud Woot*.'

Sue leaned forward. 'Oh, I'd like to hear that, wouldn't you, Ken, my dear?'

'Indeed, I would.'

Herman sighed. 'My wife was very superstitious. The story goes that *Oud Woot* was a man who lived hundreds of years ago and he defied a magician, so he was imprisoned inside the tree for eternity. The branches are his arms reaching for help towards the heavens. When the wind whistles at night, you can hear him screaming to get out, apparently.'

'That's terrifying – you can see the tree from my window.' Lil's eyes opened wide. She leaned across Albert to Maggie, who was helping herself to stew. 'I hope we'll be all right by ourselves.'

Maggie filled her plate with food. 'So, is the tree haunted? Does Old Woot creep into the house at night?'

'He'd better not.' Lil grimaced.

'It is a myth,' Maarten scoffed.' You'll be fine. But my grandfather will look after you if you need help.'

Lil noticed Marieke give her middle son a warning stare. Herman winked at Lil.

Ken's eyes flickered to Cassie. 'You should write a poem about why *Oud Woot* was imprisoned in the tree.'

Cassie nodded. 'What a great idea. I might just do that.'

Marieke opened another bottle of wine. 'Cassie, are you a poet?'

'She's a great poet,' Tommy spluttered, his mouth full of chips.

'She performs in my pub.' Duncan gave a toothy smile. 'You'll all have to come over and visit The Jolly Weaver.'

'And Cassie sings too,' DJ added.

Jake waved his fork. 'And she plays the banjo.'

Cassie picked up her glass and sipped red wine.

'Can you recite a poem for us now?' Herman asked.

'I suppose I could.' Cassie shrugged cheerfully.

'What about a poem about your mother?' Herman beamed at Lil. 'Have you written one about her?'

Maggie nodded. 'Yes, give us a poem about Lil.'

Duncan lifted his beer glass. 'What about the one you did in the pub on Mother's Day about making a cake?'

'Cake and mothers – perfect together,' Damiaan suggested.

'It's a sad poem, that one,' Lil murmured.

'Do you want to hear it, Lil?' Herman placed his hand over hers.

Lil was enjoying being the centre of attention. She beamed like an actress in camera flashlights with a golden award. 'Oh, if you insist. Cassie – what do you think?'

Cassie met everyone's eyes. 'It's a poem I wrote on my birthday years ago, when I was teaching abroad. I felt guilty about being far away from Lil, after she'd given so much of her life to bringing me up. I was far from home, feeling grateful and yet not able to repay her for everything she'd done, for all the sacrifices she made.'

'I'd like to hear that poem.' Marieke placed her hands on the table.

'Me too,' Ken agreed.

Herman's eyes shone. 'Cassie – would you mind telling us your poem?'

Cassie shook her white hair, tonight tied in a yellow band, and stood up slowly. In her rainbow top and green dungarees, she was a focus for everyone's attention. She smiled, meeting every pair of eyes.

'So, this poem is about a birthday I had when I was a child, and Lil made me a cake that took her ages. It was shaped like a doll's house with chocolate squares for windows. It had eight candles.'

She paused for a moment then she murmured, 'I'm not sure I ever told Lil how much I appreciated what she did for me. But this poem touches upon how, as a child, I wasn't really aware of how special a mum she was. It just felt normal to have such a loving mum and no dad. The poem's called "The Birthday Cake".'

She cleared her throat and began to recite, her eyes
shining, animated.
The child is eight years old today.
The cake is baked in secret, a surprise.
A gingerbread house spiced, sweet as love.
The sharp aftertaste of an absent father.
The whisk whirls in the mother's hand as she beats away
thoughts of his silent leaving,
her lacklustre life, a closed door, a single slamming.
The eggs dissolve, frothy: her life dissolved, messy.
The flour, light as hope.
The sugar, each grain a birthday wish,
the cake rising in warmth, golden, blessed as the child's
future.
She looks at her hands: cooking hands, caressing hands,
empty.
She will keep them busy, useful, fluttering.
The cake is finished, flourished, displayed.
A perfect house: rainbow roof, lollipop doors.
A candy home, sparkling with sugar.
The icing soft and crumbling, a mother's kiss,
melt in the mouth and then forgotten.
The candles flare then snuffed in one rushed blow

The cake sliced and sampled, left on the plate
The child squeals, rushes off to play. She has other things
*   on her mind.*
Absent now, like the child's father, and silence fills the
*   room again.*
Soon her child will be like him.
Gorged. Grown. Gone.

Silence followed Cassie's words, all eyes on her, all faces serious. Then Herman began to clap and everyone else applauded and cheered. A single tear rolled down Lil's cheek and Albert touched it with his long finger, wiping it away. Lil's eyes shone as Cassie sat down quietly and lifted her glass to her lips. She noticed Pat had tears in his eyes, Thilde too. Maggie had taken out her handkerchief and was sniffing and dabbing her eyes.

Marieke spoke softly. 'That was charming. Thank you, Cassie.'

Herman rested a hand on Lil's shoulder. 'Your daughter is special, like her mother.'

Teun was on his feet, holding up his glass. 'A toast, to all our mothers.'

Everyone shuffled to their feet, glasses raised. 'Mothers.'

Marieke put out a hand in protest. 'Wait, wait, before you all begin to toast and drink too much. I have the puddings to bring to the table. Who would like *mattentaart* and who would like Speculoos ice cream?'

All hands shot up and Tommy called out, 'I'll have both, please.' Lil noticed each face around the table; everyone was smiling and enthusiastic, apart from Pat and Thilde, who were still gazing into each other's eyes, and Denise, who seemed left out and was examining her fingers.

* * *

The meal was over and everyone had moved away from the dining room. Maggie tugged Albert's sleeve, coaxing him to watch television with her. Lil smiled; it was unlikely that she'd understand the language of the local channels, but she could put her feet up and doze. Albert followed her reluctantly, looking back over his shoulder hopefully, his eyes begging Lil to go with him.

Lil watched as Damiaan helped his mother to clear the table, Marieke insisting that the guests should enjoy their leisure. Teun and Maarten led the way to the games room where there was a pool table and darts; DJ, Jake, Emily, Duncan and Tommy rushed after them carrying bottles of Belgian beer. Cassie announced that she was going to write a poem about *Oud Woot*, the man imprisoned inside the tree, and Denise slunk away, saying she was going to bed. Ken had asked Sue if she'd glance over his travel guide to Amsterdam, so that they could work out in advance where to eat. Pat and Thilde had already disappeared. Lil turned to Herman hopefully. He held out a hand. 'The stars will be particularly bright tonight. Would you like to take a stroll?'

Lil pretended to think about it; she wondered if she should play hard to get, then she countered with, 'Won't it be cold?'

He shook his head. 'It is summer time – balmy nights, if you can manage the wind.' He lifted a jacket from the back of his chair and wrapped it round her shoulders carefully. 'Can we stroll now I have made you warm?'

They stepped outside and Lil took Herman's arm. He led her as they walked towards a group of outbuildings. She smiled. 'Are we going to see the chickens?'

He shrugged. 'We may see some chickens on the way, and hear some owls. But it is the night sky I think you'll enjoy the most.'

The air was chilly and there were no sounds at all other than their soft footfall. The darkness was intense. For a moment they were thoughtful. Herman paused and stared upwards at the skies spattered with little fragments of brightness. 'The heavens are very clear tonight. You can see Orion and the Great Bear.'

'Do you know all the names?' Lil asked.

'Of course. They have been my constant companions for many nights.' Herman noticed her frown and continued. 'This farm was my father's and his father's before him; I have worked on the land since I was younger than Damiaan. It was our home, when my wife Theodora was alive and we had our son, Dirk. I spent a lot of late evenings on the tractor, even into the darkness. Sometimes the constellations were my only light.'

Lil pressed her lips together. 'It must be hard losing your wife and son. You must feel very alone.'

They walked a few paces, stopping in the doorway of a large outbuilding. Lil could smell the sweet hay inside. Herman's voice was hushed. 'Of course, I miss them. We are a big family now I have grandchildren, but sometimes when I am by myself, I remember how good it was to hold a woman and to touch the softness of her hair.'

'I've forgotten how that felt, to be close to someone.' Lil's voice was determined but cracking with too much emotion as she spoke the next few words. 'I've spent all my life alone.'

'You never married?'

'I never wanted to. I suppose I never met the right man. I was better off by myself in those days. There was nothing to lose if I didn't take a risk.' Lil was thoughtful. 'Of course, there was Cassie's father and I loved him but I was only young. He was the first person I cared for and, probably, the last. After that, I didn't see the point in bothering. Men are too much trouble.'

'I hope we are not all too much trouble.'

'I've been thinking about that recently, especially since I came away on holiday. Being on your own isn't always the best way to be.' Lil examined his craggy face, the fascinating twist of his mouth as he smiled, the bushy eyebrows over glimmering eyes, and she wondered for a moment how life might have been if she'd met someone like Herman years ago. She sighed. 'Tomorrow, we'll be back on our journey, to Holland. It was nice to have met you though, Herman.'

'You don't leave the farm until the early afternoon.' He took her hand. 'So tomorrow we go into Boom and I will buy you lunch.'

Lil's eyebrows shot up. 'Don't farmers start work at the crack of dawn?'

'You are a special guest in my home.' He brought her hand to his lips. 'I will take the morning off to be with you, if you will accept.'

Lil wondered whether she should kiss him. It occurred to her that she was badly out of practice in affairs of the heart and she suddenly felt awkward. Then a noise behind her caused her to turn sharply. A young man and woman were walking together towards them, their arms around each other, their heads close, whispering quietly. Lil grasped Herman's hand tightly. 'It's Pat – and Thilde. They mustn't see us.'

Lil whirled inside the barn, behind the door, anxious that she wouldn't embarrass Pat. She and Herman stood close together in the shadows, breathing lightly, as the young couple strolled by. Lil heard Pat's low voice, soft as a caress, and the warmth of Thilde's hushed reply. Lil waited until they had passed, then she turned to Herman, her eyes shining. He reached out a large hand, smoothing her hair. She thought he might kiss her so she held her breath and closed her eyes.

Suddenly, there was a rustling noise from above. They stared up into the gloom of the shadows, where a rickety ladder led to a deep hayloft. Herman wrapped an arm around Lil and they waited: again, the sound of movement came from above, in the thick of the hay, then there was a hushed voice, a man's, a romantic whispering.

Lil heard the words from a low male voice, 'We might be missed by the others...'

And then a hooting laugh and the words, 'Don't worry, my dear...'

Lil's eyes widened. A man and woman were in the hayloft together and she'd recognised the voices instantly. She pressed her lips together to stifle a laugh: it was Ken and Sue.

18

The minibus was packed with luggage and everyone was seated inside, gazing through the window at the Goossens family, who had assembled to wave them off. Pat had been the last person on the bus, hugging Thilde and whispering a final promise in her ear. Lil had a lump in her throat as she stared at Herman, his face cheerful, the large hand raised in a final wave. Earlier they had enjoyed a quiet lunch in Boom and Herman had asked her to send him a postcard when she reached Amsterdam; he'd murmured that it would be nice to stay in touch. Lil didn't really see the point; she hadn't said so, but she knew what happened if you cared too much for someone. Frankie Chapman had been her only love; she had thought about him every day for so many years. And now she'd met Herman, now she liked him, she'd hardly said hello and it was time to say goodbye. But it had been so pleasant, another person, the attention, the affection. Lil's feelings confused her.

Tommy started the engine. The minibus was filled with excited chatter: Duncan, Emily, DJ and Jake had been into Boom to buy souvenirs; Cassie had written a poem about *Oud Woot*. Ken was telling everyone that they would be in Zandvoort, in Holland, by four o'clock and there would be lots of exhilarating things they could do before going on to the hotel for six-thirty. That evening they could choose from a variety of interesting restaurants over-looking the sea.

Lil twisted round to observe the youngsters in the back seat; Pat's usually cheery expression was glum and both DJ and Jake on either side had wrapped a protective arm around him. Lil was pleased that they weren't teasing him; poor Pat was genuinely miserable. She understood how he felt, as the minibus pulled slowly away and Lil watched Herman press his fingers to his lips and wave again. She glanced at Maggie, who had stuffed her nose in a new chapter of *Fifty Shades of Hay* and was laughing out loud intermittently. Lil sighed and leaned her head back against the seat, closing her eyes, wondering what life held for her next. Then she felt Maggie reach out a hand and take hers, a gesture of empathy. Lil squeezed her friend's fingers in thanks: Herman might have been her last chance to love someone. She was fooling herself: life had never given her an opportunity to be loved by anyone she could love back except for Cassie. She was suddenly aware of a slight pressure on her other arm and, as she sat up and blinked, she saw that Albert was leaning over, full of kindness, offering her a folded handkerchief. She took it gratefully and dabbed her eyes. He nodded and smiled.

Lil looked at Maggie again, who still clutched her hand but was completely immersed in the goings-on in the novel, her eyes bulging with disbelief. Lil remembered the soft kiss Herman had placed on her lips last night, then her mind moved to Ken and Sue canoodling in the barn. They were sitting together now, their eyes locked; Denise was on the other side of Ken, obviously trying to look uninterested, reading a magazine. Lil thought about how she had heard voices in the hayloft, and imagined that Ken and Sue were like the characters in the novel, abandoning themselves to the throes of passion in the hay. She stifled a smile.

Then she wondered again if Ken had slept with Cassie; Cassie had glossed over it when she'd asked about her sleeping alone, but what if Cassie had begun to care for Ken and if Ken was two-timing her? She glanced at her daughter, at her profile as she sat in the front of the minibus talking to Tommy, her white hair wrapped in a paisley scarf, her lips a deep red, raising a confident hand as she spoke. Lil wondered if her self-assured demeanour hid a secretly sensitive side, if she too ever felt the need for someone to love her.

The thought hit Lil for the first time, a cannonball exploding in her head; perhaps Cassie was exactly like Lil, perhaps she too had been hurt in the past, too bruised to venture back into the fray. Perhaps having no father figure all her life had left her damaged, unable to commit to relationships. Or perhaps she'd simply copied her mother, her only role model as a child; taking no chances meant avoiding the risk of being hurt. Lil wondered if it was her fault, if Cassie's feisty character was just a performance, a way of hiding the vulnerable woman beneath the veneer of self-assurance. Lil was determined to find out and protect her child.

In her peripheral vision, she saw Albert nodding in her direction. He closed one eye, opened it again and smiled; he had winked at her. Lil winked back and delved into her cat-whisker handbag and brought out a wrapped chocolate and passed it across the aisle to him. It was good to have another ally.

Tommy drove the minibus into Zandvoort past the beach, a long stretch of smooth sand fronting a line of sea, a silk scarf that seemed to have been ironed flat. The sky was deep blue apart from a few scudding clouds. Duncan muttered that it was perfect August weather and Sue, wearing a light dress, piped up that the water was very inviting. Lil noticed her hopeful glance at Ken, who was now hiding behind sunglasses. Jake reminded everyone that he and several of the others were going to the motor-racing track. DJ, in his most enthusiastic voice, asked Pat if it was possible to rent a fast car and try the track out, if he'd like to tackle the corners at speed, racing around the most infamous bend of the Dutch circuit. Pat gave a single grunt; he had no interest. There was nothing that would inspire him today. He turned to stare out of the window: he had left his heart back at the farm with Thilde Goossens.

The minibus slowed down, stopping next to the beach, and Tommy asked who wanted to get out. Albert gestured towards the door, muttering that he'd like to walk on the beach with Lil; his eyes followed her as she clambered out through the door and he stood up to follow her, but Duncan insisted that he should stay on the bus so he could go with 'the lads' to the motor-racing circuit. Albert shrugged and sat down, waving to Lil through the window.

Ken wanted to see the cars too, and Sue was eager to accompany him. Lil asked Cassie if she'd spend some time with her on the beach and Cassie nodded eagerly, threading an arm under her mother's. Maggie said she would like to sunbathe and Cassie invited both Emily and Denise to join them, arranging to meet the others at six o'clock. Denise shrugged, muttering that she didn't really care what she did, it was all equally dull, and Emily quickly offered to take her to a place where they could rent bikes. Resting a friendly arm on Denise's shoulder, she suggested that since the weather was fine, they were both wearing jeans, the terrain was flat and they'd be in Amsterdam tomorrow where the culture and city life would be fast and furious, it might be nice to cycle into the surrounding countryside and relax. Denise frowned, grumbled that she'd had enough of nature on the Goossens' farm, but shuffled compliantly after Emily, leaving Lil, Cassie and Maggie watching the minibus disappear up the road in a fog of exhaust fumes.

They wandered onto the beach where there were groups of people sunbathing and children playing ball, running and calling out to each other. Cassie produced a blanket and the three of them sat down, feeling the warm sea breeze on their cheeks. Lil took off her shoes, pushing her toes into soft sand, feeling the warmth against her bare skin. Maggie tugged out her novel and began to read more about the antics in the hay as Cassie lay down on the blanket and closed her eyes. 'Ah, this is nice.'

Lil nodded, wondering how to broach the subject of Ken.

'We'll be in Amsterdam tomorrow.' Cassie sighed. 'I want to go to the Rijksmuseum. What's on your agenda, Lil?

'Anything really.' She thought for a moment. 'I'm glad I didn't book to go to Anne Frank House though. It would make me cry. I need to cheer myself up.'

Maggie muttered, 'Your books cheer me up. There are things happening between these pages that I never knew existed. The things men and women get up to nowadays... it wasn't like that in our day.'

'It certainly wasn't,' Lil muttered grimly. 'Romance has passed me by.'

Cassie opened one eye and glanced at her mother, examining her expression carefully. She knew Lil had become friendly with Herman and assumed she might be missing him a little. She decided it was best not to ask, so she opted for a different approach. 'I might buy Jamie a present – you know, a scarf with an Amsterdam emblem on it, a T-shirt, something like that.'

'Mmm, good idea.' Lil pressed her lips together thoughtfully. 'I might send Herman a postcard. A tasteful one.'

Cassie nodded, pleased with herself that she'd given her mother a chance to air her feelings.

Maggie's eyes were still on the page as she muttered, 'I texted Brian again. Still no reply. I might take him a souvenir back though.'

Lil patted her shoulder and said, 'Make sure you buy yourself something nice while you're here, Maggie. Treat yourself. After all, this is your time, your holiday. You're only here for a few days and when you get back, you're a long time—' She stopped herself. She had almost said *a long time dead*. She tried again. 'You're a long time at Clover Hill.' She thought for a moment and made another effort. 'It's a long time until the next holiday.'

'I'm enjoying it here,' Cassie agreed. 'It's been great.'

'It's brilliant,' Maggie murmured.

Lil leapt in. 'They are a nice crowd, Cassie. How do you get on with the tennis club people?'

'They are good fun.' Cassie shrugged. 'I think Denise is a little unhappy. Sue's friendly. And Ken.'

'Oh, Ken wouldn't be my type,' Lil retorted, examining Cassie's face with narrowed eyes, intent on interpreting the slightest movement of muscle.

'No...' Maggie's voice came from beneath the book and she patted Lil's knee, a warm gesture of understanding. 'Herman's more your type.'

Cassie noticed her mother's awkward expression, so she added, 'I'd agree – Herman would be more my type than Ken would – Herman is honest, unpretentious, nice. He's more down to earth. Ken's pleasant enough, but he's not the type of man we would go for, Lil. As for me, though...' Cassie shrugged. 'I'm not even sure I have a type any more. It's been so long since I had a significant other in my life.'

Maggie grunted. 'You're probably better off without one. I might change my mind once I get home, though. It depends if Brian meets my conditions. I might write a list...'

Lil placed a palm across her mouth to hide the spreading smile. She was delighted: Maggie was becoming more assertive and, what was even more pleasing, Cassie definitely had no feelings for Ken. The fact that she said she preferred Herman showed that she approved of Lil's choice. Lil wasn't sure if Cassie suspected she'd had an emotional moment with Herman but she shook her head to dispel the thoughts; after all, that was all it had been, a moment. She turned to Maggie, who had just finished another chapter. 'Okay, let's move on, shall we?'

Maggie gazed up at the sky. 'I want to sunbathe. The sunshine always makes me feel happy.'

A gust of wind puffed sand onto the blanket and Cassie was on her feet. 'Right. Shall we find a sheltered part of the beach to sit down and I'll buy ice creams?'

'Great.' Lil reached up to Cassie, wanting to be tugged to her feet. Cassie helped Lil and Maggie to stand upright and watched while they both stretched stiff muscles.

'No, let me buy the ice creams.' Maggie hugged her handbag. 'I'm enjoying spending time with you both so much. I want to say thanks.'

Lil met her eyes. 'Are you looking forward to seeing Brian, now you're away from him? Is absence making the heart grow fonder?'

'Yes, I do miss him.' Maggie shrugged. 'I'm used to Brian. He's always there, he's like part of the fixtures and fittings.'

Lil winked. 'Like the TV and the armchair?'

'I suppose so. But I wouldn't want to be without him.' Maggie smiled. 'You know, Lil, in our day, we never gave ourselves much choice about our futures as girls. I mean, you had choices, Cassie – you learned languages, wrote songs, you travelled abroad. For me, it was always marriage and kids, that's what I wanted. Nobody ever told me there was anything else I could do with my life.'

Lil squeezed her arm. 'So, what would you like to have done, Maggie, if you had your chance again?'

'I'd probably still have married Brian and had the kids. Brian and me and the kids, those were the best times for me really, when I was happiest.' Maggie thought for a moment, adjusting her sunglasses. 'I wouldn't have minded being a movie star though.'

Lil gave an encouraging smile. 'Just like Liz Taylor. I said you look like her.'

Maggie preened, delighted. 'Do you think so?'

Cassie nodded. 'Definitely. It's great, isn't it, spending time with other women? It gives us chance to reflect on what's important.'

'Ice cream is important.' Maggie brushed sand from her dress and shoved the novel in her handbag. 'There was a sign back there for the next beach. Adam and Eva, it is called. I want to go there. It sounds like a lovely place. Very romantic.'

Lil nodded. 'Yes, let's go there and get an ice cream on the way. A walk would do my hip good – it's started to seize up.'

Cassie offered Lil and Maggie an arm each and they strolled towards the road. Maggie had been right: there was a signpost to the Adam and Eva beach, so they walked for a while, found a shop and bought vanilla cones. Maggie devoured hers while Lil licked the melting ice cream from her fingers like a contented cat. There was a dusty ramp down to the beach, a gradual descent from the road onto silver sand, faded scrubby grass on either side. Lil clung to Cassie; her eyes narrowed to watch the rolling waves in the distance. A lot of people were bathing, kicking their toes into the foam as the tide rolled in. Lil noticed a café not far away, with little tables and chairs with parasols, lots of people drinking beer and talking. Her feet touched the sand and she gazed in the direction of a bunch of young men playing volleyball, their feet pounding dust as they leapt into the air yelling, their fists punching the ball high across the net.

Lil shook her head. There was something peculiar about the beach. It was busy; there was a lot of activity; there were no children around, but that wasn't what Lil was finding strange. Cassie was smiling at something and, all of a sudden, Lil understood what was so different. She opened her mouth and gazed around, then laughter spluttered from her lips.

'They haven't got a stitch on. Everyone here is as naked as the day they were born.'

'Oh, my goodness.' Maggie breathed out, her eyes wide. 'We'd better get off this beach quickly. It's a nudist beach. I can't stay here and look. I'm a married woman.'

'Not on your life.' Lil shook her head, a delighted smile stretching her face. 'I'm not going anywhere. All these young men running around playing games, with everything out in the fresh air? It's too good to miss. Get the blanket, Cassie. We're stopping here until someone tells us to leave.'

19

Lil had cheered up considerably. She lay in bed, her eyes open, staring into the darkness. To the left, a soft snuffling came from Maggie's bed. To the right, where Cassie was sleeping, there was no sound, not even the light breathing of someone awake and thinking. Lil called out softly. 'Are you asleep, Cass?'

'No.' The reply drifted from the shadows. Then, 'Why are you still awake?'

'I was thinking.'

'What about?'

Lil took a breath. 'Guess!'

'About the naked men on the beach?'

'No. We only stayed for a few minutes. It was their private beach and, to be honest, I soon felt bored.'

'Are you thinking about how Sue elbowed everyone out of the way tonight so she could get one of the single rooms?'

'No, not that, although Sue was pretty determined to have a room to herself,' Lil replied, thinking that Sue would probably not be sleeping alone. But it wasn't Lil's secret to share; she wouldn't gossip.

'I agree. It was a good thing Denise got to share with Emily. I think Em's taken her under her wing.'

'She's a nice girl, Emily.' Lil was thoughtful. 'She was so kind to Denise today. They had a lovely cycle ride.'

'Emily is a star. She's a great football player, she keeps the boys in line. It's so tough for her too, with Alex being so far away at the moment. But she's enjoying herself, which is more than I can say for Denise.' Cassie rolled over. 'I'm not sure Denise likes me, but I'll keep trying.'

Lil considered her daughter's words, wondering how anyone could dislike Cassie. 'And are you enjoying this holiday, love?'

'I am, Lil – and I'm getting some writing done. Are you?'

'What?'

'Are you enjoying yourself?'

'Oh.' Lil took a breath. 'Yes, I am.'

'So, what was it?'

'What was what?'

'The thing you were thinking about, the thing I was supposed to guess.'

Lil closed her eyes. 'I was thinking about Herman.'

'I noticed you talking together a lot during the dinner. Do you like him?'

'He's a nice man.' Lil was quiet. 'Cassie, do you think I'm too old?'

'For what?'

'For... everything. I've come on holiday; I'm enjoying myself but – am I too old for all the other things? For a bit of love?'

'Of course not.' Cassie rolled over again; the bed springs creaked. 'None of us are too old, ever. There are some strange attitudes in the world about ageing, as if we all suddenly become too far gone for the pleasures in life. I've seen many people over the years who were old at thirty-five, their lives dominated by poverty, misery and disease. And I know inspirational people older than I am – you're one of them – who don't let age hold them back.'

Lil sighed. 'Sometimes I think I'm still forty until I look in the mirror.'

'But you're full of life, Lil – and while you are alive, you can do anything your body will let you: travel, have new experiences, even love.'

'Herman was a nice man.'

'I'm sure he still is,' Cassie agreed. 'Do you miss him?'

Lil sighed. 'I don't know. It might have been something. At least it reminded me I still have feelings.'

'We all do.'

'I thought mine had dried up a long time ago.' Lil inhaled. 'But you're alone, Cassie, with no one to love.'

'I have you.'

'You know what I mean.'

Cassie was silent, then she replied, her voice small. 'Love never really worked out for me. I suppose I was too selfish, too engrossed in what I was doing. I'm fine how I am, living with Jamie. We rub along okay.' Cassie thought for a moment: Jamie, his smile, his warm nature, his eagerness to support her, his sense of fun.

'It's not too late, love. You might find someone.'

'It's not too late for either of us, Lil,' Cassie protested. 'You should send Herman a few postcards, then invite him over to stay at Clover Hill.'

'He's probably always busy on the farm.' Lil brushed the thought aside.

'Well, see what happens.' Cassie rolled over. 'Come on, we should get some sleep. We're off to Amsterdam tomorrow. I can't wait.'

Cassie cuddled a pillow, pushed her head into the softness and was surprised to find herself imagining how it would be to snuggle

close to someone as she fell asleep. She breathed out softly and
Jamie's smile filled her thoughts.

Lil gazed into the darkness again, wondering about the journey
back home after Amsterdam and if it might be possible to stop at
the farm in Boom again. She didn't think that was on the itinerary.
She imagined running away, turning up at the Goossens' farm door
with her suitcase, staring up at Herman with his bushy eyebrows
and his lopsided grin and saying, 'I've come to stay.'

She wrapped her arms around the pillow, closing her eyes and
breathing deeply.

The minibus left Zandvoort after breakfast for the journey to
Amsterdam, which Tommy promised would only take forty-five
minutes. They'd drop their things off at the Roodhuis Hotel, a name
which was making DJ and Jake snigger together, offering loud
observations about whether the place they'd be staying for two
nights was, in fact, in the red-light district.

Ken gave a little cough. 'Our hotel's in the Jordaan area –
according to my guidebook, it's about fifteen minutes from the red-
light district, ten minutes from the Rijksmuseum and five from
Dam Square. Perfectly chosen, Tommy.'

Tommy called from the driver's seat. 'Thanks, Ken – it's all down
to my wife, Angie. She sorted out all the bookings. I'll buy her
something nice to take home.'

Duncan agreed. 'My Kerry will be getting a wonderful present
from me – Amsterdam's famous for diamonds. I might push the
boat out.'

'The boat's been out for quite a while, Dunc,' Jake observed.
'How much have you spent on beer?'

Maggie lifted up her novel; she had just finished *Fifty Shades of Hay* and was avidly reading the first page of *Frolics in the House*. Jill, the innocent young politics student, had been trapped in the viewing gallery of the House of Lords with Devlin O'Toole, the handsome but wayward son of a baronet. She called out, 'I'm not sure I want to go to the red-light district. That's where all the prostitutes are, isn't it?'

Lil nudged her gently. 'I think we'll be safe enough, Maggie.' She began to cackle. 'Unless you fancy supplementing your spending money. After all, Brian's not here – out of sight, out of mind.'

Maggie laughed back. 'Now that might be a thing. You and I, out on the town in our frilly suspenders, finding out what we've missed in life.' She waved the book. 'I'm getting a few ideas from the characters in your stories.'

Sue raised her voice. 'What is the proper word for a prostitute? Isn't sex-worker more PC?'

'Prostitute's more honest, I think.' Ken cleared his throat and adjusted his cravat. 'Oldest profession, as they say...'

Denise glanced up from her magazine. 'Whatever you call them, those poor women are exploited. I think it's dreadful.'

'It has to be their choice, if at all,' Emily offered. 'And sex worker is a better term – it's gender-neutral and less loaded...'

'It's all legal in Amsterdam, though. The women sit behind glass windows and you can choose the one you like.' DJ sat up straight in his seat and Jake gaped in disbelief.

'Is that what you're planning, DJ?' Duncan teased. 'A visit to a lady of the night?'

'Not at all. My days!' DJ's shoulders hunched awkwardly.

'We should go and have a look around the area though,' Jake suggested. 'There might be some good clubs there.'

Pat snorted. 'Women should be treated with respect. Whether

you agree or disagree with legalised prostitution, you shouldn't discuss women like they are pieces of meat.'

Everyone stared at Pat, his ears now pink. He went back to texting on his phone.

Ken's voice was light. 'Well, I think it's important we take in all the aspects of Amsterdam culture while we're there. It's a beautiful, vibrant city and the architecture is stunning.'

'Definitely,' Tommy called from the front. 'We're just entering Amsterdam now, folks. Have a think about what you all want to do when we have dumped our stuff in the hotel. We're at leisure for the day and we can eat anywhere we like tonight – Amsterdam is our oyster.'

'I don't like oysters, they remind me of snot,' Maggie observed, pushing *Fifty Shades of Hay* back into Lil's hands. 'Here you are, Lil. I enjoyed reading that. I'm – what's the term? – I'm expanding my education on this trip.'

Lil placed *Vicky the Saucy Vet* on her knee, still open at the chapter she was reading, and turned around, waving *Fifty Shades of Hay* in the air. 'Denise, here, you can borrow this – you must have read that old magazine a dozen times. It's a great novel. Maggie's just finished it.'

Denise held out her hand and Duncan passed the book back to her after pausing to examine the cartoon cover of the woman in jodhpurs waving a whip as she sat astride a man on all fours.

Denise took the book and muttered, 'Thank you. I haven't read this one – it looks rather... different.'

Lil picked up her novel, making herself comfortable against the cushions in her seat. 'Enjoy,' she muttered to herself before going back to the misdemeanours of Vicky the vet.

* * *

They arrived at the Roodhuis Hotel just after eleven o'clock. It was a beautiful five-storey building, narrow with a single room under a curved gable, the front painted a deep red. Across the road, the river nestled behind a bridge, so many bicycles nestling against black iron railings. Cassie helped Lil and Maggie down the steps of the minibus and they stood for a moment, their eyes taking in colourful barges and bending trees, their green leaves sweeping onto the glassy grey canal. Ken beamed, wrapping an arm around Sue and Denise. 'Here we are, ladies.'

Denise brightened. 'I like the look of our hotel. What do you think, *Syoo*?'

Sue pursed her lips, glancing at Ken and away again, and hooted, 'I hope they give me that little garret room at the top.'

'I want a room on the ground floor,' Maggie retorted. 'They don't have a lift in this hotel.'

Duncan was gazing around him, his face shining. 'There's a bar just across the road – they sell real Amstel beer.'

'Let's get unpacked and find our rooms,' Tommy suggested. 'Then we can explore as much as we like.'

'I'm going to visit Anne Frank House,' Denise announced. 'Who else has booked to go there? We have online tickets, don't we?'

'Five of us, my dear.' Sue spoke with authority. 'You, me, Ken, Emily and Pat.'

'I'm going to the Rijksmuseum,' Cassie offered. 'Are you coming, Lil?'

'I might just find a café and rest for a bit.' Lil shook her head. 'I'm tired. I can do the energetic stuff tomorrow.'

'I'm with you, Lil. I want to put my feet up before I see the sights.' Maggie agreed and Albert nodded, placing himself at Lil's elbow, smiling.

'We're going to find a bar with live music.' DJ wrapped an arm around Jake.

'So that leaves us to drink some Amstel beer?' Duncan grinned at Tommy.

'And just me for the museum.' Cassie sighed.

They deposited their luggage in the rooms they had been allocated for the next two nights. Lil and Maggie were sharing a room with Cassie on the first floor, next to Sue, Denise and Emily. DJ, Pat and Jake were together, next door to Duncan, Tommy and Albert on the third floor. Ken had the garret room to himself at the top, with a view he claimed was magnificent. He had winked at Sue and proclaimed, 'You can see right across Amsterdam from my little room. You'd love it, Sue.' Sue had beamed and Denise had wrinkled her nose and looked away.

* * *

An hour later, Cassie was strolling through the Rijksmuseum. She had taken the steps to the first floor, into a vast room with huge paintings lit by little overhead lamps. She wandered past an alabaster sculpture on a plinth, some china displayed in an enormous glass cabinet, highly polished oak furniture and several paintings of men in ermine and velvet, holding a sceptre, regal and composed.

For a moment she stood gazing at a painting of a shipwreck and she was fascinated by the vast swirl of sky, the turbulent blues and greys that seemed to swamp the sunshine. A ship had been tipped to one side and tiny people were jostling on the beach, insignificant in comparison to the sweeping power of the stormy sky and the grey, sucking sea. Cassie held her breath, struck by the emotional impact of the image, and read the details: it had been painted in 1837 by Wijnand Nuijen. She had never heard of him.

A voice at her elbow said something in Dutch; she turned sharply and met the smiling eyes of a man about her own age. He spoke again, and she was conscious of the intense darkness of his gaze. His hair was pulled back into a small ponytail, although it was not really long enough, tin-grey wavy strands around his ears. His skin was tanned and leathery, and he had deep lines around his eyes. He was slim, dressed in black jeans, T-shirt and jacket. Cassie shook her head.

'Sorry, *ik spreek geen nederlands...* I don't speak Dutch.'

'American?' the man asked.

'English.'

'I apologise.' His eyes swept over her, white hair wrapped in a bright scarf, long colourful dress. 'I thought you were a Dutch-woman. Your clothes are bohemian.'

Cassie frowned, words springing to her lips, speaking the first thoughts that entered her head. 'Dutchwomen aren't the only ones who wear what they like.'

He held out a hand. 'I have offended you; I am wrong twice. I apologise again.'

'No offence taken.' She took his hand. He held it in his for a moment, then released it and stood back, glancing at the painting.

'So, do you like the shipwreck painting?'

'I do – I don't know much about the artist though.'

'Nor do I, except that sadly he didn't live long enough to make many more paintings,' the man replied. 'And that he was unusual for Dutch painters of this period. He was influenced by the Romantics, and I like that. No perfectly realistic pictures of kings and queens and girls with pearl earrings, but instead the wildness of nature and the insignificance of mankind. He reminds me of your English painter, Turner. I like his work very much.'

Cassie glanced at the brief biography next to the painting. 'Wijnand Nuijen is certainly dramatic like Turner; Turner was born earlier but died later. I wonder if they ever saw each other's work.'

The man gave her his full attention. 'You know about art. I was right to talk to you, even by mistake.' He gave a little bow. 'My name is Piet Cornelissen.'

'Cassie Ryan.'

'Cassie.' He repeated her name softly. 'Are you staying here for a while, visiting? Or do you live here?'

'I'm just here for a couple of days.'

Piet shook his head. 'Just two days?' He shrugged. 'Maybe I can buy you a coffee, tell you about some places you might like to visit?'

Cassie met his eyes. 'Like museums and parks? Canal cruises? I know about those.'

'Like the Zwart Gat, a great club where they play the best music.'

'Zwart Gat? That means the black...?'

'Black hole. It's ten minutes from here. There will be some good music tonight.'

'What sort of music?'

'Jazz, Cassie. It's the best local music scene. I am on stage tonight. I will play the guitar and sing. But there are greater musicians, pianists, much better singers and they will be there, many instruments and good songs.'

'But you play too. Are you any good?'

He tucked a strand of hair behind his ear. 'Good enough to be paid for it.' He shrugged. 'You can come and judge for yourself.'

'Maybe I will.'

'So, Cassie – do you like music?'

Cassie was enthusiastic. 'Yes, I do. I dabble a bit myself.'

'That is so cool.' Piet 's smile broadened. 'Please – come and have that coffee with me and tell me all about yourself.'

'All right.' Cassie met his eyes. 'I don't see why not. Thank you, Piet – that would be very pleasant.'

His dark eyes shone. 'The pleasure is all mine.'

20

It was almost six o'clock and Lil and Maggie were debating where they should eat that evening. They had passed several Italian restaurants, a brightly lit Asian-fusion restaurant and a small taverna. Lil wasn't particularly hungry; she had dragged Maggie and Albert along the banks of the river for half an hour, stopping to point at bright barges and curved bridges, and now they were all tired, especially Maggie, who was complaining that her ankles had swollen to at least twice their normal size.

Maggie stopped. 'I bet Ken, Sue and Denise are in that floating restaurant by now, eating chow mein. Can't we go there?'

'You have to book in advance,' Lil replied.

'What about a takeaway? I could murder a pizza.' Maggie licked her lips. 'Chicken wings. A burger. Chips.' She thought for a moment. 'All of them.'

Albert shook his head and muttered, 'Beer.'

'Why don't we go back to the hotel and pick up some takeaway food on the way?' Lil suggested. 'We can sit in our room with some junk food and a few bottles and slum it.'

Albert nodded. 'Card game.'

'I can't play cards,' Maggie said. 'But I've always wanted to wear one of those trilby hats and say, "I've come up trumps."'

'I can teach you to play.' Lil nodded. 'I'm pretty handy at poker.'

'Okay, we'll do that later.' Maggie sighed. 'I'm hungry now. And thirsty.'

'Right, let's grab a cup of coffee, then we'll go back and have an evening in,' Lil suggested again. 'We've eaten at fancy places and enjoyed the local food for several days. There's a TV in our room and we can just eat out of cartons and relax and take it easy.'

Albert grinned. 'Good. Beer too.'

'We'll get beer, Albie – oh, look over there. That's perfect.' Lil broke into a broad smile.

'What's perfect?' Maggie screwed up her eyes. 'I can't see what you're looking at.'

'A coffee shop.' Lil pointed across the road. She gazed at the coffee-shop frontage and a wide grin spread across her face. 'This is where we're going. I'll treat us all.'

Albert nodded; whatever Lil suggested was bound to be right.

Maggie agreed. 'Okay. I'm dying for a cuppa. But why this place?'

'Look – what a gorgeous picture.' Lil pointed eagerly: the painted sign depicted a man, his eyes two golden stars, staring into the sky. Around his head were various planets in stunning technicolour. The café was called Stargazer; the huge sign was painted yellow, red and green; below it, the words 'coffee shop and juice bar' in black letters. The door had been flung wide and, inside, welcoming music was playing. Lil recognised it as Donovan's 'Mellow Yellow', a tune she knew well from the sixties. Cassie had often sung Donovan songs as a teenager, accompanying herself on the banjo. Lil noticed the warm golden lights behind the window, and saw there was a bar with pretty coloured strings of lights shaped like stars, and the aroma of coffee beans filled her nose, making her sigh with anticipation.

She led the way inside. Lil thought it was a lovely place: bright lights, spangly designs on the walls – rainbows, huge green leaves, shooting stars; at wooden tables, groups of young people were chattering, drinking coffee, munching cakes, using their phones.

The man at the counter with a white ponytail had a badge proclaiming his name was Henk. He was middle-aged and very tall, and his face shone with cheerfulness. Lil slid onto a tall stool; Maggie and Albert copied her. Lil beamed at Henk.

'Hello. Do you speak English?'

Henk's smile broadened. 'Yes, and French and German. Dutch too.' He met her eyes. 'Would you like coffee?'

'Yes, please – what do you recommend? I like latte.'

'We have good arabica beans. Small or large latte?'

'Large, please,' Lil replied.

'Two large ones,' Maggie added. 'I need the caffeine.'

Lil glanced at Albert. 'Three large lattes. And a cake.' She pointed her finger towards a display. 'They look nice.'

Maggie became suddenly energised. 'Ooh, chocolate brownies. I'll have one of those.'

Henk raised an eyebrow. 'You want a brownie?'

'Would one each be too much? Before dinner?'

Henk was suddenly anxious. 'I think so. Three brownies are quite a lot...'

Maggie shook her head. 'I'm sure I could manage a whole one by myself. Probably two, even three.'

'Three? Wow, so much respect,' Henk murmured.

'No.' Lil took charge. 'They are quite big and there's chocolate on the top. We'll share one between us, then we won't be too full by the time we get the pizza and chips.' She met Henk's eyes. 'A chocolate brownie, please – and can you cut it into three portions? We'll share it.'

Henk was staring at her, filled with admiration. 'Of course. And three lattes. Coming right up.'

Lil beamed at her friends. 'This is working out well. We'll have coffee, then it's about fifteen minutes' stroll back to the hotel – we dawdled coming down here, so we'll be much quicker going back – and we're sure to pass a pizza place or a takeaway.'

'What if we don't?' Maggie fretted.

'Then we'll just ring up from the hotel and order it in,' Lil announced. 'I'm quite happy to ask at the hotel desk if I can use their phone.'

Albert rubbed his hands together as Henk placed three huge white cups in large saucers in front of them. Maggie grabbed her latte eagerly and slurped, leaving a foam moustache on her top lip. Henk placed the sliced brownie on a small plate, three napkins next to three forks. As Lil handed him two notes, he met her eyes. 'Enjoy.'

'We certainly will.' Lil reached out to the plate, forked her portion and took a delicate bite.

Cassie had enjoyed a fascinating afternoon in the museum, exploring the galleries with Piet Cornelissen. They shared a similar taste in art, preferring the rustic characters of Vermeer and the agrarian peasantry of Anton Mauve to the battle scenes of Piene-man. Piet seemed fascinated by Cassie, too; his eyes widened when she told him she performed as a poet in a variety of venues and also sang and played the banjo. He was amused by her outspoken banter: she asked him openly if he often visited the museum in order to meet women and he replied that he was a Rijks Friend; his annual membership allowed him to come and go whenever he liked, and, because he lived quite locally and it gave him inspiration for songwriting, he could often be found browsing through the galleries – but never before had he thought of talking to a woman he didn't know. Cassie had given a cynical snort; she would defer judgement.

Piet had told her something about his life over coffee, his Surinamese mother and his Dutch father, his teenage years in Amsterdam and his fascination for playing and listening to live music. She, in exchange, had chatted about her wonderful mother, the American soldier father she'd never met and who had left nothing behind but an old banjo; she told him about the many years she'd spent abroad, teaching in Africa and China. They chatted about composition and favourite bands, finding that they had so much in common.

It felt natural then that after the museum, they moved on to an Italian restaurant, where they ate pasta and talked more, drinking beer, their heads close. At seven o'clock, Piet suggested that it was time to go to the Zwart Gat. He was due to play at eight and he wanted to introduce Cassie to the other musicians. She wondered whether she should go back to the hotel and change her clothes, but Piet protested that she was perfect, dressed as she was. Cassie considered her options. Lil would be fine; she was with Maggie and Albert. She sent a brief text to Emily and Tommy, asking them to let her mother know her whereabouts, joking that she still had to do this after so many years, and then smiled at Piet and said she'd love to hear him play.

The Zwart Gat was, as its name suggested, a gloomy cellar reached by several stone steps; there was a small dimly lit stage at the far end and rustic wooden tables and chairs in the surrounding gloom. The club was already almost full, but Piet found a table close to the stage where two middle-aged men were sitting drinking beer, reserving two seats. Piet's friends introduced themselves as Jan the drummer, who had sparse fair hair, and Joop the bass player, who wore a trilby. Cassie shook their hands, sat down and gazed at the stage, where a man was setting up amplifiers and speakers, running cables along the length of the floor.

They drank beer and chatted for a while, then two elegantly dressed women appeared on stage, playing guitars and singing a soulful version of 'Wild Horses'. Cassie clapped enthusiastically. Then Piet stood up and leaned over, whispering in her ear. 'It's my turn now.'

'Good luck,' Cassie called.

'Come and sing with me?'

She shook her head. 'This is your slot, Piet – I don't want to butt in.'

He met her eyes, then clambered on the stage, picking up a guitar and fiddling with the keys, checking the tuning. He leaned towards the microphone and spoke in Dutch, then proceeded to play a song about a watermelon man. His voice was gravelly and warm, and Cassie watched him carefully as his fingers plucked strings: he was talented and extremely professional. He played two more songs, 'Ain't Misbehavin'' and then a slow, sad rendition of 'Autumn Leaves'. There was an aching tenderness in his voice that made Cassie wonder if he knew the pain of lost love. She applauded him warmly as he finished and he leaned towards the mic.

'Dank u,' Piet murmured, then his eyes moved to Cassie. 'I will speak in English now. We are lucky to have someone here with us from England who is a great poet and singer. I wonder if she will come to the stage and give us one of her poems, perhaps? In English – that would be okay.' He smiled at Cassie, a teasing grin, and she stood up with a show of reluctance and wandered over to the stage, clambering up beside him.

'Cassie Ryan.' Piet waved an arm in acknowledgement of her presence next to him and everyone clapped.

Cassie lifted her hands in apology. 'Thank you. I'd love to perform a poem for you, but it will have to be in English.'

She glanced at the audience, serious with anticipation. Someone shouted, 'Give us a poem – tell us what do you think about Amsterdam.'

An idea came to Cassie. 'I can give you a poem about a place in Belgium. I wrote it a day ago. It's never been performed before – you'd be the first people to hear it. I recently stayed on a farm near Boom and there was a fascinating legend, a story about a man called *Oud Woot*, who had been imprisoned inside a tree for many centuries.' She offered the audience a hopeful grin. 'Would you like me to read the poem?'

Applause ricocheted around the room, echoing on the ceilings. Cassie reached into her handbag and pulled out a piece of paper. She took her time, aware of the eyes on her, waiting for her first word; Piet was next to her, staring in admiration. She cleared her throat softly.

> *Bark-mouthed; centuries-muffled*
> *Oak-choked, smooth limbs cankered,*
> *Feet fettered as arms strive for the sky*
> *Trunk dappled, dark mottled*
> *He twists against the wind's whip*
> *Deep wooded, stifled, he will not strain out*
> *His sin was to look – and he was locked*
> *He craved – now caged and corked*
> *Shackled, silent, muscles stilled*
> *Arms hewn for gallows; trunk sapped*
> *Eyes rage cleaved, unseen*
> *Dogs sniff at his roots and scent him there*

Now gnarled and gagged he twists,
Whispers and rots in his stillness.

There was a pause, then suddenly applause erupted from every corner. Cassie smiled gratefully, leaning towards the microphone. '*Dank u.* Thank you.'

Piet put a hand on her arm. 'Do you know the song "Can't We Be Friends?" Louis Armstrong and Ella Fitzgerald?'

'I know it well,' Cassie replied. 'But...'

Piet winked and turned his attention to the audience. 'Now we can sing a song together. It is good to have Cassie here in Amsterdam. So, I will sing this song with her, hoping that she can stay longer with us here and, if she can't stay, that she will want to come back soon.'

He began to pluck strings, his eyes on Cassie, and they sang together, Piet's gravelly voice an octave below Cassie's strong throaty swell. Cassie was enjoying herself; singing with Piet was easy. It felt nice to have a partner, a foil for her performance. Until now, she had always been alone on stage. And he was professional, a smooth, confident singer with an easy stage presence. As they returned to the table amid the cheers, he took her hand.

'Thanks, Piet, I really appreciated that.'

He leaned close to her. 'They already love you here in the Zwart Gat.' They sat down and Joop handed them each a beer. Piet moved his mouth close to her ear. 'You know, Cassie, you should stay in Amsterdam. It is a place that suits you. The people welcome you and you fit in really well here.'

'I have to say—' Cassie met his eyes '—I do like the Zwart Gat, very much.'

'Your poem was very good and your singing voice is sensational.'

Cassie shrugged. 'You're very kind...'

'No.' Piet's tone was hushed. 'You could belong here, Cassie. You should stay.'

Cassie thought of Lil, of her home; she thought about Jamie. 'I don't know...'

'Meet me tomorrow. Spend the day with me. Let me try to change your mind.'

Cassie glanced around. The club had a warmth, a friendly atmosphere; people were rocking back and forth in their seats, clapping hands softly, smiling. On stage, a young man and woman were singing a blues song. Cassie's eyes fell on Piet, the tenderness of his gaze as he smiled at her. She imagined what it would be like to live in Amsterdam, to perform there regularly, to get to know Piet better. She sighed. It was a wonderful place – she felt at home. It might be very nice indeed.

21

It was past eleven when Cassie returned to the Roodhuis Hotel. She'd have liked to stay at the club longer but she'd thought of Lil and Maggie asleep in their shared room and decided to return before the Zwart Gat closed. Piet had insisted on walking back with her. He'd invited her to meet him for lunch the next day but Cassie hadn't been sure; she'd explained that she was on holiday with her mother and they ought to spend some time together. Piet had light-heartedly replied that Lil could come to lunch with him too; it would be a pleasure to meet her. Cassie sighed, kissed his cheek briefly and promised to text him in the morning; she was already forming a plan. She'd spend most of the day with Lil and the evening with Piet. She'd tell him tomorrow.

She raced up the stairs to the first floor. There was music blaring from their room as she burst in and stopped still, staring. The TV was on loudly; there was a metal rock band in concert screeching, the screen flashing. The lights in the room were all turned off except for one glowing bedside lamp. Lil, Albert and Maggie were sitting on pillows on the carpeted floor, facing each other, frowning deeply with concentration. They were each wearing a baseball cap with the word *Amsterdam* emblazoned across the front. Albert had a matchstick between his teeth, his face a picture of pure concentration. On the floor between them playing cards had been loosely strewn, a fan of spades, diamonds, hearts and clubs. Cassie caught her breath. The room was littered with empty cartons; a cardboard box was smeared with tomato and cheese; a few stray chips lay on the floor. Beer bottles were everywhere, discarded metal tops; paper wrappers of biscuits had curled and been thrown to one side. A few chicken nuggets had been left on top of Cassie's bed on a piece of toilet paper. The room was a mess and the three card players were oblivious to the detritus around them; their eyes were focused on the playing cards.

Lil was laughing, tears streaming as she stared at Maggie, who was wearing a long blouse and a pair of pink knickers that were clearly visible above the sagging waistband of her tan-coloured tights. Her shoes and a skirt were in a heap beside her and she was blinking at her cards, speechless and confused. Lil repeated, 'Look at my poker face, everyone – you don't know what a winning hand I've got.' She held up a beer bottle, swigged from it and froth ran down her chin.

Albert wore nothing but a once-pristine white vest that had tomato smudges down the front, socks and a baggy pair of under-pants. His legs stuck out in front of him, bent at the knees. His arms and broad shoulders appeared from the top of the vest; he was peering at his cards, shaking his head and muttering, 'Read 'em and weep,' several times in a low, hollow tone.

Maggie raised her eyes and stared at Cassie, who had inadver-tently placed her hands on her hips in disapproval. Maggie made a low mooing sound and whispered, 'We're playing strip poker.'

'And I'm winning.' Lil began to laugh again until she rocked backwards and almost fell over.

Cassie moved quickly to sit beside her, wrapping a protective arm around her shoulder. 'Lil, are you all drunk?'

Lil shook her head and laughed. 'We're having such a nice time. The pizza was very tasty. The tomato was so red...'

'It was good pizza,' Maggie agreed. 'I was so hungry. I could eat another one right now.'

Cassie frowned, thinking, and then she realised. She wrapped her arm around Lil more tightly. 'What have you been up to this afternoon?'

Lil started to cackle, as if Cassie had said the most ridiculous thing. She wiped her hand across her eyes and her fingers were damp with tears. 'You should have come with us. We went into a coffee shop and the barista made us lovely lattes. Then we got some takeaway food. We were all starving. My hip doesn't hurt at all, though – that's why we're sitting on the floor playing...' She was suddenly serious. 'Cards are just so important. You can really concentrate and expand your mind. It's like we're really proper gamblers, like the ones in *Casino Royale*.'

'I'll raise you ten, if you play your cards right.' Maggie found her jokes hilarious.

'Ah, but what if the chips are down?' Lil croaked, wheezing with laughter.

'I'd love some chips,' Maggie breathed.

Lil hugged her cards. 'Look – I'm playing them close to my chest.'

'I'm a wild card,' Albert cackled and waved a sprightly leg in the air.

'I have a trick up my sleeve,' Maggie howled as she pushed a card under the cuff of her blouse. 'Oh, no, I've lost it—'

'You must have been dealt a bad hand,' Lil yelped and the three of them keeled over, one after the other, screaming, in convulsions, everything seeming much funnier than it was in reality.

'I'd better play my ace.' Cassie sighed, reaching onto the bed for the remote, turning off the television. The silence was a sudden stark contrast.

Maggie moved her head and muttered, 'Where did all the music go?'

'I am Queen of Clubs.' Lil raised her arm in the air. 'I'm trumps and I vote – Albie, you've got to take off your pants.'

'Right, then – I will.' Albert stood up slowly, tottering and smiling, his thumbs moving to the waistband of his snow-white undies, wriggling and sliding them down over his belly. Maggie started to bawl out the stripper tune and wave her arms in the air. She reached for her sunglasses and put them on, leaning forward to get a better look.

Cassie decided that she'd seen enough and murmured, 'Stop, please.' Albert stopped, clutching his pants, grinning.

Cassie gazed from face to face, meeting the eyes of each of the card players, each of them staring back at her as if they were naughty children. Then she took Lil's hand. 'Did you eat anything while you were having lattes in the coffee shop?'

'We had cake,' Maggie answered. 'A brownie.'

Albert brought a bottle of beer to his lips and muttered, 'A chocolate one.'

Lil piped up. 'We sliced it into three bits. We had a bit each. It was very nice although I thought it tasted a bit funny at first.'

'Oh, Lil, you've no idea what you've eaten, have you?' Cassie said, then she stood upright, folding her arms. 'Right, the poker game is over. Lil, Maggie, I want you to get into your beds. Albert, you need to go back to your room. I can take you...' She paused; her phone had started to ring. She caught her breath. 'Oh, no – I said I'd call Jamie this evening and I forgot. Lil, get yourself to bed. I'll take this outside, in the corridor – I'll be back in a minute...'

She stepped into the hallway, leaving the door ajar behind her, and murmured, 'Hello – I'm so sorry, Jamie...'

'Cassie,' his anxious voice came back. 'I waited but I didn't hear from you.'

'Yes, sorry, I—' Cassie's mind raced, deciding she wouldn't tell him yet that she'd met Piet Cornelissen and had dinner with him. Cassie had been too busy enjoying herself and she felt awful that she'd forgotten to phone him. 'I was about to call you.'

He sounded tired. 'I was just going to bed.'

Cassie's voice was confidential. 'Jamie, you wouldn't believe what happened tonight – I came into our room and Lil and the others were in a ridiculous state. They'd been in a coffee shop and bought a dope cake and got themselves completely stoned.'

Jamie drew an audible breath. 'Cassie, that's unbelievable – your mother's in her eighties.'

'I think they only had a little. But they were all sitting on the floor, eating pizza, drinking beer and playing strip poker.'

She expected Jamie to laugh, but he hadn't caught the infectious mischief in her tone. Instead, his voice was quiet. 'So, have you been out somewhere nice?'

'Yes.' Cassie's voice was full of enthusiasm. 'I went to a club. I sang and performed a new poem.'

'Did it go down well?'

'Oh, yes.' Cassie recalled the audience's applause. 'I met some locals – a local – a guy called Piet. He's a singer, a musician, really good.'

'Oh.' Jamie was quiet on the other end of the phone, then he said, 'Good for you. I'm so glad you're enjoying yourself.' She heard him inhale steadily. 'I hope Lil will be all right. She'd better stay off the wacky-baccy for the rest of the holiday, though.'

'Definitely,' Cassie agreed.

Jamie waited a second too long. 'Right. Well, I'm off to bed now.

I'm glad your performance went down well. We can talk tomorrow. You must be tired.'

'Yes, I am, a bit,' Cassie admitted. 'I wish you'd been there.'

'I'd have enjoyed that. We'll catch up tomorrow. Sleep well, Cass. Goodnight.'

'Yes, you too...' she began, but he had ended the call.

Cassie stood on the landing, the phone still raised in her hand, wondering if Jamie had felt troubled by her words. She shook the thoughts away; she was imagining it. She'd call him tomorrow and ask him how his day had gone. She knew she could cheer him up; he was probably not enjoying his time alone. She stood still for a moment, thinking. Jamie was a priority; she desperately didn't want to hurt his feelings. She missed his warmth, his steadiness and his support, his friendly voice – for a second, she thought about ringing him back. But now wasn't the time to talk to him: it was time to go to bed.

Cassie moved quietly back to her room, cracking the door open a little to see how the land lay. She expected Lil, Maggie and Albert to be still playing cards. She thought with a grin that she wouldn't be surprised to see Albert stark naked and Maggie ready to strip off while Lil waved her hand of cards triumphantly and encouraged them to hurry up. Instead, there was silence in the room. Cassie stepped inside. The floor was still covered with debris, pieces of pizza, empty cartons, greasy packaging. The smell of fried food and beer was in her nostrils as she gazed around. Maggie had fallen onto Cassie's bed, still wearing sunglasses, clothed in blouse and tights, and was asleep, her mouth open. Lil and Albert had tumbled onto Lil's bed, Albert in his tomato-spattered underwear, and they were both slumbering like babies, their arms round each other and a smile on their lips. Cassie covered them both gently with a blanket from Maggie's bed, lifted the faux-fur coat from a chair and placed it over Maggie's chest, and wondered what to do.

She would clean her teeth and her face, pull on her pyjamas and slide into the third bed, Maggie's, under the single sheet, and hope that she'd fall asleep quickly. There would probably be a spare blanket or two in the wardrobe, at the top. She was tired – it wouldn't be hard to doze off, and she could resolve the fallout from her mother's drug-fuelled binge with her gambling friends in the morning. Cassie glanced fondly at her sleeping mother, who was curled up on the bed, her expression angelic, Albert's nose nuzzled into her neck.

Then the thought of life in Amsterdam came to her, the excitement of performing at the Zwart Gat. She imagined herself living in her own flat in Amsterdam, such a vibrant city; she'd make new, exciting friends. She imagined getting to know Piet Cornelissen. He was certainly interesting. She glanced around the room as Lil snuffled softly in her sleep. Cassie exhaled deeply. It *would* be an interesting place to live.

The next morning at breakfast, the attention was on Albert, who hadn't returned to his room all night. By breakfast time, everyone knew that Cassie had texted Duncan before midnight to tell him that his father had fallen asleep and was going to spend the night with Lil and Maggie. The banter was flying fast across the table before he arrived, innuendo about Albert's *ménage à trois* and him still being a player at eighty-one years of age, that there was life in the old dog yet. Tommy was telling everyone it was because the three of them had crossed the Minnewater bridge in Bruges together, over the river of love.

Ken politely asked everyone to refrain from making jokes as Albert and his lady friends would soon be down from their room. This caused even more hilarity from everyone except Pat, who told everyone that it wasn't right to mock those who had genuine feelings for others. Then Lil, Maggie and Albert arrived for breakfast, baffled and tired, and a huge whoop echoed around the breakfast room, Tommy waving his fists in the air and DJ and Jake cheering and singing 'Pass the Dutchie', a song that confused Lil, Albert and Maggie, although everyone else smiled, seeming to know that the word 'Dutchie' was a euphemism for marijuana.

Lil sat down, rubbed a hand over her brow and muttered, 'I'm exhausted. Just pass me a cup of coffee,' and the laughter erupted again. Lil reached for the jug and filled her cup. 'Well, yesterday was interesting. I slept like a log though.' She nudged Albert. 'I was a bit surprised when I woke up this morning and found Albert next to me.'

Albert grinned, his face shining with delight, and patted her hand. Maggie reached for a plate of ham and bread. 'I'm still starving. We must have been playing strip poker until all hours.'

'Strip poker?' Sue boomed, her eyes wide, whisking a flowing scarf over her shoulder. 'And did I hear right, my dear? You were eating cannabis cakes?'

'You should have been there, Sue,' Lil admitted. 'It was quite a party.'

'It was,' Cassie agreed. 'It took me an hour to clean up the mess this morning.' She gazed fondly at Lil. 'You certainly had a good time.'

Maggie's eyes shone. 'I can't remember when I last laughed so much.'

Denise managed a smile. 'I think I'll join you next time.'

'Oh, there won't be a next time,' Cassie promised.

Tommy raised his coffee cup. 'On that note, I've arranged a canal trip for us all this morning. Then this afternoon, we can do as we wish.'

'I'm going shopping for souvenirs.' Maggie tapped the table with her fist. 'I need to get something nice for Brian.'

'I have a postcard to send to Herman...' Lil mused.

Pat nodded. 'I'm getting Thilde something special.'

'And I have to buy something for the wife.' Duncan sighed.

'I'm tempted to try out Lil's coffee shop – what do you think, *Syoo*?' Denise suggested defiantly, noticing Ken glance her way.

'We could all go for a coffee,' Ken said cheerily. 'I want to visit a local bookshop too.'

'Pornography?' Jake whispered too loudly.

Ken looked insulted. 'Contemporary literature, nothing more,' he insisted, and DJ guffawed.

Sue patted Ken's hand. 'I'll come to the bookshop with you, Ken, but I have to be back for half past two – I've booked myself an appointment for a manicure and a pedicure at a beauty parlour. And a facial. A bit of luxury will be so nice– two hours of bliss.'

'You're so lucky.' Denise glanced at Ken. 'My poor nails have been bitten down to the quick just lately. And I haven't been sleeping at all well.'

'You need one of those brownies,' Maggie suggested.

Tommy took charge. 'So, what about dinner tonight? Who wants to go where?'

'I want to eat at the Zingende Appel,' Emily replied. 'It's a wholefood place near the red-light district.'

'Me too,' Pat agreed. 'Thilde told me about it, she's been there several times – it's really trendy.'

'We'll go.' DJ nudged Jake. 'It's not far from a club I know about and we're going clubbing afterwards.'

'We'll go to the Apple place too, shall we?' Lil asked Maggie and Albert. 'I like hanging out in trendy places in Amsterdam.'

Ken nodded. 'Maybe we should all go together? Wholefood might be just what we all need.'

'That would be nice, Ken,' Denise returned his smile.

Tommy clapped his hands together. 'Shall I book for all thirteen of us tonight at seven?'

'Twelve of us.' Cassie put her phone away. 'I'm spending the morning with Lil and then I have a date in the evening – I'll be eating somewhere else.'

A roaring sound not dissimilar to a labouring cow came from DJ and Jake, intended to imply that Cassie was involved in an illicit romantic liaison. She rolled her eyes.

'I don't think I would like to date anyone on holiday.' Denise made a disapproving face. 'After all, what would be the point?' She waved a paperback book in the air. 'That reminds me, Lil – thanks for the loan of this novel about the stables. I loved it. It certainly made me think about life and romance. Can I borrow the next one?' She glanced at Cassie momentarily, who had raised her eyebrows. 'No, I'm not the one-night-stand type.'

'You can have *Frolics in the House*, Denise – I've just finished it,' Maggie offered. 'It's even better than *Fifty Shades of Hay*, especially the ending when Devlin O'Toole gets his punishment from the whole front bench.'

Ken shook his head. Denise was gazing at him on one side and, on the other, Sue was smiling, her eyes shining. He coughed. 'So, Tommy, when do we go on the canal trip?'

'We'll finish breakfast and then we'll be off sharpish. We'll spend a couple of hours on board. Then we can all go shopping.'

'I can't wait.' Lil reached for more toast. 'I'm enjoying it here. I think I could get used to Amsterdam. It's my new favourite city in the world. I could live here.'

Cassie sighed and her eyes drifted towards her mother. 'Me too,' she muttered, sipping coffee thoughtfully.

22

A well-modulated male Dutch voice announced that the boat was just about to travel beneath the Skinny Bridge, one of the most famous bridges on the Amstel. 'The Magere Brug or Skinny Bridge connects the banks of the river at Kerkstraat, between the Keizersgracht and Prinsengracht. The central section of the Magere Brug is a bascule bridge made of white-painted wood. The present bridge was built in 1934.'

The passengers leaned out of the windows of the long white boat, cameras and phones clicking, framing stretches of the grey river, the curve of the bridge, the tall narrow houses in the background below deep blue sky. Pat tapped Lil's hand.

'We text each other all day, dozens of times. Thilde is feeding the cows at the moment.' He exhaled. 'I wish she could have come with us to Amsterdam.'

Lil smiled, meeting his sad eyes. 'She's a lovely girl.' She raised an eyebrow. 'So, do you think she's the one, Pat?'

'She is.' Pat was dreamy. 'I've liked other girls, dated a few times but no one has ever been like Thilde. We just – connect.'

'I can see that.' Lil glanced out of the window as they sailed beneath the bridge, darkness filling the boat and then brightness. She gazed into the steel-coloured water. Another barge glided by.

Pat took a breath. 'Thilde says Herman asked after you.'

'Yes.' Lil stared towards the banks, where cycles were lined up against dark railings and a tree dipped its branches into the murky river. 'He's a nice man.'

'He asks about you every day.'

'I'm going to send him a postcard.'

'Lil?' Pat's cheeks were pink. 'I'm going to go back to see Thilde in a few weeks. I'm going to ask my dad for some time off work. He's a chippy, a carpenter; we work together, Stott and Son.'

'Do you think he'll mind?' Lil's brow wrinkled. 'I mean, you've just had one holiday and you'll be asking for another...'

'I know. He can be a bit grouchy. Business was a bit bumpy a year ago, but we're back on track now. I just thought, if I went to Belgium for a few weeks to see Thilde – that you'd like to come along? To see Herman.'

'Thanks.' Lil was thoughtful. She recalled the warm smile, the bushy brows, the light touch of his arm. 'I might just do that, Pat.'

Pat nodded. 'I'll tell Thilde – just that I asked and that... you might.'

'Mmm.' Lil turned her attention back towards the river, the guide's voice in her ears explaining that they were approaching another bridge. Her eyes found Cassie, chatting to Emily; Ken was flanked by Denise and Sue, both gazing up at him; Duncan was talking to Albert and Maggie but neither of them were listening, both staring into the river. Lil's own thoughts filled her mind; it might be nice to go back to Boom, to the Goossens' farm, to get to know Herman better. She gazed at Cassie again and wondered about the man she was meeting later. Lil remembered that he was called Piet and that he was a musician, but she knew little else. She felt the old familiar anxiety creep along her spine and into the back

of her neck and she forced a grin. She would never stop being
Cassie's mother, whatever their ages.

* * *

They stood on the roadside, by the riverbank, as the cruise boat
glided away; everyone was making decisions. Duncan, Tommy and
Albert were going to find a bar and have a swift drink. Ken wanted
to buy books and Sue insisted he take her with him. Denise was
going back to the hotel to read. The youngsters were going shopping for souvenirs by themselves so Cassie shepherded Maggie and
Lil towards a parade of brightly coloured shops. 'Right – let's get a
list in our heads, shall we? So we don't miss anyone out?'

'I'm going to buy something special for Brian.' Maggie smiled.

'What about some boxers or a posing pouch? It might ignite his
passion,' Lil joked.

Cassie exhaled. 'There are lots of souvenir shops here. I'm going
to buy Jamie a sweatshirt and I have to buy myself a mug. I've some
friends I want to get a few small gifts for, Cathy and Mark and—'

'I want to get some stuff for me, so that I can remember my holiday,' Lil said decisively. 'And maybe something for Herman and I
might get Keith something...' She was thoughtful for a moment.
'I'm going to buy a present for Jenny Price too.' She nodded, her
face serious. 'Yes, I'll get her a little something. I bet she misses the
random acts of kindness.'

Maggie's eyes were swivelling from shop to shop. 'Right – shall
we all meet back here in half an hour? Then maybe we can all have
a cup of coffee?'

'Good idea,' Lil agreed. 'I can shop better by myself.'

'All right.' Cassie's brow clouded, a moment's anxiety. 'I'll be
standing right here in exactly thirty minutes. Don't go too far –

make sure you don't get lost. And I'll pick the coffee shop today and buy the coffee. There will be *absolutely no more brownies*.'

Maggie was already wandering away. Lil gave Cassie a peck on the cheek and was gone too. Cassie stood by herself, making a mental list of gifts she wanted to buy. She thought about Jamie, and wondered if he was still missing her. He had texted her earlier that he was going to the theatre this evening with Mark and Cathy, so she needn't ring until tomorrow. That was convenient, Cassie thought, as she'd be having dinner with Piet tonight. It would be better if she didn't let Jamie down again by ringing him too late or forgetting about him altogether, as she had yesterday. He was a proud man, confident on the outside but sensitive and easily hurt; it was clear that he was very fond of her. Cassie was very fond of him too.

She decided she'd buy him the bottle of wine he'd requested to share, and some presents that might show him that he was impor- tant. When they were back, she'd get in touch with some of her contacts and arrange to perform at several venues across the UK and ask Jamie to go with her. He deserved a break and she'd spoil him, take him out to dinner, make a fuss of him. She was looking forward to seeing him again.

Cassie turned and walked past several shops, the frontages packed with a gaudy range of gifts. She paused to gaze at beer mugs, T-shirts, clogs, windmill models, windmill clocks, windmill plaques. She wondered what cheap souvenirs Maggie and Lil were currently buying. She lifted a T-shirt in bright orange, emblazoned with the word Amsterdam, then pushed it back on the rail with so many more. She turned to walk away and stopped suddenly. A couple was strolling past, holding hands: a tall, elegant man and a short, slim woman with dark hair. She recognised the woman's tinkling laugh as she clung to the man, reached up on her toes and kissed his lips before they sauntered away. Cassie put a hand to her mouth to hide a smile: it was Ken and Sue.

Cassie, Lil and Maggie returned to the Roodhuis Hotel with their shopping. Lil and Maggie decided that they were going to have a snooze; yesterday's antics and the late night had left them feeling tired. Cassie was going to shower and change; she was meeting Piet at five o'clock. Once inside their room, Maggie pulled off her shoes and fell back onto the bed.

'I'm all shopped out – presents for Darren, Ross and Paul and Gemma and their partners and their kids, and something for Brian.'

Lil nodded. 'I just bought a variety of souvenirs and a few things for myself. Cassie, when you go out to spend time with this man you've only just met, can you post my card to Herman? I'm going to write it now.'

Cassie thought she heard a note of irritation in her mother's voice, but she decided to ignore it. 'Of course, Lil.'

There was a pause, then Lil said, 'Where are you eating out tonight with Piet or Paul or whatever he's called? You could have invited him to the Zingende Appel and I could have met him, checked that he was suitable for my girl.'

Cassie pressed her lips together to prevent a smile. 'Piet's cooking dinner – I'm going to his place.'

'Oh, isn't that a bit risky, Cassie?' Maggie opened her eyes wide. 'He might be dangerous.'

Cassie was incredulous, but Lil shook her head. 'Maggie has a point, love.'

'It'll be fine...'

'Well, you hardly know this man – he could be anybody.' Lil paused from writing her postcard, pen in the air.

'More to the point, will you be safe?' Maggie fretted. "He might be a sex maniac, like the politician in Lil's book...'

'I should be so lucky,' Cassie joked and immediately regretted it, noticing Lil's anxious expression. She sighed. 'He's just a nice man who likes the same sort of music that I do. He's fine.'

Lil frowned, staring at the postcard on which she had written 'Dear Herman'. 'Cassie, do you remember going to that rock concert when you were about seventeen, to see a band with a boy with a ridiculous name?'

'The Obliterated with Biff Baker from my Philosophy class at school. I thought he was lovely until he kissed me. He was the sloppiest kisser I ever met – he dribbled all over me. It put me right off,' Cassie remembered, smiling.

'You didn't get home until two in the morning.'

'We were sitting in his car for an hour discussing Aquinas' five arguments about the existence of God.'

'I sat up for half the night waiting for you to come in – I was worried to death about you. Then you came home with a love bite on your neck.'

Cassie wrinkled her nose. 'Oh, I got that during the band's encore.'

Lil scratched her soft white hair. 'What ever happened to him, Biff Baker?'

'He married a vicar's daughter and became a social worker.' Cassie went over to Lil and hugged her. 'And I turned out all right, didn't I?'

Lil squeezed her daughter affectionately, her eyes shining. 'The best daughter anyone could have had.'

'No grandchildren, though,' Maggie grunted.

Lil's eyes flashed. 'I have my Cassie. I don't need anyone else.'
She was suddenly anxious. 'So, what about this Pete Corny Son?'

'Piet Cornelissen, Lil, and it's just dinner.'

'He might seduce you in his den...' Maggie's eyes were round.

Cassie shook her head: Maggie had been reading too many of
Lil's books. 'No, I've got to be home by midnight, or I'll turn into a
pumpkin. Isn't that right? That's what you used to say to me when I
was a teenager...'

'You do what you want – you're all grown up now,' Lil
murmured, then she gazed up from the postcard and beamed. 'You
just have a lovely time, Cass. We're on holiday. That's what we're
here for, to enjoy ourselves.'

'Why would she turn into a pumpkin?' Maggie asked. 'Do you
mean like Cinderella's coach?'

'Like me,' Lil muttered. 'I stayed out late once with a handsome
soldier and that turned me into a pumpkin. I just grew and grew.'
She winked at Cassie. 'But at least I got you...'

* * *

It was fifteen minutes to five as Cassie stepped onto the landing,
calling goodbye to Lil and Maggie and closing the door crisply. Her
hair was freshly washed and wrapped in a pink scarf; she was
wearing a long floral dress and smelled of jasmine. She was ready
for her date. She paused as the sudden noise of a door opening
further down the corridor caught her attention, and she watched as
a man emerged from the room occupied by Sue, Denise and Emily.
A muscular woman with auburn hair, wearing a long T-shirt that
came to her thighs, rushed out and embraced him passionately.
Cassie held her breath, watching the couple kiss. Denise hugged
Ken for the final time before he checked the timepiece on his wrist
hurriedly and rushed upstairs to his garret room.

Cassie descended the narrow flight of steps to the front entrance. As she stood in the doorway, she encountered Sue on her way in, who seemed excessively delighted to see her.

'Cassie, I've just had the most wonderful time at the beauty salon. Do you like my nails? The colour's called Peach Passion.'

Cassie glanced at her outstretched hands with immaculate nails. 'Lovely.'

'Are you going somewhere? Did I hear that you have a date? Is it a local man, from Amsterdam?'

'Piet. He's a musician. I'm having dinner with him.'

Sue caught her breath. 'You don't waste any time, do you, my dear?'

'Pardon?' Cassie frowned.

'Oh, you know.' Sue waved her flawless hands. 'Amsterdam. It's a perfect place for an *amour*. I mean, I know that's a French word, but when you're away from home, a little fling might be just what the doctor ordered, don't you think?'

Cassie pressed her lips together. She thought of Ken creeping guiltily from the room next door but decided it was better to say nothing.

'You look nice, Cassie – you smell nice too.' Sue waved her newly painted fingers. 'A girl has to look her best, especially when she wants to impress a man. And, you know, you might not be the only one around here who has a beau on her arm. I'll see you tomorrow – and you must tell me all about the date with Piet.'

Sue tripped away; Cassie could hear her feet tapping on the wooden staircase as she ran back to her room. She crossed the road, negotiating a passing car, and suddenly felt sorry for Sue and Denise. Someone's feelings would certainly be hurt.

Cassie recalled Sue's deliriously optimistic voice a few minutes ago and Denise's enthusiasm as she had clutched Ken in a final embrace outside her room. There was clearly something serious going on between Denise and Ken *and* between Ken and Sue. It would end badly. Someone was almost definitely going to suffer, Cassie decided sombrely. She recalled her own past, the two long-term relationships she'd had: how both Mo in Dakar and Jon in Guangzhou had loved her for a while and she had loved them back, then she had become restless. They had found her too independent, too headstrong and unwilling to commit. So she had moved on.

Cassie strolled along the busy street, her handbag over her shoulder, lost in thought. She wondered if Piet would be her type, creative like herself, a partnership of two similar people drawn together by their love of music. She pictured them writing songs, singing in harmony, and for a moment she imagined herself living in Amsterdam, performing at the Zwart Gat. Then she crossed the road and Jamie's smile popped into the space in her thoughts, and she found herself smiling back.

23

Lil was still talking about the wonderful food as she left the restaurant with Maggie. They couldn't agree: Lil said the buddha bowl she'd eaten with rice and beans and hummus had been delicious, Maggie replied that the sweet potato and quinoa burger had stuck between her teeth and the portions were too small. Lil suggested that they walk back to the hotel together and stop off in a supermarket so that Maggie could buy some crisps, and she cheered up. DJ, Jake, Emily and Pat had gone to a club. Both Pat and Emily had been on the phone through most of the meal, Pat chatting delightedly to Thilde and Emily frowning anxiously as she struggled to get a connection on her phone to Alex, her boyfriend.

Lil had noticed that both Sue and Denise had dressed impeccably, both smelling of strong fragrances as they sat across the table from her on either side of Ken, who wore a smart blazer, a turquoise cravat and a crisp shirt. Sue and Denise were both trying to persuade Ken to sample some of their delicious food, holding forks to his mouth, competing to tempt him with tasty morsels.

Tommy and Duncan had gone to a bar with Albert; the wholefood restaurant did not serve alcohol and Duncan had asked aloud what was the point of eating well if you couldn't wet your whistle at the same time?

Ken, Sue and Denise had taken a stroll down the river, hoping to go on a short night cruise on the Amstel. Lil had asked to go with them – she was fascinated by the way both women were competing for Ken's attention and wanted to find out who was winning – but Maggie had said that she was tired and she wanted to look at some of the gifts she'd bought, especially Brian's, so Lil reluctantly accompanied her back to the hotel. She wished Cassie were there. There was so much she wanted to share: the mystery about Ken having two admirers, the anxiety about Emily as she gave up trying to contact her boyfriend, the romantic message she'd sent on a postcard to Herman earlier, but most of all she wanted to know how Cassie was getting along with her new man friend. Lil felt irrationally anxious. There was no reason why she should feel uncomfortable – she had never met Piet but she trusted her daughter's wisdom perfectly – but she had worries, spiders wriggling beneath her skin.

Maggie's voice was pulling her from her thoughts. '...and a T-shirt each for the girls and a couple of mugs with "I heart Amsterdam" on and a lovely windmill clock, a clog windchime and some chocolate...'

'That's nice.' Lil grinned.

Maggie tucked an arm through hers, still chattering. 'And I bought something really nice for Brian. I mean, it's a bit naughty but this is the first time in all our married life we've been apart, except when I was in hospital having the kids, so I thought I'd get him something special... and it wasn't cheap...'

They had turned a corner into a street with bright lights; loud music boomed from brightly lit shops and bars. Many windows were illuminated by soft, red glowing lamps. Lil saw a figure move in one of the windows. A woman stood up, wriggled and turned, then sat down again. Lil caught her breath. 'Maggie, we're in the middle of the red-light area.'

Maggie stopped and stared at her friend. 'Oh, no – should we go back?'

'Why ever would we do that?'

'Someone might proposition us.' Maggie was aghast with fear.

Lil laughed. 'I'm eighty-two and you're only a few years younger, Maggie. We'd have more chance of being propositioned if we paid the clients.'

Maggie was still horrified. 'But what about Fifi Bagatelle, the madam in the bordello in *Frolics in the House*?'

'What about her?'

'She had sex with lots of the men... and she was seventy...'

'No, she didn't – she ran a brothel. She just took the money.'

'So – all these ladies in the windows. Who takes their money?' Maggie gaped.

'I've no idea.' Lil stopped to admire a statuesque woman in a bikini, long dark hair over her shoulders. 'These ladies are very beautiful.'

'But look at this place, Lil – it's so busy, and listen to all that loud music.' Maggie hugged Lil's arm. 'I think we should go back to the hotel as quickly as we can.'

'Let's not go just yet.' Lil's eyes were bright with curiosity. 'I've never been to a red-light district before. This could be really interesting.'

* * *

Cassie followed Piet onto his houseboat, moored at the side of the river. The outside was plain wood, with several hanging plants on the narrow deck. Downstairs, Cassie felt as if she were cocooned: the living room immediately felt cosy and warm, the walls were red, covered with bright paintings and mirrors with oak frames, and the floors were carpeted with richly coloured rugs. In the main cabin, a table was set for dinner, a low golden lantern hanging from the ceiling, and a stove with a small fire glowed in the corner.

'This isn't what I expected. It's very cosy and bright.' Cassie was impressed as Piet led her into a galley, the walls covered with mosaic tiles. Terracotta pots on shelves held a variety of culinary herbs: rosemary, parsley, coriander, thyme. A pan simmered on a small cooker and a bowl of salad, the tomatoes and leaves glossy with dressing, had been placed on the worktop next to a chilled bottle of white wine and two glasses.

Piet raised an eyebrow. 'Can I show you round? After I have poured us a glass of Pinot Grigio?'

Cassie nodded, accepting the glass he offered her, and followed him through the living area up a small flight of stairs to a galleried room. The walls were painted white and guitars stood next to amplifiers. Shelves were lined with books and Cassie was immediately struck by how organised everything seemed. She smiled. 'So – this is home? It seems very comfortable.'

'I have lived here for seven years now.' Piet waved an arm around, indicating his guitars. 'I have all I need and I am happy. Shall we go back downstairs?'

Cassie sat at the table while Piet served the food, a steaming bowl of risotto and a colourful salad.

'A simple risotto – mushrooms, peas, garlic, cream. I hope you will like it.' He topped up her glass and sat down opposite.

Cassie gazed around the living room: more books, more guitars, all tidily arranged. A window looked out onto the Amstel. She made a mental note to gaze through it later as the lights of the city reflected against the water, streaks of colour writhing with the lilt of the boat; she decided it would be lovely. Piet read her thoughts.

'After we have eaten, I hope we can take our drinks onto the deck and watch the city as it celebrates the night time.'

Cassie lifted a fork and began to eat. The food was creamy and delicious. 'This risotto is very good.' She noticed Piet watching her, his fork in mid-air. 'Thank you for inviting me.'

Piet smiled, a subtle movement of his lips. 'I have ulterior motives.'

Cassie raised an eyebrow, remembering the warnings Lil and Maggie had given her earlier. Piet wasn't exhibiting danger signs, certainly not yet, but she was alone on his houseboat, the river all around them. 'Oh?'

'I want us to write a song together after we have eaten dessert.' He chewed slowly. 'We can take instruments up onto the little deck, open a bottle of brandy and compose something wonderful.'

'I'd like that.' Cassie murmured.

'Then perhaps we can talk about you and your music, your poems.' Piet pushed his food away, half eaten. 'And what it might take to persuade you to stay here in Amsterdam, at least for a time. Or maybe you might want to come back in the future and we could play some music together.'

'Perhaps.' Cassie reached for her wine. 'Amsterdam is a very inviting city.'

Piet stood up, pushing his chair back, and moved around the table to stand behind Cassie, putting his hands lightly on her shoulders. 'And you are a fascinating and talented woman,' he muttered, his cheek against her hair. 'I think we could be a wonderful partnership. It is good to share your company. There is so much we might share together, Cassie. What do you think?'

Cassie closed her eyes and leaned back in her chair. It was very nice, the meal, the wine, the cosy houseboat, the prospect of composing interesting music with Piet on deck while gazing at the city lights dancing against the dark water of the river. But as for anything else beyond this moment where she sat at his table, feeling his breath against her neck, she had no idea at all what she wanted.

Lil dragged Maggie down the street, stopping to gaze at the beautiful women in the windows, bathed in red light. A particularly stunning woman, tall and slender with auburn hair, was surrounded by a purple light; in the window next to her, a small woman was sitting on a stool, dark hair piled on her head, wearing silky underwear, knitting. Around them, people walked past, many oblivious, pausing to go into shops and cafés, and Lil marvelled at how normal it all seemed, to be strolling past a parade of women dressed as if they were entering a beauty contest. But the women weren't smiling; they seemed calm and composed as they stared out into the busy street, almost uninterested.

Lil paused at a large window to gaze up at a striking woman with lacy underwear, olive skin and blonde hair, who had just eased herself from her seat and stretched her legs and arms, as if she'd been sitting in one position for too long. She saw Lil gazing at her and winked. Lil waved back, a slight movement of her fingers. The woman indicated to Lil by raising a languid hand that she should stay where she was. Then she picked up a coat from a hook on the door behind her, wrapped it around herself and moved smoothly on stilettos towards the exit.

A few moments later, the woman, wearing the coat over her underwear, was standing next to Lil, rummaging in her pockets. She spoke in perfect English. 'I saw you looking at me and I thought I'd come out for a chat and a cigarette.' She took out a packet from her pocket and immediately placed a cigarette between red lips.

'Don't catch your death; it's not as if you've got enough clothes on to keep you warm,' Lil warned her. 'Mind you, if you keep smoking those things, you'll kill yourself anyway, so I don't suppose it matters.'

The woman breathed out a steady stream of smoke and held a hand out to Lil. 'Anouk. That is my name.'

Lil studied her. She was exquisite, with flawless skin and almond eyes. She pushed her blonde hair back, one simple careless movement, as if she didn't know how elegant she was, as if she didn't care.

'Lil,' said Lil. 'And this is Maggie.'

'Hello, Anouk.' Maggie was staring in disbelief.

'Pleased to meet you.' Anouk took a desperate drag on her cigarette. 'Are you English?'

Maggie nodded and indicated the cigarette. 'Is that the wacky-baccy?'

'No.' Anouk frowned. 'This is instead of my dinner. I must get back to work soon. I can't eat – I put on weight so fast nowadays.'

Maggie nodded. 'I know the feeling. But you're slim. Do you eat many chips? There seem to be a lot of them here in Amsterdam.'

'I have a year-old baby.' Anouk shrugged. 'My body has changed so much since childbirth.'

'We do suffer, we women,' Lil agreed.

Anouk was halfway down her cigarette. 'So, you are tourists?'

Lil nodded. 'Yes, but we're not looking for a prostitute.' She was suddenly serious as she brought a hand to her mouth to cover her blunder. 'Oh dear – I probably shouldn't have called you a prostitute.'

'I have been called much worse.' Anouk shrugged and Lil wondered how she could be so calm.

'That's terrible,' Maggie breathed.

'So,' Lil asked. 'Why are you a prostitute, sex worker, lady of the night – whatever the right term is?'

Anouk raised an eyebrow. 'I would hate to work in an office from nine to five or serve beer in a bar or be a bank clerk. Besides.' She blew smoke through delicate nostrils. 'My mother cares for my daughter in the evenings so I can come to work most nights without paying for a childminder.'

'Is the money good?' Lil asked. 'Doing what you do?'

'I get a lot of clients, repeat clients.' Anouk dropped the finished cigarette and ground it into the concrete with the toe of her stiletto. 'It depends what service they've asked for, how much money I make, but it's pretty good. I can't complain. I make fifty euros for fifteen minutes of sex.'

Maggie almost choked. 'Fifty euros?'

'Anouk?' Lil's mouth was pursed, a question ready. 'Are you – is it safe? I mean, there's nobody treating you badly or stealing your money?'

'Oh, it is all legal and regulated here in Amsterdam.' Anouk tugged her coat around her shoulders against the gust of wind funnelling down the street. Her hair blew across her face. 'On a good night I make five, six hundred euros. I am happy enough.'

Lil noticed someone brush past her elbow, a short middle-aged man in a heavy coat. He had square shoulders and his hair was all bristles. He raised his hand in Anouk's direction and she spoke to Lil without acknowledging him.

'I have a client now so I must go. It was very nice to meet you, Lil and Maggie.' She reached out a hand and touched Lil's arm.

'Take care of yourself, Anouk,' Lil called, but the woman had disappeared through the doorway, the burly man following behind her. Lil sighed. 'She was very nice, wasn't she, Maggie?'

'Fifty euros for fifteen minutes?' Maggie marvelled. 'And I've done it for nothing all my married life. Mind you, Brian and I adored each other once. It was like floating on a cloud, just being in his arms.'

'And I've just avoided it all my life – sex, love, commitment.' Lil sighed. 'Do you know, Maggie, the older I get, the less I understand matters of the heart.'

'I know what you mean.' Maggie stared ahead as they walked. 'But I've been married for ages and I think I understand the meaning of love. It's not like in those books, all romping in the hay and fun and frolics. And it's not about a single night of expensive passion like Anouk and her client, not for me. It's about trust and respect and caring for each other. You know, someone who makes you a cup of tea because you need one and then puts a biscuit on your plate when you don't ask for one, like an extra bit of love.'

'Is Brian like that?'

'He used to be, Lil. He used to be so sweet; he'd kiss me every morning and say, "My beautiful Maggie, I'm so glad you're mine," and he'd whirl me in his arms. But not for the last couple of years. It just sort of stopped.'

'That's what makes me so cross.' Lil pressed her lips together. 'He has forgotten how to be a proper partner. He should treat you like a treasure, a beautiful woman, like he's lucky to have you. All women should be treated like that.'

'They should.' Maggie slowed down as she thought. 'Have you ever been treated like a film star?'

'Once.' Lil spoke softly. 'Twice, if you count Herman.'

'He was a nice man, Herman. Do you love him, Lil?'

Lil shook her head. 'I might have, given time.'

'I love Brian.'

'I hope he's missing you right now, this very minute. Then when you're back, he'll shower you with attention and love. That's what you deserve.' Lil tucked her arm in the crook of Maggie's elbow as they walked in step. 'But it's been fun, being on holiday. Life's full of interesting people, isn't it?' They increased their pace. 'Herman, Brian, Cassie's new friend Piet, Anouk. All living different lives. I suppose that's why travel expends the mind. Come on, Maggie. I'm exhausted. Let's get back to the hotel and have an early night.'

They walked in step together, turning around a corner into a stiff breeze. 'We could get some crisps,' Maggie muttered, gazing longingly towards a mini supermarket.

Lil inhaled loudly. 'I can smell frying chips on the air. That's got to be more of a celebration of life than a packet of cheese and onion crisps. We're on holiday. Besides, it's only twenty minutes back to our hotel and if we're tired, we'll hail a taxi. I'll buy you a bag of *frites* on the way.' For a moment she was thoughtful. 'They will probably be the last chips we'll ever have in Amsterdam. We're off again tomorrow, back to Belgium. And who knows if we'll ever come back here again?' Lil sighed as they approached a brightly lit shop with a neon sign that advertised The Best Chips in Amsterdam.

'The best chips.' Maggie smiled. 'We deserve the best, don't we, Lil?'

'We do.' Lil tugged Maggie towards the strong smell of frying food. 'You've got to make the best of it all while you can, Maggie. Eat chips now, that's my motto. Who knows what life will serve us up on our plates next?'

24

Cassie pushed her dish away. 'That was a delicious sorbet, Piet. I couldn't eat another mouthful.'

He refilled her wine glass. 'Shall we have a chat about lyrics for a while and then go up on deck and put some tunes together?'

'Great idea.' She moved over to the small sofa, sinking into soft cushions. 'What shall we write a song about?'

'You? Me?' He was sitting next to her, his elbow against hers, a notepad in his hands. 'Don't all songs come from ourselves?'

'I suppose so.' Cassie was thoughtful. 'I've been trying to write one about pollution but the subject is too big. Anything I try to say sounds trite.'

Piet scratched his head. 'When that happens to me, and it does a lot, I always start from someplace else.' He raised an eyebrow. 'How about I make coffee and bring the brandy glasses while you tell me more about yourself? Maybe that way, we can find a way into what we'll write.'

He touched her arm affectionately, then moved across to the kitchen area, rattling a coffee pot, putting beans in a grinder machine. Over the noise, he said, 'You're close to your mother?'

'Lil? Yes, we've always been close.'

'She's Lil, not Mum? Why is that?'

'She had me when she was a teenager and I've never called her anything else.' Cassie gazed at Piet, at the muscular movements of his back as he busied himself in the kitchen. 'I never met my father. He was called Frankie Chapman.'

'But you're Cassie Ryan, after your mother?'

'Frankie was an American soldier. He was called away before my mother even realised she was pregnant. He never knew about me.'

Piet glanced over his shoulder. 'Was that difficult for you as a child, having no dad?'

'No.' Cassie wrinkled her nose. 'I never had any male figures in my life as a child.' She sighed. 'Sometimes you never miss what you've never had.' She watched him pour coffee. 'You had a more normal family though, Piet – a mother, a father?'

'Yes, I had two parents, but our family was not normal. My parents argued a lot: my father was very kind, keen on music, and my mother was very strict and believed in formal education. They had different hopes for me. In the end, they both got their way.'

'How do you mean?'

'I am a musician, as my father wanted, with a formal training, like my mother insisted upon. I am glad for it though.' He sat next to her, offering coffee in delicate cups. Cassie took one and sipped slowly.

'So...' Piet put down his cup and picked up his notepad. 'Where shall we start?'

Cassie glanced through the little window, noticing the movement of the water, a dark swirl tinged with the silver glimmer of the moon. 'Let's start with the river.'

'Okay. What about the river?' Piet met her eyes. 'What shall we write down?'

Cassie leaned forward. 'You live on the river. It holds you, it rocks you when you sleep. It takes care of you, as if it's nurturing you. Don't you have a special relationship with it?'

'Oh, yes.' Piet was thoughtful. 'I often go out on deck at night when it's quiet and stare into the dark depths of the Amstel. If I have a problem, the river is consoling – like a silent friend – because it is a constant thing, always there, always a form of security. I've even spoken to the river at moments when I've felt alone.' He raised his eyebrows. 'Do you do that, Cassie? Speak to something around you when you feel lonely or when you are in need of a friend?'

Cassie shook her head. 'Oh, no, I have Jamie for that.'

'Jamie? He is your brother?'

'Not at all. He's my...' Cassie searched for the right word. 'He shares my house.'

'You are very close?'

'Very.' Cassie closed her eyes. 'He's my best friend, if you don't count Lil. He knows me so well and he's always there for me. We've lived together for two years and he's put up with my creative tantrums when I'm writing, my diva behaviour when I'm performing; he's organised, he's patient. He's a calming influence...'

'Are you lovers, you and Jamie?'

'No, not at all,' Cassie protested, as if the idea was ludicrous. 'He's a great bloke though. You'd like him.'

'I'm sure.' Piet nodded, his eyes not straying from her face. 'So, let's think about our song now. We can write about something or someone we can confide in, we feel close to, like Jamie, like the river, always there, a perpetual friend, loyal...'

'Great idea, Piet, let's stick with the idea of something inanimate that we can share our thoughts with...'

He took a breath. 'I tell the river my hopes and fears. It hears my happy moments and it is there when I am sad. I have even shed tears into the river.'

'Let's start with that, shall we? Tears in the river?'

'That's good, Cassie. *Tears in the river, each time that I cried.*'

'*You know all my troubles...*'

'*You heard when I sighed...?*'

Cassie was suddenly excited. '*You know all my secrets; you keep them all deep. You whisper them softly to rock me to sleep.*'

'It might work. We might be able to do something, using a minor chord, something really sorrowful and emotional...'

'We could develop the story, Piet – the river keeps the man's secrets and what does he do in return? Betrays it, pollutes it. Like lovers, the river is the constant one and the man is fickle, the one who doesn't care...'

'That's it!' Piet leaped up and grabbed Cassie's hand. 'Come up on deck and we'll take the instruments and the brandy. We've got this.'

She met his gaze, her own eyes shining. 'We certainly have.'

* * *

It was past two in the morning. Cassie and Piet were sitting on deck, him strumming a soft melody, their voices in harmony, powerful and plaintive. Piet turned to Cassie.

'We should record these songs now.'

Cassie closed her eyes. 'I'm glad I texted Tommy. There's no way I'd have got back to the hotel tonight. Lil would have worried.'

'It's great working with you, Cassie.' Piet grinned. 'We have one song finished and we've almost completed the second. I think the folky one about the old man in Amsterdam who sits on the bank staring at the moon asking for forgiveness will be my favourite.'

'I only like love songs if they are sad,' Cassie mused.

'You have been disappointed in love?'

'Not really.' Cassie shrugged. 'I have dabbled, but never really had my fingers burned. I walked away before I let it happen.'

'You have not taken many chances, then.' Piet's smile was mischievous. 'I have been burned many times. I think I am going to be burned again.'

'How is that?' Cassie asked. 'Are you in love with someone now?'

'I could be, very easily.' Piet's eyes shone. 'But I suspect she loves someone else.'

'You need to talk to her, tell her how you feel.'

Piet shook his head. 'Yes, but tomorrow, she will leave me; she will leave Amsterdam. She will go back to the man I think she secretly loves, back to Jamie.'

Cassie caught her breath; she suddenly realised that Piet was talking about her. She shook her head. 'I'm flattered, Piet...'

'I was going to ask you to stay on for a while in Amsterdam, as my guest on this houseboat. Tonight, I had planned to write songs with you, to convince you how good we are together...'

'You *have* convinced me.'

'As songwriters, yes, certainly. But...' Piet took her hand. 'Of course, I wanted more. I thought you and I...'

'I can come back to Amsterdam. We can write more songs; we can play more music together...'

'Yes, we will, and I am so pleased to have met you. But I think we will only ever be friends.'

'No one knows what the future holds.'

'I do. I saw your face when you were talking about your Jamie.'

Cassie waved a hand. 'No, you're wrong, Piet. Jamie and I have known each other for ages.'

'Then you do not know yourself. You think yourself a free spirit, but I saw it, how you feel about this man.'

Cassie shrugged. Piet's words had found a mark and suddenly

she dared to wonder if he was right. Jamie was loyal; she had taken him for granted. But she had never thought before that her feelings might develop beyond friendship. Now she was not so sure and the idea left her stunned and blinking.

'I think you are in love with him, Cassie.' Piet picked up his guitar. 'But I will live. I will explain it all to the river, how I met a special woman, how I started to fall in love with her, how I was convinced after so many disappointments in love that I had finally found someone...'

'We should never give up, Piet – there's always hope.' Cassie's voice was soft; she was still baffled by her own feelings. 'The river knows that. It's always there for us, holding us safely in its arms.'

She gazed out into the water slapping against the houseboat. In the distance Amsterdam glowed, a mixture of reds and yellows, the lights reflecting soft light on the river. She thought about Jamie again, how he was a part of her life, one she couldn't be without. She wondered if that was love, if it was the sort of honest, safe, reliable love she needed.

Piet played some soft notes on the guitar, his fingers deft; it was a poignant melody. He began to sing softly.

> An old man of Amsterdam stared up at the moon
> Asking why does love always leave me so soon?
> He sat there alone, his head in his hands
> Wondering why only the moon understands.

Cassie joined in, her voice swelling with emotion, louder than Piet's deep tone.

> The moon looked on silently, so far away
> As the old man of Amsterdam decided to pray

As he asked for forgiveness, he started to cry
Why am I so low while you are so high?'

'That was really great, Cassie – the best song I have written in a long time.'

Cassie met Piet's glistening eyes as he played the last few notes on the guitar, and her own suddenly began to fill. Without thinking, she threw her arms round him and hugged him. Her voice was soft in his ear. 'I'm so glad I met you. And we will meet again. After all, I came to Amsterdam and I met someone who could become a good friend. Isn't that much, much more important than a one-night stand or a brief fling?'

She felt his arms around her and his shoulders began to shake. She wondered if he was sobbing but, when he raised his head, he was smiling, his face bright with happiness.

'Yes, we are friends – good friends who are beginning to under-stand each other. Perhaps if you come to Amsterdam to visit me again, you can stay for longer and I will organise some opportuni-ties for us to play music together. I think we could work well; we could get to know each other better and maybe one day we will be the firmest of friends,' he offered. 'And where you have a friendship, you can always have hope for something more.'

* * *

The time was well past four o'clock in the morning. The room was dark, the blackness churning around her like the depths of a river. Lil blinked and glanced at the shadow of a bed. Maggie was asleep, making her usual soft sniffing sound, a gentle flow of air out of her nostrils. Lil rolled over. On the other side of the room, Cassie's bed had not been slept in.

Earlier, Tommy had knocked at the door while she and Maggie had been struggling into pyjamas and cleaning their teeth. Maggie's eyes had widened like a bolting colt at the harsh knock. It had been late at night and Lil had immediately feared the worst: bad news, a stranger at the door. Cassie needed her. Lil had answered on the second, more persistent knock and, when Tommy had said Cassie wouldn't be back that night, she'd pretended that she was already complicit in her daughter's plans, waving her hands in protest.

'You really didn't have to come and tell me. I knew already. But thanks for passing on her message, Tommy. She'll be having fun, I'm sure.'

The uncomfortable feeling that had penetrated her skin and delved deep into her gut as soon as she had closed the door was still with her hours later, as she stared into the darkness. Lil knew that Cassie was not coming back to the hotel; she knew that she was with Piet, that they were sharing time together. Lil was not worried about what she knew, but what she didn't know made her imagination swell like a hurricane. She didn't know how Cassie felt about Piet, or even if he was a trustworthy, nice man. She didn't know if Cassie was safe, if she was all right and, a terrifying thought, if she was enjoying herself, would she now start to form an attachment to this man; would she want to move to Amsterdam, to live there with him?

Lil thought about Herman. She had liked him very much. She had wanted to see him again. She had enjoyed his company, the conversation, the human contact and the warmth of his smile, the touch of a hand. But she would always put her daughter first. Had Herman begged her to live with him on his farm near Boom, she would have said no; she'd have returned home with Cassie.

Lil wasn't sure about Cassie, though. What if she wanted to stay in Amsterdam, with Piet? It would be natural, Lil thought – Cassie was still young, she was still adventurous. As her heart thudded in her chest, she screwed up her face tightly so that she wouldn't let out a sob, Lil knew that she was being selfish. She would never stand in Cassie's way. But the thought that followed made her gasp: she wasn't sure how she would manage to survive from day to day without her daughter now.

25

At breakfast, there was a lot of discussion about the empty chair at the table. Denise appeared very anxious to know the details. Frowning, she asked, 'Who's missing? Who hasn't come down to breakfast?' and then, more brightly, 'So Cassie didn't stay in her room last night? You mean she didn't come back to the hotel?' and finally, with obvious curiosity, 'Are you sure you've heard from her, Lil? She hasn't eloped or been abducted by her mystery man?'

Lil ignored her, concentrating on chewing her bread and cheese, pouring coffee for Albert, who was on the right side of her, and chattering loudly to Maggie, who was on her left. Finally, Tommy, dressed in an 'I Heart Amsterdam' T-shirt that was several sizes too small, turned to everyone and said, 'Right, let's put an end to the gossip. Cassie texted me at eleven o'clock last night to say she wouldn't be back; I passed her message on to Lil. Yes, Cassie stayed out all night. She's an adult. If you want to know any more, then ask her yourself, all right?'

Denise played with the sugar in the bowl throughout breakfast, hardly touching her food, while Sue ignored her and chattered loudly to Ken.

Just as Lil and Maggie had finished packing their cases, Cassie bustled into their room, a broad grin on her face. 'Sorry I'm late – did you get my message?'

Lil glanced up from folding her underwear. 'Yes, Tommy told me you'd texted him that you weren't going to be back until after breakfast, so I didn't worry.' She held Cassie's gaze for a moment. 'Everything all right, love?'

'Everything's fine, thanks.' Cassie smiled. She picked up her suitcase and began to arrange her clothes.

'You're a dark horse,' Maggie observed. 'So, did he seduce you, your Dutchman? Or...' She leaned forward. '... did you seduce him first?'

Cassie winked at Lil and held up a red bra. 'Perhaps I should have worn this last night.'

'Did he chase you round his bedroom, Cassie?'

'He has a houseboat, Maggie.'

'Ooooh.' Maggie's eyes gleamed. 'I bet the boat rocked like mad.'

'Oh, it certainly did. We rocked the boat all night.' Cassie noticed Lil's troubled face. 'Piet and I sat on the deck until the early hours, writing songs. He has a mini recording studio and we laid some tracks down. I have a couple of copies – you can listen to it.'

'That's nice.' Lil couldn't help but be relieved.

'The music really worked – we collaborate well. Our voices sound good on the tape. I was really pleased with what we achieved.' Cassie yawned. 'Then we ate breakfast, drank even more coffee and I came back here.' She sighed; her eyes were tired. 'I'll grab a couple of hours' sleep on the bus.'

'Oh, is that all that happened? No passion?' Maggie was disappointed. 'Well, my case is packed. I'm ready to go. And I've put Brian's present in my handbag for safekeeping. Do you want to know what I've got him, Lil?'

Lil sat on her suitcase, compressing the lid while Cassie leaned over and clipped it shut. 'Tell me later. We need to get downstairs, Maggie. We said we'd meet Tommy by ten and it's almost quarter past.' She raised an eyebrow. 'Denise seems fascinated by your love life, Cassie. She talked about nothing else at breakfast, where you were and why you hadn't come back and who you'd been seeing.'

'Perhaps she's not getting any action herself,' Maggie suggested, her eyes wide.

'Or quite the opposite...' Cassie couldn't help herself. 'Perhaps she's got nothing but love on her mind.'

Lil seized the opportunity. 'Why? What do you know? Tell me all about it.'

'Yes, spill the beans,' Maggie added.

Cassie clicked her case shut. 'All in good time.' She checked the room: it was tidy and nothing had been left behind. 'All in good time. We should go downstairs now. We don't want to be late for our journey to Ghent.'

* * *

On the bus, Lil asked Cassie to take the window seat next to her; Denise sat in the front with Tommy, unhappy that it was the only seat left, and Ken was ensconced at the back with Sue. Maggie sat herself between Emily and Pat and offered them chocolates from her handbag, then proceeded to read *Vicky the Saucy Vet*.

Lil tucked her hand under Cassie's arm. 'So, tell me all about your man friend, Piet.'

Cassie closed her eyes, enjoying the soft thrum of the wheels on the road beneath her; it was rocking her to sleep. 'Only if you tell me about Herman,' Cassie murmured.

'He's a nice man. I like him. If he lived in England, in Salterley, I might let him take me out.' Lil glanced slyly at Cassie. 'But he doesn't.'

'Did you kiss him, Lil?'

'Only once. So...' She gave another sly sideways glance. 'Tell me about Piet.'

'I like him. He's a good man. And a great musician. We get on well.' Cassie paused, peeking at Lil through one eye. 'I suppose if he lived in Salterley I'd see him again. But he lives in Amsterdam.' She sighed, her eyelids heavy. 'I said I might go back there in the autumn. A professional visit. We'll play a few gigs together, then I'll come home again.'

Lil took her daughter's hand. 'Did you kiss him?'

'Once...' Cassie mumbled. 'I just kissed him goodbye.' Her eyes closed and gradually her breathing became the soft snuffle of sleep. Lil smiled and held Cassie's hand tightly in hers.

She took out her new novel: *I, Sex Robot*, a story about an energetic young android reporter in the year 22,000 who teleports through time in order to research and collect information about famous Lotharios from the past. Lil had read the first chapter and was intrigued to know how racy Roberta Bott would get on with her new darkly handsome beau, George, Lord Byron, an apparently dangerous young man who lived in the early 1800s. She glanced over her shoulder, listening to Sue's monologue about Belgian chocolate to Ken, who had his sunglasses on and appeared to be asleep. DJ and Jake were still chatting about Amsterdam and how they'd enjoyed the club scene so much they were going to return later that year. Duncan was snoring loudly and Albert, who had been staring ahead of him, turned to Lil and held out a large, flat hand. She grinned back, delved into her cat handbag and passed him a chocolate. Emily was reading a book; she gazed up and caught Lil's eye.

'I've almost finished this, Lil. Do you want to borrow it?'

Lil nodded and called back, 'Is it any good?'

'Oh, yes.' Emily brandished her novel. 'It's called *Birdsong*. It's set in World War One. It's really very moving.'

Lil was interested. 'Is there any romance in it?'

'Lots – Stephen and Isabelle have a passionate affair.'

Lil waved *I, Sex Robot*. 'I'll swap you for this one when I've finished it.'

Ken leaned back in his seat and touched his silk cravat. 'I'm thinking of writing a novel about a gifted young Dutch painter. He moves to the south of France and paints landscapes but his life is troubled by psychotic delusions...'

Cassie murmured in her sleep. 'Van Gogh...'

Suddenly, Pat let out a yell. 'Lil – I just had a phone message from Thilde. She's managed to take a day off work – she's going to meet me in Ghent. We're going to spend the whole day together. Isn't that great?'

'Oh, that's wonderful news.' Lil beamed. She thought for a moment, then added, 'How will she get to Ghent from Boom? Is someone driving her there?'

'No, she's getting the train,' Pat called. 'It takes an hour and a half. She'll be able to stay until late.' His cheeks were flushed. 'That's fantastic, isn't it?'

'Fabulous.' Lil grinned, and turned back to stare at her book. At her side, Cassie was snoozing, her head against the window. Lil continued to read her chapter. Roberta Bott and Lord Byron were in his chamber, naked, and he had just spoken to her in a deep, testosterone-fuelled voice, offering such romantic words that Lil marvelled at them:

> She walks in beauty, like the night
> Of cloudless climes and starry skies;
> And all that's best of dark and bright
> Meet in her aspect and her eyes.

Lil let the book drop on her knee and, in her imagination, Roberta and Byron faded away and she and Herman were standing in the room together in their places. They gazed at each other, eyes locked, and Herman repeated the words, 'She walks in beauty like the night...'

Lil sighed. It could have happened, once upon a time, many years ago, but she had been far too busy to think about herself as the years had whizzed by from one to the next. She hadn't wanted to risk heartbreak and, besides, independence had suited her. But now Lil wondered if life had passed her by, if love had passed her by. Frankie had been the only one, and it was too late for any of that now.

* * *

Two hours later, at half past two, eleven of the travellers were sitting by the window of a café, drinking hot chocolate, staring out at the passers-by and talking amongst themselves excitedly. Sue was delighted with the hotel, a smart building, which comprised a house from 1517 and an old cotton factory from 1857, overlooking the Leie river, where they had already left their luggage.

'I have the most wonderful room all to myself – it has an en suite and a wonderful view of the river. Ken's room is next to mine. He says he can see the belfry from his room.'

Emily was sipping thick chocolate from a huge cup, licking her lips. 'I want to visit the seventh century abbey this afternoon. It's amazing.'

'St Bavo's? There's so many beautiful things to see around the town,' Cassie agreed. 'But I think we may have missed the Friday market.'

Duncan shrugged. 'The bars are all open.'

Sue waved a hand happily. 'Ken has told me about a bar called

Dulle Griet's – named after the Breughel painting. I want to go there, my dear.'

Tommy gazed around him. 'Where is Ken, by the way? I need to organise tonight's meal.'

Jake elbowed DJ and sniggered. 'Denise isn't here either.'

'Ken will be here soon – he wanted to talk to someone at the hotel about his room. He was asking for some extra towels, I think.' Sue sniffed. 'Denise has a migraine.'

DJ elbowed Jake, who winked and clapped a hand over his mouth.

Pat rubbed his hands together. 'I'll be leaving you all in a moment. Thilde will be here any second. She's going to meet me outside.' He ran a hand through his hair. 'Don't book any meals for me tonight, will you, Tommy? I'm spoken for already.'

Maggie piped up. 'Where are we going to eat?'

'We're sorting all that out now, over our hot drinks.' Tommy held up a pen. 'Right, who wants to—?'

'Ah, here's Ken,' Sue called, waving a hand.

Ken rushed into the café, an apologetic expression on his face. 'Sorry, everyone – that took longer than I intended.'

Sue stood up, her voice loud. 'Shall I order you a drink, Ken?'

'Oh, no, thanks.' He offered her a quick smile and turned abruptly as Denise appeared in the doorway. She looked flushed and happy.

'My migraine's gone. I feel much better now.'

Ken touched her elbow gently. 'What will you have, Denise?'

She met his gaze and arched an eyebrow. 'Oh, something wicked, full of Belgian chocolate.'

'Really, my dear?' Sue was appalled. 'Isn't chocolate bad for migraines, Denise?'

Denise glanced at Ken. 'Oh, I find a little of what you fancy does you the world of good, *Syoo*.'

Lil pressed her lips together, trying not to burst out laughing. It was most entertaining, the way others' secret lives and liaisons were unfolding on this trip. Lil was enjoying it almost as much as her romance novels.

Suddenly, Pat leaned over and grasped her elbow. 'Lil – I'm going now. Thilde's here. She's outside.'

'That's lovely.' Lil beamed, not really sure why Pat was announcing the fact of Thilde's arrival only to her. 'Have a great time, Pat.'

Pat's grasp on her arm became tighter. 'Come out and say hello.'

'In a minute.' Lil picked up her hot chocolate, bringing the creamy drink to her mouth. 'I don't want this to get cold...'

She narrowed her eyes as she stared out of the window. Thilde was waving, happy, her dark curls blowing in a gentle breeze. Pat was already on his feet.

'I'll see everyone later.' He turned to Lil. 'Well, are you coming?'

'With you and Thilde?' Lil frowned, confused. She shook her head and moved her eyes back to the window, where the sound of Thilde knocking gently against the glass had caught her attention.

Lil heard Cassie murmur, 'Go on, Lil. Go off and have some fun.'

Lil stared at Thilde, who was waving again and smiling excitedly. Behind her, a tall man had appeared; he was wearing a hat and a smart jacket. Lil recognised the bushy brows and the twist of his grin. All of a sudden, she was flapping her arms and calling out.

'Herman! Herman!'

She turned to Pat and grasped his sleeve, tugging herself to her feet. 'Come on, Pat – let's get a move on. I've got a date with a handsome man and I don't intend to keep him waiting.'

26

Lil didn't want the evening to end. They were sitting at a table overlooking the river Leie, having shared a pizza. She was having a wonderful time. She watched Herman carefully as his lips touched the beer glass, as he brought food to his mouth and chewed slowly, as his eyes met hers and he smiled his lopsided grin. She beamed back and gazed towards the river that was dark and smooth as glass, reflecting the tall houses and wide bridges as black images in the water. The sky overhead was pale, streaked with white, stringy clouds. She heard a church clock strike seven. Herman dabbed his mouth with a napkin.

'So, Lil, I hope you had a good day today. Which part was your favourite?'

Lil saw the glimmer in his eyes. She pretended to think hard, waving a finger as if in doubt. 'Well, the boat trip was lovely, especially because you made sure we sat at the front. Seeing all those historic buildings, the winding canals and the beautiful fronts of the houses. I loved that.'

'So, the boat trip was best?'

'I enjoyed the deep-fried peas you bought in the café. Maggie would have loved them.'

Herman nodded. 'The *kroakemandels*.'

'And it's gorgeous here, this little restaurant right next to the river.' Lil closed her eyes. 'I was tired after walking around the town. It's good to sit down and I like this food. It's not too fancy.'

'So, eating here in the restaurant is your favourite part of the day.'

'No, it isn't at all and you know it!' Lil's expression was one of mischief. 'I'll never forget the moment I looked up from my hot chocolate in the café and there was Thilde at the window waving, and, behind her, you were standing there smiling. My heart just jumped. It was such a lovely surprise.'

'I agreed with Thilde and Pat that I wouldn't tell you I was coming.' Herman sat back in his seat. 'I was taking a chance that you'd be pleased to see me again.'

'Of course I was pleased,' Lil retorted. 'I just naturally assumed you'd be at work on the farm, that you'd be too busy to come and see me.'

'I am seventy-eight years old,' Herman announced. 'I spend most days driving the tractor but today I wanted to see you. Besides, I have three strong grandsons who can do the heavy work now.'

'Yes, I suppose you deserve to take things easy. Farm work must have been tough all your life.' Lil thought for a moment and then she nodded. 'It's a funny thing, old age, isn't it, Herman?'

He frowned. 'Why funny?'

'I mean strange-funny. You know, most of the time I forget I'm old. I'm just me, Lil, doing what I do and then I look in the mirror or my hip aches or I'm tired or it takes me longer to do something...'

'Or you walk into a room and forget what you came there to find,' Herman added.

'Yes, that too – that happens all the time and I think I must be

losing my marbles.' Lil sighed. 'I'm really lucky, I suppose – I'm
healthy, I've never been ill, I've always been active. There are a lot of
people our age and younger who are less fortunate.'

'Age is at first a number,' Herman murmured. 'Yes, it is an accu-
mulation of years, a big number. I will never run a marathon now
or go skateboarding. I know my limitations. But it is also an attitude
of mind, keeping options open, doing what we can and living life to
the full.'

Herman lifted a large hand and placed it over Lil's. She enjoyed
the feeling of her smaller one being covered, encased and warm.
She frowned, a thought floating into her mind. 'But the big difference for me now I'm in my eighties, Herman – well, I often wonder
how long I have left. I mean, you don't think about dying when
you're thirty, when you're busy living life at a fast pace. But sometimes I think to myself, "Well Lil, today's another day and you're one
day closer to death." And it makes me feel terrible.'

Herman raised his bushy brows. 'So you worry about dying?'

'I do. I worry about what it will feel like and what will happen to
Cassie when I'm gone and, do you know, Herman, sometimes I can't
believe that it will really happen? But I know that it will, of course.
Life will suddenly stop. There will be no more Lil, just a shell that
was once me, a body, but it'll be empty and the bit that was me will
have vanished. And that's it, all done, finished, forever.'

Herman exhaled. 'Perhaps anxiety is what makes us feel old.'

'Don't you worry about dying?'

'No, not any more.'

Lil examined his expression and suddenly felt sad. 'Because you
lost your wife? Because you watched her die? And your son too?
Surely that makes it worse.'

'Watching Theodora die was sad. When Dirk died, and I had
lost two people I loved, I became very aware of my own mortality,
yes.' Herman wrapped his fingers around Lil's, holding them firmly.

'After that, I had a health problem myself. For more than a year, I battled with prostate trouble and I wasn't sure if I would recover. It slowed me down and I could have given up several times. But I fought it and I was lucky.'

'You're very brave,' Lil breathed.

'I am no longer afraid.' Herman shook his head. 'I am lucky to be here and, as life goes on, I find more ways to be happy. And now I have met you. I would never have believed that such a fine woman would come to stay with me on the farm and that I would find myself at this point in my life with such strong feelings.'

Lil opened her mouth, about to protest that she had to return to England, that their friendship would be brief or, at best, one maintained at a distance. But instead she said nothing. She didn't want to change the happiness on Herman's face. She didn't want to spoil the moment for either of them, so she simply smiled.

Herman's grin broadened. 'Well, we have an hour before I have to be at the railway station with Thilde. What would you like to do?' Lil shrugged. Herman gave a small cough. 'We can stay here and have another drink. Or maybe we can take a walk...'

'Oh, yes, let's have a short stroll.' Lil brightened. 'We can sit on a bench somewhere and watch the barges drift by. I'd like that.'

Herman stood slowly, offering Lil his arm. 'Come along then, *mijn schatje*. Let's have some quiet time together by the river before I go home.'

Twenty minutes later, Lil and Herman were leaning against the railings of a bridge, watching a barge disappear beneath them. The glassy water split as the boat surged forward, leaving a trail of diminishing ripples in its wake. A child on the boat waved and Lil raised her hand in acknowledgement. Herman wrapped an arm around her shoulder.

'I like Ghent,' she breathed. After a pause she added, 'I like

Bruges, and Boom. I like all of Belgium. It's all so clean and charming, picturesque and pretty.'

Herman was gazing at her, giving her his full attention. 'Ghent is beautiful in the evening but in the autumn particularly it is quite special. When the skies are dark and the moon is over the river, the reflection in the water...'

'It sounds nice, autumn in Ghent.'

'Perhaps you would like to spend some time here?'

'In Ghent?'

He nodded. 'We could visit many cities. We could spend time at the farm.' His voice was low, gravelly. 'Each season on the farm is beautiful. The freshness of spring, the warmth of the summer and in autumn there is the harvest. The long evenings become short nights and sometimes the winters can be harsh and we sit by the fire and it is very cosy.'

'It sounds lovely, Herman.' Lil snuggled closer to him. The silence hung heavily on the air as she waited for his next sentence.

Then he whispered the words she had been expecting. 'Cosy is better when there are two of you.'

Lil nodded. She thought of Clover Hill, of her warm little flat filled with her own things; she thought of Maggie and Brian next door watching the old programmes on television, of Jenny Price downstairs; Lil imagined her office empty, a chance to sneak in and make a mischievous call on her phone. She thought of Cassie just down the road, popping over to visit her whenever she needed something. Yet she enjoyed Herman's company, his arm around her; she wasn't sure if she wanted to be alone any more.

She imagined Cassie and Piet last night on his boat: what if Piet had asked Cassie to stay in Amsterdam and she had said no because of Lil, because she felt responsible? Lil forced herself to gaze up into Herman's face, his kind eyes, his warm smile.

'Are you asking me to visit you?'

He paused. 'I'm asking you to visit and perhaps one day you may want to stay.'

'I'd have to leave my old life behind...' Lil's voice trailed into silence. A huge lump had swollen in her throat and she swallowed it to prevent tears from coming.

'I can give you my home and my heart in exchange.' Herman's voice was a whisper.

'I'd have to... give it some thought...' Lil had no idea what to say next.

Herman grinned. 'That's all I can ask. When you go home and think of me, maybe I will just be a memory. But...' He gave an expansive shrug, wide shoulders heaving. 'Maybe you can accept my invitation to come back to visit in September and maybe – what is the expression? – we can take it from there.'

Lil nodded. 'Maybe we can.' She wrapped her arms around him and leaned against his shoulder as he kissed the top of her head.

'It is time now,' he muttered. 'I have a train to catch. But we won't forget each other, Lil. We won't forget this day.'

'No, Herman,' Lil said sadly. 'No, we won't.'

* * *

Cassie was lying on the bed, a notepad in her hand, thinking about writing a poem. She wondered if she could write one about Piet and her evening on his boat in Amsterdam. She wrote the title 'Regrets' and then drew a line through it. Emily, her current roommate, was resting on the other bed, reading *Birdsong*. Cassie wrote down another title, 'My Friend the Stranger', considered it for a moment and then crossed it out. She sighed.

Emily glanced up. 'You okay, Cass?'

Cassie nodded. 'Life's complicated. Yes, all's fine, thanks.'

Emily went back to her book and mumbled, 'You should have my life if you want complicated...'

'Do you mean Alex?'

'Alex, yes.' Emily put down her book and rolled on her back. 'We're supposed to be announcing our engagement at Christmas.'

'That's wonderful. Why is that complicated?'

'I'm not sure complicated is the right word.' Emily stretched out her arms. 'It's just difficult. I haven't seen him since the beginning of June. That's over two months now.'

'It must be so hard,' Cassie said sympathetically.

'I'm glad I came on this trip. The boys are such great company and the football game was awesome. Daytimes are fun, but then at night time by myself, I start thinking about Alex and I hope he's all right over there. It's so far away, Cass.'

'But you talk on the phone a lot?'

'When we can.' Emily seemed sad. 'But recently...'

Cassie's phone buzzed by the side of her bed. She picked it up. 'It's Jamie,' she muttered. 'Sorry, Em – I'll just take this on the stairs.'

Cassie rushed out onto the landing, leaving the door open behind her. She sat on the top stair leading down towards the ground floor.

'Hi, Jamie. How are things?'

'Cassie! Things are fine. How's Ghent?'

Cassie was pleased to hear him sound so cheerful. 'It's great here – you'd like it. I have so much to tell you when I'm back. I wish you'd come with us.'

'Lil wanted you all to herself.' Jamie's voice was mischievous. 'How is she?'

'She's having a great time. Apparently, she was in the red-light district last night chatting to the sex workers...'

'You let Lil loose in the red-light district?' Jamie seemed both amused and shocked.

'Oh, she and Maggie had a great time.' Cassie made her voice breezy. Her thoughts moved quickly; she was asking herself why she hadn't just told Jamie about her dinner on Piet's houseboat. She changed the subject. 'Anyway, what's the latest from home?'

'I bring some good news.' Jamie sounded bright. 'There was a call on the landline this morning from someone in London, Hammersmith actually, wanting you to do a poetry and music gig there in November. I said you'd call them as soon as you were back. I didn't want them to spoil your holiday by ringing your mobile or emailing you. But a gig in London on November the fifth might be lovely.'

'We could make a week of it – I can call a few people and do a few more venues while I'm there.' She thought for a moment. 'I know – I'll write a poem specially for Bonfire Night.'

The line was quiet, then Jamie's voice came to her. 'I miss you.'

'I'll be home in a few days.'

'I'm looking forward to it. The place is quiet without you here.'

Cassie laughed. 'Enjoy the peace while you can.'

He didn't return her laugh. 'Come home soon.'

'I will,' she murmured softly.

'Bye, Cass.' There was a click and Cassie put her phone in her pocket with a sigh, clambered up from the step and made her way back to her room, imagining Jamie lying on the couch, whispering into the phone and then turning his attention to the television.

Emily was lying on the bed on her front, her mobile phone clutched in her fist. Cassie stood in the doorway, about to make a comment about Jamie when she realised Emily was sobbing. Cassie moved to the bed and put a hand on Emily's shoulder.

'Em? Is everything all right?'

'No. I don't know. I don't think so.' Emily sniffed. She rolled over and sat upright, her face streaked with tears, and took a shuddering breath. 'I just tried to ring Alex. It's the third time I've phoned today. I can't get an answer.'

Cassie sat on the bed next to her. 'It must be difficult to get through. I mean, it's a long way away and phone connections...'

'He rings me when he can: I hear from him at least twice a week. But it's been days now and I've heard nothing.' Emily spoke softly. 'It's really unusual to hear nothing at all for such a long time.'

Cassie placed a friendly hand on her shoulder. 'I'm sure there is a logical explanation.'

Emily wiped a hand across her brow. 'Yes, thanks, Cassie – I'm sure there is too. It's just – I can't help worrying when I hear nothing – all the stories he's told me of life out there and... normally, I'm so strong but this time, I don't know, I feel fretful. Maybe it's because I'm away from home and not busy at work and I have more time to think about things...'

Cassie threw her arms around Emily, her cheek pressing against the soft hair. 'Try not to worry. I'm sure he'll call as soon as he can. Meanwhile, focus on enjoying your holiday. We have a couple of days left. We'll have a lovely time then we'll all be home and you'll find out everything will be fine.'

'Yes, thanks – you're right.' Emily pulled Cassie close again, a desperate hug. 'I'm just being silly. It's just – it's such a horrible feeling when you are away from someone you care about...'

'It's not silly at all.' Cassie shook her head, understanding a little how Emily felt. She was thinking about Jamie. He was missing her; it was more than just needing company. He wanted to be with her. And Cassie was looking forward to seeing him too. The thought filled her with astonishment as she recalled Piet's words on the barge. 'You think yourself a free spirit, but I saw it in your face, how you feel about this man.'

Cassie felt the stirring of an unfamiliar emotion. Jamie was warm, easy-going, handsome; he was loyal, kind-hearted. He didn't seem to find her too independent, too headstrong and opinionated. He had mentioned the possibility of a gig in London and, suddenly, the prospect of him accompanying her seemed very exciting. Cassie breathed out, wondering why she felt happier, more alive and filled with a sense of purpose.

* * *

Lil clambered up the stairs, Pat beside her, their expressions mournful. Pat groaned. 'Why does it hurt so much when you have to leave someone you love?'

Lil sighed. 'Did you and Thilde have a great time today?'

'It was just brilliant, Lil. It makes it even harder to be apart now.'

Lil decided it might be better to say nothing. They had almost reached the landing, Lil walking slowly; her hip suddenly felt stiff and aching. Then she heard a noise. A little way down the corridor, Denise's door opened with a furtive creak and a man emerged from the darkness. Lil suddenly went into *Charlie's Angels* mode. She imagined Brian watching the crime-fighting Angels from his armchair and she was on the screen; she decided immediately that she was the tough one with sleek dark hair. She pulled Pat back into the shadows of the wall and pressed a finger against her lips.

They watched in silence as Ken stood upright, stretching his arms over his head as Denise's door closed with a sharp click. He paused for a moment as if thinking or waiting. Lil met Pat's eyes as they each put a hand over their own mouths to stifle a simultaneous guffaw.

Ken took several steps forward, coming closer to Lil and Pat, who held their breath and flattened themselves against the wall. Ken paused outside another door and tapped lightly. In seconds, the door opened and an eager arm appeared, grasping Ken around the neck. Sue emerged in a thin nightgown, clinging to Ken, reaching up on her toes to kiss him. Ken allowed himself to be tugged into Sue's room. The door closed with a clunk.

Lil turned to meet Pat's grin. 'It seems someone is getting plenty of action tonight, Pat, even if we're not.' She laughed softly. 'Ken and Sue and Denise, the eternal triangle. Well, I never! Someone ought to write a book about it.'

Pat shook his head. 'Maybe Ken will put it in his next novel.'

'They kept that little liaison a big secret.' Lil winked.

'Secret?' Pat pressed Lil's arm affectionately. 'No way. Everyone on the bus has known about the goings-on between those three for days. The only problem is...' he winked '... Sue and Denise have no idea.'

'Poor Sue and Denise.' Lil's eyes shone. 'I feel so sorry for both of them, Pat – when they find out about Ken's exploits, there will be some fireworks... and goodness knows who will get hurt in the blast.'

27

The breakfast table was arranged with bread, sliced Gouda and ham, jams and honey, and pots of tea and coffee, but not everyone was hungry. Emily toyed with her coffee spoon, stirring her drink with glazed eyes, eating nothing. Pat devoured several slices of bread and cheese, but his half-closed eyes showed that his mind was elsewhere and he had little to say when DJ and Jake quizzed him about his date with Thilde, preferring to answer, 'Ah, that's just for me to know,' to everything.

Ken seemed tired, smiling sweetly at Sue to his right and glancing warmly at Denise to his left as they both tried to tempt him with morsels of food, offering extra coffee to keep his energy up. Duncan had a hangover and wondered if the hotel could provide him with a couple of fried eggs so that he would feel better. Tommy was as ravenous as ever, declaring he needed the extra calories to drive to Dunkerque, where they would be spending the day. Emily sighed and Denise added, 'Oh, no, not more dead men in graves.' Emily's eyes suddenly filled with tears and she stared at her fingers. Denise gazed at Ken hopefully, whispering a suggestion in his ear that no one else could hear.

Lil couldn't concentrate on food; her mind was filled with choices for her future, what she might do, where she might go. Maggie, on one side of her, stole the cheese from her plate with an eager stab of a fork while Albert, on the other, kept smiling and refilling her mug with tea from the steel pot.

Cassie watched Lil carefully from across the table, determined to ask the right questions later, when she'd had time to rest. She also decided that she'd sit near Emily today and provide a bit of emotional support; the poor girl looked as if she needed a mother at the moment and Cassie thought she might be the nearest thing.

Once everyone was installed in the minibus and the luggage stowed in the back, Tommy turned around from the driver's seat, Ken relaxing in the seat next to him, his face flooded with relief. Tommy coughed loudly, ready to give one of his speeches. His tone was deliberately jolly, as if he sensed the torpor around him.

'Well, campers, how are we all?'

DJ and Jake cheered, but there was little response from the others. The mood was listless and uninterested. Outside the bus, the air was cold and the sky was a swirl of pale grey, straggling clouds hanging low as if it might rain. Tommy offered everyone his most endearing smile, his belly thrust forward, full of bluster like a stand-up comedian.

'Right, everyone. I want to discuss our itinerary for today.'

Jake cheered and DJ called out, 'Take Dunc to the nearest boozer.' Duncan had fallen asleep again, his head on Albert's shoulder.

Tommy took a breath. 'I was thinking, it's a bit chilly today so we might want a change of plans. I was going to take us to Dunkerque first, but it'll be freezing on the beach, so I thought we might go straight to Le Touquet, where our hotel is, and spend some time in the town there.'

'What's of interest there?' Maggie asked.

'All sorts of things: it's a holiday resort. So, there's a market for shopping, mini golf, an equestrian centre. There's a beach, a nice spa, a museum of fine art...' Tommy cast his eyes towards Sue for approval. 'So, shall we go straight to Le Touquet?'

Ken turned around, addressing everyone behind him. 'I think Tommy's idea is a good one. It's a very French holiday centre, very charming and relaxed, so we can choose to do all sorts of different things before we set off to Honfleur tomorrow, which will be our final day.'

Sue boomed cheerily, 'Don't forget, Ken, we've booked a dinner for everyone in Honfleur tomorrow evening, a final meal to round off the visit.'

'Of course, *Syoo*. I'm chipping in too,' Denise replied. 'Ken's arranged it already. It's in a lovely hotel.'

'I know,' Sue retorted. 'I helped him to choose it.'

'I made the final choice,' Denise insisted.

Ken wiped a hand over his brow, his eyes red-rimmed. 'So, Le Touquet it is?'

Duncan had woken up. 'There's a big casino there, isn't there? Let's go, then, Tommy – we'll give Dunkerque a miss and go straight to the coast and have some fun.'

Emily gave an audible sigh and lifted her novel in front of her nose. Cassie, who was seated next to her, whispered something in her ear. Lil picked up her copy of *I, Sex Robot* and gazed at the photo she always kept in the crease of her book: Frankie Chapman, his cheery smile, his arm around her. She smoothed the glossy surface with a finger and stared at the book.

In the chapter she was reading, the intrepid investigative android-journalist Roberta Bott had whizzed back in time to France in 1660, where Charles the Second, the English king-in-waiting, was lying low, living a life of debauchery. Lil had just read the chapter where Roberta accompanies Charles to his boudoir; he had removed all of his clothes, and was naked but for his long black wig.

Lil closed her eyes and wondered about Herman: if she should go to visit him at the farm in Boom, if she would sleep in his bedroom with him. She thought about how it would be to spend time with him, not just a fleeting holiday but several weeks, months. She had to admit, it was the company, the warmth, the conversation she craved most; she relished the idea of someone who would share things, who would listen to her and enjoy her funny stories. For a moment she felt sad; her roller-coaster life had been busy and full of fun but now, having met Herman, she understood how nice it would have been to share and to enjoy another's company. But maybe it was too late. She was used to her own space, her routine. Perhaps she couldn't change now, even for a chance of something that might bring happiness.

As she'd left Herman, she'd promised to send a card from Salterley and he had begged her to consider his invitation to come to the farm in September. She hadn't said no. She could make her mind up later, when she arrived home. She might feel differently when she was back in Clover Hill.

The hotel was welcoming and comfortable, and the sleeping arrangements were exactly as the previous evening. Cassie had wanted to keep an eye on Emily, who seemed glad to share with her. Sue and Denise were eager to grab the single rooms, although Ken offered to swap his single room with someone who hadn't yet enjoyed the experience of their own private space and the privilege of peace and quiet. Both Denise and Sue had been quick to point out that everyone else was happy sharing with who they had shared with yesterday and that Ken should definitely have his own room. Ken had agreed, although his expression was one of tired resignation.

In the afternoon, the weather had perked up, the skies still grey, but the air was warmer and the sunshine squeezed through gaps in the clouds. The group stood in the town centre, discussing what they would do until dinner that evening. DJ and Jake wanted to play mini golf and they insisted that Pat go with them. Pat said he'd go if Emily went. Cassie offered to accompany Emily, who was pale and had said very little all morning. Sue insisted that Ken take her to the fine art museum and Denise was adamant that she wanted to go there too, particularly with Ken, who was so knowledgeable about art and just about everything else. Lil was watching carefully and thought she detected an unfriendly glance pass between the two women. Duncan and Tommy had already left to make the most of their afternoon in the casino. Maggie wanted to try mini golf. She turned to Lil.

'I've never played before, but I've always fancied myself as a golfer, with one of those hats and the bright checked trousers. Come on, Lil – let's see if we can beat the youngsters. I'm going to play. Besides, I need someone to caddy for me. I have Brian's present in my handbag and I need someone to keep an eye on it.'

Lil shrugged. She wasn't keen on the idea of hitting a tiny ball with a stick then walking after it. But there was little else on offer, and Maggie was so keen, dressed in sunglasses and a straw hat. In truth, Lil would have preferred to sit down in a café and watch the waves roll onto the sands and away again, but she was happy to support her friend. She sighed. 'All right, Maggie.'

She felt a pressure on her arm and noticed Albert standing next to her. His eyes sparkled and he was wearing a tie and a smart shirt beneath his coat. Lil thought he looked dapper. His voice was like the soft sound of dry leaves underfoot. 'We're going for a walk, Lil.'

Lil faced him, frowning. 'Pardon?' She was astonished; he'd rarely spoken anything other than a few monosyllables.

'Lil and I are going for a walk.' Albert's mouth turned up in a smile as he offered his arm. 'No golf. Just a walk, both of us together.'

* * *

Arm in arm, they walked slowly towards the beach. Lil wondered who was leaning on who as Albert shuffled beside her, but they were in step and he was smiling.

Lil squeezed his arm. 'Well, this is pleasant, Albie, me and you.'

He nodded, offering a charming smile. 'It is.'

'So, what shall we do?'

'Cup of tea? Cake? Explore?'

'I like all of those,' Lil murmured.

They were close to the beach, the rush of the waves in their ears. Lil stopped to gaze at the flat sandy beach, the undulating scrubby grassland behind, and the deep blue line of the sea. She spotted a beach-shack-style café and pointed. 'Shall we go there?'

Albert nodded. 'We shall. That would be lovely.'

They sat inside the café; it was warm and smelled of brewing coffee. Lil was aware of the happy cries of two wriggling children at the table next to them and the nonchalant parents, who were oblivious, involved in a deep conversation in fast French. Lil pointed. 'I bet Duncan was just like that.'

'A cheeky little lad, Duncan was. His mother spoiled him rotten.' Albert's smile broadened and Lil noticed a glimmer in his eye. 'We both did.'

A waiter brought tall mugs of hot chocolate and a piece of apple pie for them to share. Lil muttered, *'Merci,'* and the young man replied, 'My pleasure,' in perfect English. Lil reached for her drink eagerly and noticed Albert watching her, his eyes steady. He was handsome, caring; he had a ready grin, and Lil thought how easy it was just to look at him, to share his company. She wrapped her hands around the cup to warm them, enjoying the comforting burning sensation against her skin.

'Albie?'

He raised his eyebrows.

'I've noticed – you don't say much.'

Albert nodded; again, the charming smile. 'That's right.'

'Why?'

Albert reached for his drink. Lil watched as he brought the hot chocolate to his lips, sipped slowly and replaced the mug on the table. 'Two reasons.'

'Oh?' Lil leaned forward, intrigued, and forked a piece of pie into her mouth.

'First of all, I'm an old man.'

'What's that got to do with it?' Lil retorted.

Albert raised his shoulders in answer. 'I don't have much to say. Most people are not really interested in me nowadays.'

'That's awful.' Lil helped herself to more pie before quickly adding, '*I'm* interested.'

'I know.' Albert's ready smile returned. 'You're a very special lady, Lil.'

'So, what's the other reason? Why you don't say much?'

Albert cupped a hand to his ear. 'I got clouted round the head a lot as a kid. Now I'm deaf as a post in one ear.' He appeared to find it funny, as he added, 'And the other one's not as good as it was.'

Lil raised her voice. 'I'll have to make sure I speak up, then.'

'It's not too bad if there's just me and you.' Albert winked. 'The hearing's not so good in big crowds, with all the background noise.'

'Well.' Lil sat up in her seat. 'It's just me and you, then.' She glanced at him, his smart shirt and tie, his handsome face. She was beginning to enjoy herself. 'We've got time away by ourselves– I didn't really want to play mini golf anyway– and we've got a few hours until we have to go back to the hotel for dinner. So, this is where we have some fun.'

'Fun,' Albert repeated. 'I couldn't agree more.'

'So, what shall we do?' Lil asked. 'It's too cold to sunbathe; I don't do horse-riding; Ken and Sue and Denise will be up to their tricks at the museum and I've no intention of going to a casino – strip poker is as far as I go with gambling. So – what's it to be?'

'I have just the thing.' Albert rubbed his hands together. 'Perfect for two youngsters like ourselves.'

'I'm intrigued.' Lil leaned forward. 'What do you have in mind?'

'I noticed it on the way to the beach – just a few minutes' walk from here. I haven't been to one for years. Come on, Lil.' He pushed away his half-filled cup. 'Let's show the kids how it's done, shall we?'

Lil guzzled the last of her hot chocolate, swung her bag onto her shoulder and eased herself upright. 'All right.' She clutched his arm as they walked towards the door. It felt very nice to be escorted by a good-looking man whose eyes gleamed with a sense of mischief. 'Where are we going?'

Albert's face shone with delight. He had Lil on his arm and the promise of a splendid afternoon in her company. 'We're going to the funfair.'

28

The rhythmic sound of the machinery, a dull throbbing of engines, thundered in their ears as they approached the little fairground. Ahead, Lil could hear the squealing of children having fun, being spun and hurled into the air on waltzers and big dippers. A variety of smells filled her nose: the oil of moving machines, the sizzling aroma of frying onions, the sweet sugar of candy floss. Lil tucked an arm through the crook of Albert's and offered him a questioning glance.

'So, what will we do first? The dodgems? I can drive.'

They were surrounded by brightly coloured stalls where men and women were touting for custom, calling out to attract attention, waving arms to persuade bystanders to choose a lucky dip or to hook a fish on a pole. Albert tugged Lil towards a shooting gallery, his face suddenly animated. He waved at a young man with slicked-back hair who called him 'Monsieur' and handed him a rifle in exchange for several euros. Lil edged behind Albert as he lined up a shot and she whispered in his stronger ear, 'Are you any good at this?'

She felt a movement of his shoulders, then there was a popping sound, a crack of metal against metal, then another and another. Lil watched as Albert knocked five tin cans from the shelf, each one flying backwards and disappearing into darkness.

Lil gasped. 'You're very skilful at shooting.'

Albert nodded. 'The upside of being deaf is that your eyesight compensates.'

The lean attendant with oiled hair approached and waved towards a shelf full of prizes. There were piles of stuffed toys: pink fluffy pigs, koalas with huge black eyes, long-legged frogs, and tangerine-billed ducks wearing red striped pyjamas. Albert waved his fingers towards a huge panda bear, nodding his head when the stall owner touched it. He passed the panda to Lil. 'I got this just for you, dear Lil.'

Lil clutched it in her arms. 'Thank you, Albie. I'll treasure it.' She inhaled. 'Can you smell the hot sugar? Shall we get a toffee apple?'

'It'll stick to your teeth.' Albert raised his eyebrows.

'What about candy floss?' Lil tugged him towards a stall where a young woman was swirling a stick loaded with a cloud of pink sugar, spinning it into a ball. A bright sign nearby offered *barbe à papa* for three and five euros. Albert delved into his pocket, brought out a note and offered it to the young woman, who extended the sugary cotton candy stick towards Lil. She stuck her tongue into the pinkness, watching the shade deepen to a dark rose. Her tongue fizzed, the candy stuck to her lips and she sighed. 'I haven't had candy floss since I was a child. Have some.'

Albert took a bite. The candy floss plastered itself to his nose. 'I forgot just how sweet this stuff was. It'll ruin your teeth.'

'Only the few that are still my own,' she countered and they both laughed. Lil pulled a swirl of candy floss from the stick, rolled it into a gooey ball and pushed it into her mouth, repeating the action to fill Albert's mouth with pink sugar.

They walked on as loud music assaulted their ears, Cyndi Lauper singing 'Girls Just Wanna Have Fun'. They passed the waltzer and Lil hesitated by the dodgems. 'How about a ride on the cars?'

Albert shrugged. 'My bones aren't as strong as they were. What about a ride with no impact?'

'What did you have in mind?'

The music boomed louder now with a new song, Wizzard's 'See My Baby Jive'. Lil pulled a face. 'I haven't heard that one for ages – it takes me back.'

Albert gazed up at the Ferris wheel, the top pod scraping a low-hanging grey sky. He sighed. 'What do you reckon? Could we see the whole of France from up there?'

'There's only one way to find out,' Lil replied.

'We might even be able to see the sea and far across the channel.' Albert's eyes were misty.

'Come on, then.' Lil tugged his arm, feeling like a child. She instantly recalled being seven years old at a fair in Oxfordshire, jerking her father's arm in the same way, her eyes hopeful that he'd buy her a penny ride. With a jolt she realised she hadn't thought about that moment in over seventy-five years. Lil hugged Albert, a spontaneous excited squeeze. 'Come on, then – my treat.'

Lil and Albert huddled together in the little pod that rocked as the Ferris wheel began to turn. Lil felt a tickle in her tummy as she was propelled upwards and she gazed at Albert, who wrapped a protective arm around her shoulders. The ground suddenly appeared a long way below them, the people small as insects. 'Tiger Feet' by Mud blared from speakers, then another song in French, the volume increasing as they descended past the huge loud speakers and becoming more distant as the wheel took them higher. Then, momentarily, they stopped at the top and Albert pointed a finger. Lil felt instantly giddy as she followed the line of his direction across the striped canvas tops of fairground stalls, over rooftops towards the deep blue strip of sea and the expanse of grey sky.

Albert pointed. 'There's home, beyond the sea, Lil.'

'And here we are in France on holiday.' She hugged the panda, her trophy from the shooting gallery. 'It's wonderful.'

'It is now,' Albert muttered. 'I was very uncomfortable during the first few days – I didn't like the atmosphere in the battlefields. My dad was injured in the Second World War. I lost two uncles. The whole place made me feel very sad.'

'It was sad – and very atmospheric. But we've had such a good time here, haven't we?'

'Oh, we have.' A soft light glimmered in Albert's eyes as he watched her. 'And when you get back? What then? Will life be the same?'

Lil sighed. 'I don't know.' She thought for a moment 'I hope not. This holiday has made me rethink my priorities.'

'Priorities?' Albert's voice was hushed.

'It's been so refreshing to travel, to meet new people, to experience the outside world. I needed this holiday. I needed to live a little.'

He nodded. 'And how are you living a little?'

'I'm having fun, every minute.' Lil replied. 'I have spent quality time with Cassie and with my best friend, Maggie – and now with you. It feels nice to be special, and with someone special. I never realised how much it made a difference.'

'And the farmer.'

Lil gazed into Albert's eyes for a sign that he might be jealous of Herman. She found none, just a kind warmth, an interest. She gazed out towards the ocean and sighed. 'I don't know what I will do about Herman. He's invited me to visit him in the autumn. I could go.'

Albert smiled. 'Wait and see how you feel when you're home again.'

He wrapped an arm around her and she leaned back, enjoying the human contact, the delicious feeling that someone was close by, someone who would offer her friendship and warmth. The Ferris wheel began to descend again, making her stomach lurch. Albert's grip on her shoulder tightened.

The wheel reached the bottom and began to ascend again, the pod swinging back and forth as Lil held her breath. Life was exciting. A new thought filled her mind: life took you to the bottom of the wheel's rotation; for a moment you were still and in limbo, as she had been before the bus trip came along, and then suddenly you were on the up, as she had been whisked away to France and Belgium and Holland. She hadn't expected anything other than continuity, stability, but now she was rising up towards the clouds, being rocked back and forth, perfectly safe but also a little insecure, heady, suspended and waiting, lifted off her feet in mid-air.

Lil exhaled. Life could be interesting like that. She had been alone, managing to get by, happy enough; but now she was riding high, with uncertainty rising around her and it was exciting. Handsome Albert was next to her, his arm around her shoulder, and not so many miles away on a farm in Belgium there was a very pleasant man who'd promised to wait for her, who had told her he cared. Lil had heard often that life's opportunities, and especially men, came along like buses: there was nothing for such a long time, then they'd turn up in twos.

* * *

'Fore!" Maggie yelled. She had no idea why she'd shouted 'Fore!' except that she associated it with thwacking a ball with a club and she was feeling pleased with herself: she'd just beaten everyone at mini-golf, twice. She had discovered a new talent – and she had enjoyed every moment of the game. She adjusted her sunglasses and her hat, raised the golf club over her shoulder and posed, triumphant. She felt like a movie star, like Liz Taylor. And she knew she looked well: she was more relaxed, more self-assured. Having fun suited her much better than watching Brian gaze at the TV. And she was sure, thanks to Lil, that things would be very different when she was back home again at Clover Hill. DJ lifted his club, his face in a mock-morose grimace, and he groaned.

'You've won again, Maggie. You're a golf wizard. You're unbeatable.'

Cassie smiled. 'It's probably time to head back to the hotel.' She gazed at her phone. 'It's almost six and we all agreed we'd all meet up back there before dinner...'

She glanced at Emily, who was staring at her feet, hands in her pockets. 'You must be hungry, Em. You've hardly eaten anything all day.'

Emily forced a grin. 'I'm starving, Cass – you're right. We'll have a nice time tonight. I don't want to be a wet blanket. I ought to cheer up and stop being such a mope.'

Cassie lowered her voice. 'It's hardly surprising, though. You must be worried. You still haven't heard from Alex?'

'Oh, this has happened before a couple of times.' Emily sighed. 'I worry that I don't hear anything for days and days, and then, all of a sudden, he phones and it's fine; he's been out on some sort of manoeuvre or there's been an embargo on communications – there's always a good reason.'

DJ and Jake approached and DJ spoke softly. 'We'll look after you, Em. Don't worry.'

Emily nodded. 'I know I can rely on you two. But please don't say anything to the others. No one else on the bus knows that I haven't heard from Alex in days. I don't like to make a big deal of it.

I'm sure it will all be fine. It's just tough, you know. I'm trying to enjoy myself but all the time there's this nagging feeling, wondering if he's okay.'

Jake's voice was sympathetic. 'We've been neglecting you a bit, sorry. We've been trying to cheer Pat up – he's been down in the dumps too.' He thumped DJ on the arm. 'The course of true love and all that...'

'Never runs smooth,' DJ finished.

Pat was engrossed, staring at his phone and thumbing a message. DJ rolled his eyes and muttered, 'He's missing his Thilde.'

Maggie lifted the golf club hopefully and called, 'Don't we have time for just one more round of golf?'

Everyone else groaned in unison.

Cassie spoke softly. 'We've got to tear you away, Maggie – we're going back to the hotel. But it's free drinks for you tonight – you've beaten us all.'

'Free drinks would be nice.' Maggie was pleased with herself. She glanced around expectantly. 'I wish Lil had seen my moment of glory.'

Jake pointed into the distance. 'She's gone off with Albert.'

DJ nodded. 'And Ken's with his two girlfriends at the gallery.'

Emily grinned. 'Come on, then, boys – let's get back and we'll have a really fun evening. I promise to stop being grumpy.'

'Here's Duncan.' Maggie waved an arm towards two figures slouching towards them. 'And Tommy. I wonder if they won lots of money at the casino.'

'I don't think so.' Cassie shook her head. Both men were walking slowly, heads down. She murmured softly, 'They'll get it in the neck from Angie and Kerry when they are home if they've squandered the family fortunes.'

Pat had finished his text. 'Are we going back to the hotel now?'

'How do, all?' Tommy came to a halt.

'Did you win millions at the casino?' Maggie was hopeful.

'Nah, we both lost far more than we should have,' Tommy grumbled. 'We ought to know when to stop by now, Dunc.'

'But we'll live to fight another day, Tom,' Duncan offered. 'Not like that poor lad in the newspaper.'

'What poor lad?' Pat asked.

'I picked up an English paper in one of the shops.' Tommy waved a *Daily Mirror*. 'I thought I'd find out about all the news back home. It's not all good though. Some poor soldier in the Middle East has been killed...'

Emily stood still as stone. Her face had suddenly lost all its colour. Cassie spoke gently. 'Can I see the paper, Tommy?'

Tommy passed her the newspaper, indicating the headline on the front page, and the map showing the region where the event had happened. Cassie scanned the article as fast as she could, searching for a name and finding none, then she read aloud.

'A British soldier has been killed and three others were injured in the attack on the Taji military camp, north of Baghdad. No names have yet been released.' She glanced at Emily, who was trembling. 'Em?'

Emily whispered, 'That's where Alex is...'

DJ, Pat and Jake had surrounded her, their arms around her.

Cassie spoke softly. 'Em, I think you should ring home.'

29

Cassie was sitting in the hotel bar, a glass of wine on the table next to her notepad. She was attempting to write a poem about November the fifth. She had written several words so far and circled them: bonfire, fireworks, children, Guy Fawkes. She crossed them out one by one and put the end of the pen to her lips, thinking.

She had been in the bar for several hours, and was currently sipping her second glass of Merlot. She'd watched Ken sneak out with Denise at half past six, a protective hand against her back as they'd made for the exit, presumably going out to an early dinner together. She'd waved to DJ and Jake as they'd brought in some takeaway food to share with Pat and Emily. Cassie sighed. Poor Emily had phoned her own parents as well as Alex's, who lived nearby. They were all in the same excruciating position of knowing nothing and fearing the worst. Emily hadn't wanted to go out to dinner and her friends were rallying round with pizza and beer. Tommy and Duncan had taken Maggie for a fish supper. She had been delighted, dressing up in a long flowery dress, glittering jewellery and sunglasses, a wide smile on her face as she'd saun-

tered through the bar between the two men, waving a hand like a
movie star.

Cassie had decided to eat alone after a hotel receptionist
contacted her to say that she'd received a message from Le Papillon,
a Michelin-starred restaurant in a huge local hotel; they'd phoned
by request of a Lilian Ryan to tell her that she was dining there this
evening and would be home late. Cassie had raised an eyebrow and
asked if there was bar food available in the hotel and ordered a
salad for herself. That had been three hours ago; it was half past
nine now.

Cassie had watched Ken creep into the bar with Denise just
before eight o'clock; he'd glanced ruefully in Cassie's direction,
although Denise's gaze had been only for him. Cassie had scribbled
a few lines about fireworks popping and children gasping and
bonfires roaring and crossed it all out. She'd muttered, 'Fatuous
rubbish,' to herself and swallowed a mouthful of wine. Fifteen
minutes later, Ken had reappeared with Sue, who had immediately
noticed Cassie and waved frantically, yelling, 'How good to see you.
Ken and I are going out for a pizza. We thought we'd keep it low-
key tonight, since we're all having a huge meal tomorrow to celebrate together.'

Cassie had wriggled her fingers in greeting. 'Enjoy your pizza,
Sue,' her eyes sliding from Sue's glowing face to Ken's sheepish
expression, wondering how much he had already eaten on his
dinner date with Denise.

Now, over an hour later, she brought the wine glass to her lips,
thinking she might have a coffee before retiring to bed. It occurred
to her that she might write the bonfire poem from Guy Fawkes'
point of view. She thought perhaps he had a story to tell, so she
wrote the title 'Gunpowder Plot' and underlined it. Her phone
buzzed: it was Jamie. She held it to her ear. 'Hi, you.'

'Cassie, just a quick one – I don't want to spoil your evening.'

'You're not spoiling anything – I'm dining alone.'

'Oh?' Jamie's voice was tinged with concern. 'Is everything all right?'

'Fine.' Cassie decided she wouldn't tell Jamie about Emily, how her boyfriend had been incommunicado for nine days now and how everyone feared the worst. Instead she said, 'Lil's out painting the town red. She's dining in a Michelin restaurant and I'm waiting in the bar for her to come back.'

'You're being the parent, then?' Jamie sounded amused.

Cassie nodded, although she then realised Jamie wouldn't be able to see her. She exhaled. 'I don't mind. I want her to enjoy her holiday.'

'But you should be enjoying yourself too, Cass.'

'I am.' She sat upright, immediately enthusiastic. 'And I'll be home soon. Maybe you and I can go somewhere...?'

'I've been thinking about this bonfire tour. I have contacted a couple more venues who seem genuinely interested in booking you and there are several others who'll get on board. I think we might be able to organise at least seven nights in London, maybe more.'

Cassie nodded. 'That would be good.'

'We'll finalise it when you're back.'

'Perhaps we can invite some guests along to perform.' Cassie was full of enthusiasm now. 'I could ask Piet, the man I met in Amsterdam...'

'You met someone in Amsterdam?' Jamie's voice was suddenly filled with anxiety.

Cassie hesitated for a moment too long. 'I mentioned him to you. He's a musician. We had dinner. We wrote a song together – two songs. I told you...'

'I didn't realise you'd had dinner.' Jamie's tone was hushed now.

'There was nothing much to tell.' Cassie tried a different angle, determined to sound positive. 'Perhaps you and I could go to

Amsterdam later this year, Jamie. You'd like Piet – he'd like you too. He's very creative.'

'That's good.' Jamie's voice was soft. 'I'm glad you're having such a great time, Cass.'

'Oh, I am.'

There was a pause, then Jamie's voice was in her earpiece; he was clearly attempting to sound more cheerful and unconcerned. 'Well, I just wanted to tell you that we could put a good tour together. I hope I didn't disturb—'

'No, of course not – it's good to hear from you...' Cassie thought about adding that she was looking forward to seeing him, but he was speaking again hurriedly.

'Okay, I will see you soon – all's fine here. I've got a physio-therapy appointment tomorrow and I'll probably rest afterwards.'

'I hope it goes well, Jamie; please don't – oh!' Cassie noticed two familiar figures walking into the bar, arm in arm, their heads close together. She called, 'Lil. Over here.'

'I'll talk to you soon, Cassie. Bye.' Jamie's voice was low, then the phone clicked. Cassie sighed and placed it on the table; it was too late now to tell him that she was missing him. Lil and Albert were approaching, Lil hugging a giant black and white stuffed toy. Cassie stood up, throwing her arms out for an embrace. 'Where have you been, you dirty stop-out?'

Lil turned to Albert. 'Could you get us all a drink?' She thrust a hand into her handbag and brought out her purse, shoving it in Albert's hand. 'You paid for dinner so this is on me. I'd like a white wine and Cassie will have a red one and buy whatever you want for yourself, my dear.'

Albert's gaze was tender; his fingers folded around the purse and he moved off towards the bar on his mission. Lil sat down, pushing the panda in the seat next to her.

'We ate at the Papillon. It means butterfly. Cassie, it was so posh and so expensive and so nice. But I told them that Albie and I were celebrities.'

Cassie reached out and grabbed Lil's fingers, taking them in her cupped hands. 'What did you eat?'

'Oh, the menu was all in French but the waiter was ever so nice – he asked us what we liked and he suggested things. I had white fish in a sauce, with so much butter in the sauce that Keith at the Kaff would have had a heart attack on the spot. Oh, and the puddings! I had a creamy pudding on a square plate with all sorts of sauce and squiggles on it, and, the wine, Cassie. I've never had wine like it. We had a bottle of white wine and it was like drinking a mixture of sunshine and honey.'

'You had a good time, Lil.'

'I wish you'd been there. But we didn't book – we turned up and when I said we were celebs, they offered us the best table. We'd been to the fairground and we were hungry so we thought we'd treat ourselves.' She waved a hand towards the panda. 'Albie won this for me on the shooting gallery and we went on the Ferris wheel...'

Cassie thought about asking her mother about Herman, wondering if she'd forgotten all about him, given this sudden new friendship with Albert, but Albert had just arrived at the table, holding a small tray of drinks: two glasses of wine and a pint of beer. Cassie noticed his hands trembling beneath the weight of the load, so she leaped up, taking the tray from him. Albert sat down next to Lil, placing the panda gently on his knee as if it were a child. Lil reached over and took his hand. 'We've had such a wonderful time, haven't we?'

Albert nodded, cupping a hand to his ear. 'Oh, we've enjoyed ourselves.'

Cassie reached for her glass and held it up. 'To all the good times to come. To more fun holidays.'

As they clinked their glasses together, Cassie saw Lil's eyes shining with happiness. Albert's lips curved in a wide smile. Cassie recalled Pat's sad face, Emily's anguished eyes, Jamie's troubled tone when she'd mentioned having had dinner with Piet. Cassie sighed, aware that there was little she could do to soothe the sad feelings of so many people she cared about, and she wished that, somehow, everything could magically be made all right.

* * *

The next morning, the sky was overcast, heavy clouds hanging low; light rain spattered the grimy windows of the minibus. Ten people were huddled in different seats, having forsaken their previous arrangement. Tommy was trying to work out who had not yet arrived, the itinerary clutched in his hand. Lil was sitting closer to the back seat next to Albert, sharing chocolates, her novel on her knee. In front of her, Maggie was sitting next to Duncan, already falling asleep, her head on his shoulder. Tommy frowned.

'Ken's missing.'

Sue and Denise were sitting alone on opposite ends of the aisle, an empty seat next to each of them, their hands resting lightly on the fabric, saving the space. Denise piped up, 'Ken didn't come down to breakfast.'

'I knocked on his door early this morning, my dear, but he didn't answer,' Sue added, adjusting the flowing scarf she wore.

DJ suggested, 'He's probably tired.'

Jake agreed. 'This holiday seems to have really taken it out of him.'

Then Sue and Denise chimed together, 'Here he is,' and both patted the seat next to them. Ken clambered onto the bus, his face haggard and his eyes tired, collapsing next to Sue. Denise's eyes were like daggers.

Tommy's frown deepened. 'So, who else isn't here? There's still an empty seat.'

Emily's voice called from the back seat. 'Pat's missing, Tommy.' She clutched the copy of *Birdsong* in front of her, sunglasses hiding her sad eyes.

Cassie, in the front seat next to Tommy, gazed around the bus. 'Has anyone seen Pat this morning?'

'He had his own room.' Jake shrugged. 'We saw him about half an hour ago at breakfast, eating bread and cheese. He was a bit quiet.'

'We shared pizza last night but he didn't drink much – he seemed quite quiet then too. He didn't seem like himself at breakfast, either.' DJ was perplexed. 'I hope he's all right.'

Tommy glanced towards the hotel entrance. 'Here he comes.'

Pat placed his luggage on the ground before he scrambled on the bus. He turned to Tommy and spoke quietly. 'Tom, can I have a word?'

DJ yelled from the back, 'Come on, Pat. You're keeping us waiting.'

Pat whispered to Tommy, leaning towards the driver's seat, then he turned around slowly to gaze at the rest of the passengers, staring at each pair of eyes. It took him a while to speak, then he muttered, 'I'm not coming.'

Jake's voice was a raucous bawl. 'What do you mean, you're not coming?'

DJ called out, 'Get your backside down here, Pat Stott – you're holding the bus up.'

'I'm not coming back with you.' Pat's cheeks were pink; his ears glowed. 'I've decided.'

Cassie put a gentle hand on his shoulder. 'Do you need a lift to the station to catch a train to Boom?'

'I've called a taxi – well, the hotel did it for me. It'll be here in ten minutes.'

'I don't get it.' DJ's face was anxious. 'Why aren't you coming with us?'

Pat pushed his hands into his jeans pockets and took them out again. 'I'm getting a train to Ghent, then I'll change and get one to Boom. Thilde will meet me.'

'But why? Why aren't you coming home?' Jake frowned.

Pat scratched his head. 'I want to stay here.'

'Have you spoken to your dad, Pat?' Emily's voice was hushed.

Pat nodded. 'I talked to him last night on the phone. He wasn't pleased. He needs me for work – we have jobs booked next week, chippy work, a kitchen to install. He wasn't happy at all. But I told him why. I said I had to go to see her. I think I might stay there if I can.'

Duncan was puzzled. 'But how will you manage? You can't speak Flemish or French...'

'I can.' Pat beamed. 'Cassie taught me some words. *Bière, bier, pintje.* I'll get by.'

Suddenly, DJ, Jake and Emily rose from their seats in unison, rushing to the front of the bus and hugging Pat in a group squeeze, their heads down.

DJ murmured, 'Good luck, mate.'

Jake added, 'Don't come back if you don't want to.'

Emily agreed. 'Perhaps you can work on the farm there.'

'That's what Thilde said,' Pat spluttered. He lifted his head and his eyes shone with tears. He clutched his three friends hard in his arms and gulped back a sob. 'Text me, Jake, DJ, won't you?' He turned to Emily. 'I hope you hear something from Alex soon – that it's all okay.'

They hugged for a moment longer, then Pat wriggled away and down the steps, towards his luggage, then he was standing in the road, gazing up at the passengers through mud-splashed glass. Rain was spattering the ground. Cassie closed the door and Tommy started the engine as Pat mouthed something that looked like, 'See you all – good luck,' and the minibus slowly pulled away. Through the back window, Pat was still waving an arm, his face creased in a sad but determined smile.

30

The passengers were lost in their own thoughts as the minibus sloshed through muddy puddles on the road. Tommy called over his shoulder, his voice full of enthusiasm, 'We'll be in Honfleur in a little over two hours.' When no one replied, he tried again. 'It's a lovely place, the prettiest port on the coast. There's lots to do – there's a beach, nice architecture, shopping, a garden of personalities with busts of famous people.'

He waited for a response but still none came. He offered his parting shot. 'Deauville, a few miles away from Honfleur, has a massive racecourse – we could all go and bet on a few horses.'

He was met with silence. Duncan was asleep, his head on Maggie's shoulder; she was snoring softly. DJ was slumped across Jake's knee, his seat belt at full stretch; they were both dozing, sketch pads in their arms. Emily and Lil were reading; Albert was munching a bar of chocolate. Ken was leaning away from Sue, who was frowning and applying lipstick, gazing into a small mirror in her hand. Denise was engrossed in the final chapter of Lil's novel, *Fifty Shades of Hay*. Tommy turned to Cassie, but she was busy scribbling ideas for a poem that had just popped into her head. He turned the radio on and listened to a jangling pop tune.

At twelve-thirty, Tommy pulled into the car park of the Hotel Myrtille, a pretty, white-fronted building with hanging baskets crammed with red flowers on each side of the door. There was a soft rustling behind him in the bus: people waking, stretching, putting things in bags; he was suddenly filled with optimism. 'Right, here we are. I booked us all a light lunch in the hotel for one o'clock.'

Denise's voice came clear and strong from behind him. 'Oh, I don't know that I want much lunch. We have a big meal organised for this evening.'

Sue fiddled with her scarf. 'Well, I'm hungry. I've no idea why, but my appetite has been really huge during this holiday.' She beamed at Ken.

'I'm careful with my figure, *Syoo*.' Denise wrinkled her nose. 'Some people might not care if they pile on the pounds, but I've always been fastidious.' She smiled in Ken's direction. Ken had turned to stare out of the window and was muttering something to himself about the hotel being clean and well cared for.

Sue gave a triumphant cry. 'I never put on weight, my dear. I play tennis and keep myself fit...' She tilted her chin towards Ken. 'I love all forms of exercise.'

DJ coughed loudly from the back seat. Tommy tried again, twisting around and waving his arms towards the passengers.

'So, we'll have lunch and then we're at leisure until this evening. The celebration meal has been booked at the Table des Fleurs. It's a very nice place – and it's all free.'

'It's hardly free, Tommy.' Sue was gloating. 'It's courtesy of three of us and the tennis club.'

'It will be wonderful,' Denise insisted. 'Ken and I and, of course, you as hosts.'

'I chose the place because they do a wonderful *poisson sauvage au beurre noisette,*' Ken purred. 'I'm definitely having that with a glass of chilled Chablis.'

Sue shook her head. 'The problem with eating fish is that it stays on the breath afterwards, Ken.'

'I'll make sure I have the fish too.' Denise wriggled coyly in her seat. Sue gave her a hard stare and Ken returned his gaze to the window.

'I like the Calvados apple brandy they have in this area,' Maggie piped. 'I'm taking a bottle or two back home for myself. Brian's not having any, though. I've already got his present – it's in my hand-bag.' She raised an eyebrow mischievously. 'Would anyone like to know what I've got him from Amsterdam?'

'A posing pouch?' Jake bawled.

'Is it black lacy underwear, Maggie?' DJ yelled.

'A nice bottle of wine?' Emily asked tactfully.

'No, it's something he'll really appreciate,' Maggie gloated.

'Shall we get off the bus now, everyone?' Tommy asked quickly and Cassie put a hand to her mouth to cover her smile, remembering how she'd assisted him in the lingerie shop to buy the right size for Angie. Cassie had picked out the perfect set, while Tommy stood behind her, his face crimson, euros folded in his palm.

After lunch, Lil, Cassie, Albert and Maggie wandered into the Jardin des Personnalités. The rain had stopped but the ground was soggy underfoot; their shoes quickly coated with mud. Beyond the clusters of flowers, between the huddling rails, the grey sea stretched for miles. Albert pushed an arm through Lil's and nodded his head towards the ocean. 'Look, Lil – we can see home from here.'

Cassie took Maggie's elbow and guided her towards an

alabaster bust of a man with an old, sad face, raised on a pedestal, surrounded by a bush of white roses. 'Do you know who this is, Maggie?'

'Is he French?'

'He is.'

'Then I've no idea...' Maggie shook her head. 'Maurice Chevalier?' She tried again. 'De Gaulle?' Her final attempt. 'Napoleon?'

'It's Charles Baudelaire.' Maggie shrugged. 'He's a poet.' From the corner of her eye, Cassie noticed Lil and Albert wandering towards the exit. 'Would you take a photo of me standing next to him? A minor poet next to a famous one?' She smiled at her own joke.

Maggie took Cassie's phone and turned it upside down. 'What do I press?'

Cassie put a gentle hand on Maggie's. 'That button there – just touch it lightly with your finger. Take a couple.'

Cassie stood next to the bust of Baudelaire and posed, a hand on her hip, her body tilted to one side, a hand out as if performing. With her hair blowing beneath the blue paisley scarf wrapped around her head, long jewelled earrings waving in the sea breeze, she was as flamboyant as the poet next to her. Maggie took a few photos. Suddenly she yelled in surprise, as if she had been stung. 'Ahh, Cassie – something's happening with your phone – it's shaking in my hand – here, quick!'

A panicking Maggie tossed the buzzing phone to Cassie, who caught it and held it to her ear. She put a thumb up to Maggie to signal that she was taking a call.

'Hi, Jamie – I wasn't expecting to hear from you. How are you?'

Jamie's soft voice came back, muffled by the breeze and the rushing waves. 'I'm okay. How's France?'

'I'll be home soon. Oh, and I've started writing my Guy Fawkes poem from his viewpoint. It might be a good one.'

Jamie sighed, his voice a little anxious. 'That's great, Cassie. I wouldn't have called you, but you've just had a visitor.'

'A visitor?' Cassie's thoughts filled with the possibility of Piet turning up at her house, luggage and guitar in his hand. She frowned; she didn't recall giving him her address. 'Anyone we know?' She laughed. 'A tax inspector? Amazon?' Jamie didn't return her laughter.

'A man called David. He was American. He said he really needed to see you and that it was personal, important.'

'Really?' Cassie's eyebrows moved towards her hair. 'I don't know anyone called David.'

'He seemed very keen to talk to you, Cass. I told him you were away – I didn't say where you were. He said he'd call back in a couple of days.'

'Did he say what he wanted?' Cassie was intrigued.

'He didn't want to talk to me – he said he wanted to talk to you personally.' Jamie sounded anxious. 'I've no idea what about.'

'It's a big mystery, then,' Cassie replied.

'He was on holiday from the States – that was all he said. He was in his late fifties or sixties, dark hair, blue eyes, spectacles, slim, tanned.'

'Sounds interesting,' Cassie quipped and instinctively she thought Jamie might be hurt by her remark so she added, 'But he's not important. We'll sort it all out when I'm back. How are you, Jamie? Do you miss me?'

'More than you'd know. I just thought you'd be able to throw some light on the mystery visitor...'

'Not really.' Cassie decided to change the subject. 'So, what are you up to today?'

'Not much – sitting in the living room with earphones on. I was listening to some music – Béla Bartók, Satie.'

'Oh, Erik Satie's around here somewhere too,' Cassie observed.

'I'm in a garden with lots of busts of famous people – we haven't come across Satie yet.'

'It's chilly here, in the breeze.' Maggie shuffled her feet. 'Where's Lil? Shall I go and get us an ice cream?'

Cassie nodded, and then whispered in the phone. 'I'd better go, Jamie – don't worry about this visitor – we'll sort it all out when I'm home. I'll see you soon.'

'Yes, soon, Cassie.'

'Lots of hugs,' Cassie added, and he was gone. She turned brightly to Maggie. 'Shall we go and get that ice cream?'

Maggie beamed and they made their way towards the exit, Maggie in sunglasses, craning her neck to search for Lil. Cassie pushed her hands into her jeans pockets and was thoughtful. The American man called David was a mystery. She wondered if he was someone she'd met when she worked abroad, and simply forgotten about. It occurred to her that the only American she knew of was her father, Frankie Chapman. She wondered if that could be the link. For a moment, her head was buzzing with thoughts about who the visitor could be, then she noticed her mother and Albert in the distance eating ice-cream cones, and she waved and shouted, pushing thoughts of the unknown David to the back of her mind.

* * *

Lil, Maggie and Cassie were in the room they shared, deciding what to wear for the celebratory evening dinner. The restaurant was just a short walk from their hotel; Tommy had asked Ken to choose somewhere close by so that they could all have a few drinks and walk back to the hotel. Maggie was keen to impress. She held up a long dress in cobalt blue.

'What do you think? Is it the Liz Taylor look? I brought this for a special occasion and tonight seems exactly the right time to wear it.'

Cassie gazed at the dress with interest. 'Beautiful colour – it will match your eyes, Maggie.'

'I want to stun tonight. Just like I intend to stun Brian when I get home.' Maggie beamed, flattered. 'I'm practising being irresistible. What are you wearing, Lil?'

'I don't know – I can't decide.' Lil sat down on the end of the bed, sinking into the softness of the mattress. 'I feel like the girl who hasn't got a thing to wear.'

Cassie sat next to her mother, draping an arm around her. 'Can I lend you something?'

'Oh, your clothes will swamp me.' Lil pulled a face. 'I'm all skin and bone now.'

Cassie surveyed her thoughtfully. Lil's mouth was turned down; her shoulders were drooping. Cassie understood. Lil wanted to make an impression this evening; she wanted to shine and now, as she sat on the edge of the bed, forlorn, her confidence was ebbing away. Cassie brightened – she had an idea. She rubbed her hands together. 'Let's all go as the French flag.'

'That's barmy, Cass.' Lil was frowning. 'I haven't got a flag...'

'No, I mean that Maggie has a beautiful blue dress. I have a white silk trouser suit thing, which I can glam up. And then there's this red dress...'

Cassie whisked a crimson dress from the wardrobe; it was long, sweeping, made of crushed velvet.

'I'll look like an artery.' Lil's mood had sunk completely.

'You'll look hot,' Maggie suggested.

'No – imagine, a nice belt, some red dangly jewellery – you'll be fabulous.' Cassie waved the dress as if she were luring a bull. 'Come on – you won't know if you don't try it on...'

'She's right.' Maggie rubbed her hands together. 'We'll make an entrance like film stars, the three of us, glamorous in red, white and blue.'

Lil shrugged. The bait had been set. She smiled slowly. 'All right, give it here and let's try it on. We'll all go to the dinner dressed as the Marseillaise.'

Cassie smiled. 'You mean the Tricolore, Lil, but never mind. Come on, girls, let's get ready – tonight we're going to knock 'em dead.'

31

The group had been given the upstairs room of the Table des Fleurs all to themselves. Ken was pleased with his choice: the room was beautiful, with white walls and low-hanging chandeliers. There were candles flickering on the round table, which was covered with a damask cloth scattered with rose petals, and was set for thirteen people, although there would only be twelve diners. Pat had arrived in Boom and, according to DJ, he was reunited with his Thilde and had sent everyone his best wishes for the evening.

A vast window revealed a charming view of the sea, a skeletal ship in the bay, the sun hovering above a stretch of golden water. The diners took their places, Ken sitting down first and Sue and Denise moving to either side of him. Ken was dapper in a grey suit; Sue's long, translucent pink dress had a plunging neckline. Denise had chosen a short little black number, dark stockings and high heels. Everyone had dressed in their best clothes, the men in smart suits and the women in their most glamorous attire. Maggie was stunning in the cobalt-blue dress and sparkly earrings. Cassie wore the fitted silk trouser suit, the white jacket buttoned, a huge silver chain with a heart at her throat, and Lil stole the show in her belted crimson velvet dress and a black feathered fascinator. With Cassie on one side and Albert, in a black suit and red dicky bow, on the other, sitting at a table with bowls piled with soft bread rolls, wine and silver service, Lil felt like royalty.

Tommy, in a crumpled jacket, opened proceedings by waving at the waiter, who brought in glasses of Kir Royale for each guest, then he stood up, gave a formal little cough and said, 'Right. Good evening, everybody. I'd like to thank the tennis club members, Ken, Sue and Denise, for organising tonight and treating us to this lovely celebration meal in such a wonderful setting. We have had a great holiday, I'm sure you'll all agree, and this will be a perfect evening.' He raised his glass. 'To us all – to our successful holiday.'

Twelve people raised their glasses in the toast. Cassie glanced at Emily, beautiful in a lacy vest top and shiny black trousers. She was trying to smile, sitting between DJ and Jake, laughing at their jokes, then her face became sombre again. Cassie sighed; there was clearly still no news about Alex.

The food arrived, efficient waiters placing plates on the table: soup or pâté, followed by a choice of white fish, pigeon, or mush-room stroganoff, then desserts: sweet cherry clafoutis, champagne sorbet, Tarte Tatin, double-chocolate soufflé, and finally cheese, biscuits and coffee. The conversation at the table became louder and more excitable with each course. Lil was forcing huge spoon-fuls of pudding into Albert's mouth and he was smiling and hand-some, enjoying the attention, cupping a hand to his ear. Lil turned to Cassie. 'Albie can't hear in these noisy groups. It's a shame. It's best when there's just me and him.'

Cassie raised an eyebrow. 'Maybe when we're back home, we could take him for a hearing test and get an aid fitted.'

Lil nodded. 'That would be good.' She grasped Albert's hand in a gesture of affection. 'You'd like that, wouldn't you?'

Albert nodded enthusiastically although Lil thought he probably had no idea what she'd said to him, but his complicity was a gesture of pure trust. Lil kissed his cheek and offered him more soufflé.

Maggie waved a hand through her freshly washed hair. 'I didn't tell you all – I've heard from Brian.'

'He's phoned you?' Lil was suddenly interested.

'He texted me.' Maggie brandished her phone.

'How many times have you texted him since you've been on this holiday, Maggie?' Lil frowned. 'And he's just got around to replying now?'

Maggie protested. 'He wrote me a beautiful text. It was romantic.'

'Brian's being romantic?' Lil raised an eyebrow. 'That's really good news. I hope he's going to treat you like a goddess now.'

'Oh, everything is going to be so much better.' Maggie turned to Cassie. 'Read what he put, what he texted to me. Real words of poetry.'

Lil squeezed Maggie's hand in support as Cassie took the phone and began to read.

'He begins "Dearest Maggie…"'

'Dearest – that's a good start,' Lil agreed.

Cassie continued. '"I miss you very much. Come home from Germany soon. I'll be waiting for you with the kettle on. Love, Brian."'

'Germany!' Lil frowned. 'He's not very good at Geography. But really, Maggie – this is perfect. Going away on holiday and leaving him behind was such a good move. He's started to appreciate the wonderful woman that you are.'

Cassie's voice was serious. 'I think that's really lovely.'

'I thought so too.' Maggie folded her arms. 'He hasn't really ever texted me before and he hasn't made me a cup of tea in years.'

'Well, let's hope he's a changed man.' Lil put a thumb up in triumph. 'When you get home, he'll be on his knees with a red rose between his teeth... or his buttocks.'

'I hope so...' Maggie sighed. 'I've bought him a present too. I hoped he'd start to notice me again when I came away on holiday. And I'll make sure he does.' She reached for her wine and drained half a glass, holding it out to Cassie to refill. 'I don't think he's said anything romantic since we moved to Clover Hill...'

'Maggie, this is the turning point.' Lil squeezed her hand again. 'When you're back at Clover Hill, Brian has to accept that there are new rules and he must promise to change. He can't slip back into bad habits.'

'I know.' Maggie thumped the table defiantly. 'I'm a new woman now, with new needs and expectations.' She met Lil's glance anxiously. 'Will you help me to stay strong when we get back, Lil?'

'Of course I will. And so will Cassie.' Lil smiled. 'That's what friends are for.'

'Friends.' Tommy was on his feet, clanking a spoon against a wine glass. 'My friends. I want to say a few words.'

Jake, all in black, and DJ, lean in a smart suit, groaned in mock-horror. Tommy's face was an exaggeration of seriousness and responsibility. 'Friends, it falls to me, as the organiser of this holiday, to do several things. Firstly, to say thank you to Ken and Sue and Denise...'

Sue patted Ken's hand; Ken looked uncomfortable. Denise was cross; the order of names had offended her. Tommy continued, oblivious. '... for hosting this wonderful meal.'

Duncan was on his feet. 'Friends, we won't forget this holiday. Some of us started as strangers and we all got to know each other so much better. We have had good times. We had a football match – and lost. We've been to many and various places. There have been a few ups and downs...'

DJ called out, 'Pat fell in love and went back to Boom.'

Jake yelled, 'You ran into that woman's car before we even left the car park, Tommy.'

'Yes, well...' Duncan gazed around him. 'There have been some incidents, but it's been a really lovely time. We've all got to know each other so well.'

Denise placed a hand over Ken's; Sue, at exactly the same time, grasped his other hand. Ken shuffled in his seat. Tommy turned to Cassie. 'Come on, Cass – we need a song.'

Cassie rolled her eyes. Tommy, who had drunk several glasses of wine already, showed her his most earnest expression. 'Please, Cass – a song about friendship. You can do it.'

'You want me to make up a song on the spot, just like that? I haven't brought any instruments.' She gaped. 'Honestly, Tom—'

'Please. Pretty please.' Tommy clasped his hands together. 'A song about friendship? Just for us? For tonight?'

DJ and Jake chorused, 'Friend-ship, friend-ship,' their fists rhythmically pounding the table.

Cassie sighed, muttering, 'I'd have preferred some advance notice,' then she smiled good-naturedly and stood up, sweeping her gaze around the table, already in performance mode.

'Right, if I've got to do a song extempore, then you all have to learn the chorus first and sing it with me later.' She scratched her head, thought for a moment and then launched into a cheerful song.

> *There is nothing else like friendship*
> *An inspiration, that's friendship,*
> *Unite the nation with friendship,*
> *We'll always be good friends.*

Hands clapped in applause, deafening cheering, then Cassie

yelled, 'Okay– you have the tune now. I'll do the verse and you can all follow me in the chorus. All right?'

Each face at the table shone with happiness; a jolly clapping accompanied Cassie as she sang:

> *Although love may often come and go*
> *Friends are there when we feel low*
> *We're best of friends so let it show*
> *We'll always be good friends.*
> *Whatever life may send our way*
> *However hard the working day*
> *However far we all may stray*
> *We'll always be good friends.*

Cassie hollered, 'Now the chorus – it's your turn.'

Every voice rose, each person swaying from side to side in unison, as hands were joined around the table.

> *There is nothing else like friendship*
> *An inspiration, that's friendship,*
> *Unite the nation with friendship,*
> *We'll always be good friends.*

A huge cheer exploded, echoing around the room. Faces were glowing and the room was full of laughter. Maggie was suddenly emotional, wiping away a tear; Lil and Albert kissed; DJ and Jake thumped each other's arm. Sue was in awe as she whispered to Ken, 'Did she really just make that up on the spot?'

Tommy rose to his feet. 'That was wonderful, Cassie. It hit just the right note.' He guffawed at his own joke. 'And, on a serious note, I'd like to thank everyone for such a wonderful time and also express our huge thanks once again to Ken and Sue and Denise, who treated us to this wonderful meal.'

Ecstatic applause rang out, along with more cheering. Maggie, her handkerchief still in her hand, was smiling and clapping. Only Denise seemed sombre; as she rose to stand up, she was hesitant, a little apprehensive. 'I have something I'd like to say.'

Someone shuffled their feet; someone coughed, then the room was silent. Denise glanced in Ken's direction and then began to address everyone else. 'I know that now may not be the best time, but then, when is, with these things?'

She laughed, too high and too loud, the effect of nervousness and two large glasses of wine. The expressions around the table were puzzled. She tried again.

'We were all talking about friendship – singing about it together...' Denise glanced warmly at Cassie. 'And we've all become close on this trip – people I wasn't so sure about at first, I have come to admire and – to count as friends.'

Denise held up her glass and smiled in Cassie's direction, then she took a breath. 'However, it has to be said – some of us have become very close indeed.'

She gazed at Ken, who was wiping perspiration from his brow, his shoulders hunched uneasily. Denise continued. 'As I was saying, *very* close. I wasn't looking for love, on this holiday.' She tittered softly, then became serious. 'I've been let down badly, as some of you may know – my ex-husband cheated on me with another woman –and, in truth, it's made me a little cynical, a little dour, in fact. But someone has come along in my life since we came away on this holiday and changed all that forever.'

Sue was frowning deeply; her mouth had turned downwards. Ken had blanched to the colour of the tablecloth.

'Ken,' Denise cooed. 'My own darling Ken. Thank you for making me so happy, for finding me, for loving me, for saving me.'

Ken squeezed his eyes shut. Sue rose to her feet slowly to face Denise. For a moment, she couldn't speak, then she thundered, 'What on earth are you talking about?'

'Ken.' Denise was ecstatic. 'He and I are lovers.'

'What did you say?' For a moment Sue's mouth hung open. Her eyes were missiles, forcing Denise to blink. 'What did you just say?'

'Ken and I are—'

'I heard what you said.' Sue bared her teeth. 'But that's complete rubbish. Ken and *I* are lovers.'

Denise blinked again, swished her hair in a gesture of defiance, then she retorted, 'You can't be. We've been lovers since Zandvoort.'

'Oh, well, that's easily resolved.' Sue huffed and folded her arms. 'Ken and I first made love in Boom. Undoubtedly, I have the earlier claim, Denise.'

'I don't think so, *Syoo*,' Denise retorted. 'Since then, he's obviously changed his mind.'

Ken slumped over the table, his head on his arms, as Sue and Denise squared up to each other on either side of him, their cheeks scarlet. For a moment, it seemed that they were going to hit each other. In the moment's silence when everyone was watching, gaping in disbelief, suppressing the beginnings of a smile, Lil reached out to a basket where soft bread rolls were piled. She took one in her fingers, holding it like a cricket ball. Her hand flew behind her head and she launched the roll towards Ken, missing him completely, yelling, 'Time to change up the mood – time for a bun fight!' The roll bounced onto the table.

Jake grabbed a roll and hurled it, shouting, 'Buns away!'

DJ threw a hunk of bread through the air, screaming, 'Rock and roll!'

Maggie caught a flying piece of bread in her palm; she lobbed it towards Duncan, yelling, 'Fore!'

As Sue and Denise began to shriek insults at each other, many pairs of hands reached across to bread baskets and rolls began to soar into the air, hurled at anyone who was in the way, as chaos descended. Screams of joy, laughter and raucous howling accompanied each fling. Suddenly Emily rose from the table and rushed out of the room.

Cassie glanced at Lil, who was having the time of her life, her face contorted in mischief as she caught flying bread in the air with one hand and flung it back to the other side of the table. Cassie moved quickly from her seat and across the room, through the open door.

She found Emily leaning against a wall in the hallway, pallid, clutching a mobile phone in her hand, breathing deeply. Cassie watched her for a moment, then grabbed her arm. 'Emily. Are you okay? What's happened?'

Emily turned slowly, tears in her eyes, and held up the phone. 'It was a call from the camp near Baghdad.'

For a moment Emily couldn't speak. Cassie squeezed her shoulder. Time stood still. Then Emily inhaled and collapsed into Cassie's arms, sobbing uncontrollably. She gulped another desperate breath, raised her head and muttered, 'It's Alex. He's... he's all right.'

32

The next morning, at quarter to twelve, Cassie lay on the bed in her hotel room, her eyes closed, thinking. Lil was on hers, in the same position, doing the same thing. On the third bed, Maggie had fallen asleep. Three hours ago, breakfast had been almost funereal; Ken had not been there, neither had Sue, Denise or Duncan. Albert had been the most talkative person at the table, passing plates of bread, asking, 'Anyone for a roll?' and bursting into wicked laughter.

Lil and Maggie hadn't felt particularly hungry; they'd drunk black coffee, both lost in their own thoughts. Tommy, DJ and Jake had eaten everything they could find: yogurt, cheese, bread, jam. Emily had been serene and smiling, sipping tea: Alex was safe and well, although she'd explained sadly that his troop had been involved in the skirmish that had been reported in the newspaper and the details about what had happened would emerge later.

Cassie opened her eyes and sighed, without moving her position, her head resting on two thick pillows. She muttered, 'Are you awake, Lil?'

Lil murmured softly, 'I'm resting. Worn out. Last night was – what's the modern word DJ and Jake use? Epic.'

'It was a memorable evening. It's a good job we cleaned up the mess. By the time the manager came in to close up, the place was as pristine as when we first arrived.'

'The bun fight was good fun,' Lil murmured, smiling. 'It's a shame this holiday's ending. Mind you, I felt so sorry for Sue and Denise. It was an awful way to find out that you're being two-timed.'

'There may be some fallout on the bus today,' Cassie observed. 'It's not all over yet.'

Lil nodded. 'Poor Sue and Denise. Ken turned out to be a bit of a cheat, stringing them both along like that.'

'I'm not so sure.' Cassie was thoughtful. 'Things can often be more complex than they appear on the surface. All three of them are lonely. In situations like this, it's usually just all about human beings trying hard but getting it a bit wrong.'

'Yes, you're probably right, love,' Lil agreed, and began to think about Herman and Albert and whether she would have a proper romance with one of them, neither of them, or even both. There was a case for each option, she thought. Lil was sad for a moment; she had no real experience in these matters to help her. Perhaps her feelings would change when her life returned to normal back in Clover Hill. Maybe she would ask Cassie what she thought about it all.

But Cassie was deep in her own thoughts, recalling her conversation with Jamie on the phone yesterday. Who was the mysterious David who had come to visit her? Was someone from her past about to rear their head? Cassie would have to sort it all out when she returned to Salterley but for now it was an enigma, an itch she couldn't help but scratch. She was shaken from her thoughts by a sharp knock on the door.

Lil called out, 'Come in,' but her voice was too feeble to carry so Cassie leaped up and opened the door. She was surprised to see two women standing together, both holding out cardboard cups of coffee.

'Sue, Denise. I didn't expect to see you,' Cassie murmured.

Denise seemed anxious. 'Hello, Cassie – may we come in?'

Cassie nodded and stood back, ushering them inside the room.

Lil greeted them warmly. 'Well, I didn't expect to see you two here together. I hope we're not going to have Catwoman versus Wonder Woman round two. Come in. How are you both?'

Maggie sat up slowly, blinking. 'Denise, Sue – are you all right? Where's Ken?'

Sue handed a cardboard coffee cup to Cassie and Denise passed one each to Maggie and Lil. Sue shrugged awkwardly. 'We've come to apologise...'

'For ruining your evening,' Denise completed her sentence. 'And for being a complete cow to you in Belgium, Cassie.'

'Oh, you didn't ruin the evening. Quite the opposite.' Lil beamed. 'Although I'm glad to see you're both friends now. I was worried...'

Maggie was puzzled. 'I thought you'd hate each other – given that you've both been having an affair with the same man.'

Sue and Denise glanced at each other uneasily. Cassie put a hand on Denise's shoulder. 'Sit down for a moment. Thanks for the coffee.' She indicated her bed. 'How can we help?'

Sue sank onto the soft mattress and rubbed a hand over her face. 'Denise and I have been talking.'

'You might even say we've been comparing notes,' Denise added, flopping down next to Sue.

'We went for breakfast together in town this morning...'

'So that we could talk things over, woman to woman We had a lot to discuss, didn't we, *Syoo*?'

Sue nodded. 'We've decided – we come first and women have to stick together. Men are nothing but trouble, my dear. Ken's a player and he played us both off against each other. But he won't get away with it.'

'My ex was a scumbag.' Denise seemed rather pleased with herself. 'And Ken's no better than he was. We have learned a valuable lesson. *Syoo* and I are now the best of friends.'

'I'm glad.' Cassie sipped her coffee. 'Have either of you spoken to Ken about this?'

'Oh, no, we wouldn't do that.' Denise's lips clamped together firmly.

Sue agreed. 'We wouldn't give him the time of day again, to be honest.'

'Or the time of night?' Lil asked with a smile.

'He's let you both down.' Maggie frowned. 'I expect he's really embarrassed.'

Sue shrugged. 'I've no idea how he feels. And I honestly don't care.'

'*Syoo* and I have decided to sit together on the bus,' Denise said. 'And we'll ignore him.'

'I see.' Cassie was thoughtful.

'So, we wanted to apologise, Cassie. And to say how good your entertainment was last night, my dear.'

'Thanks, Sue.'

'We've apologised to everyone else already – and bought them all coffee,' Denise explained.

'So, we'll be leaving the hotel at half one – we have to be at the ferry port around three thirty.' Cassie made a soft humming sound. 'Is anyone going to speak to Ken about this before we go, to clear the air? It might be awkward on the bus...'

'I don't care about Ken at all,' Sue snapped. 'I hope he does feel awkward.'

'I despise him now, after what he's done to us,' Denise added.

Cassie exhaled slowly. 'I'll go and see him, shall I? I expect he's in his room, reading. I'll tell him that you two would like some space and I'll sit next to him on the bus – so that he doesn't feel totally ostracised.'

'He doesn't deserve anyone to be so nice to him after he's been a randy cheat,' Maggie spluttered.

'Too right,' Denise agreed.

'I'm thinking of all the passengers and Tommy, who organised this trip, and Emily, who probably doesn't need anything to upset her equilibrium.' Cassie put out a hand, touching Sue's arm. 'I'll make the peace, you two can sit together on the bus and Ken won't feel outnumbered.'

Maggie was alarmed. 'He might try to seduce you too, Cassie – be careful.'

'I think that boat has already sailed,' Cassie suggested. She saw Maggie's alarm and added, 'His charm doesn't work on all of us.'

'Has he tried it on with you too?' Sue was aghast. 'The scoundrel!'

Cassie shook her head. 'He's just a lonely man.' She examined her fingers thoughtfully. 'Why don't you all go out and have some lunch? I'll pop to Ken's room and have a chat with him, clear the air.'

'Be careful,' Maggie warned, her brow wrinkled with anxiety.

'Oh, no, Ken better be careful.' Lil grinned, raising her coffee cup. 'He'd be wise not to cross our Cassie.' She turned to Sue and Denise, her face triumphant. 'Ken's a Lothario, hanging around her room with a bottle of champagne and two glasses. But my Cassie's no pushover. If she says she'll talk to him, you can believe he'll get a good talking-to – and nothing more.'

Sue and Denise exchanged glances, puzzled.

'So, we have a plan.' Cassie smiled. 'Could you bring me a sandwich back, please, Lil?'

'Of course I will, love. Right, let's go and have some lunch.' Lil stood up, ready to go. 'Maggie and I will treat you – a girls' lunch together. Sue, Denise, we'll go and grab a pizza somewhere and you can tell us all about Ken. After all—' she winked at Cassie '—I may need to pick up a few tips.'

* * *

The luggage was safely stowed at the back of the minibus and the passengers in their seats. As they had promised, Sue and Denise sat together near the front. Jake and DJ were quietly at work, sketch pads on their knees, earbuds in, listening to music. Emily was reading. Ken leaned his head against the window halfway down the bus, a book in front of his face, while Cassie sat next to him scribbling in her notepad. Maggie was across the aisle and Lil was reading the last chapter of her novel, *I, Sex Robot*, the treasured photo of Frankie pressed between the pages. Roberta Bott was in her time capsule on her way home, having come to the scientific conclusion that men throughout history hadn't changed that much at all. In front of Lil, Albert was dozing, a smile on his lips, a spare seat next to him. Duncan sat in the seat next to Tommy at the front.

Tommy was wearing a Belgian football shirt that was at least two sizes too small. He called out, 'Right, we're leaving Honfleur and we should be in Cherbourg by half past three. We'll whizz through customs and on to the ferry. It's a three-hour sail then, once we're off the ferry, it's about five and a half hours, but we'll have a stop. That means we'll be getting home quite late. You should all have something substantial to eat on the ferry and try to get some sleep.'

'I'm not looking forward to that long drive back,' Lil grumbled. 'I've got cushions but I'll get ever so stiff in my hip.'

'Lil?' Maggie was concerned. 'What did he mean, we'll whizz through customs?'

'They won't care about a bunch of British tourists in a minibus,' Lil explained. 'They'll just check our passports. It's not as if we're drug smugglers.'

'Oh, right.' Maggie caught her breath and glanced at her handbag.

Cassie gazed up from her writing. 'We'll have dinner on the boat and a walk around, stretch our legs. We'll stop for a coffee on the way back to break up the journey.'

'And we'll need plenty of toilet visits too,' Lil added.

Maggie hugged her handbag anxiously, her mouth drooping. 'I'm not looking forward to this at all.'

Ken leaned over kindly, offering an opened bag of toffees. Cassie took one, Lil delved in and pulled out two wrapped sweets, handing one to Maggie. 'Here, Maggie, you look a bit worried. Chew on this. It'll cheer you up.' Seeing her friend hesitate, Lil added, 'Go on – it won't turn you into Ken's concubine.'

Cassie winked at Ken, who looked very embarrassed and offered her another toffee.

* * *

Two hours later, as Lil gazed out of the window at the drizzle, she saw a sign for the ferry port and frowned. There were things she wanted to talk to Cassie about, important things. She glanced over towards her daughter, who was shaking her head in refusal as Ken offered her another sweet. Maggie leaned over, taking two. Lil tapped her friend's knee. 'Maggie, would you let Cassie sit next to me, just for a while?'

'All right.' Maggie nodded good-naturedly, unclipped her seat belt, struggled across the aisle into the seat Cassie had just left, and plonked herself down next to Ken. She glanced a little nervously at his crisp blazer and cravat and clutched her handbag firmly against her chest.

Lil tucked an arm through the crook of Cassie's. 'I want to buy some new books to read, Cassie. Will you help me?'

'Of course.' Cassie closed her eyes. 'What sort of thing do you want?'

'Romances – something about tender feelings. And strong characters, especially the women.'

'No more bonking books, then?'

'No, I've had enough of them for the time being.'

Cassie hugged her. 'We'll get you some nice new books – there are some very moving romances, some great stories about realistic relationships.'

Lil took her opportunity. 'The thing is, you see, I was wondering...'

'About Albert?'

'I'm becoming very fond of him, love. He's very nice.'

'I know he's nice, Lil...' Cassie took a breath. 'But...?'

'But I like Herman too. I mean, he's a long way away. I know a bird in the hand is worth two in the bush so – do you think Albie would mind if I kept Herman just for the holidays?'

'You'll have to ask him,' Cassie suggested. 'Why don't you wait and see how you feel when you get home?'

'Good idea.' Lil closed her eyes, thinking about herself in an embrace with one man and then the other. She kept her lids shut and murmured, 'Nothing for years, no love at all, and now I'm old, I've got two...'

Cassie sighed. 'You're never too old, Lil.' For a moment, she saw herself at her mother's age and wondered what the future would bring. She thought fondly, she might still be living with Jamie. He was in her thoughts most of the time now. They had arrived at the ferry port and the minibus had slowed down; they were in a queue.

Across the aisle, Maggie had put on her sunglasses; she was still hugging her handbag, staring ahead. She thought that if she didn't make eye contact with the passport officer, she might be safe. Then she felt the need to talk, so she nudged Ken gently. 'I'm looking forward to seeing my husband, Brian, when I get home. We've patched things up.'

Ken coughed lightly. 'You must have missed him while we've been away, Maggie.'

'Oh, I have. And I think he's missed me. I've made a list of everything I want him to do from now on. Lil has been wonderful – she persuaded me to go on holiday so he'd realise how much he loves me.' Maggie noticed Ken was holding out the sweets again. She took the whole bag. 'So – I've got him a present.'

'That's nice,' Ken said politely. 'What did you buy for him?'

'It's in my handbag.' Maggie turned anxious eyes in his direction. 'In fact, I'm a bit worried about what I've got. It's very special. I'm not sure I'm allowed to take it home...'

'How do you mean?'

Maggie leaned close to Ken. 'Well, I've heard that the customs don't take kindly to people bringing some things through – alcohol, cigarettes and the like.'

'What did you buy him?' Ken allowed himself a smile, finding Maggie's concern endearing. 'A bottle of Dutch gin?'

'No.' Maggie's voice was low and confidential. 'It's something completely different. I'm not sure I should have bought it at all. A nice young man in the street in Amsterdam sold it to me. It cost me a lot of money but he said it would make Brian a very, very chilled-out man...'

33

The customs officer was already on the minibus, checking passports. He was short with a large stomach, a dark blue shirt, sparse hair and a clean-shaven face. His eyes were small and penetrating as he stopped to check Sue's and Denise's passports. The customs officer then paused in front of Lil and Cassie, held out a hand and said, 'Passports.'

Lil noticed that he seemed very serious. She wondered whether to offer him a chocolate triangle, then she glanced down at his belt and saw the holster and the pistol and decided against it. She handed over her passport and waited while he stared at her for a moment and returned it without a word. Cassie passed her document to the man and smiled. *'Voici, monsieur, mon passeport.'*

The customs officer glanced at her, returned the passport and turned to Maggie and Ken. Lil noticed he had the words *Douane* on the back of his shirt in large white letters. Beneath his arms were dark sweat patches. Ken handed over his passport and murmured, *'Merci.'*

The customs officer turned to Maggie. 'Madame, your passport?'

Maggie had started to tremble. Her hands had become large and cumbersome, and they refused to do as she was asking them to do. As she whisked off her sunglasses, fumbled in her handbag and tugged out the passport, she pulled with it a wrapped package that flipped into the air in a somersault and landed in the aisle at the feet of the customs officer. Maggie gasped and started to babble.

'I'm sorry. Sorry. It's not mine. It fell into my bag by accident. I don't know where it came from. It's just funny tobacco. I didn't buy it in Amsterdam. It's not illegal, is it, officer?'

The customs officer picked up the package and stood up very straight, leaning back on his heels so that his stomach protruded. He held the package to his nose and inhaled deeply. He glared down at Maggie, his brows lowered, and he sniffed the package again. He leaned over her imperiously. '*Est-ce le vôtre, ce paquet?*'

Maggie was confused; she'd started to perspire. She wiped sweat from the top of her lip and raised her voice. 'It's not mine. I don't know how it came to be there. I don't want to go to prison.' Her face crumpled.

Ken pressed her hand gently. 'Leave it with me, Maggie. I speak a little French.' He gave a little cough and addressed the customs officer. '*Excusez-moi, monsieur – le paquet est à moi – je l'ai acheté pour... la médecine.*'

The customs officer frowned. His voice was very stern. '*Venez avec moi, s'il vous plaît, monsieur.*' He turned to Tommy, whose hands were frozen at the wheel, horrified. '*Vous tous, restez où vous êtes.*'

The customs officer's hand touched his holster; he stood back as Ken slid past Maggie and moved to the front of the minibus and down the stairs. The customs officer followed him, turning to growl at the passengers, '*Vous tous, attendez. Je reviendrai,*' before he disappeared.

There was no sound in the bus for several seconds. Everyone

held their breath and exchanged glances, then Maggie said, 'Oh dear. Was that my fault?'

'What on earth happened?' Tommy gasped. 'What did he say? What's going on?'

Cassie stood up. 'Ken's just talking to the customs officer...' She exhaled. 'We have to stay here and wait.'

Sue was distraught. 'What's happening to Ken? Has he been arrested?'

'What was in the package, Maggie?' Cassie asked quickly.

Maggie's lip trembled. 'Special wacky tobacco. It cost me a lot of money. I bought it for Brian from a young man I met in the street in Amsterdam when I was shopping. I told him my husband smoked, so he said this was especially good and he could roll his own cigarettes with it – he said it was a wonderful present and it would make him chilled out and happy.' Maggie started to cry. 'I had a funny idea it might be something I shouldn't have bought when he told me to keep it safe in my handbag and not tell anyone where I'd got it – and now Ken's in trouble.'

'Why is Ken in trouble if it's yours?' Denise asked.

'Is it cannabis?' asked DJ.

'Marijuana.' Jake added.

'One of them, both even, I think.' Maggie wiped perspiration from her brow. 'Oh dear... poor Ken. I feel so awful.'

Lil handed Maggie a handkerchief from her cat-whisker handbag.

'Ken told the customs officer it was his and he'd bought it for medicinal purposes,' Cassie explained.

Duncan was flabbergasted. 'Why ever would he do that, the idiot?'

'Because he wanted to save Maggie,' Denise explained. 'He's being heroic.'

'And now he's in trouble,' Sue wailed.

'Lil, can you sit next to Maggie and look after her?' Cassie grabbed her bag. 'I'm going out to talk to the customs officer. I'll explain it's all been a mistake.'

'We might miss the boat,' Tommy muttered, gazing at his watch.

'That's the least of our problems, I reckon,' Duncan mumbled. 'Ken's going to prison for drug trafficking.'

Cassie pushed cushions round Lil and Maggie. 'Are you comfortable?' They nodded and she announced to the passengers. 'Right – I'll be as quick as I can. I'll explain it all and hopefully they'll let us go.'

'Be careful, Cassie,' Maggie blubbered. 'The customs man – he had a gun.'

Cassie winked and headed towards the steps. As she descended, the breeze blew her white hair in a cloud around her head. Out of the window, they could all see Ken standing opposite the customs officer and another, taller man in identical uniform. Cassie went up to the men and spoke directly to them and they turned, suddenly interested. Cassie was waving her hands, speaking forcefully. The shorter, burly officer put his hands on his hips and began to shout.

'Oh dear,' Lil sighed. 'I don't think it's going well.'

Albert eased himself up and moved to the empty seats across the aisle from Lil, sinking into a chair and reaching out an arm to hold her hand. Maggie was now sobbing onto Lil's shoulder, wailing about everything being her fault and how she'd spoiled everyone's holiday. Lil was making soft noises to comfort her as Emily rushed forward, pushing a bar of chocolate into Maggie's hand, promising her that everything would be fine.

Sue's voice echoed around the bus, over everyone else's excited chatter. 'They might try to keep Ken here and lock him up. He'd be convicted for smuggling. He'd go to prison.'

'We'll explain that he's not responsible, *Syoo*. We'll stand by him.'

'But then we'd get Maggie into trouble – we can't put her in the firing line, Denise.'

Maggie began to sob harder. Lil wrapped her arms around her friend, promising that Cassie would sort everything out. Tommy was suddenly concerned. 'The next thing they'll do is drag us all off the bus. They'll strip-search everyone. They search for drugs everywhere on your naked body, you know – and I mean, everywhere.'

'They won't put their hands on *my* naked body,' Lil affirmed. 'That's definitely not happening.'

'Nor mine,' Maggie wailed.

'Perhaps they'll bring the sniffer dogs out?' Duncan gasped.

'I don't like fierce dogs.' Maggie's sobs grew even louder. Albert took the bar of chocolate with shaky hands and divided it into three, pushing a third into his own mouth.

DJ said, 'It's only a bit of dope. It's not much – just a bit for personal use. They'll let us off.'

'They might not.' Jake wrapped an arm around him. 'We're the young ones here – I bet they'll blame it on us.'

DJ put a hand to his forehead. 'I've been stopped on suspicion before and I'd done nothing...' He thought for a moment. 'Poor Ken.'

'Think positively.' Emily smiled warmly. 'We'll all be on our way soon. Cassie will sort it out.'

Tommy folded his arms. 'We'd better hope so. We should be on the boat by now.'

Another customs man strode onto the bus, standing at the top of the steps, his hands on his hips. '*Vous tous, descendez maintenant.*' He waved towards the door.

'What did he say?' asked Tommy.

Emily sighed. 'He said we all have to get off.'

The ten remaining passengers clambered out of the minibus and stood in a circle. It had become cold outside; although the rain had stopped, there was an icy wind from the ocean. Ken was led into an office by the two other customs men. Out of nowhere, two more uniformed customs officers, a man and a woman, with two Alsatian dogs on leads, clambered onto the bus. The group huddled closely as Tommy wailed, 'They are searching the entire bus for drugs.'

Cassie walked over to Lil and Maggie grabbed her arm, distraught.

'Are we going to be stripped?' Her grip increased. 'Are they going to search us?'

'There's no need to panic.' Cassie rubbed Maggie's shoulder affectionately. 'I think we can sort this out. I've said there is nothing else on the bus – they are just checking.'

DJ's face fell. 'This is serious.'

'Cassie – what's happening to Ken?' Denise asked worriedly.

Cassie sighed. 'I'm hoping they'll believe that Ken bought it to help with a medical problem he's pretending to have.' She shrugged. 'We'll see what they say.'

'He didn't say it was all my fault?' Maggie grasped Cassie's arm in desperation.

'No, it'll be fine, Maggie.' Cassie offered a smile. 'When we get out of this one, though, you'll owe him a huge bottle of something special.'

'Oh, yes.' Maggie gasped, turning to hug Lil for comfort. Albert wrapped an arm round them both. The three of them shivered; the drizzle had begun again. The customs officers with the dogs scrambled off the bus and rushed back into the office and Cassie followed them.

Lil watched as several figures moved jerkily, arguing with each other inside the office while Ken hung his head. She saw Cassie lay a protective hand on his arm and say something earnestly to the portly customs officer, who appeared to reply angrily. Lil caught her breath, anxious for her daughter. Another customs man, the tall one, spoke to Ken and he uttered a few words, then Cassie was speaking quickly, waving her hands to explain the problem. Suddenly, both customs officers turned their back on Cassie and a three-way argument seemed to break out.

Tommy murmured, 'She'll have to be quick. We have to be on board in twenty minutes.'

The door swung open and Cassie was outside. The group crowded around her as she put her hands on her hips. 'Right, everyone. We have a solution. It's not ideal but it's the best I can do. Ken will sign something to say that it's his package, even though it isn't, and we'll be charged a fine, then they'll let us go.'

'That's good.' Duncan was relieved. 'How much?'

'Two hundred and twenty euros.'

'I don't have enough money.' Maggie gasped.

'We'll split it, my dear,' Sue insisted. 'Twenty euros each. Then we'll take Ken away from here and get on the boat.'

'You can't pay my fine,' Maggie wailed. 'It's all been my fault.'

'You're my best friend, and we've had a great holiday,' Lil soothed. 'It's all been worth it.'

'Oh, Lil, you're wonderful.' Maggie looked suddenly relieved.

'Friends,' Albert insisted with an encouraging smile, reaching inside his overcoat. 'We stick together.'

'Exactly.' Denise was searching in her purse. 'We've shared this holiday and it's been wonderful. Now, come on, everyone, cough up – it's twenty each.'

'Thank you – thank you.' Maggie greeted each person with pure gratitude.

Tommy was gripping his wallet. 'We'd better hurry up.'

Lil pushed forty euros into Cassie's hand. 'That should cover my and Maggie's contribution.' She watched Cassie walk away with a fistful of euros; she noticed how efficient she was, how assured her stride as she pushed open the office door, approached the customs officer and counted the notes onto his desk. Next to her, Ken was peering through the window, his face pale and haggard, but Lil thought she could see an expression in his eyes that looked a great deal like relief.

Moments later Ken staggered onto the minibus amid a round of loud applause, Cassie behind him, pulling the door closed with a bang. As Ken took his seat next to Maggie, who was gazing up at him as if he were a blessed saint, Tommy started the engine, pushed his foot hard on the accelerator and grimaced. 'Let's get out of here.'

The minibus thundered up the bumpy ramp, a woman in an orange jacket waving at Tommy frantically, and as he parked he put a hand to a damp brow and muttered, 'We only just made it.'

The tired troupe of passengers staggered up the stairs to the bar and fell exhaustedly into soft red seats around a large table. Duncan and Cassie rushed off to order drinks, coming back with a brandy each for Maggie and Ken, and glasses of wine and beer all around. Maggie, Sue and Denise were all staring at Ken, their eyes shining with admiration although Ken, for his part, looked exhausted.

Lil whispered to Cassie, 'He'd still be locked up in France without you, love – you're the one who should have all the credit.'

'All I did was speak a bit of French.' Cassie waved a hand, making the bow around her hair wiggle. 'The customs officers were quite reasonable really, once things were explained. Besides, I've often been told I'm too outspoken and headstrong. I'm glad I can put it to some use.'

'I'm going to buy Ken a bottle of champagne, to say thank you. And, Cassie – you were marvellous. You must be so proud of her, Lil.' Maggie was thoughtful. 'Now I'll have to get Brian something else for a present – I've no idea what to get him now.'

'There's a shop on the level below.' Emily grinned. 'We'll all go down in a bit, Maggie – me and you and DJ and Jake. They need to buy presents for their mums.'

'We forgot,' DJ explained sheepishly.

'I'll come with you too,' Lil offered. 'I want to get some books and some CDs. Maggie, we should buy Brian some nice music. He might like that – a change from watching the goggle-box.'

'Oh, yes.' Maggie smiled, happy again. 'That's a good idea, much better than cigarettes and certainly better than dodgy substances for him to use to roll his own.'

Duncan banged the table with his fist, making the beer in his glass slosh towards the top. 'We'll be home this time tomorrow – you'll all have to join me in The Jolly Weaver for a complimentary drink or two.'

'What a lovely idea, my dear,' Sue agreed. 'I might invite other members of the tennis club. We can share some wine and tell everyone all about this holiday.'

Ken was sheepish. 'Don't tell them *everything*, please.'

Denise touched his arm tenderly. 'You've been a hero, Ken.'

Sue agreed. 'I'm so glad we're all friends again. We can put all that silly business behind us.'

Ken's face flooded with relief and at last he managed a smile. Jake glanced at Cassie. 'Hey, you'll have to write a song about this holiday, Cass.'

Cassie rolled her eyes. 'Now that would be an epic story, wouldn't it?'

Lil snuggled up to Albert. 'Shall we go and find something to eat soon?'

'We'll all go,' Duncan enthused. 'All of us together, one happy throng.' He nudged Tommy. 'I'm so glad we're not going to end the holiday tonight. Everybody can meet up in The Jolly Weaver tomorrow night – it'll be a special party for Ken, to celebrate his heroism.'

Ken gave a polite cough. 'That's very kind, Duncan. But it was really Cassie we should all thank. If it hadn't been for her, I'd probably still be in the customs office – or worse.' He shuddered at the thought.

'Dunc doesn't really care about having a party.' Tommy laughed cynically. 'We're only invited to The Weaver to keep the peace. Kerry will kill him when she finds out how much money he's spent on beer orders while we've been away.'

Duncan gazed down at his pint, his cheeks glowing: Tommy had hit a nerve. Then he broke into a smile and he said, 'Kerry will be fine – I bought her some earrings in Amsterdam. We'll have a great party.' He gazed at everyone around the table. 'After all, this has been a special holiday – and we've become such good friends. We can't let it all go as soon as we're back home in Salterley.'

Cassie sipped her wine thoughtfully; tomorrow they would be back home again. She would have to resolve the mystery of David. She wondered who he was and how he knew her; she'd had a strong suspicion about his identity, from the moment Jamie had mentioned where he had come from. Then she imagined Jamie welcoming her when she walked through the door. She had to admit, she was looking forward to seeing him so much. She swallowed a mouthful of wine and sighed; she had some thinking to do.

34

Inside the minibus, not far from Portsmouth, the night skies dark all around her, Lil felt wrapped in warmth, rocked by the low rumble of the engine. She closed her eyes, resting against the cushions Cassie had carefully placed around her, nestling into the comfortable softness. She thought about the new books and CDs in her shopping bag; she had some fascinating new romances to read, her own new copy of *Birdsong* and new music to listen to, some of the composers whose busts had been in the *Jardin des Personnalités* in Honfleur, and she was imagining giving away the presents she'd bought. She visualised Jenny Price finding an oversized mug with 'I heart Amsterdam' on it in her office. This time, she'd know it was from either Lil or Maggie.

And Keith the chef would love the chocolate cookies she'd bought him in Ghent, the Belgian butter biscuits. Lil was looking forward to seeing Keith and Jenny again. It would be nice to be back home.

Then Lil felt a hand cover hers, fingers pressing the soft flesh of her palm, and she opened an eye to see Albert gazing at her, handsome and kind. She noticed the tenderness in his eyes, the shining light, the gentle curve of his smile and she wondered how many times in her life someone had looked at her that way. Not many; not enough. Lil squeezed Albert's hand with affection, showing him that she felt the same way. She'd never really known what it felt like to have someone on her side, someone to care. It felt wonderful.

But what life had been like in the past wasn't her concern now. It was all about the time she had left, what she'd do with each day. And tomorrow evening she and Albert were going to meet at The Jolly Weaver and their life in Salterley would unfold from there. Lil sighed. She still wasn't sure what she'd do about Herman.

* * *

In the passenger seat next to Tommy, Cassie was gazing at the road. They were passing the exit sign for Bere Regis, bright in the headlamps. She stretched out her legs and glanced at her phone. Jamie had texted. She told him not to wait up, but he was insisting that he wanted to be there when she walked in through the door, even though it would be way past midnight.

Cassie replied that he should go to bed; she would see Lil home first and make sure she was settled, so it was likely to be very late indeed. Jamie replied quickly with a smiley face icon and an x. She assumed he would be sitting in his armchair watching something on television, a brandy in his hand, his eyes tired. He'd read her text then he would grin, ease himself slowly up from his seat, turn the set off with a flick of the remote and make his way upstairs. Cassie flexed her shoulders, wriggled and snuggled down in the seat. She would be home soon. Holidays were wonderful, but it was always good to get back to your own space, your own bed, and start to plan the next trip. And it would be lovely to see Jamie again, to hug him, feel the warmth of his arms around her. Cassie had to admit, she'd had a special time with Lil, but another holiday might be nice, a different sort of break altogether, one where she and Jamie could spend some time together, where she could tell him about some thoughts she'd had on her mind for several days now.

* * *

Back in her own bed, Lil slept until past midday. She woke, feeling strangely comforted by the sweet scent of her pillows, in the small, warm room with the white walls, her own familiar things on the bedside table. She stretched her body, conscious of the aches in her hip, and immediately felt hungry, so she wriggled into clothes and decided to go across the road to the café and flirt with Keith. On the landing, she thought about knocking on Maggie's door. It was ajar and music was playing loudly inside, a lively tune on a violin that made you want to dance a reel. She hesitated and listened more carefully: there was the soft tinkle of laughter. Lil stood still; the music rose and fell. She couldn't resist it – she pushed the door wide and gazed at Maggie and Brian, dancing to the sweeping music of Paganini. Lil was amazed: the television was off and there was a fresh smell on the air, the scent of flowers, of sweet peas.

Lil watched in silence as Brian and Maggie twirled in each other's arms. The music whirled and fizzed, then faded to an ostentatious ending, a whizz of the bow against strings. Maggie and Brian gazed at each other as their feet moved nimbly. Lil clapped her hands softly, a smile on her face.

Maggie whirled round. 'Lil, nice to see you. Brian and I were just enjoying the violin concerto.'

Brian draped an arm around Maggie. 'It's good to have the old girl back again.'

'Old girl?' Maggie wriggled under his embrace, smiling. 'Brian has missed me, you know.'

'She's a new woman, Lil. I don't know what you did to her while you were out in Germany but it's done us both the world of good.'

'Germany, indeed.' Maggie tittered, her eyes shining. 'Now Brian's talking about us going on holiday together to Italy, aren't you, love?' She faced him again, taking up a dance position. 'We might even be able to dance to the real Paganini.'

'I doubt it, he died over a hundred and fifty years ago,' Lil muttered to herself. Then she raised a hand. 'Italy would be wonderful. You'll be a jet-setter, Maggie. Now I'm going to get some brunch – I'll see you both later.'

'See you soon,' both dancers chorused as they rose up on their toes and swirled round; a new track had started and they were instantly lifted by the swelling tune of the violin.

* * *

Cassie was hunched over the steering wheel of her car, her thoughts racing: she had a lunch appointment in a little bistro in Exmouth, a fifteen-minute drive from her home. She was meeting David at one o'clock. She'd phoned him earlier that morning and they'd agreed on a venue where they could share lunch and have some time to speak together. He had come over from Denver in the USA; he was currently on vacation, he said, and he wanted to share some information that would be mutually beneficial. He believed that Cassie would find it most interesting.

Jamie had been a little fretful; he'd wanted to accompany Cassie, in case it was some sort of scam, but Cassie had suggested that he remain at home. They'd been delighted to see each other, immediately squeezed in a tight embrace, but Jamie had seemed tired and he'd mentioned the numbing sensations in his hands. Cassie had fussed over him, wanting him to rest. After all, she'd promised him, with a peck on the cheek as he stood in the kitchen wearing a fetching grey Amsterdam sweatshirt, she'd accompany him to The Jolly Weaver that evening and they'd be able to spend quality time together. He was not to worry. Besides, she was interested in what David had to say to her and it was clearly private; it concerned only her. There was something about his warm tone, the confidential way he spoke, that invited her to believe that he was genuine. That, and his surname.

* * *

Cassie's hunch had been correct: she knew it was him instantly as they faced each other inside the café. David was a little taller than she was, a little younger, with piercing blue eyes behind rimmed spectacles, and dark wavy hair. He had an easy smile as he introduced himself, holding out his hand and taking Cassie's; his accent had a soft inflection.

'Pleased to meet you, Cassie. I'm David Chapman.'

'Well, shall we sit down?'

They sat opposite each other at a white square table near the window, gazing out towards the sea wall. The sky was a crumpled, faded grey; droplets of rain spattered the window. David placed his iPad carefully on the tablecloth and raised his eyebrows, picking up the menu. 'Well.'

Cassie said, 'I can recommend the lasagne.'

'I like the idea of a Manhattan panini – Monterey Jack cheese is just about my favourite thing in the world.'

'Then I'll try it too.'

Cassie waved to the waiter, gave her the order and turned her attention back to David. 'So – David – how can I help you?'

'Maybe we can help each other.' David raised dark eyebrows. 'Does the name Chapman mean anything to you?'

'It does. Frankie Chapman was my father.'

David nodded. 'Frankie Chapman is my father too.'

'So, he's still alive?'

'He is.' David pressed a button on his iPad and showed Cassie a photograph. An ageing man was grinning from the depths of an armchair, a red and white baseball cap on his head. He was shrunken beneath his jacket, his face lined, his eyes deep set.

Cassie sighed. 'So that's Frankie Chapman. That's my father.'

'Yes, it is.'

She met his eyes. 'Well, I have some questions. First of all, how did you find out about me?'

David was quick to reply with a question of his own. 'Is your mom still alive? Lilian Ryan?'

'Very much so,' Cassie said.

'My father knew nothing about you until recently. He's not been well. He had a stroke a couple months ago and he's convalescing in a nursing home in Kansas. He started talking about a woman he once knew, Lily Ryan, and how he'd met her in Oxfordshire when he was stationed there after the war. He asked me if she might still be alive and that's where my research started.'

'They were both very young.' Cassie glanced up as the waiter placed two paninis on the table and walked away. 'My mother was seventeen when I was born.'

'I researched online and you both came up. I was shocked to find that Lily had given birth to a daughter. My dad was named as your father on your birth certificate.'

Cassie shrugged. 'I've always known he was my father. Of course, I never met him.'

'He'd like to meet you. He'd like that very much, Cassie.'

'And Lil?' Cassie shook her head. 'What about her?'

'He asked after her...'

'And what about your mother, David?'

'My mom died last year,' David said sadly. He took a bite of his panini. 'I'm married to Joni; we have two sons, Aaron and Reuben, and a granddaughter, Hannah.'

David waved his iPad, scrolling through more photos as he showed them to Cassie. A striking, flaxen-haired wife standing next to David; two tall sons with dark curly hair, one wearing spectacles; a small blonde girl in various poses, clutching a teddy bear, reading a book, playing with a puppy.

'Do you have a stepfather, Cassie? Siblings? Children?'

'No, there's just me and Lil – it's always been that way.' Cassie lifted her panini and put it back on her plate. She wasn't hungry. 'She never married and nor did I.'

'Ah,' David murmured. 'Dad will be really surprised to know that Lily is still around. He was called away from Heyford, where he was based in the American camp, all those years ago. He didn't even have time to say goodbye, I guess; he came back to Denver and then, in time, he met my mom and they had me.'

'While Lil was bringing up a toddler whose father didn't know she existed.'

David raised his eyebrows. 'You must feel a little bitter, Cassie, your mom too. I guess you have every right.'

'No.' She shook her head. 'We aren't made of that stuff. Lil and I did just fine – we're still doing fine. It was never a problem – we didn't need Frankie Chapman.' She examined a fingernail, then stared out of the window. 'I'm glad Frankie had a good life, though. I'm glad things worked out for him.' She thought for a moment. 'Does he still play the banjo?'

'He used to, a lot, but not now.' David's eyes met Cassie's. 'But I do. I play live gigs sometimes. Why do you ask?'

'He left a banjo behind when he rushed back to the USA. Lil passed it on to me.'

'Do you play?'

'Yes, to audiences, just like you do.' Cassie smiled. 'Well, David, Frankie has given us a gift we both share.'

David met Cassie's eyes, his face hopeful. 'Can I meet Lily? I'd like to, very much. After all, she's the mother of my half-sister.'

Cassie decided that she liked this man; he was well intentioned and good-hearted, but the news was so sudden, so overwhelming. She'd take her time. She wasn't ready to open her arms to a new brother and a new father, not yet. Lil was most important: how she might feel, what she would want to do. Cassie was unsure how she might react after so long.

'I'll have to ask her first.' Cassie exhaled slowly. 'I've no idea what she'll say, after all these years. It's her call.'

Cassie put a hand to her head, thinking. Lil had loved Frankie Chapman; she'd never loved again after he left. Cassie wondered how her mother would take the news after all these years, how she'd feel about the shrunken man in the armchair, the red and white baseball cap pushed on his head. Lil remembered him as a dashing soldier, the charming young man in the photo, dark curly hair, a smart uniform, eyes shining with affection and a warm grin. She shoved her plate away, the food untouched.

'I'll go and see her now and then I'll call you.' And as an afterthought, she murmured, 'Can you send me his photo, Frankie's? The one of him in the armchair? I think I might need it.'

35

Lil was munching toast in the Kaff while Keith the chef was munching Belgian butter biscuits covered with chocolate. He handed Lil another plate of wholemeal toast with lashings of butter and a steaming cup of tea. 'Here you are, Lil. Get your laughing gear around this little lot.'

Lil reached for the toast. 'Thank you, Keith darling.'

'My pleasure. I have to say, these biscuits are delicious. I'm going to have a go at making some myself. Belgian, aren't they?'

'They are indeed – that's the meaning of life, you know.'

'What is, Lil?'

Lil grinned, her lips moist. 'Butter.'

She opened her copy of *Birdsong*, smoothing out the black and white photo with her fingertip before she started to read. She'd been fascinated by the opening chapter, the mysterious house that led to the river Somme: she could imagine the dark shadowy corridors and hear the whisper of footsteps from the past.

The café door opened wide and Cassie rushed in. Lil glanced up from her novel and called to Keith. 'More tea and toast, please, darling – with lashings of butter.'

'Coming up, gorgeous.'

Cassie sat next to her at the table. 'How are you, Lil? Tired?'

'Not at all,' Lil lied, closing her book. Her hips and legs were aching after the long journey yesterday, but she wasn't one to grumble. 'Well, it seems you can't keep away from me, Cass.'

Cassie scrutinised her mother, trying to work out how she was feeling. Cassie wasn't sure quite how to begin her story. She took a breath. 'Lil, I've just had lunch with a man called David.'

'Ooh, nice.' Lil grinned, leaning forward. 'Handsome, is he? Jamie will be jealous, I'll bet.'

'He's called David Chapman.' Cassie watched her mother for signs of how she'd take the news. 'He's from Denver.'

'Chapman?' Lil sat back in her seat, the colour starting to drain from her face. She lifted her hands to her mouth and her fingers were shaking. Cassie put an arm around her mother who felt small, frail, vulnerable. Her breath came in a short gasp, then she whispered, 'Frankie?'

'He's Frankie's son, Lil.'

Lil blinked. It was difficult for her to take in. Cassie noticed her thin eyelids, the heavy veins in the back of her hand, the way her lips pursed in confusion. Then the question came, her voice a dusty croak, a question she had been asking herself for so long but had not dared to utter the words. 'Is Frankie...?'

'Still alive, yes.' Cassie nodded, gauging her mother's reaction. Lil closed her mouth with a snap of teeth and exhaled. Cassie waited for the next breath to come and, eventually, Lil sighed softly.

Keith arrived with the tea and toast, but Lil didn't notice as his tattooed hands placed the tray on the table.

'Frankie. After all these years.' She was quiet for a moment and Cassie waited, taking her mother's hand in both of hers.

Lil met her gaze and Cassie was surprised by how diamond-hard her mother's eyes were, how they glittered with an emotion

Cassie had never seen before. Her voice was low. 'He married, then? He had children?'

'Just a son.' Cassie studied her mother's frozen expression of horror; she decided not to mention the grandchildren, Aaron, Reuben, and the great-granddaughter, little Hannah. Lil had missed out on all that; she didn't need to know about Frankie's family. She watched her mother pick up her cup and bring it to her lips, her hands still trembling, and Cassie lifted her own drink, sipping warm tea. Then she said, 'Do you want to see a photo of Frankie?'

Lil nodded. Cassie pulled out her phone and opened up an attachment. Lil took the phone from her hands and stared at the image, her lips moving silently, forming unspoken words. Then she murmured, 'He's changed – he's old now.'

'The years have passed, Lil.' Cassie wrapped an arm around the small shoulders.

'Is he married?' Her voice was a whisper.

'Widowed.'

'Does he know I had you? That you're his child?'

'He didn't. But he does now.'

Lil was lost in thought for a moment, her lids closed. Then she muttered, 'Is he still here, the son?'

'He's here for two more days. Do you want to meet him?'

'No.' Lil's answer was immediate, forceful. 'But he's your half-brother. I suppose you want to get to know him better.'

'I might.' Cassie shrugged. 'But this is about what *you* want, Lil.'

Lil took a breath. 'I want to talk to Frankie. I want to ask him some questions. I want to see him.'

'You want to go to Denver?'

'I don't know. It's a long way. It was all such a long time ago. I just want to – to see him.'

'I can try to set you up a video call, on a laptop. Would you like that?'

'Yes, I would. Can we do it now?'

'Not now. Not straight away. I'd have to talk to David. Maybe we can set it up for later this afternoon? Denver is seven hours behind us so, if we were to chat at six o'clock, before we go to the pub, it would be eleven in the morning there. How does that sound?'

'It sounds all right.' Lil put her hands to her face, long fingers pressing against her cheeks. 'Cassie, I want to talk to him by myself. I mean, I want him to meet you, to know who you are...'

'I'd like to meet him.'

'But when you've spoken to him, can you give me some time by myself? Just a few minutes?'

'Of course.'

Lil leaned back in her seat. She could feel her heart beating, fluttering like a trapped bird, knocking hard at her chest. She turned her gaze on Cassie, her eyes half closed, exhausted. 'I'd like to get a couple of hours' sleep first, love. I think the bus trip has caught up with me.' She held out a weak arm. 'Would you give me a hand back to my flat? I'm tired.'

Cassie nodded, helping her to stand up, picking up her novel. The black and white photo slid to the floor and Cassie bent down quickly and stared at her mother and father together, so many years ago, Frankie's disarming smile, Lil's expression of uncertainty. She replaced it gently between the pages and wrapped an arm around Lil, helping her to shuffle forwards. 'It's best to have a rest for a few hours. I'll set up the chat and pop round this evening.' Cassie offered a cheery grin. 'Then we'll go to The Weaver, shall we? I'll drive you there and we can relive our holiday and have a nice time. Albert will be there.'

'Albie?' Lil's mouth formed the words, confused, her eyes glassy.

'Come on, let's settle you down. No wonder you're tired out, all this information, seeing him again after all these years.'

'Tired... all these years,' Lil agreed and allowed herself to be

shepherded across the road and back to Clover Hill. Her mind was
confused, buzzing with too many thoughts.

Fifteen minutes later, her head was on the pillow. She sighed
softly and her eyes closed straight away. Cassie smoothed the soft
white hair and placed a kiss on her brow. Lil's skin was damp.

'Sleep well, Lil – I'll be back soon.'

Cassie moved quietly from the bedroom, through the living
room to the door, closing it behind her with a click. She stood still
for a while on the landing, thinking. It had been a shocking day.
She had acquired a father, a brother. She was feeling a little
stunned herself; she noticed that her pulse was racing. Cassie imagined how it must be for her mother: sixty-six years of silence, and
suddenly Frankie Chapman was alive, smiling at her from a photo,
a red and white baseball cap on his head. Cassie frowned. Her own
discovery that she had a father who was still alive, and a half-
brother, had stunned her. She couldn't imagine the turmoil of
emotions exploding like fireworks inside Lil's mind, making her
heart pound.

She glanced at a clock on the landing wall – it was almost half
past two. Cassie would go home and talk to Jamie. He'd offer kindness, warmth, and the thought made her throat swell with emotion.
Her mind was filled with the image of Frankie, her father. She
wondered what she would say to him, what he would be like,
whether she would even like him, whether she might feel resentful
and blame him for all the missed years. Perhaps it was his fault that
she could never settle down? Perhaps his absence had damaged her
emotionally, made her afraid to commit? Cassie took a breath, then
another, and calmed herself. She'd be fine; she'd support Lil. She
set off for the stairs. As she passed Maggie's flat, the swirl of a violin
being played sifted from beneath the door with the faint scent of
sweet peas.

* * *

Lil was dreaming; it was vivid, in Technicolor. She was dancing to music, a fiddle was playing, and she was young, her hair dark and long to her waist. She was wearing a floral blouse, off the shoulder, a long dirndl skirt; her legs and feet were bare. Her arm was in the air as she waved a tambourine in time with each step. The breeze lifted her hair; she was outside, dancing in a field that smelled of woodsmoke and flowers – even in her dream she could hear the loud, vibrating music, smell the sweet scent of a log fire – and her dancing was frantic, animated, but she was strong, sturdy, in control.

Lil twirled and the skirt spread wide like a bell, her feet pivoting beneath her. A man approached; he was handsome, with a charming smile and dark curly hair. Lil tilted her chin, raised an arched eyebrow and, with a single word and a flash of her eyes, invited him to dance. He took her hand and they whirled round together; she could smell his warm scent, feel the heat of his body; his fascination with her was tangible and she threw her head back, confident in the power she had in her movements and in her control over this man who clearly adored her.

The man's arm was around her waist. Of course, it was Frankie, and Lil's dreams swelled with the recognition of old emotions, desire, longing, anticipation, danger. They were dancing, their bodies pressed together, and Lil realised that they were moving too close to the fire. The violin cry became louder, it swelled as the heat of the fire warmed the flesh of her legs. Then the tambourine slipped from her grasp, a fast rattle of metal and then there was a roar, a wind, a whoosh of flames as it caught alight and began to crackle. The blaze was suddenly around them; they were trapped inside leaping tongues of red heat. Lil was choking, her vision blurred by hot clouds of silver smoke, and Frankie had disappeared. In her dream, her voice called his name over and over until her cry became the loud wail of a violin, a melody out of control. Then there was silence.

36

Jamie had been desperate to come with her; he had held Cassie's hand in both of his, gazed anxiously into her eyes and told her that, after sixty-five years of having no father, she needed the support of someone who cared for her when she talked to Frankie for the first time. Cassie couldn't disagree, but she had explained to him softly that she wanted Lil's feelings to come first. She'd spoken to David, arranged to set up the video call between Lil and Frankie, who was in a nursing home and would be helped throughout.

Although Jamie's intentions were good and he'd wanted to support Cassie, there would be time for that later. This was Lil's moment. She would need all the help Cassie could give her when she spoke to Frankie; she would finally have the chance to lay her ghosts to rest. There was so much that had been unresolved for so long. Jamie had conceded that Cassie was right; he'd be in The Jolly Weaver at seven-thirty and he'd have a pint of best bitter waiting for her.

Cassie's fingers were on the door handle, her laptop under her arm. She pushed her way into Lil's flat and stood in the little living room, furnished simply with two armchairs and a small table. It was fifteen minutes to six. The room creaked softly, then was quiet. Cassie took a breath: Lil wasn't awake yet. She set up her laptop on the table. She'd wake Lil in a moment, settle her in an armchair, pop into the kitchenette and make her a cup of tea. She fiddled with wires and buttons. It was ten to six. Lil needed to get ready.

Cassie moved towards the bedroom. The door was ajar and Lil was sleeping, resting on her back in exactly the same spot as Cassie had left her. Cassie approached the bed and gazed at her mother, the soft white hair spread on the pillow, lids rounded, her mouth slightly open. Cassie's thoughts drifted, as they often did, to a time when her mother would be no more; Cassie would find her lying in bed exactly as she was now, her face at peace, and she knew instantly, like the jab of a spear to the heart, how much she would miss her. She approached the bed and took Lil's hand, cool in her own, the skin paper-thin to the touch. She pressed it gently. 'Lil?'

Lil did not move, her head resting on the pillow, her hand in Cassie's. Then her eyelids fluttered and she exhaled softly. 'I've been dreaming – I was fast asleep.'

Cassie crouched down. 'You need to get up, Lil. Remember, you've got a chat with Frankie.'

'Oh. Oh, yes.' Lil opened her eyes wide, struggling to get up. 'Oh, I wanted to look my best.'

Cassie took her hand. 'Put some lipstick on. He'll only see your top half.' She wondered how much Frankie would be able to see at all: the figure in the armchair had appeared frail and small. She helped Lil to sit up and swing her feet out of the bed. 'Right, tell me what you want and I'll get it for you.'

'Cassie.' Lil turned watery eyes towards her daughter. 'I'm a little bit scared.'

'I bet.' Cassie pressed her hand. 'To tell you the truth, so am I. But we'll talk to him together first, then I'll leave you alone for ten minutes so you can – reminisce.' She took a breath. 'After that, we'll both go to The Jolly Weaver and have a stiff drink.'

Lil nodded, standing on wobbly legs. Cassie put an arm around her and felt her shaking, her body like a butterfly against glass. Cassie hugged her. 'We'll be all right. We have each other. That's what matters – that's what has always mattered.'

Once she was ready, Lil sat in front of the screen, squinting, making her eyes small. She could see a fuzzy shape, a man in an armchair, something red on top of his head. A voice spoke, an unseen person, telling Frankie to say hello. Cassie squatted next to Lil, taking her hand, and spoke clearly, aware with each word how absurd it sounded. 'Hello, Frankie. I'm Cassie Ryan. I'm your daughter. I have Lil here with me, my mother.'

Frankie stirred, leaned to one side then tilted forward, his face filling the screen. 'Hello, Cassie. So nice to meet you.' His voice was thin, a single reed, tremulous. Cassie took a breath.

'I'm pleased to meet you too.'

He shifted around in his seat and then raised a hand, a bony finger. 'I'm sorry, Cassie – sorry that I never knew. I wish I had. I missed out – we both did. But I'll make it up...'

Cassie shrugged. She decided to move the conversation forward. 'I have Lil here with me, Frankie...'

'Lily?' Frankie gave a little cough. 'Hey, Lily – is that you?'

Lil leaned towards the screen nervously. 'Hello, Frankie.' Her heart thudded in her chest – he still had the power to do that to her. She stared at him: the same eyes, the same charming smile. His face was thinner, older, and she couldn't see his hair for the red and white baseball cap pushed down on his head.

'How are you, Lily?'

'I'm fine, Frankie.'

'You're looking good...'

Lil exhaled. 'You too.'

Frankie gave a little cough. 'I've been unwell. I had a stroke. They are very kind to me here. I'm a lot better than I was...'

There was silence, then Lil muttered, 'That's good.'

He leaned forward, and his eyes were filled with water. 'I'm so sorry I left you when I did, all those years ago. They called me back to the States and I had less than twenty-four hours' notice. I should have come to see you, to tell you I was leaving, but I was a coward. It would have hurt us both so – I just left without saying anything.'

'I heard you'd gone back home from one of your friends, from one of the other soldiers at the camp. I went to the base, trying to find you. You didn't even leave an address so that I could write and tell you what had happened. I was all alone.'

'I'm so sorry. I was young, foolish. It was wrong to do what I did.'

'It was very wrong.' Lil wiped a tear from her cheek with a knuckle. 'But you left me my best treasure. You left me my Cassie.'

'I wish I'd known...'

Lil's little voice rose. 'We didn't need you. We managed by ourselves. My daughter is a clever girl – she's worked in Africa and China and then she came home again and we look after each other. She's a poet now; she performs all over the country.'

'You raised her well.'

'She was mine to raise, Frankie.' Lil's voice was firm. 'No one else's. I put her first. I did a good job, all by myself.'

'I'm so sorry,' Frankie muttered. 'I can't make it up to you. I wish I could.'

'You can't,' Lil called out, then she was thoughtful for a moment. 'It's in the past. I'm glad I saw you again. Time has moved on.'

'It has, Lily. We're old people now. I'm all alone – I'm widowed.'

'I may be old, but I don't let it hold me back.' Lil pressed her lips together. 'I've just been on holiday.' She spoke firmly, tilting her chin. 'I have been to Amsterdam and Belgium and France with my daughter and my friends. I have a new gentleman friend – he's called Albert. He's a fine man.'

Cassie squeezed Lil's hand. Lil took another breath and continued. 'It worked out well for me. I'm in nice sheltered accommodation. I have enough money from my business. I have friends, I have my health, a good life. I can't complain.'

Frankie nodded. 'It's good to see you again.' He put a hand to his face. 'I'm glad you're well – I'm glad things are all right for you now.'

'And you, Frankie. How's life treating you?'

'I'm fine... a little lonely – David is often busy and he lives a couple hours away. I see his family sometimes but life's, you know, quiet.'

Cassie murmured, 'Life's never quiet around Lil.'

Lil suddenly remembered. 'Oh, Cassie – I said I was going to talk to Frankie by myself. I'd forgotten you were here. I'm glad you stayed, though. I'm glad you're here.'

'I'm always here.'

Frankie inched forwards, pressing his nose against the screen. 'Cassie, are you still there?'

'Yes.'

'Do you need money? Does Lily need money? I've no use for all of it now...'

'We're fine.'

'I spoke to David. I asked him...' Frankie seemed suddenly sad. 'Will you be able to come visit me here, Cassie? I'd like to meet you, to get to know you.'

'That would be nice.' Cassie glanced at Lil. 'I can't promise anything right now, though.'

Lil took a breath. 'You go, love. You go and meet Frankie.' She began to laugh and cry at the same time, tears rolling down her cheeks. 'You should go and visit him, say hello, get to know your father while you can. After all these years, it's about time you had one.' Lil wiped her eyes, smiled at the screen and patted her soft hair. 'Well, it was nice to meet you after such a long time, Frankie. I wish you all the best. There are no hard feelings, as they say. I'm going to sign off now. I have to get ready. I'm meeting my friends in a while and my gentleman friend, Albert. I hope you'll have a pleasant evening too. Goodbye. It was nice to catch up, after so long.'

Frankie murmured and the screen fizzed, became fuzzy and was blank. Cassie raised her eyebrows. 'Well, that was Frankie Chapman.'

Lil wriggled in her seat and exhaled, her hands forming little fists. 'Well indeed. Now everything's all done and dusted, as they say. Time marches on and we can move forward.'

'How are you feeling?'

Lil wiped her eyes and when her hand came away, her face was defiant. 'I thought I'd be heartbroken, seeing him again after so long. I've thought about him every day since he left me. I suppose I was always in love with him. That feeling never went away, not even after you left home, Cassie. I still thought of Frankie as the only one I'd care for.'

'And now?'

'Now I don't feel anything at all. He's an old man. I don't recognise him any more.' Lil took a deep breath. 'Of course, I know he's a memory I'll never forget. He was my Frankie; he's lived in my heart for so long. But that man I've just spoken to is different now; he has had a life of his own that has nothing to do with me. Frankie's changed, and I've changed. And now I know that I want something else. There are things in my life I'm still looking forward to, and they don't include him any more.'

'That's good to know, Lil. I've found out about my father and you've put the past behind you. It's been good for us both to talk to him.'

'And what about you, Cassie love? Was it a shock, meeting him after all this time?'

'It was, at first.' Cassie shrugged, her eyes gleaming. 'I've always been your daughter, Lil, the apple of your eye – feisty, too outspoken. I never had a father figure – you were my role model, both mum and dad, and I didn't need anyone else. As a kid, I copied how you were. So I couldn't settle down with one man either. How could I? But now, I suppose I've got the bit of the jigsaw that had been missing. I can meet Frankie, connect with a past I never knew. Now maybe I can move forward too.'

'You're right. I'm glad we spoke to him, and I'm glad you were there with me the whole time. But that's done now – we'd better get going. I need to put my glad rags on. We're off down the pub. I dare say there's a glass of something on the table already with my name on it.' Her eyes shone. 'I've finally put Frankie behind me. Come on, I've got things to do, people to meet, fun to have.'

37

Chairs had been set up around two tables that were pushed together. Two seats were empty. One seat was for Pat, a pint of bitter set down in front of the vacant chair, placed there by Tommy, who had photographed it and sent it to him in Boom. An immediate reply showed Pat at the dinner table with the Goossens family, his arm around Thilde, all of them holding glasses aloft and smiling. He looked serenely happy.

Lil stared at the photo on the screen, seeking out Herman, who was sitting between Marieke and Damiaan, a hearty grin on his face. She thought of Herman, on his tractor, at home. She reached for her glass of wine, forming a plan.

Duncan's seat was empty; he was busy at the bar with Kerry, serving customers, pulling pints. Lil could see his smile as he cracked jokes. She glanced around the table; everyone was there. Ken was drinking red wine, sitting between Sue and Denise, all smartly dressed, relaxed and happy. They had been joined by several other members of the tennis club, who listened with interest as Ken expounded the architectural delights of Bruges. Emily, her hair in a ponytail, was talking football tactics to Jake and DJ, one dressed in black and the other in a smart shirt and designer jeans; they had played a five-a-side game earlier and won easily. DJ and Jake were keen to discuss two girls who had apparently been eyeing them from the touchline. Then Emily explained to everyone at the table, her eyes round with relief and happiness, that she'd spoken on the phone with Alex earlier. There had been a terrible crisis in Taji, a tragedy, but the marines would be returning to the UK soon. She'd hear all about it when he was back on leave, and she couldn't wait to see him again.

Tommy sat next to Jake, trying to tell his wife, Angie, an athletic woman with short blonde hair, about a goal he'd saved that afternoon. Now Pat was no longer keeper, Tommy had been moved to the position between the posts and his place as defender had been taken by a local lad, Kevin, who was a talented header of the ball and a much better tackler.

Maggie sat with Brian, drinking wine and chatting. Brian was chewing gum frantically, trying his hardest to give up smoking. He was pleased with himself: he'd started dancing – he was loving the new exercise – and he was going to save the money he used to spend on cigarettes to take Maggie on holiday to Italy. Lil patted her hand. 'You'll have a wonderful time.'

'It's all thanks to you.' Maggie beamed. 'You've brought me and Brian back together again.'

Brian agreed. 'I can't thank you enough, Lil. My Maggie's a transformed woman. Look at her. She looks like a movie star. She's my very own Liz Taylor.'

Lil smiled. 'You can always buy me a drink, Brian. And Maggie and I will still be going for girls' nights out together. We developed a few habits while we were away – gambling, drinking, having fun...'

'Too right. We aren't going to give that up.' Maggie squeezed Brian's hand in hers.

Cassie and Jamie were talking quietly, their heads together. Lil listened carefully, trying to catch the gist of what they were saying; she'd heard the word 'Father' and another word, 'David', and she noticed Cassie's eager expression, the one she'd seen many times when her daughter had been a child, and she knew at once that Cassie intended to go to the USA and visit Frankie. Lil didn't mind; she turned to Albert, gave him her full attention and murmured, 'Would you like another beer, my sweetheart?'

Albert nodded, reading her lips. The background noise in the bar was quite loud and distorted, especially as Alice Springs in her dangling-cork hat had just launched into a tuneless version of 'Down Under'. At that moment, Kerry arrived at the table with a tray of drinks, which she declared were on the house, from Duncan. A large diamond twinkled in the lobe of each of her ears as she set the drinks down. She grinned at Cassie. 'Will you do a number for us on stage next, Cass? Duncan asked if you would…'

Cassie waved a piece of paper. 'I've scribbled a quick song.' She indicated a black instrument case next to her. 'And I've brought the banjo.'

'Fab,' Kerry cooed. 'And you are all coming to the Belgian Beer and Stew night on Friday?'

'Wouldn't miss it.' Jake grinned and thumped DJ's shoulder.

Duncan helped Alice Springs to descend from the little stage, as she wobbled on her heeled boots. Then he took the microphone. 'Thanks, Alice, for your rendition of the well-known song by Men At Work. But now we're not going "Down Under". Quite the opposite. As you know, a group of us recently went on a coach trip to Europe, thanks to our good mate Tommy Judd. And, as it turns out, he may be organising another later in the year, a Christmas-shopping trip in Cologne.'

'When all the beer you bought runs out?' Kerry quipped good-naturedly.

'I'm going with him next time,' Angie yelled, tucking an arm through Tommy's. 'I want some diamond earrings like Kerry's.'

'What about the lacy undies I bought you?' Tommy whispered, his cheeks suddenly reddening as he realised that DJ and Jake had overheard and they began to cheer raucously.

'So,' Duncan yelled, trying to restore order. He gazed around the bar, all the tables filled with customers. 'We all had a really good time, although it was very eventful. Maybe next time we'll take a full-size coach and you can all come with us. No more getting arrested at customs, though.' He winked in Maggie's direction and she winked back.

There was a rousing cheer from every table. Glasses were raised. Duncan spoke into the mic. 'So, I've asked Cassie to give us a song. Here she is with her song about our holiday bus trip.'

Cassie was next to him, holding the banjo. Her hair was wrapped in a black, yellow and red ribbon, the colours of the Belgian flag. Her dress was a patchwork of red and black velvet. She grinned. 'I've written this little ditty specially for Tommy, Duncan, and all the others who came on a very eventful trip.' She gazed at rapt faces and added, 'If you can pick the tune up, please do sing along.'

Applause echoed around the room as Cassie plucked a few jaunty notes, allowing the twanging rhythm to establish itself as a tune, a few people clapping along. Then she began to sing, her voice strong and persistent, her eyes twinkling with mischief:

> We took a bus trip 'cross the sea
> A much-needed break for Lil and me
> We went to France, to Bruges city
> The ale was good, the buildings pretty
> Then Amsterdam, canals, good cheer,
> And wacky brownies, too much beer.

A howl of protest came from Duncan and Tommy, their wives good-naturedly nodding in agreement. Cassie rode the wave of yells and applause and continued with a cheeky grin.

> *We played football at the farm*
> *Enjoyed the food, the beer, the charm...*
> *We said goodbye to our friend Pat*
> *Who fell in love – well, fancy that!*
> *In France, good food across the table*
> *We threw rolls, all drunk and quite unstable*
> *Detained at customs with Maggie's dope*
> *Ken came to the rescue – heroic bloke –*
> *We paid the fine and rushed to the boat*
> *All so relieved to be back afloat*
> *Then Tommy drove us safely home*
> *And now, wherever we may roam*
> *We've memories we'll always treasure*
> *And friendships that will last forever.*

A loud cheer resonated around the bar. Denise banged the table and yelled, 'Well done, Cassie.'

Ken raised his glass and everyone else copied, chorusing, 'Friendship.'

Cassie stepped gingerly from the stage, the banjo held aloft, amid deafening applause, and waved enthusiastically to the crowd, blowing kisses. She sat down next to Jamie, put her banjo away and whispered, 'It's not technically the best song I've ever written.'

His head close to hers, he replied, 'But it's probably one of the most popular in The Jolly Weaver, and today that's what counts.'

'It certainly is, Jamie.' She sat up, tucking a hand through the crook of his arm. 'Have you thought about what we discussed earlier?'

He nodded. 'Do you really want me to come with you to the States to meet your father?'

'I do. It's going to be a big deal for me, having a father. It's important to have him in my life – and you're a huge part of my life already.' She met his eyes, her own shining with affection. 'I rang David. We can stay with him and his wife in Denver. Then we can hire a car, visit Frankie in Kansas, and take some time for ourselves to travel around. The area is beautiful, apparently. The weather in August is lovely, and there may even be snow on the Rockies.'

'I may not be much good at hiking up mountains,' Jamie protested.

Cassie raised an eyebrow. 'We'll walk at your pace, or take the car. And we'll be back in the UK in time for my poetry tour in October and November – the Guy Fawkes tour. I'm looking forward to that.'

'Cassie.' Jamie took her hand solemnly. 'I don't want you to invite me to go with you just because of what I said last night – that I missed you while you were away more than I can say. I won't be baggage...'

'I thought about what you said a lot too, since I came back. And you're definitely not baggage.'

He took a deep breath. 'Then what am I? What am I to you?'

'You're special.' Cassie took his face in both hands. 'Very special. And I care – I care a lot.'

'So, when we go to Denver together, what will I be there? Your housemate? Your friend? Or something more...?'

'You, Jamie Anastasiou, will be wonderful. Let's just go to Denver. Let's have a good time. Let's just forget about labels, about whether we are friends, partners, lovers, and let's see what happens.' She offered him a wink. 'Sometimes life has a way of showing us that the people we see every day are the ones who are dearest to us, that we love the most. Like you – and like my mother.'

She cocked her head towards Lil and Albert, who were gazing into each other's eyes. Lil placed a small kiss on Albert's mouth, a brush of skin against skin. Cassie turned to Jamie and gave him a similar peck, a warm touching of lips. 'Let's see where life takes us. I think we're both going to enjoy the journey very much.'

Jamie leaned over and took her hand, holding it to his cheek, then he raised his glass. '*Yamas*, as my dad used to say. To the journey, my dearest Cassie – to you and me, and to whatever the future brings.'

* * *

The next morning, Lil stood in her flat, thinking. There was something she needed to do. She took a deep breath, then she was ready. She reached in her pocket for a scrap of paper, peering at the numbers that had been carefully written on it. Then she picked up the heavy receiver of her phone and dialled each one in turn. There was the sound of intermittent ringing at the other end. She waited; they'd be having breakfast.

Then a deep voice answered. '*Met Herman...*'

Lil caught her breath. She'd expected Marieke to answer, but she had no idea why; Herman's voice had taken her by surprise. She faltered. 'Herman?'

There was a pause and then he replied, 'Lil? It is you?'

'Yes, it's me...'

The voice came back in her ear. 'It is wonderful to hear from you.'

'You too.' For a moment, her resolve weakened. His tone was resonant, affectionate. Then she said, 'I hope you're well.'

'Oh, yes,' he replied. 'I am working hard as ever. But now we have Pat to help us here. I hope you too are well, Lil.'

'I am, very well, thank you. Herman, I wanted to say to you...'

'Yes?'

'I had such a lovely time with you in Belgium.'

Herman was silent on the other end. Lil knew that he knew what was coming next. Then he simply said, 'Yes. I had a good time too.'

'Herman, Belgium is a long way away and you're a lovely man and I'd love to come and see you again and we could be great friends and have lots of fun but...' She took a breath.

'But, just friends, Lil? Is that what you are telling me?'

'It is.'

'I see.' Herman was silent for a moment. 'I suppose it is difficult, with you being so far away.'

'Yes.' Lil sighed. 'But we can keep in touch, phone each other occasionally – that would be nice.'

'It would. Friends is nice. I would like that.'

'That's good.' Lil nodded. 'Now that's straight. Well, goodbye, Herman and – thank you.'

'You will ring me again?'

'Oh, yes, of course – if that's all right.'

'It's perfectly all right. It's good to have a friend.' He paused, then his voice came softly. 'Goodbye, Lil.'

'Goodbye, Herman.'

Lil sighed, reached for her cat bag and wandered down to Jenny Price's office. It was just past eight o'clock and Jenny wasn't there yet. Lil stealthily tried the door handle and it opened easily so she took a furtive peep up and down the corridor to make sure no one was coming and stepped inside. The coast was clear. She left the door ajar.

Jenny's office was untidy. Lil reached into her bag and pulled out the 'I heart Amsterdam' mug and the packet of Belgian choco-lates, placing them carefully on the desk. She gazed around, then hurriedly collected the stray pens and pencils, dropping them into the empty biscuit tin from the mixed selection she'd bought last Easter. She didn't have much time. She reached for a tissue and wiped the surfaces, picking up a chocolate wrapper and an empty tray that had been last night's fish and chip takeaway supper. Lil pushed the rubbish in the overflowing bin, thinking that she might buy Jenny a new one, a larger one with a flip top. She gazed at Cliff Richard on the 2019 calendar: as Mr August, he was playing with a striped beach ball, wearing red shorts, smiling with pearly teeth.

Lil turned sharply, hearing the sound of loud heels clacking in the distance. She rushed out of the office and closed the door, moving a few steps away, loitering theatrically as Jenny turned the corner and walked quickly towards the office. She frowned. 'Good morning, Lil. May I help you?'

Lil didn't miss a beat. She offered an innocent expression. 'I wanted to ask you – how's your car?'

Jenny almost smiled. 'My brother-in-law looked at it for me. Tommy Judd rang me last night and I told him not to worry – it's only a slight dent in the bumper, so...' She raised her eyebrows. 'Did you and Maggie enjoy your holiday?'

'It was wonderful, Jenny. You should go sometime – a break would do you the world of good.' Lil's eyes twinkled. 'Ah, and there's something else I wanted to discuss with you...'

'Oh?' Jenny raised her eyebrows.

'I have a visitor coming tonight. A gentleman friend.'

'A gentleman?' Jenny's eyes bulged. 'I see.'

'He's called Albert Hopkins. We're dating. We're going to have a takeaway meal and some wine.' Lil took several steps and began to saunter away.

'Oh,' Jenny replied, amazed as she stood in the corridor watching Lil stroll towards the staircase, a swing in her walk even though it made her hip ache. 'And, Lil – will Mr Hopkins be staying late into the evening? Only, the rules state that, for the security of all residents, the outside door is to be locked at half past ten.'

'Albie and I are having a romantic dinner together in my flat,' Lil called over her shoulder, swishing round to meet Jenny's astonished gaze. 'There will be music and flowers, sparkling wine and chocolates, dancing and smooching.'

As she rounded the corner, her foot on the first step, she raised her voice as loudly as possible, turning her head to maximise the volume of her words as they echoed off the walls.

'Oh, and one more thing, Jenny – just so that you know – you can lock the front door whenever you like. Albie will be staying the night.'

ACKNOWLEDGMENTS

Thanks to my agent, Kiran Kataria, for her wisdom, professionalism and integrity.

Thanks to Amanda Ridout, Nia Beynon, Claire Fenby and Megan Townsend at Boldwood Books.

Huge thanks to Sarah Ritherdon, editor extraordinaire.

So much appreciation to everyone who has worked hard to make this book happen. I'm so grateful to designers, editors, technicians, magicians, voice actors, bloggers – thanks to you all.

As always, thanks to the many people who continue to encourage me, the many friends I haven't hugged in months.

Thanks to Solitary Writers, Avril's Writing Group, all at Radio SoundArt, especially Julie Mullen and Martin Seager, Radio Somerset, Planet Rock, and to the generous community of Boldwood writers.

Much thanks to the talented Ivor Abiks at Deep Studios.

Special thanks to our Tony; to Kim, Ellen, Angela, Norman, Bridget and Debbie.

Love to my mum, who showed me the joy of reading, and to my dad, who proudly never read anything.

Love always to Liam, Maddie, Cait and Big G.

Warmest thanks to my readers, wherever you are. You have helped to make this journey incredible.

ABOUT BOLDWOOD BOOKS

Boldwood Books is a fiction publishing company seeking out the best stories from around the world.

Find out more at www.boldwoodbooks.com

Sign up to the Book and Tonic newsletter for news, offers and competitions from Boldwood Books!

http://www.bit.ly/bookandtonic

We'd love to hear from you, follow us on social media:

facebook.com/BookandTonic

twitter.com/BoldwoodBooks

instagram.com/BookandTonic

Made in United States
Orlando, FL
03 November 2021

10191728R00193